I'm an Irish author who is addicted to writing romances featuring damaged, moody, book boyfriends searching for their happily ever after.

Visit K.A. Finn online:

www.kafinn.com
(trailers, excerpts, artwork, playlists etc)

Facebook: kafinnauthor

Instagram: kafinnauthor

Additional links: linktr.ee/kafinn

Also by K.A. Finn

Nomad Series (Space Opera)

Ares

Nemesis

Perses

Chaos

Mania

Cronus

Blackjacks Series (Paranormal Romance)

Breaking Phoenix

Reviving Davyn

Defying Shep

Broken Chords (Rockstar Romance)

Broken Rock (Tate)

Fractured Rock (Gregg)

Split Rock (all band members)

Crushed Rock (Luke)

Shattered Rock (Dillon)

Twisted Legends (Folklore Retelling/Romance)

North Bound (Nick/Santa)

Masters of Havoc (Dark Romance)

Rook's Awakening

STONE WOLVES BOOK 1

SORCHA

K.A. FINN

Cover design by Getcovers

www.getcovers.com

Published by Cooper Publishing

cooperbookservices@gmail.com

ISBN: 978-1-914177-73-6

This one is for me! Why the hell not? I deserve it.

DEAR READERS,

SORCHA is a dark paranormal romance set in the brutal and hidden Level Three wolf-shifter prison in Ireland. This world isn't for everyone. It includes elements of torture, assault, injury, captivity, violence, slavery, death, control, kidnapping, forced proximity, brutal injuries, graphic language, and sexual activities (male/male/female).

Readers who may be sensitive to these elements, please enter the prison with caution.

Now, are you ready to meet Sorcha, Bannon, and Quill?

Wolves / Whelans

Murtagh 'Murt'
Conal 'Con'
Garret
Sorcha
Fionn

Vampires / Blackjacks

Quillan 'Quill'
Bannon
Phoenix 'Nix'
Court
Davyn 'Dav'
Shepherd 'Shep'
Bastian 'Bas'
Fallon
Willow
Ethan Croft

Humans

Fletcher 'Fletch'
Isabella 'Izzy' (Shep's mate)
Thea (Davyn's mate)

BANNON

When you take a life, things can't continue as though nothing happened. Unless you're used to murdering, there's no way your own life could possibly continue as normal. There would always be a price to pay for losing control in that way.

He just wasn't expecting the price to be so high.

Bannon looks straight ahead at the imposing mansion, unable to take his eyes off his new *home*, which seems to close in on him as the boat nears land.

Sitting in the middle of a private island off the Hook Peninsula in Wexford, Ireland, his new residence is as far from inviting as you can get. But it's not supposed to be. It would hardly be a prison if it gave off homely vibes.

At his feet, the large duffle bag holds everything he owns. Not much for someone in his sixties. But sixty to a vampire is nothing. He looks like he's in his late twenties at the most.

The boat pulls up at the jetty, the suffocating dread building in him, as one of the guards secures the boat to its mooring.

'Come on. Move!'

He gets to his feet, not wanting to irritate the guard who accompanied him from the mainland.

Trying hard not to lose his balance as the waves cause the boat to lurch, he climbs out and walks along the wooden jetty. The three storey house towers above him, as he follows the silent guard around the back of the house, until he finally stops at a door in a one storey annex.

The guard gestures for Bannon to go through the door first, which he then locks behind them. Bannon follows him down the corridor, until he comes to a stop at a door with the number twelve in digits on a plaque to the side. The guard unlocks the door and holds it open for him.

Bannon steps inside and looks around the small but clean room. There's a bathroom to the right, with a bed, desk, and wardrobe taking up the other side. The window is at eye level, thick bars covering the glass.

The door shuts behind him with a loud bang, startling him. He drops his bag on the ground, then lowers onto the bed, the suffocating sensation threatening to take him over. He closes his eyes, imagining he's somewhere else - anywhere else - rather than here.

But this is where he is. It's where he's going to be until he's released... if he's ever released.

BANNON

He barely slept, nightmares keeping him company until it was time to get up. He'd been given the schedule by the guard in the boat last night, and is determined not to get off on the wrong foot with anyone here. He was going to behave and not cause any problems. Hopefully that way, his time will pass without incident.

He's just lacing up his boots when there's a firm knock on his door. He opens it to find a tall female standing outside. She's dressed in the uniform of a guard, her straight blonde hair tied back in a ponytail, her blue eyes hard and cold as she looks him over. 'Bannon?'

He nods and holds out his hand, pulling it back when she merely glances at it before crossing her arms. 'I'm Duna. Second in command.' She points down the corridor. 'Breakfast. Come on. Can't be late.'

He obediently follows the guard along the corridor to the canteen around the corner. 'Help yourself.' Duna walks away, leaving him facing a counter with various fried food and cereals. Bannon picks up a plate, filling it with sausage, eggs, and bacon, before taking one of the empty seats at the end of the table, where other guards are already seated.

The conversation lulls as he sits, Duna and the other males already tucking into their breakfast looking over at him. He focuses on his breakfast again, hoping they won't engage him in conversation. It works, Duna and the other guards talking amongst themselves after an awkward minute of silence.

Bannon picks at his breakfast, moving the sausage and eggs around his plate with his fork. He's not really hungry. Nerves don't usually get to him, but today is different. Today he's taking up his new post as a guard in one of the Raven King's hidden prisons.

It doesn't matter that he's outside a cell instead of inside one. He'd rather be anywhere on the planet than here, but he doubts anyone is on the island by choice.

He brushes a crumb off his black uniform sleeve. Like everyone else at the table, he's going to be tasked with keeping the prisoners in line. Lucky him. He hasn't got a clue what's expected of him. He's completely lost in a world he knows nothing about.

There are five males in the room along with Duna. From what they're saying he guesses some of them have just finished their shift. He presumes there is a night and a day shift.

He glances up as another male strides into the room, silencing the chatter without saying a word. Bannon tries not to stare at him, but he can't help it. Whoever he is, he's the sort of male you can't help but look at, no matter what. He's built like a tank and looks about as serious as they come.

The newcomer settles into the seat opposite Bannon, then glares

10

over when he catches him staring at him. His eyes are two entirely different colours - one navy and the other green. For some reason that fact just gives extra weight to his cold glare.

'Bannon?'

He nods quickly, deciding not to offer his hand to this guard.

'I'm Quillan, but I prefer Quill. I'm the head guard. Your new boss.' He nods down at Bannon's breakfast. 'Eat that. Shift starts in ten minutes.'

Quill gets up and grabs some breakfast, before settling back in the seat opposite Bannon again. 'What?' Quill asks, catching him looking for the second time.

Bannon shakes his head and concentrates on his breakfast again, the bacon, sausage, and eggs suddenly unappealing. Duna moves up beside Quill, then spends the next few minutes giving him the report from her shift.

So, as Bannon had guessed, there are two shifts. Duna and some of these guards must have covered the shift just coming to an end, handing over to Quill and his team for the rest of the day.

Bannon risks another quick look at his new boss, before focusing on his breakfast again. Tattooed and pierced, Quill is big and about as intimidating as you can get. His dirty-blonde hair is tied back in a bun, but a few strands have escaped, which Quill tucks behind his ear, as he drinks his coffee.

Tattoos stretch from his fingertips to his neck, and his lip, nose, both eyebrows, and both ears are pierced. Bit brave for someone who works in a prison, but then again, Bannon doubts anyone would mess with Quill. He certainly doesn't look like someone you should cross.

Duna stands, picking up her plate and sliding it into the dishwasher. 'That's me done. I'm hitting the sack.' Quill nods at her before she leaves the room, then silently finishes his breakfast, while the other guards continue their conversation at a slightly lower volume. As soon as he finishes, Quill clears away his things and leaves the room.

11

Bannon quickly shovels some food into his mouth, then puts his plate in the dishwasher. He follows the three guards out into the corridor leading from their accommodation block to the prison a few metres away, as they hurry to catch up with Quill.

They file into a room at the end, taking their seats facing a table. Bannon sits at the back and tries not to fidget in his seat as he waits for the meeting to begin. Quill props himself up on the edge of the table as he checks his clipboard.

'Before we get started, this is Bannon,' he says, nodding to the back of the room. Bannon smiles nervously as everyone slowly turns to give him a quick glance. 'He's joining the team from today,' Quill continues, still not looking up from his clipboard. 'Now, back to business. I'll keep the roster the same as last week,' he says, his attention on the page in front of him as he writes something down.

He finally looks up, crossing his arms as he looks over the room. 'The Warden isn't expecting any new inmates until next week so it should be quiet until then. That's all for now. Dismissed. Newbie! Hold back.'

Bannon glances nervously at Quill as the rest of the guards head off to start their shift, briefly nodding at him as they pass by. The silence seems endless as he waits for his boss to acknowledge him again. But he continues to read through a document on a clipboard, completely ignoring Bannon.

A good five minutes later, Quill drops the clipboard to the table with a crash that makes Bannon jump. He turns his hard eyes towards Bannon and examines him like he's something that just crawled out from a crevice in the wall.

'The Warden told me you can't talk.'

It's not a question, so he doesn't answer. Not that he could. He subconsciously runs his fingers along the raised, lumpy scar stretching from under his chin to his chest. He's mute. Has been since he was savaged by a wolf eight years ago. He can hear just fine, but you'd think he was deaf the way the rest of the world talk about him, right in front of his face.

Quill is actually one of the few people he's met to look him in the eye as he speaks to him. In an ideal world everyone would know sign language, but this is far from an ideal world. This is a world where no one is interested in even attempting to *hear* what he has to say.

'I take it that scar on your neck is the reason for that. The Warden said to keep an eye on you around the wolves. Am I going to have a problem with you?'

Bannon shakes his head, unable to break free of Quill's cold glare. He wasn't expecting the Warden to tell Quill that, but as it has been mentioned, he might as well acknowledge it. He isn't a fan of wolf shifters, but no vampires are. For generations, vampires and wolf shifters have been enemies. He doubts anyone remembers why they fell out in the first place, but no one is brave enough to step out of line and make friends.

In any event, he'd be last on that list. His dislike goes deeper than a generational issue. A wolf took his voice from him. No *warm handshake and all is forgiven* coming from him any time soon.

Quill frees him from his glare, turning his attention to his own weapon that he has just taken from the safe., checking it before he holsters it.

'You must really have pissed off someone if you've been sent here. Vampires run the prison, but you know all the inmates are wolves, right? Only wolves.'

Bannon nods again. It's something he's been trying to psyche himself up for since he heard about the prison. He's not sure how it's going to play out for him. Time will tell.

Quill glances over at him, his eyebrows drawn as he crosses his arms, and perches on the edge of the table. 'Do you know sign language?'

Bannon nods enthusiastically as a small glimmer of hope grows at the thought that someone here might be able to understand him.

'Don't get excited,' he says, killing off that hope before it can fully take hold. 'I asked around. No one here knows it. Keep it to nods and shakes of your head. I won't be having any *deep and meaningfuls* with you. You're here to listen to me, not the other way around.'

This isn't quite the start he was hoping for. He's just getting more depressed as the day goes on.

'There are two shifts - night and day. Wolves are more active during the day, so that's the shift that needs more supervision. That's our shift. Duna and two guards look after the night shift when the dogs are locked up. You'll be working with me for the moment so I can step in if needed. As for your extra ability, what the fuck does *'can manipulate fire'* mean?'

This is the part Bannon wasn't looking forward to. It's not something easily explained without a voice. To add to the awkwardness, Quill raises his eyebrows again, clearly waiting for him to find some way of explaining himself.

Bannon shakes his head as he reaches for his notebook and pen. Quill watches as he writes a short explanation. He passes the notebook to Quill who reads it aloud. 'I can create fire, but it takes a lot of energy. I can usually control it. Send it in different directions. Make it burn hotter or extinguish it completely.'

He passes the notebook back to him. 'Fuck! You keep that under control and to yourself. You hear me? The last thing I need is this place going up in flames because you're too weak to keep a handle on it. I could do without that paperwork.'

Being called weak isn't something he appreciates, but he doesn't react. He's perfectly capable of controlling his ability. He's only lost that hold once and it was in exceptional circumstances.

Circumstances that have now led him to this place.

'Did you hear me or what?'

He nods at Quill, disliking the male more by the minute. He might be nice to look at, but he's clearly someone who doesn't take any nonsense.

Quill pushes to his feet, then walks back over to the gun safe. He passes Bannon a weapon, watching in silence as he checks it is clean and ready to fire.

Quill nods approvingly which helps ease some of Bannon's nerves.

'I don't usually do this,' Quill says, lowering his voice even though they're alone. 'I'm going to give you some advice to help you survive out there. Whatever you do around the prisoners, don't let on you can't talk. If they sense a weakness they'll use it against you. We're not expected to have chats with them, so it shouldn't be a problem. Be the strong silent type. You don't need to talk, because you say what you need to say by just being there. Lay on the *don't fuck with me* vibe.

Bannon nods, the nerves he felt a few minutes ago coming back again.

'Good. Now for the official rules. There are only a couple, but I expect them to be obeyed without question. I don't give a fuck about any vampire and shifter feud. In here we're guards and prisoners. It's not personal and it needs to stay that way. I expect my guards' control to be firm, but not excessive. If I see any heavy-handedness, I will come down on you like a tonne of fucking bricks. Do you understand?'

He nods again, but Quill isn't looking at him.

'Fuck! Forgot,' he says, looking back at him. 'You with me so far?'

Bannon nods, hating that he's already pissing off his new boss.

'Second rule. No forcing yourself on any of the prisoners. Don't look so shocked. It happens. Some of the guards have regular fuck partners. As long as it's consensual I really couldn't give a damn. But if I hear of anyone taking advantage, they will be removed from the island, after I remove their dick from their body. I won't have that kind of shit going on. Are we clear?'

He nods quickly. Having that sort of relationship with any of the prisoners hadn't crossed his mind for even a second. The worrying part is the way Quill is talking, he's under no illusions that he has carried out that punishment in the past.

Quill takes a step forward, narrowing the distance between them, bringing Bannon nearly nose-to-nose with his boss. 'Third rule. The Warden owns the island, but I am in charge of the prison. Do everything I say without question. I don't repeat myself, so make sure you're hanging on my every fucking word. You understand?'

He nods again.

'Good. Let's get this fun day underway.' Quill walks over to the door, pausing to look at Bannon over his shoulder. 'Are you coming or what?'

Bannon falls into step beside Quill, matching his long strides along the corridor. 'There are three of these prisons in Ireland,' he explains as he marches along the corridor to a heavily bolted door at the end. 'Level One is similar to a regular human prison. Inmates mix with each other, higher numbers and less security. Level Two has fewer inmates with tighter security. You get moved from Level One to Level Two if you're giving the guards problems.'

He stops at the door and turns to face Bannon. 'We're Level Three. Twenty-three of the most dangerous wolves in the country. Apart from exercise, meals, and showering, they stay in their cells. A few who keep pushing the boundaries stay in their cells for mealtimes. Each prisoner is in here for life. Only the Warden knows what they're here for. None of our business. As soon as they step through the door, they're all equal. No names - just a number. There's only one way they're getting out of here, and that's when we bury their bodies behind the prison. One way ticket.'

He nods when Quill glances at him over his shoulder.

'You make any sounds at all?'

Bannon shakes his head, suddenly feeling more self-conscious than he has for a while.

'This is going to be fun,' Quill mutters under his breath. He places his palm against a panel at the side of the door and the light above them turns green. Bannon hears the heavy clunk of locks disengaging, and the door swings open.

The air surrounding Bannon takes an unpleasant turn. He

swallows back the retch that threatens to have him vomiting all over Quill's boots. It's stale sweat, rancid bodily fluids, and suffocating humidity.

Quill briefly laughs at his reaction. 'You'll get used to it. The Warden isn't keen on providing luxuries like air conditioning.'

Or even a window by the smell of the air. It's all-consuming and he's been here for less than a minute. Trying to breathe through his mouth just results in his tongue becoming coated in the foul smell.

As Quill leads him down into the underbelly of the prison, Bannon's heart races. He hasn't even seen an inmate or a cell yet, and he already knows this is Hell.

They've gone down another level before Bannon finally sees some sign of life. One of the guards he had breakfast with, approaches with an inmate. The wolf prisoner is wearing a black jumpsuit, his dark eyes sunken in his pale face. He may be here because he's a hardened criminal, but the wolf moves to the side, his gaze dropping to the floor as Quill passes.

Quill leads him to a double door - two yellowed windows giving him a glimpse into the canteen on the other side. It looks like most of the inmates are inside, eating their breakfast.

Quill glances over his shoulder, waiting until Bannon looks at him before he speaks. 'You ready to meet the dogs?'

Bannon licks his lips, then nods. Whether he is or not doesn't matter. This is his job. This is his life now. He either faces it head-on or ends up on the other side of the bars.

Quill places his palm against the door, pushing it inwards. 'You'd better be, 'cause these ones bite.'

QUILL

From the far side of the canteen, Quill watches his new guard moving through the room, throwing his best *don't fuck with me* look at the inmates. He'd been working with Bannon one-on-one for a week now and is impressed.

He might just have to admit that the new guard he had dismissed as a liability on paper, was so much more than he had originally thought. In fact, he's out-performing some of the longer serving guards. He's eager to learn, taking in everything he's told and putting it into action.

Quill walks around the edge of the room, his attention moving between Bannon and the inmates. Everyone is behaving, eating their food, talking quietly to each other. Apart from showering and brief exercise, this is the only time they see each other. Some take advantage and talk. Others remain in silence, their minds lost or broken.

As he passes by, each inmate lifts their attention from their meal and conversation to look at him. They're wary of him. Fear him. Respect him. If they didn't when they came in, he soon put them in their place. It was easier that way. Easier to keep control of the prison and keep everyone relatively safe. While he's not afraid of using force when necessary, beating the living daylights out of prisoners wasn't top of his to-do-list.

After doing a lap of the room, he takes up position by the door, facing the low tables, his arms crossed. He catches Bannon looking at him, but his frown convinces him to look away. He's caught him doing that a few times since that first morning at breakfast.

It's probably his eyes that are drawing his attention. He's had unwanted attention and stares his whole life because of his different colour eyes. They are unusual, but not unheard of. It doesn't stop people looking though.

But there's something different about the way Bannon is staring over at him. Maybe he's wary of him too? Maybe worried he's going to fuck up and Quill will come down on him like a tonne of bricks. He chews on the ring piercing his lip, as he continues to watch Bannon.

If he's being honest, he thought he'd have told the Warden to reassign the new guard by now. He was convinced the Warden had made a mistake. Who hires a mute guard? He has no idea what the fuck the Warden was thinking. Maybe he hadn't even looked at Bannon's file? Quill wouldn't be surprised.

Or maybe, like most of the other guards here, whatever Bannon did to earn himself a place on the island, means a small detail like being mute doesn't matter?

Whatever the reason, it's Quill's job to make sure Bannon doesn't get himself killed. Quill is the only one in the prison who actually gives

19

a damn about keeping the place running smoothly. Duna too, to a certain extent, but her life is slightly easier than his. She rarely interacts with the inmates on the night shift. Lucky her. She had handpicked the guards working with her, so she understood the importance of having the right people in place.

If the wrong guards were brought in, people could get hurt. The Warden wouldn't give a fuck about that. But *he* does. It's his life on the line if things go wrong. Inmates have killed guards in the past. His job is to make sure that doesn't happen on his watch.

It's a crappy and seriously thankless job, but it's a job he takes pride in. Or does most of the time. It's all he has. When all of his guards make it back to the dorms unharmed, it's a good day in his books. If the inmates were in the same position, he's even happier.

Only time will tell if Bannon will be an asset to the team, but so far so good.

If he can keep it together, keep a hold on that anger he senses inside the male, he might have a chance. Bannon may have tried to keep his scar hidden, covering it with his shirt collar as much as possible, but you'd have to be blind not to see it. From the portion he can see, Quill can tell it's fucking huge.

The male is damn lucky to be alive. He saw the teeth marks left when his flesh was torn apart. It must have been a wolf. Quill can't think of anything else that could have left a scar like that.

Fuck knows how he survived, but the fact he did is something he gets credit for. He must be strong, determined, a fighter.

Getting off that boat and walking into the prison just reinforces how strong he is. Not that he had a fucking choice. But, so far, he's not letting his justified fear of wolves get to him - not on the outside anyway.

Bannon's lip twitches as he glares down at the wolves. He's letting his fear out as anger and, in here, that's the only way to do it.

'Finish up!' Quill shouts, spurring everyone into action. The inmates quickly finish the last remnants of their food, before standing and lining up at the door in front of him. In silence, the wolves make their way back to their cells, Quill and his guards making sure everyone is locked away, before they head back to their side of the house for their own meal.

The other guards talk amongst themselves, leaving Bannon out of their conversation. Not that he can really blame them. It's not going to be easy to include him. Quill hangs back before he steps into the kitchen, stopping Bannon at the door. 'You hungry?'

Bannon pauses, not sure what exactly Quill is asking.

'It's not a trick question. Are you hungry or not?' Bannon shakes his head. 'Thought not. I was the same for the first few weeks. Seeing the dogs eating turned me off my grub too. I'm going to hit the gym. You coming?'

Bannon nods eagerly, so Quill heads past the kitchen to the small but well-equipped gym. There's another one in the prison that the inmates can also use from time to time, but Quill prefers this one. He unbuttons his shirt, laying it across one of the benches before taking off his boots, then stands at the edge of the padded mat in the centre of the floor. 'You any good at hand-to-hand combat?'

Bannon nods and holds up one finger.

'Once? You've fought once?'

Bannon nods again, momentarily looking to the ground in front of him, before meeting Quill's eyes again.

'Fuck! Not good enough. You'll need more experience than that. If the inmates kick off, they'll be coming at you full force with their bodies. You need to be able to face up to them, take them down without getting hurt. Shirt and boots off then get on the mat.'

He bites back the unexpected smile at the look of horror on Bannon's face. He's worried he's about to get well and truly annihilated.

He might be right.

4

QUILL

Twenty minutes later Quill holds out his hand, helping to pull Bannon off the mat. His new guard had spent a lot of the time down there, but even though he looks deflated and pissed off with himself, Quill is seriously impressed. For someone with no combat experience, he did well.

He throws Bannon a towel from the cupboard, wiping his own face as he sits on one of the benches. 'You did good.'

Bannon glances over at him, as he massages the back of his neck. He doesn't believe that for a minute. Quill thinks it's kind of refreshing that Bannon's not up his own ass. So many vampires he's worked with develop this superiority complex when they start here.

The power gets to them after a while. There's nothing he detests more than people who think they know it all. They're the ones he enjoys watching fail - which they all do at some stage.

'Hey!'

Bannon slaps the towel against the wall in frustration, then looks sideways at him.

'I said you did good.'

Bannon shakes his head, then points to the mat and then to his back.

'Yeah, you were on your back for most of it, but you didn't give up.'

Bannon storms over to his shirt, taking the notebook and pen from where he left them. *You killed me.*

Quill again just manages to hold back the laugh. 'Not quite.'

Bannon shakes his head, scribbling again before holding out the notebook. *I want more training.*

Fuck! This male is seriously impressing him. 'Every day before your shift. I'll train you for an hour.'

Bannon squeezes the notebook in his hands as he nods. When he smiles, Quill isn't on the ball quick enough to restrain his own smile before it escapes. Bannon looks around the room as he absently rubs the scar on his neck.

Quill has been around so many vampires and wolves over the years who thought they were strong. But this is strength. Surviving whatever he went through, and facing life with no voice every day is true strength.

Quill gets dressed again, slipping his shirt back on, then sits down to deal with his boots. It's been a while since he looked forward to training with anyone. He usually worked out alone, because everyone else just ended up pissing him off.

He gets the feeling Bannon will be different. With a bit of training, Bannon will be one hell of a guard.

Bannon walks with him back to the prison so they can let the inmates out in smaller groups for some exercise. Bannon falls in with the other guards, herding the wolves into the yard, as if he's been doing it for years.

This is probably Quill's favourite time of the day. He prefers being outside. The prison stinks, is either too hot or too cold depending on what room they're in, and there are too many other bodies around him.

It didn't matter what side of the bars you were on, the place is still Hell. It's slightly overcast today, so there's no need for his sunglasses to protect his eyes. He's the only Prime vampire in the prison. The others can deal with sunlight for a few hours before it gives them trouble. He can only manage an hour or so. Then his eyes sting and he gets a rotten headache. Joys of being pure-blood.

Quill curses to himself when his mobile rings in his pocket. He turns away, facing the wall as he answers the call. 'Yes sir?'

'I'd like a brief meeting with you Quillan.'

The phone line goes dead. Perfect! There goes his slightly good mood. But when the Warden summons, he has to obey. He walks over to Bannon. 'I'm meeting the Warden. Stay here with the others.'

Before Bannon can nod in response, he leaves the yard and heads to the dorms. His heart races as he climbs the stairs leading from the guards' section of the house to the upper levels of the mansion.

He pauses at the Warden's door, composing himself before he knocks.

'Come in.'

He takes a long breath, then opens the door, before closing it behind him and taking up position in front of the Warden's desk, standing straight and tall with his hands behind his back.

As usual, the Warden doesn't acknowledge his presence. The power-hungry vampire is all about respect and making sure others know their place. The Warden turns the page of his book, ignoring him as he continues to read. He'll just have to wait until the Warden is ready.

He's glad he worked out before he was called in. Being left hanging like this isn't doing anything for his mood. He's never acted out or disrespected the Warden, but has been sorely tempted on more than one occasion. He's got a job to do and this is just wasting his time.

The vampire is easily in his third century, his hair greying slightly at his temples. His features are sharp, his cheeks and eyes sunken in his pale face. His expensive shirt is open at the collar, the diamond cufflinks at his wrists glinting when they catch the light.

After a good six minutes or so, the Warden finally turns his book over, placing it on the desk in front of him. He gets to his feet and walks over to Quill, stopping in front of him.

'Quillan. Good to see you.'

Until he met the Warden, he actually liked his full name. But now, hearing him say *Quillan* in his soft voice gives him the creeps.

'How is the new guard coming along?'

'Well sir. He seems competent, but it's early days.'

The Warden nods as he turns one of his expensive cufflinks. 'You will make sure he fits in.'

It's an order so he nods.

'And the fact he's a mute isn't causing problems?'

For some unknown reason, the Warden calling Bannon *a mute* irritates him. 'No sir. We're working around it. He doesn't need a voice to do a good job.'

The Warden nods again, his eyes travelling over Quill's body as the silence stretches on. Quill keeps his attention on the oil painting behind the Warden's desk. It's of some ancestor, but anything is better than looking at the Warden himself.

'That's good to hear. We have a new inmate arriving tomorrow. From all accounts she's a feisty one. Her track record includes numerous injured guards and a clear lack of respect for authority.'

'Yes sir.'

'I want you to break her, Quillan.'

That gets his attention. He looks down at the shorter Warden. 'Sir?'

'She needs to be controlled. That's what you excel at. Others have failed to get her to comply. I want you to use whatever means necessary to break her.'

Quill doesn't know what to say to that. He's hurt prisoners before. It's part of the job. But what the Warden is asking him to do is more than just keeping order. 'Break her how, sir?'

The Warden shrugs nonchalantly. 'Flog her. We both know how effective that can be.'

'Sir, I don't think—'

Quill's cheek stings like fuck when the Warden slaps him hard, his heavy ring tearing his skin. 'What gave you the impression I want you to think? You follow my orders. Do exactly as I say. Do I make myself clear Quillan?'

He nods, biting back the growl that's desperate to launch itself in the Warden's face. 'Yes, sir.'

The Warden smiles as he walks back around his desk, picking up his book when he sits. 'Glad to hear it. I don't like when you defy me Quillan. Don't do it again.'

'I didn't mean any disrespect, sir.' Fuck, the words burn as he forces them out. 'It won't happen again.'

'Glad to hear it,' he repeats. 'Off you go. I expect to see results Quillan.'

On that note, the Warden dismisses him by getting back to his reading.

Quill leaves the room, gently closing the door behind him instead of slamming it like he wants to do. He rubs the side of his face, his cheek still burning from the slap. Fucker needs to be taken down hard, but he's not the vampire to do it. Far from it.

Instead of going back to the prison, he locks himself in his room, far away from everyone else who could hear him, as he shouts in rage, kicking the wall beside his bed.

He doesn't want to torture anyone. It had nothing to do with the fact he's dealing with a female. He'd raised his hand to more than his fair share of male and female wolves in his role. It's not something he's proud of, but also not something he's going to dwell on for too long. They all did things they're not proud of in here.

He knows from experience that gender didn't matter when it came to unruly prisoners, but that didn't mean he was a monster. He wasn't going to hurt her for no reason. That's not how he does things.

Unfortunately, it's not his call. The Warden will be checking on him. No matter how much it sticks in his gut, he's going to have to do as he's told.

BANNON

Strangely enough, today was a good day. He didn't think he'd have many of those on the island. It didn't have *that* feel to it. But working out with Quill at lunch was actually fun, and that was entirely unexpected. When Quill mentioned training, his initial thought was that he was going to completely embarrass himself in front of the boss he desperately wants to impress.

Quill is the key to his survival here. If he can get on the head guard's good side, or at least not on his bad side, he would be okay. Quill is a good boss, but he worked him hard, running him through his daily duties quickly and efficiently. It was taking time, but Bannon thinks he's getting a handle on the head guard. He's firm and strict, but nothing he's done so far hinted that he was unfair in any way. He genuinely seemed to be focused on keeping the prison running smoothly without any problems for either side.

In his position he could easily take things too far. With these wolves here for life, Quill could let his guards have their way with them without any repercussions. It's how he expected the prison would be run when he was first told about the place. He never thought it would have the order it does - and that's down to Quill. The head guard can more than hold his own against anyone.

From the minute he stepped on the mat, Quill put him in his place again and again. The head guard was savage, his movements methodical and his attack relentless. Bannon has no doubts Quill could have done a hell of a lot of damage if he really wanted to, and had restrained himself during their training, but he's still sore and bruised from the encounter.

An encounter he was convinced Quill would consider pathetic and weak.

Instead, the guard had complimented him. That recognition helped his crippling self-doubt lessen slightly. He didn't care what the other guards thought of him. They didn't think it was worth acknowledging him because of his disability, so to hell with them. But Quill had talked to him. Even knowing he couldn't respond easily, he still spoke to him as if his opinion mattered.

Plus, the head guard made eye contact as much as he could when he spoke to him. He's not used to that. It's like he wanted to make sure Bannon understood each task, without having to get a vocal confirmation that would never come.

Bannon liked that.

It's a small thing but made a world of difference to him. When he lost the ability to speak, he lost more than just his voice. He lost his ability to make himself heard in so many ways. It was like he suddenly didn't have an opinion, or anything to offer. Conversations took place around him while he listened on the sidelines.

He's still the same person. He still loves literature, art, old movies, good food, even better company. Still adores taking out his motorbike and heading off with no plan in mind. Just riding until he runs out of road. He desperately missed his bike and the freedom it offered.

Instead of getting lost in his head, he decides to go for a run before going to bed. After changing into joggers and a tank top, Bannon makes his way through the house to the back entrance which leads to the beach.

The island that the Warden owns is stunning in almost every way. But, having a secret prison under the magnificent house is a blot on the otherwise breathtaking location.

He takes the path to the beach, thankful to find he's alone. Bannon waits until he reaches the shore where the large rocks fall away to finer shingle, before breaking out into a run. This is the only time he's truly happy. Truly free.

He does a few laps of the beach, then after checking that he really is alone, strips down to his boxers before walking into the sea. The cool water is refreshing after his run, helping to clear his mind of the turbulence that's always with him.

He powers through the water alongside the shore, his thoughts wandering to places he tries to keep away from. He misses his old, much simpler life. Misses his family. Bannon's scar burns when he thinks of them. He lost his family and his voice in that one blood-filled night.

Dark thoughts replace his temporary happiness. Well, that didn't last long.

He pushes out of the water and gets dressed, struggling to slide on his clothes over his wet skin. As he's heading up the beach he spots Quill. *Shit!* How long has he been there? He was alone when he went in the water, so Quill must have arrived while he was swimming.

The male is further down the beach, standing on the stones at the water's edge, staring out at the sea. He either doesn't notice or doesn't bother acknowledging Bannon. It is his downtime too, so there's nothing to say he even has to be polite to Bannon.

30

He should turn and head back to his room, leave Quill in peace, but he doesn't. He stays watching him from just out of view. The head guard is impressive in so many ways. His hair is loose, the blonde locks sweeping across his face in the breeze. He's removed his work shirt, leaving on the black tank top with his combats.

Quill is confusing him. Bannon is over sixty years old and has only ever been with females. He'd be lying if he said he didn't look at males from time to time, but looking is very different to acting. And he's never taken that step. Never really wanted to explore that aspect of himself.

Everything about his life had been torn apart when he was savaged. Being attracted to males as well as females is probably just another symptom of his new confused life.

Maybe.

As he watches Quill, he realises for the first time how sad the male appears. His broad shoulders are slumped, his arms hanging by his side. In front of the other guards, and certainly the prisoners, he stands tall and sure of himself. But out here, alone on the beach, some of that front has slipped away.

As the head guard, his job is to run the prison and make sure everyone knows what they have to do. That doesn't leave much space for opening up, chatting, or relaxing. Maybe this is the one place on the island he can be himself. Somewhere to cast off all the rules and regulations he has to live by inside the prison.

Maybe that's something they have in common with each other. This is their escape.

Maybe he should stop thinking like that before he gets too carried away. They're not kindred spirits by any means. Quill is his boss and he's a new subordinate who should just mind his own fucking business and do what he's told.

He has no idea how things work on the island. He's only been here a week. Quill has been here for decades. Bannon can't imagine what Quill has seen, heard, and done in that time. It doesn't bear thinking about.

Bannon is about to turn around and go back to his room, when Quill pulls off his top and wades into the sea. Seems they might have another thing in common. But instead of swimming, he arches his back and releases his stunning wings.

His vast navy wings straighten behind him, showing Bannon the deep green flesh covering the front of each wing. Two-tone wings are not uncommon, but he hasn't seen many in his lifetime. Quill's wings perfectly match the colours of his eyes.

He watches as the head guard slowly lowers his wings into the water and just stands in the sea, looking out over the horizon, the cool water swirling around him.

In that moment, Bannon has never missed his voice more. He has the overpowering urge to ask Quill what's wrong. Maybe...

Maybe what? He can't blur the lines here. Quill is his boss and he's a mute newbie who doesn't know how things work around here. The last thing he wants or needs, is to get on the wrong side of the head guard in his first week - especially after he offered to train him.

And if he's having some sort of vampire equivalent of a midlife crisis, is Quill really the male he wants to explore that with?

Absolutely not! There's no question of that.

Bannon turns away before Quill catches him staring again. It was bad enough being caught over breakfast on his first day. He climbs up the beach, stepping onto the grass surrounding the house.

'You need to keep away from him.'

He stumbles, nearly knocking into a tree, when Duna appears out of the shadows that always seem to surround the ancient house.

She must be on a break from her shift. Duna walks over to him, her arms crossed as she comes to a stop in front of him. 'Quill is off limits.'

Bannon shakes his head, desperate to stop this conversation.

'I just need you to listen,' she says, dropping her voice low. 'I like you Bannon. I think you're decent. Probably one of the few decent ones in here. That's why I'm talking to you right now, so you need to listen to me.

'Keep away from Quill. Work with him. Do what he tells you to do. Then leave him alone. The Warden keeps a close eye on him. Believe me, you'd do best to avoid any attention from that high up.'

Bannon points down the beach to Quill then back to her, as he raises his eyebrows. If they're in a relationship, a part of him doesn't think he wants to know. But Duna quickly shakes her head.

'Me and Quill?' She laughs as she shakes her head. 'No. He's a decent male, but he's my boss. Just like he's your boss. It's not happening. Do you understand?'

He hears her loud and clear, although he's still not sure why he's even entertaining this conversation. Probably because he's absolutely positive Duna could break both his legs if she wanted to.

'Good.' She slaps him hard on the back as she walks away. 'Good talk.'

Bannon watches her disappear around the corner of the house, then glances over his shoulder.

Quill is still in the sea, but instead of looking out over the horizon, his head is down, his eyes closed as the waves break around him.

Bannon knows he should steer clear. He didn't need Duna to tell him that. The problem is he's not sure he wants to.

SORCHA

She peers up at the monstrous house as it appears out of the mist surrounding the island. Her previous two homes didn't look anything as lavish as this one does. Maybe this time she'll have a full suite with a private bathroom?

As if!

Sorcha releases a snort as she laughs to herself about that, earning a stern glare from one of her two guards. To hell with him! After this long in chains, she's going to laugh about whatever the fuck she wants to laugh about. Maybe they'll think she's insane and give her a nice, padded cell?

The boat docks, and when the engine is shut off, she could almost imagine she's just at the beach, listening to the waves lapping against the shore. But then she's shoved in the back and ordered to walk.

She growls at the asshole guard, before pushing to her feet and making her way unsteadily up the boat to the front. The other guard hauls her out of the boat and orders her to stand on the wooden dock, while the second one climbs out of the boat and stands behind her.

'Walk Wolf!'

'You know what? I don't think I want to.'

She nearly laughs aloud at the look on their faces. Idiot vampires weren't expecting her to refuse.

The one in front of her tries again. 'Move!'

She doesn't get a lot of excitement in her life anymore, so she's not about to pass up on this opportunity. 'Nope. I'm quite happy here, thank you very much.'

After looking at each other for moral support, they decide to take things up a level. The one at the front grabs hold of her arm, while the one at the back gives her a good push. With her wrists chained together she doesn't have a lot of room to move, but that's never stopped her before.

She throws her elbow back, catching the guard in the gut, sending him down to his knees. When his mate turns around to see what happened, she head-butts him, breaking his nose, blood spewing down his face.

Distracted briefly, the guards do nothing as she launches herself along the jetty. She's not going to get far. She knows that, but it's not going to stop her from trying. She hadn't survived this long just by accepting her fate.

With the vampires getting themselves together and hot on her heels, she jumps off the path onto the beach, racing across the stones as fast as she can. It's difficult to keep her balance with her hands restrained, but she's managing to put some distance between them.

To her left, the house towers above her, taking up most of the island with its sheer size. Maybe in the daylight it's stunning, but in the moonlight, it's an ominous presence, its eerie shadow following her along the beach.

Then she hears voices from her left. The guards from the boat are catching up with her. She screams as another large vampire suddenly bursts through the trees and throws himself at her. They crash to the ground, the male getting the upper hand for a moment.

On her back, and on the stones, she peers up at the vampire. His brown eyes are glowing, his fangs visible through his parted lips. He's obviously been through the wars himself at some stage. There's a thick raised scar running from under his chin and down his neck.

She smiles at him as he pins her wrists to the ground. 'Well, hello there gorgeous. If you wanted some alone time, you just had to ask.' He frowns and momentarily loosens his grip on her wrists. Sorcha shoves off the stones, flipping them both over.

She drives her restrained hands against the side of his head, dazing him as he tries to scramble to his feet. She pushes upright, desperate to put some distance between the vampire and herself before he can right himself.

She screams as a ball of flames erupts in front of her. Sorcha veers to the right, covering her head with her hands as the asshole releases another burst in her direction. Fucking vampires and their powers! At least he's not trying to kill her, just stop her. She doubts he's missing her by accident.

She risks a quick look behind her. He's gaining ground, his hands engulfed in flames as he pounds across the beach. Something momentarily blocks out the moonlight. She glances up and knows her cards are marked. One of the blood-suckers is up there. Might as well make her final push a good one. She'll play with these fuckers as long as she can.

But her fun doesn't last long. A huge vampire drops to the ground in front of her. He straightens, his green wings stretched out to either side, blocking her escape. She skids to a halt, sizing up her adversary.

This one won't be taken down like his friend. Everything about this vampire is menacing. He'll be the one to take her in. So be it. At least it's not one of those idiots on the boat. That would have just been insulting.

He flaps his wings, showing the navy skin covering the back of them. The thick black, razor-sharp, talons catch her attention as he moves them. She might want to make things difficult for these bloodsuckers, but she's not keen on being on the receiving end of one of his talons.

For a vampire this one is impressive. His eyes glow intensely, the unusual blue and green orbs the same colour as his wings. His blonde hair is tied back from his face, but the chase has freed some of the locks.

'Where the fuck do you think you're going Wolf?'

His deep, husky voice is the perfect match for him. 'It's such a lovely night. I thought I'd have a little moonlit run on the beach.'

He sneers at her, his lethal fangs making a brief appearance. She doesn't want to get up close and personal with those either.

Then he hits her with a taser he pulls out of his back pocket. The shock sends her to the ground, convulsing as her system is hit with a surge of voltage. The vampire crouches down beside her, his huge wings blocking out the light from the moon, leaving her staring up at his glowing eyes.

He punches her hard, and the last thing she hears is his voice coming from somewhere in the darkness. 'Welcome to Hell.'

QUILL

That was a fucking shit-show. In all his years at the prison, a prisoner transfer has never gone as badly as that one just did. He grabs a new shirt from his locker, pulling it on as he tries to calm down. One female wolf shouldn't have been able to get the better of those two vampire guards. They're just lucky they don't work for him. If they did it would be their last day. He doesn't tolerate idiots.

Quill flexes his fingers, but he's still wound like a spring. He glances over at Bannon, cleaning his head over at the sink at the side of the locker room. The guard has an impressive cut on the side of his head where the wolf hit him. It didn't stop him from taking chase though.

He's getting the impression it would take more than a punch from a wolf to take him down.

'You okay?'

Bannon nods as he dabs the cut with a cloth.

'You did good out there. I've got to say that power of yours came in useful.'

Bannon smiles as he nods, then goes back to cleaning the cut.

Before he met him, Quill was convinced Bannon would be a liability. Catching Bannon looking at him over breakfast that first day had just affirmed his initial feelings, but not for the reasons he thought.

The new guard is seriously good-looking.

He can't even pretend he wasn't looking himself that morning. He found his attention lingering on Bannon long after he'd looked away in embarrassment. But Quill hadn't looked away. He took the opportunity to have a long hard look at his new guard.

His brown hair and brown eyes matched perfectly, unlike his own freaky odd-coloured eyes. Bannon's not a Prime, but he's big enough to be one, which is a plus around here. You need to be able to look after yourself in this dump.

Watching from the sky as Bannon threw those fireballs at the wolf, he realised how deadly the mute vampire is. Fucking lethal in fact. Any worries he may have had about Bannon keeping control of his power had disappeared in that moment. The precision and control he showed on that beach was evident. He's more than got a grip on his power.

He looks over at his new guard again. He's done cleaning his wound. Time to get back to work. But this next part he has to do alone. 'When you're done, help the others with checking the cells.'

Bannon frowns, no doubt wondering why Quill is ditching him again. But, part of the perks of being in charge means he doesn't have to explain himself. Comes in useful at times like this.

He grabs gloves from his locker before shutting it and walking away from Bannon. As he heads towards the interrogation room Quill tries to calm his mind, but it's not an easy task. The Warden didn't give him anything to use against the wolf. No reason for wanting to break her, apart from her behaviour in previous prisons.

The sadistic bastard just wanted to throw his weight around. Prove he could control what others before him couldn't, which is a fucking joke. He rarely comes down to mix with the wolves and vampires living under him. Wouldn't want to get any grime on his expensive shoes.

He nods at the guard standing outside the door, dismissing him without a word. Both of them know what she's been brought into that room for. There's nothing else to say. He opens the door to find her hanging by her wrists from a heavy hook embedded in the ceiling, her toes barely touching the concrete floor. She's been stripped of her prison uniform, leaving her in her underwear. That wasn't his request. Someone else took it upon themselves to do that.

The wolf turns her head towards him, the blindfold hiding her eyes, but he can feel the venom in them through the material.

'Are you my welcome party?'

She is feisty. Quill stands in front of her and gets into the right frame of mind. He's done this countless times. He can do it again. He glances up at the camera over his head. It's directed at the wolf, giving the Warden front-row seats without having to get a spot of blood or dirt on his expensive suit.

'Do you do this for all new arrivals, or am I just lucky?'

'We do things differently in Level Three. I need to make sure you understand that.'

'Ah. The taser-shooting blood-sucker.'

Feisty doesn't come close to the correct description for this one. Quill picks up the leather whip, the weight of it in his hand dragging him down. He's glad she is blindfolded. He couldn't do it if she was looking at him.

She ran, Quill. She ran and hurt one of your men. Punish her for that. It's a weak reason, but it's all he's got.

She smiles at him, grabbing onto the chains supporting her. 'Go on then. What are you waiting for? Make me understand.'

He circles her, the whip dragging along the ground behind him. He can hear her heart beating rapidly in her chest. She can probably hear his too. Time to get this over and done with.

He pulls his arm back, then strikes out. The leather snaps against her back, and she arches away from him. He hits her again and again, her shouts of pain increasing with each snap of the whip.

SORCHA

She won't cry. Not yet. The tears will come. They always do sooner or later. But she won't give them the satisfaction.

But she's so fucking close.

She'd been hurt so many times since she found herself in prison, but nothing compared to what that guard did to her last night. Or was it today? Who knows how long she's been here for? She'd lost consciousness after a while, and for that she's grateful. Not that it makes the slightest bit of difference to the pain. It's all consuming, like fire coursing over her back.

She's still in her underwear, the cold stone wall she's now restrained against only adding to the excruciating pain from the flogging. But here is better than hanging from the ceiling of that other cell.

Don't let them win Sorcha.

It's a mantra she's been chanting to herself for years, but it's becoming difficult not to give in. Her new *home* is smaller than her last one, which doesn't help to improve her day. Being half naked isn't helping to improve that either. The stone walls are damp and cold, the concrete floor ingrained with years of dirt, dried blood, and she dreads to think what else.

The only light is coming through a yellowed piece of plastic or glass covering a small window in the door. Aside from her less-than-comfortable metal cot with sheets that were probably white when they were new many moons ago, is a small table with a plastic chair.

But it's the item in the corner between the table and the small metal sink that has her on the verge of tears. Instead of a toilet, there's a metal bucket.

She very much doubts the guards will deal with whatever she puts in there. Something else to look forward to.

Then she hears the locks disengage. Time for more fun and games. She pushes her fear deep down inside her, letting her inner bitch take control. She instantly recognises the two vampires as the ones who chased her down on the beach.

'About time.'

The two vampires glance at each other, before the blonde one leans back against the small table, resting his hip on the edge as he checks the paperwork. While Blondie looks at his paperwork, his companion gives her a thorough once-over. It could just be exhaustion, but she could swear he's surprised, maybe even shocked, by her appearance.

'Inmate Sixty-four,' the blonde one says.

'Asshole. I thought using a taser on me was a low blow, but the flogging might just have changed my mind.'

He glances up at her before looking at his mate. Nope. The brown-haired one had no idea about what had happened. Blondie isn't happy about her mentioning it. Fuck him! She pushes herself upright so she can use her arm to brush her long dark hair back from her forehead.

'Did you really think blindfolding me would hide your identity? I'm a fucking wolf you idiot! I have an exceptional sense of smell. I'd recognise your stench anywhere, and knew who you were as soon as you spoke.'

He glares at her but doesn't react.

'Oh, and my name is Sorcha.'

'Sixty-four,' he continues, ignoring her. 'Four years in Level One, four in Level Two. Now you're here.'

Eight years? She had no idea it was that long. He catches the surprise on her face before she hides it. 'Injured sixteen guards—'

'Nineteen.'

'What?' he asks before he can stop himself.

'That number should be nineteen. Those two guards on the boat.' She nods over to the silent guard, winking at him. 'And you. How's the head? Hope I didn't hit you too hard.'

She smiles at the vampire, catching the flash of his fangs as he glares at her. Clearly, he doesn't forgive her.

'You'll get twenty minutes exercise a day,' Blondie continues. 'Shower once a week. Because of your moonlit run on the beach, you've lost your meal privileges.'

'Meal privileges? You mean eating in this place is a privilege?'

'Yes. Being allowed to breathe the fucking air in here is a privilege.'

She blows out a long breath. 'Whoa. That's intense. You on a bit of a power trip or something?'

He straightens, his snarl echoing in the small cell.

'I'm the head guard so yeah, you could say that.'

She pushes her back against the wall, trying to take some pressure off her wrists. There's a strong chance he's just going to leave her chained to the wall in her underwear. He's not about to cut her any slack. 'Well, well, well. The head honcho himself. I'm honoured. Or are you the big bad guard dog? The big gun sent in to control any unruly prisoners?'

'Having me in your cell isn't a good thing.'

'Ah, I get you. And what about him?' she asks, smiling over at the other vampire who is still standing by the door with his arms crossed. 'What's his part in this game?'

'This isn't a fucking game!' the head guard roars, his temper rapidly running out. He pushes off the table, leaning over her with one hand against the wall. He peers down at her, but she keeps smiling at him. 'I'm going to have fun breaking you.'

'Give it your best-shot guard dog. I look forward to more private time with you and your whip.'

She can nearly see him biting his tongue to hold back whatever response he wanted to give her. Instead, he unlocks the chains attaching her to the wall, leaving the bands around her wrists to stop her shifting into wolf form.

'Now what?'

He pushes off the wall, putting some distance between them. 'Now you sit and stay.' He nods to the chair tucked under the small table. 'Uniform is over there.'

He backs out of the room, shutting and locking the door behind him and his friend. 'Sit and stay until when?' she asks, already up and at the door, refusing to sit and stay as ordered, but he's gone. She peers through the small window but can see nothing except the stone wall outside her cell.

Moving slowly due to the pain, she shuffles over to the table, pulling the black jumpsuit from the chair. The thought of putting the rough material anywhere near her raw back isn't appealing, but the cell is freezing so she's just going to have to suck it up.

Thanks to her wolf blood, she should be healed in a few hours, but until then it's going to hurt like hell. Sorcha reaches behind her, wincing as she brushes her fingers against her skin. They come away covered in blood. 'Damn it!' If this prison is like the others, she'll get one uniform and have to make do. She'd prefer not to start off with it covered in blood.

Taking the small cup from the sink, she fills it with water and gingerly trickles it over her shoulder and down her back. As soon as the water hits her wounds, she hisses, trying not to make too much noise. There's no way she's going to do or say anything to show how much pain she's actually in. She won't give the head guard that satisfaction.

BANNON

He shouldn't be here. If Quill finds out he came back to the wolf's cell, he'll be in a world of trouble. But he couldn't keep away. He just had to check on her again before he finished his shift.

She hadn't endeared herself to him from the first moment he threw himself on her. His head still hurts from where she struck him. It was actually his fault she was able to hit him. She distracted him briefly by calling him gorgeous. It had done the trick though - as she planned.

She'd used that moment of distraction to get the upper hand on him.

At least Quill hadn't been angry at him for his performance on the beach. Hearing that Quill was impressed by his powers was a pat on the back he didn't know he needed. At least if this is Bannon's life from now on, he wants to do a good job.

The entire interaction between the wolf and Quill was strangely amusing to watch. He could be totally wrong, but he could swear that Quill was as thrown by her attitude as he was.

A part of him had been looking forward to seeing her again. He wanted to see how being locked in a cell for a few hours had taken her down a notch or two. But he hadn't known that Quill got there first.

When she had a go at Quill for flogging her, Bannon had heard the words. They all went in. But that didn't mean he accepted what he was hearing. He had no idea Quill did that to her. As much as he didn't want to believe it had happened, there was no denying the pain she was in. She may have been trying to hide it, but he could see it. He knows pain and knows what it looks like when someone else is experiencing it.

Since he left her cell, he'd considered asking Quill why she was flogged. Was she punished because she tried to escape? He can't think of another reason Quill would do that. Unless it wasn't Quill who made that decision. The Warden could have ordered him to do that to her.

Whoever made the decision to punish her like that, he believes their plan may have failed. The wolf giving Quill attitude was far from broken, far from tamed. She was still very much fighting. Something he has to give her credit for.

Remaining totally quiet, hidden in the shadows outside her cell, he peers in the small window in the door and watches as she tries to clean her wounds. His own scar burns as the water runs down her bloody back.

Quill didn't just hurt her. He tore her back to pieces. This was so much more than a quick flogging as a punishment. Not that he would ever condone flogging any of the prisoners here. But like everything else in his new world, that's something that's out of his control.

Everything he thought he knew about Quill fades as he watches the blood trickle down her back.

Of course she tried to escape when she was brought here. No one can blame her for that. It may have been done with a little too much sass for Quill's liking, but did that really deserve a brutal flogging?

She brushes her waist-length dark hair over her shoulder to keep it out of the way as she tries to get dressed. Even in this light he can see the pain in her green eyes. That was something he noticed about her from that first moment he straddled her on the beach. Her eyes are a deep, clear green. The same colour green as Quill's eye and his wings. Why he's making that association he doesn't know.

He frowns when he hears her quietly sobbing to herself, as she painfully pulls her jumpsuit over the wounds. Bannon walks away before she notices him, the pain she's in hitting him harder than he expected it to.

She's a wolf. He shouldn't care that she's suffering. But as much as he hates her species, he's not a cruel male. He's made mistakes in his life, but he knows they were mistakes. He'd still like to believe he's a good male. He'd never be one to take pleasure from another in pain. Wolf. Vampire. Human. Animal. It makes no difference to him. Pain is pain.

He sneaks back into the dorms and makes it to his room without bumping into anyone. He doesn't know how he'd react if he saw Quill. Sometimes, not being able to make small talk has its advantages. He doubts he'd be able to pretend everything is okay.

Bannon strips out of his uniform, suddenly feeling dirty. He steps into the shower letting the hot water wash away the shame and regret.

Tomorrow is another day. He needs to get himself together before training with Quill tomorrow before his shift. Just like him, that wolf needs to learn how things work in here. Life on this rock is hard. It doesn't matter if you're a guard or a prisoner. At the end of the day, they're all here because they have no choice.

QUILL

Instead of eating with the rest of the guards that were on the early shift with him, Quill takes his dinner back to his room, so that he can eat in private. He's not a people person. Never has been. And it's not like there's anything remotely interesting to talk about working here. They're all in the same situation. Apart from the one weekend a month when they're allowed off the island, every one of the guards lives and works here.

He's spent all day every day with most of the guards for so long, they've run out of things to say to each other. Until Bannon arrived on the island, his life was monotonous.

Fuck this! He's got no appetite. He changes into his workout clothes and leaves his room, taking the back corridor. He's not avoiding Bannon, he just doesn't want to bump into him. Working with him is going to be fucking great if he's worried about passing him in the corridor!

As soon as he leaves the prison, it feels as if a weight has been lifted when he smells the fresh sea air. It doesn't matter how many times he showers, the stench of the prison refuses to leave him. Except when he's out here. It's the only place he escapes it... escapes everything... escapes the life he's living. The life he detests nearly as much as the stench inside the building.

While he's out here, for a short time, he's free.

Quill picks his way along the rocks lining the boundary of the house, then drops down onto the beach. As soon as his trainers hit the rough sand he takes off, powering along the beach, desperate to put as much distance between himself and that building as possible.

He can't get what he did to that wolf out of his head. He'd been asked to do a lot by the Warden over his years here. So why is that one task refusing to leave his thoughts?

Probably because it hadn't had the desired effect.

The wolf had continued to front-up to him, disrespecting him, pushing his buttons. He'd flogged her for so long she'd passed out from the pain, yet she still didn't give a damn what she said to him. She's got guts and that's something he can't help but respect.

She actually amused and interested him more than any prisoner has for as long as he can remember. He's never had an inmate like her before, and quite a few have passed through the doors of the prison. As bizarre as it sounds, she's like a breath of fresh air he didn't realise he needed. Everyone else does what they're told. For the most part, his life was like a Groundhog Day. Occasionally someone would try their luck, but it was few and far between.

It's not like he wants there to be disruption. The prison needs order and control. But having that little spark of defiance is a pleasant change to his otherwise monotonous life.

When he heard she'd run rings around the guards from the other two prisons she was in, he'd assumed they were idiots. Wolves are typically stronger than vampires, but the vampires working in the prisons should be trained and more than capable of controlling the prisoners. They should be able to control one female wolf.

After spending the short time he has with her, he now realises how she was able to get the upper hand on the other guards. Like Bannon, she has an inner strength that's impossible to miss or to ignore. She is a fighter through and through.

Her defiance, her brazen squaring up to him was the most fun he's had for years. He's clearly lost the plot. He's only one-hundred and fifty-three. Too young for Blood Fever to have taken hold. Maybe he's losing his sanity? Being locked away on this island would easily do that to anyone. He'd seen it happen to many prisoners and some guards over his time here.

She needs to break though. He *needs* her to break. His well-being depends on being able to do his job. He'd made his report to the Warden, putting in basic terms what he had done to her, even though he knew the Warden had been watching it all as it took place. The Warden had seemed pleased by Quill's actions and told him to continue.

Continue what?

Beating her for no reason?

After two encounters with her he knows one thing - she's not going to be easily broken. That makes his job so much more difficult. The Warden won't let up until he gets his way. Neither will she.

So where does that leave him? Stuck in between two uncooperative, strong-willed people who are determined to make his life so much more difficult.

Fuck both of them! This is his time. His time to get away from all of that. Pushing thoughts of the Warden and the wolf from his mind, he picks up the pace. But as he runs, his mind takes him on a completely different track. Another one he has no business venturing down.

Bannon.

You'd have to be an idiot not to have noticed his face when the wolf mentioned the flogging. It doesn't bother him that Bannon was shocked. But the fact that Bannon had *such* a reaction isn't sitting well with him. Things like that happen in the prison. There could come a time when Quill orders Bannon to do something he won't want to do. Quill tried to take care of any of the more brutal tasks himself, but there was the odd time he needed help. If he can't depend on Bannon to do what's needed, they may have a problem.

He can already tell Bannon is off with him after he heard what happened with the wolf. Even with no voice, the male seems perfectly capable of making his feelings known. He usually prefers to train the new recruits personally, but might have to make an exception in this case if Bannon continues to have a problem. He's got enough on his own plate without dealing with Bannon's issues.

He slows down, coming to a stop at the far end of the beach where the sand fades away to be replaced by huge boulders lining the Warden's private dock.

End of the road. Nowhere left to run.

'Fuck!'

His roar is swallowed up by the wind coming off the sea. So much for running away from his problems. His mind is refusing to let him escape.

He turns to face the sea as he catches his breath and tries to calm himself. Since the day he was brought here, he's fought for everything he's got. And he's got fuck-all except his position in the prison and the respect of his guards. It was enough. It wasn't what he wanted from his life - far from it, but vampires in his situation should be grateful for anything they can call their own.

But now...

He shakes his head, frustrated and irritated by the predicament the Warden has put him in. Just when he thinks he's got a hold on his life, the Warden throws something else at him. It's almost as if the asshole is testing him, pushing him to his limits, seeing if, like the prisoners on the other side of the bars, he'll break.

Maybe he will? Maybe if he can't break this wolf, the Warden will break him instead. He's never failed before, but he's never had someone as stubborn as that wolf to deal with.

He looks through the alarmed wire fence to the Warden's jetty and the expensive speedboat bobbing in the water. This fence is all that separates the Warden from the lives he's lording over. A light turns on in the room at the top of the mansion, overlooking the jetty. A shadow approaches the window so Quill steps back, getting lost in the trees at the edge of the beach.

The Warden sips his red wine as he watches the sea. Quill bares his teeth, the growl rumbling deep in his chest as his fangs extend. He glares down at the thick bracelet around his wrist, momentarily tempted to tear off his hand so he can remove it. But that won't do him any good. The damn thing would just be fitted again.

Before he's noticed, Quill turns away, punching a tree with his fist as he passes by. He could run forever, and he'll never be able to escape this life. He'd give anything to see his father again. They didn't always see eye-to-eye. That was his fault. His father worked for the Raven King. He laughs harshly to himself. *Worked* is the wrong word.

Like the Warden, the Raven King wasn't keen on letting his employees have free will. He tried to get his father to leave, to escape, to stop being so damn obliging. But Fergus refused to rock the boat. After working for the Warden, Quill now sees why his father kept his head down and just survived.

He wishes he could apologise for giving his father such a hard time about it. But he wishes a lot of things could be different. Quill straightens his shoulders as he approaches the door leading back into the dorms. It's nearly time for the inmates to get their dinner. He'll order Bannon to deal with the wolf. Pull rank and keep away from her until he has to try and break her again.

11

SORCHA

When she hears the door being unlocked, she doesn't bother getting up from her bunk. She doesn't even bother looking around. If that asshole head guard wants to break her, he's going to have his work cut out for him.

She knows the routine well enough by now. After eight years she should. Besides, if this is to be her home for the rest of her life, she needs to figure out how things work in this prison. She found her feet in the other two prisons after a few days. Initially some of the guards decided to be a little too friendly with her. But that stopped after a few broken fingers and noses. Things seem to be playing out the same way here.

Arriving in style as she had, probably helped solidify her

reputation. She doesn't know if the head guard had told the other guards to keep away, or if the threat of broken bones had done the trick, but, apart from Blondie and his silent friend, stay away they did.

And for that, she's grateful.

The worst thing that you can do in these places is draw attention to yourself. It's also detrimental to appear weak and a pushover. She had shown both the guards and the other prisoners that she wasn't someone you mess with. She'd spent so long in solitary over the years that she barely knew what was going on in the prisons around her.

Solitary had become a part of her life. She had spent a fair bit of time there in the last prison. Being alone in the dark is a hell of a lot better than being in with everyone else in the main prison. In solitary, she just has to worry about the guards. Out there, the odds would be less in her favour.

The tray of food is placed on the small table against the far wall but, instead of leaving, the guard stays in the cell, looking at her. She can feel his eyes on her as she faces the wall, pretending not to care about the scrutiny.

She takes a deep breath and pauses, opening her eyes as she sorts through the scents. It's a male vampire, his scent familiar somehow. She takes another breath. This one smells good. Not just his cologne, which is deep and rich with spices, no, it's the male himself who has a pleasing scent, which is strange. She's not usually so drawn to the scent of a vampire.

Sorcha slowly rolls onto her back, her healing skin tender under her weight. It's the asshole's friend. He's tall and broad, but most of the vampire guards are. His dark hair is cut short at the sides and back, but longer on top, hanging over his forehead. His brown eyes are locked on her, but he's not making her feel uncomfortable. Quite the opposite, actually. If anything, he seems to be a little confused.

'Well, hello again. How's the head?'

His eyes narrow, but he doesn't reply.

'You're not still upset about the other night, are you? You nearly had me there for a bit.' She pushes upright, leaning forward so she doesn't brush her back against the stone wall. 'I have to say that thing you did with the fire was - wow! Seriously impressive. I take it you were trying to miss me, or else it might not have been quite so impressive?'

Still no response.

Another guard appears in the doorway, his broad body blocking out the little light shining in from outside. She keeps the smile on her face, even though having the head guard back in her cell makes her nearly nauseous.

This prison is just like the others in that regard. Each one has a well-trained guard dog, running the prison for the vampire who actually owns it. From what she's seen of the male so far, one thing is clear - he's an emotionless asshole. But they all are. What do you expect from a group of filthy vampires?

'Well, where's your whip today?'

He snarls briefly at her, before getting himself together. *That's right dickhead. I'm going to keep biting back.*

He steps into her cell, his hand on his gun as he peers down at her. Yeah, he's pissed off she's not bowing at his fucking feet.

'What exactly are you looking at?'

The smile he gives her nearly wipes her own smile off her face. He's got huge fangs that he likes to keep flashing at her. 'I'm looking at absolutely nothing.'

She doesn't know how, but he manages to make that sentence sound so degrading.

'Ten minutes to eat, then we'll take you out for exercise.'

She sits up in the bed and spreads her legs, the ill-fitting black jumpsuit doing nothing to help the seductive image, but she's bored and likes annoying him, so why not? 'You can take me for *exercise* here if you want.' She winks at his silent friend. 'Both of you.'

Blondie growls, clearly not amused by her offer. His friend, however, hasn't got a clue where to look. And she actually doesn't mind him looking. For a vampire, he's not too bad. Neither of them are, compared to her past captors.

But Blondie puts an end to her fun when he grabs her by the arm and shoves her onto the plastic chair by the table. He grips the back of her head, pushing her face close to her dinner. He holds her nose just above the food as he growls in her ear. 'Eat your fucking food Wolf, or go without! I couldn't care less.'

He gives her one last shove for good measure before releasing her and taking a step back.

'Oh, I know that. Asshole!'

He doesn't react. If he's in charge he's going to remain calm and level-headed, which is probably what you want in a facility like this. But it also means he's going to do whatever he needs to do to keep things running smoothly.

This one won't allow himself to be pushed. She won't be able to irritate him. Won't be able to push his buttons. The stoic vampire doesn't have any worth pushing.

'So does your friend have a name?'

'Officer Bannon,' he replies, watching her eat the meagre and tasteless dinner. Calling what's in front of her *food* is being incredibly kind. It's beyond terrible. There is something that was possibly a piece of bacon at one stage in its life, with a side order of under-cooked potato. Not quite a gourmet dish but it's all she's getting today, so it's going down whether she wants it or not.

'He not talk for himself?' she asks as she fights with the meat.

'Eat your food.'

She holds up her plastic fork, waving it in his direction. 'Eating! I'm Sorcha by the way, in case you missed that when I was brought in. So, Blondie, what's your name?'

He frowns, the corner of his lip twitching just above the piercing. Well, well, well. Maybe she can push a button or two.

'Officer Quillan.'

She smiles sweetly at the two of them, still refusing to be all timid in front of them. 'Nice to meet you, Bannon and Quill.' She smirks as she says his name, hoping it irritates him that she shortened it and dropped his title. But it doesn't seem to bother him, which just irritates her instead.

'You going to shut up and eat?' he asks.

Sorcha shovels more food into her mouth. Whatever it is, or was, it's dry and chewy.

'So, aren't I the lucky one, Quill?' she says, once the food finally breaks up enough to be swallowed. 'I'm such a menace that it takes two big male vampires to control me. That's a bit of a kick in the balls for you two, isn't it?'

'Stop smirking when you call me Quill. If you wanted to piss me off, you could have kept calling me Quillan.' He leans over her, his massive body dwarfing her. 'Eat your fucking food!'

'Yes, sir!'

The small kick she gets at his snarl brightens up her day that little bit more. She might not have won on the name front, but she still annoyed him. It's childish, and will probably just put her further into his bad books, but to hell with it.

She glances at Bannon, before stabbing another piece of rock-hard meat with her fork and putting it in her mouth. Bannon is completely out of his depth here. It took less than a few minutes to figure that out.

He may be nearly as big and intimidating in appearance as Quill, and that nasty scar on his neck helps add to the front he's clearly putting on, but she can see that there's still some emotion in his warm brown eyes, and that's something he'll need to lose if he's to truly fit in.

He must be new.

That innocence won't last. A few weeks working here and he'll be dead inside like all the other guards. Just another soulless, intimidating, mindless drone - obeying orders and pushing people around. Just like Quill.

And that's a huge shame.

Quill isn't unattractive by any means, but his job, and this place have obviously taken its toll on him. His odd-coloured eyes were no doubt stunning at some stage, but now show no warmth. Nothing at all, actually. She doubts he ever smiles, not that there's a lot to smile about in here. But it's the menace surrounding him that intrigues her more than it should.

There's something about him that screams *back off*.

And she has no doubt everyone does.

Except her, which doesn't make sense considering how he's treated her. But that's not really a surprise, is it? He's a vampire. They've been persecuting wolves for centuries. Why should it stop now?

Maybe she could have stopped what he was doing to her by begging him, by whimpering and pleading with him. But that's not in her nature. Not by a long shot.

She places the plastic fork back on the paper plate. 'I'm done. My compliments to the chef. It was excellent.'

Quill roughly pulls out her chair and gestures to the door. 'Get up.'

Sorcha gets to her feet then walks over to him.

'You forgetting something?' Quill says, as she reaches the door. 'Get your bucket.'

Sorcha looks over her shoulder at her *toilet* and grimaces. 'What! Really?'

'Yes, really. You clean up after yourself. You can either bring it now, or leave it for another day, or another week. I couldn't give a fuck. It's you who will have to live with the stench.'

She picks up her bucket, rejoining Quill and Bannon at the door. With Quill taking the lead and Bannon behind her, she is guided through the gloomy corridors, desperately trying not to bump her bucket into either guard or herself.

However bad the other prisons were, this is a new and degrading low. Quill stops suddenly, nearly getting the contents over the back of his legs. As much as she'd enjoy that, his punishment wouldn't be worth the few minutes of payback.

He glares at her before opening the door to a small exercise yard. It may not be an open field or a vast mountain range, but right now, it's paradise in her otherwise miserable life.

She closes her eyes and takes a deep breath. The fresh salty scent of the sea brings a smile to her lips. In the distance, she can hear the crash of the waves on the beach. It's such a relief after the stench which is ingrained in the very walls of the prison. Who knows how many decades of filth have been left uncleaned. Judging by the odour, it's been a very long time.

She curses as Quill shoves her in the back, pushing her forward so he can close the door. 'Hey! Watch it! I nearly dropped my bucket.'

'Then you would have been on your hands and knees cleaning it up. The drain is against the back wall. Empty it and wash it out, then leave it at the door.'

When she doesn't immediately move, he steps closer, dwarfing her with his huge body. 'Don't make me repeat myself. I can always turn you around and march you back inside?'

'No.'

'Then do what I said.'

She flashes him a smile before walking away from him, over to the drain. After washing out her toilet at the tap over the drain, she drops the bucket back by the door and stands to attention in front of him. 'Now what?'

'Now walk!'

He growls as she curtseys to him before she turns away from him and starts walking around the perimeter of the yard. She's going to try to enjoy her time in the fresh air before she's dragged back into her cell again. Deep inside, her wolf howls, desperate to be released. Every day her wolf grows a little quieter, a little more distant. Being locked up for years will have that effect on someone.

How much longer will she be able to feel her wolf? What if she wakes one day and it's gone? What if her link to that side of herself dies if it isn't released for nearly a decade?

She couldn't bear that. Couldn't bear to lose such a massive part of herself.

Ignoring her two guards, she walks around the courtyard in the centre of the building, desperate to keep the tears as deeply buried as her wolf is. She won't show weakness in front of the guards. Won't give Quill the satisfaction.

The monstrous house towers above her on all sides. Is the owner of the prison up there somewhere, sitting in his lavish room, while his prisoners live in despair under his feet?

She scratches at the metal bands around her wrists. The two cuffs match the ones around her ankles. If she tried to shift into her much larger wolf form, she'd lose her hands and feet when the bands cut into her. She'd seen a desperate male wolf shift a few years ago, and she can still hear his screams in her head as his hands and feet were amputated by the bands.

A tear runs down her cheek as she continues doing her laps. She's trying so hard to stay strong and defiant in front of the vampires, but she misses her wolf. Misses her old life. But more than that, she desperately misses her brothers.

The pain is almost a physical thing, always there like a heavy stone in her gut. Murt, Con, Garret, and her twin, Fionn, are more than her brothers. They are also her best friends.

They fought regularly, as most siblings do, but she loved each of them dearly. Having three older, seriously over-protective brothers did bring its own challenges at times, but they always had her best interests at heart.

It's Fionn who she misses the most, however. She is the older twin by twelve minutes, so she calls him her baby brother. Fionn hated that nickname, which is exactly why she kept using it. She loved winding him up whenever she could. But they were incredibly close, and being away from him means she's missing a large piece of herself.

62

The worst bit is knowing he's experiencing the same loss she is. The five of them are linked to each other. All shifter clans are the same. But her connection to Fionn is so much stronger. Being without him is like missing an arm or a leg.

She knows Murt will be turning over every single stone looking for her. He always took the big brother/clan leader job incredibly seriously. Level-headed and dependable in stressful situations, her brother is a natural leader. But if you get on his wrong side, you might as well dig your own grave - because that's where he'll send you.

She smiles as she does another lap. How she'd love to witness her brothers tear this place apart.

But they need to find her first. After all this time, the odds of that happening are diminishing by the day.

MURT

Murtagh Whelan grips the branch, pulls his body up, holds, then slowly lowers again. In front of him, two of his brothers, Conal and Garret, are sparring, while Fionn is buried under the bonnet of their beat-up truck, trying to fix it. Again. The damn thing is broken more often than it runs.

It's how most days go here. Since being banished to Mount Leinster on the border between Carlow and Wexford in Ireland, they've been surviving... barely. Stuck in a fucking shite Groundhog Day with no hope of escape.

They didn't have much before they were shunned, but at least they had land and property. They had freedom. They had a life. Now they're restricted to a few kilometres, are living hand to mouth, and call an old static caravan *home.*

That last part is the bit that's proving to be the largest hurdle they need to overcome. Having the four big, usually frustrated, angry wolves in a very cramped space is a nightmare. It's a fucking miracle they haven't killed each other yet.

It might still happen. Garret and Con aren't the easiest to live with.

He finishes his pull-ups, dropping to the ground and picking up the towel from the grass. He checks the time, grimacing to himself when he realises it's nearly time for work. He had managed to get a few hours bar tending in the local pub. They needed some way to keep food on the table, and there weren't many options in the village at the foot of the mountain.

When four men moved in overnight, it had raised a few suspicious looks. With no identification or official paperwork of any kind, job options were few and far between. They had to take whatever they could get.

This isn't how he had imagined his life would play out. The Whelan clan is one of the oldest, one of the original wolf families. As the Elder of his clan, Murtagh should be sitting with the rest of the clan Elders. Instead, he's pulling pints for a few Euro in the local pub.

He had never been *in favour* with the other clans, but this is fucking humiliating. He wipes his face with the towel as he watches his brothers. *He* did this to them. *He* made the decision to help the Blackjacks take down Davyn's father - The Raven King. *He* took a knee before Davyn, swearing his allegiance to the vampire.

Either of those events would have been enough to put himself and his clan on the wrong side of the Elders. But both? Well, he's kind of surprised someone hasn't tried to take them out permanently. But it's not even lunchtime yet. There's still time.

'Hey Murt!' Fionn calls. 'We've got company!'

He pauses for a second, wondering if he had just tempted fate by letting that thought cross his mind, before joining his three brothers at the edge of the field. They keep behind the side of the caravan, watching the brand-new BMW pull up at the far side of the fence bordering the field. Murt peers around the corner, breaking into a smile when the driver and passenger doors open. 'Fuck me!' he says, stepping out from behind the caravan. 'What the hell are you doing here?'

Davyn's mate, Thea, hurries over to him, throwing her arms around his neck when he lifts her off the ground. 'Hello yourself. It's so good to see you again Murt.'

He returns her hug before placing her back on the ground, then holds out his hand as Fletch walks over to them. 'Nice to see you again Fletch.'

'You too Murt. How's your leg?'

He rubs his hip. 'Still sore when it's cold. Davyn's father got me good with that damn stake.'

'That he did. So, you're probably wondering what we're doing here?'

'You could say that. Before you explain, might be best we take this out of the open. Can't say we're not being watched.'

He leads them into their temporary accommodation, clearing clothes from one of the bench seats so they have somewhere to sit. Thea and Fletch eye their new home with a small degree of pity which he ignores. He's carrying enough guilt as it is, without letting their opinion get to him.

'I suppose you want to know how we found you?' Fletch says as the four brothers squash onto the seats next to them.

'Can't deny it crossed my mind,' Murt says. 'I take it that you know what happened to us after we got back to Ireland? No way you would have tracked us to here otherwise.'

'When Davyn lost contact with you, we started to search for you,' Thea explains. 'It took a bit of digging, but we found mention of a punishment given to wolf clans who don't play by the rules.'

'And naturally you thought of us, seeing as we're always toeing the line and all that,' Garret says with a grin.

'You have been known to do things your way,' Fletch says. 'It wasn't much of a push to realise you'd got into a spot of bother by helping us.'

'You could say that. So, why no vampires paying us a visit? Why just send humans?'

'We thought vampire activity in the area could land you blokes in more trouble,' Fletch says. 'So here we are. What the hell happened to you after you left us?'

Murt settles back on the thin cushion. 'You got it in a nutshell when you said that helping you lot got us in a spot of bother. We associated with vampires, which the Elders didn't take too well, and here we are. Lost our land, property, money. All gone.'

'Why didn't you tell us?' Thea asks.

'It's our problem. We knew when we agreed to help that it would probably bite us in the ass. We wouldn't change what happened. The Elders just took this as their chance to get rid of us. We're not on the best of terms. Haven't been for too long to count. They just used this as a reason to get rid of us once and for all.'

'But part of the deal was that Davyn will protect you. You could have contacted him.'

'Wolves don't go cap in hand to vampires. It's not how we work. We're grand.'

The feisty human crosses her arms and hits him with a serious look. 'Grand? Really? You're honestly going to try to convince us that you're grand?'

Murt has always liked Thea, but she's sticking herself into a situation she knows nothing about. 'The Elders aren't going to just sit back and hope we stay where they put us. They'll be watching to make sure we stay within a ten-kilometre radius. If we leave here, my brothers could be in danger again.'

Garret growls at him, but he ignores him. He'll deal with whatever issue his brother has once they're alone. 'So why did you come looking for us?' he asks Thea, trying to get back on track.

'Do you remember Fergus? He was Davyn's father's assistant?'

The brothers nod.

'Well, he's been really helpful over the last few months. He gave us all of The Raven King's journals and ledgers. It seems Dav's father knew a bit about the practices and rules relating to wolves.'

'And that brought you to Mount Leinster?'

'And it brought us to Mount Leinster.' Thea's face turns solemn for a moment. 'I'm so sorry this happened to all of you. Is there anything the Blackjacks can do to help?'

'In fairness, Thea, they've done enough. And I mean no disrespect by that. We knew what we were doing. But I'm guessing you being here isn't just a social call?'

Fletch nods. 'It's mainly to make sure you guys are doing okay, but there is an ulterior motive to our visit.'

'I've been spending the last few weeks collating all the information from the journals,' Thea says, taking over from Fletch.

'What sort of information?' Murt asks.

'Lists of names mainly. Davyn's father liked to keep track of every vampire he put in the pits. From the notes, it seems he took vampires and some wolves from the villages around the castle. There was mention of some prisons too, as well as the fighting pits.'

'What sort of prisons?' Con asks.

'We don't know,' she says. 'The information is sketchy at best. I've only scraped the surface of the journals, but from what I can make out, he sent vampires to the fighting pits and wolves to the prisons. Perhaps your sister found herself in one of the prisons?'

The four wolves look at Thea. 'What do you know of our sister?' Garret asks.

'We know you have a sister and that she's missing,' Thea says. 'Nix sent us here to see if you would be willing to come with us to Dav's castle. The Blackjacks are looking for the prisons and thought you might like to help. The castle is well guarded, and everyone there is loyal to Dav. He'll guarantee your safety.'

68

Murt takes a second to process that. In all honesty, he assumed when he swore allegiance to Davyn, that would be the end of it. He hadn't planned to see the vampire again, let alone go back to that depressing castle.

His brothers look at him, but no one speaks. They're waiting for him to take the lead. 'Can you give us a minute?'

'Of course.' They go outside, leaving Fletch and Thea in the caravan while they speak in private.

'Do you think Sorcha is in a prison?' Fionn asks before they've come to a stop. They're all desperate to find her again, but Fionn even more so. His twin is a part of him. Without Sorcha, he's incomplete.

Murt leans against a tree and crosses his arms. 'It's the best lead we've had for a hell of a long time, and it would explain how she just vanished. We've torn this island apart looking for her. If there are secret prisons, there's a chance we could have missed them.'

'So, do we leave here? Go with Thea and Fletch back to Davyn's castle?'

He doesn't know how to answer Fionn. Leaving Mount Leinster could bring the Elders back to their doorstep. The second they leave the area they've been banished to, the Elders will know. The fuckers have eyes and ears everywhere. It would be a one-way trip, so they have to be damn sure it's the right decision. *He* needs to make sure it's the right decision. Murt already lost his sister. He can't put his brothers in danger too.

'Oh, knock it off Murt!'

Con's remark takes him by surprise. 'Excuse me?'

'I can see what you're thinking. We all can. You're fucking transparent! You're blaming yourself for Sorcha and don't want to risk us now by taking us away from here.'

'Hang on—'

'No, you shut up and listen for a second,' Con interrupts. 'Sorcha disappearing wasn't on you. It wasn't on any of us. She went for a run, Murt. None of us could have known she wouldn't come back. But we're not going to find her sitting on our arses in this shithole.'

'We don't belong here, Murt,' Fionn says. 'What we did... it doesn't deserve this punishment.'

'So, you're saying you want to go with them? You want to risk bringing the Elders to our doorstep?'

Con shakes his head. 'Fuck them! We got down on one knee in front of Davyn. We should be using him.'

Murt laughs at that. 'Davyn isn't a vampire you *use*.'

'Use his protection then,' Con says. 'That castle is a fortress. Like Thea said, we'll be safe there. We can't breathe here. We're always on edge, waiting to be taken out by either the Elders, or a rival clan. We need a break, Murt. Staying here is going to be the end of us.'

Con usually has a point when he does decide to share it. It's just not an idea Murt is completely on board with. If they leave here, the Elders will find out. No question. But if there's even the slightest chance Sorcha is in one of those prisons, they can't find her alone. Having the Blackjacks and Davyn's men to help will make an impossible task possible.

'You know what it means for us if we do leave here? You know we'll be signing our death sentence.'

'We did that the minute we took a knee in front of Davyn,' Garret says. 'We get you're trying to protect us, but we can't hide forever. Your leg is healed. We've spent months training. We're in the best shape we've been in ever. Now is the time to come out of the shadows Murt.'

He looks over at the makeshift home and battered truck. His brothers are right. They've been hiding here for too long. The only reason they didn't put up a fight when they were sent here was because he was injured. They needed breathing time for him to heal after the last battle, to regroup and figure out what their next move would be, but mainly to keep them safe.

He's ashamed to admit that. His brothers aren't cowards. Never have been. They are highly trained fighters. He trained them himself.

'You're right. Fuck, you're right! I've been afraid to put you all in the line of fire again. It was the wrong decision.'

'Fuck that!' Garret says. 'It was the right decision at the time. But that time has passed. You trained us well. Let's go and claim back our lives. Let's go and find Sorcha.'

Garret holds out his clenched fist in front of him. Fionn places his on top, followed by Con. Murt rests his fist on top, the Whelan crest tattooed on his hand scarred, but still clearly visible. Each member of the family has the exact same tattoo. They're proud of their heritage. Proud of who and what they are. What the fuck are they doing hiding in the shadows like this?

Murt nods, then walks back to the caravan with his brothers beside him. Thea and Fletch are leaning on the car and Thea is smiling. She knows their decision before he says a word.

'So, are four wolves moving into the castle?'

He looks to his brothers before nodding. 'Yeah, Thea. It looks that way.'

13

SORCHA

'Wakey, wakey, Bitch!'

She comes awake with a gasp as freezing water is blasted at her. Sorcha fights to breathe through the shock, but the cold is all-consuming. The water shuts off, and she blinks, trying to clear her eyes. She's still hanging from the ceiling of the interrogation room, but it's not Quill in front of her. It's the female vampire.

She only sees her when Quill isn't working, so presumes she's on the opposite shift to him. Sorcha isn't sure who's worse. They're both as bad as each other.

The vampire grips her face, sneering at her as she squeezes her jaw. 'Nice sleep?'

Sorcha spits on her, but the vampire barely blinks. 'I really hope

Quill lets me play with you next time.'

She takes a step back and gestures to the guard with her. He lifts Sorcha down, and together, they drag her back to her cell. They dump her on her back on the cold, dirty concrete. The female crouches over her, her fangs on full view as she sneers down at Sorcha. 'Sweet dreams.'

She swings at Sorcha, then darkness takes over.

When she wakes again, her flesh is burning, the fire spreading over her back with every breath. She wants to lose consciousness again, to drift off to sleep and not wake up for another few hours. Or ever. But the cold won't let her sleep. She looks over at her uniform. Someone had left it on the back of the chair while she was out of it.

The first flogging she gets. She'd stuck her finger up at his authority by trying to escape. It wasn't an excuse for what he did, but it could be a reason.

But last night was unprovoked. She thought she had been spared, but it appears he was just biding his time. Waiting for her to eat, have her exercise, then settle into this shit cell for the night before he had sent that sadistic vampire for her.

But did he need a reason to do whatever the hell he wants to do? She could look at him the wrong way, and that would be enough. She rolls onto her side, working up to getting off the floor and getting dressed, but the pain stops her. She cries to herself, burying her head in her arms.

He's going to break her. Quill is going to be the one to do it. All because he's punishing her for nothing. There's nothing she can say or do to stop him. How can you stop it happening, when you don't know why it's happening in the first place?

This time was so much worse than the last time. This time he didn't speak. Didn't utter a word before, during, or after. And she'd tried to engage with him. She knew it was Quill. Even with the blindfold on she knew him, knew his scent.

Maybe it was because, this time, that female vampire had stayed with him. Quill had been the one to hurt her, but that female had watched, silently getting kicks from what her boss was doing.

'You have to keep fighting. Don't let them win.'

Her words echo in her small cell as she agonisingly manages to drag herself over to her bed, where she lies face down, unable to get to her feet. Who is she kidding? It's only a matter of time before they do actually win.

She thought she knew how things worked in this world. She was wrong. There's no sense to what Quill is doing, or being ordered to do. It was senseless. Since she arrived, she's behaved. Apart from some talking back she hadn't given the guards any real problems.

Maybe this is just the way her life is going to be from now on.

After drifting off to sleep again for a few minutes, she finally manages to push herself upright. Moving is the last thing she wants to do, but it's either that, or suffer the cold on top of everything else she's going through.

The room spins as she straightens, adding pain to her constant hunger which is a new and fun combination. Before she falls, doing more damage to herself, she lies back on the bed, squeezing her eyes shut until the room stops turning.

Hopefully, food will come soon, and, fingers crossed, it will be Bannon and not Quill who delivers it. She has no interest in seeing that blonde-haired asshole, or that bitch again any time soon. Compared to his boss, Bannon didn't come across as being a dick.

He hasn't said a word to her. Apart from rugby tackling her to the ground on the beach, there was no interaction at all. He could easily have burned her to a crisp that first day, but he didn't even attempt to hurt her. He used his powers to slow her down, nothing more.

She'd seen vampires use their freaky powers on occasion, but Bannon's powers are something she's never seen before. Racing after her, his hands engulfed in flames, he'd looked like something out of a superhero action film. Well, apart from the small detail that she was the one he was trying to capture.

She picks up on his scent before he gets to her door. It's Bannon. Like the first time, his brown eyes target her as soon as he steps into her cell. He's confused by her. That much is clear. Perhaps he was told she's a blood-thirsty wolf? That she'd tear him limb from limb if he got too close.

Which she could... if she wanted to. Growing up with four brothers helped her learn from a young age how to stand up for herself. How to hit where it hurts.

His eyes drop, looking away from her as he carefully places the tray on the table. Well, that's new. Is he embarrassed because she's in her underwear? 'Apologies for my appearance. I wasn't expecting company.'

It takes her a few attempts, but she eventually gets to her feet, using the chair to pull herself upright. Instead of dragging her over to the table, like the grumpy head guard did the last time he was in her cell, he picks up her uniform and holds it out to her. This guard is almost gentle in his manner, perhaps less confident. But that will come with experience and time.

'Thank you. I think the heating is broken in this place. It's freezing.'

He tilts his head to the side, the frown growing. He can't figure her out and it's annoying him. Good. She likes to keep her guards on their toes. Sorcha manages to pull the jumpsuit onto her legs, but that's as far as she gets. Her hair is stuck to the still oozing wounds on her back. She'll eat first, then deal with them. She dreads to think what's ingrained in the cuts after lying on the filthy floor.

Sorcha sits and peers down at her food. It's not exactly a banquet. Two dried slices of bacon and a piece of dry toast. 'Oh yum. Where should I start?'

He frowns at her, then turns his attention to the food. Bannon looks as thrilled by the food as she does.

'I don't suppose you have any ketchup on you?'

He licks his lips, and Sorcha feels the heat rising to her cheeks. It's been too long since her body responded to anything. Clearly, she's been locked up for so long that even a vampire is turning her on.

He's new. That's the only reason you're acting like a hormonal teenager.

The guard shakes his head once and she laughs. It wasn't a serious question, but he took it as if it was.

'Too bad,' she says, focusing on the food instead of his lips. The bacon is dry and chewy, but it's food so she can't really complain. Sorcha turns in her chair and peers up at Bannon as she tries to break down the rubbery bacon in her mouth. 'Have you worked here long?'

Nothing except another impressive frown. Seems this is one of the less chatty guards. As she chews, her eyes move from his face to his neck as something attracts her attention. She remembers seeing the scar running down his neck when he had her pinned on the beach. It's a nasty wound, thick and lumpy as if the skin had been torn as opposed to cut.

'What happened there? You cut yourself shaving or something?'

Even as she says the words she knows she's gone too far. Even an idiot would know the scar was from a potentially life-threatening incident. Belittling it was a wrong move on her part.

Which he backs up when he tilts his head to the side, dropping his gaze from her to the corner of the table. Something in his face changes, anger suddenly coming to the surface.

She backs away when the flames ignite on his hands. Sorcha jumps aside, briefly forgetting her wounds, as he grabs the tray of food, flinging it against the wall, the bacon smouldering when it lands on the cell floor.

Bannon stares at the tray for a few seconds before hurrying from the cell, slamming the door shut behind him.

'Good job Sorcha.'

She jumps to her feet when the door opens again less than a minute later. 'I'm sorry if I...'

But it's not Bannon. It's Quill. *Shit! Shit! Shit!*

'Go on. You're sorry about what?'

'Nothing.'

'Sir or Officer.'

'Nothing, *sir*.' She snaps out the title even though she knows he'll take it badly.

He charges into her cell, pushing her back against the table. 'One of my guards just stormed out of here. What the fuck did you do, Wolf?'

'I tried to talk to him. That's it. It's not my fault he's sensitive.'

'Sensitive?'

'I asked him about his scar, and he decides to set my dinner on fire, then throw it against the wall. I get one meal a day, and he just cremated it!'

'I guess you shouldn't have pissed him off then, should you? Next time, you'll behave and keep that mouth of yours shut.'

With one final impressive snarl, he heads over to the door.

'Quill! Hey! Officer!' But he's gone, locking the door before she's even halfway across her cell. She beats on the door, not that it will do much. He's already gone.

'Fuck!'

No food and no exercise. That leaves a hell of a long time in here with nothing to do. She takes a deep breath, sorting through the variety of unpleasant smells surrounding her. But Bannon and Quill are gone. Their colognes fading, being swallowed up by all the other smells far too fast. It's getting more difficult to zone in on their individual scents. She should be able to smell them long after they leave. But within a few minutes, they're gone.

That can only mean one thing. Her wolf is weakening. Does that also mean that her connection to her brothers is weakening, too? Will they be able to find her at all if that connection is gone? Even if she does somehow manage to get out of here, will she ever be able to shift again?

She shuffles back to her bed, her back throbbing, then gingerly pulls up her jumpsuit over the wounds, before she lies down on her side, curling into a ball. Why did she say that to Bannon? It was below the belt, even for someone in her situation.

Crying won't do her any good. It's not going to give her food. It's not going to open the door and set her free. But right now, it's the only thing she can do.

14

BANNON

That was a mistake. A stupid rookie mistake. If Quill finds out he lost control like that with a prisoner, he would be in so much trouble.

Bannon paces the empty kitchen in the main house as he rubs his neck, the thick scar burning under his palm. He detests the scar. As if it wasn't bad enough having his voice torn from him like it was, he was left with a constant reminder of what happened.

Of course she was going to mention it at some stage. There's nothing else to notice in that miserable cell. And she didn't say anything negative about it. Okay, so it was a smart comment, but what else does he expect? She's not in here to make friends, or worry about other people's feelings.

It's not the first time it had happened and, in here, it won't be the last. He shouldn't have reacted the way he did. It's not her fault he has the scar. It had nothing to do with her.

He had felt his powers stirring inside him as soon as he saw her sitting in her underwear, broken and bleeding. He was angry. So far beyond that, even. He didn't sign up for this. Didn't think prisoners would be treated in this way. She had only just healed from the last time Quill flogged her. And he has no doubts it was Quill who beat her again. Not one doubt in his mind.

He leans on the countertop, cursing to himself when his hands ignite again. He needs to get a hold of himself. She's a wolf.

She's a scared, lonely, trapped wolf who is alone in this nightmare. He has to stop thinking of her like this. The only well-being he should be concerned about is his own. He closes his eyes, focusing on his breathing, doing everything he can to calm down before he's caught.

'What the fuck is going on!'

Quill's voice startles him out of his thoughts. He lifts his hands, realising a little too late that Quill's hand is now resting on the red-hot countertop beside him. Quill curses as the fire burns him, scorching his flesh.

Fuck! Fuck! Fuck!

Seeing Quill's skin redden, and the smell of burnt flesh in the air extinguishes his fire in a split second. Bannon turns on the cold tap, reaching out to grab Quill's arm so he can run the water over his hand.

'Get the fuck away from me!' Quill uses his other hand to shove Bannon aside, before sticking his burnt hand under the running water. He hisses in pain, his glowing eyes hitting Bannon as he breathes heavily through the pain.

He turns away from Quill, trying to avoid his glowing eyes. Quill is furious with him. He's not the only one. He's furious with himself.

'Don't you dare turn your back on me!'

Bannon turns around to face Quill. The guard's eyes are cold and hard as he glares at him. He holds up his hand, showing Bannon the scorched palm. 'What the fuck was that?'

Bannon opens and closes his mouth, momentarily forgetting he has no voice.

Quill angrily points to a notebook and pen sitting on the counter. 'Write it down. Now!'

Bannon fumbles for the paper, dropping the pen as Quill's furious glare weighs down on him.

'I don't know what the fuck the Warden was thinking when he hired you. Write! Now!'

Well, isn't this a great start to his new job! Totally humiliated, Bannon jots down a brief explanation, all the time Quill's words about how much of a mistake the Warden made, still ringing in his ears.

He hands the notebook to Quill who takes a few seconds to read what he wrote.

'I was attacked by a wolf a few years ago. It killed my family and tried to kill me. I survived but the injury was too severe. I lost my voice. She asked about the scar. Made a stupid joke about it. I shouldn't have reacted the way I did. It won't happen again. I am so sorry about your hand. I didn't know you were there. I didn't mean to hurt you. I swear.'

Quill's dark eyes lift to meet his, then drop to focus on the scar peeking out from under his collar. Bannon freezes as Quill turns off the tap and steps closer, then slowly unbuttons the collar so he can see the injury.

Quill's uninjured thumb grazes his skin next to the scar and Bannon instinctively tenses. He can barely stomach touching the scar himself, so doesn't understand how Quill can go near it. But Quill isn't in a rush to get away from it, or him. His fingers linger on his skin, his mesmerising eyes focused on Bannon's neck as he gently brushes his thumb along his skin.

Bannon knows he shouldn't like how it feels, but he does. A lot.

This place is screwing with him. Something about it is throwing him off track. Between the wolf and Quill, he's struggling to do what he's here to do. Struggling to remember who he is. Struggling to keep a hold on his powers. Quill reads the words again, his tongue running along his bottom lip, brushing over the two piercings as he frowns at the page.

What would it be like to kiss his pierced lips?

That foreign thought nearly knocks him sideways as heat rushes to his cheeks. Where the fuck did that come from? What if Quill heard? That's ridiculous. He knows it's completely impossible. Still, Bannon can't shake the embarrassment that envelopes him.

Quill drops his hand, and Bannon instantly misses his touch. He's probably just missing touch, full stop. He hasn't had much, if any, physical contact since he was injured.

Quill folds the piece of paper then slips it into his pocket. 'Fuck!' he mutters under his breath. He looks down at his burned hand, slowly shaking his head as he stares at it. His flesh is already healing. Bannon is just grateful Quill is a Prime. His pure blood will help him to heal fast.

'Okay. I'll dispose of that piece of paper where no one will find it. As for this,' he says, holding up his hand. 'It didn't happen. I'll be healed in a few hours. But I swear if you ever turn your powers on one of the guards - on me, again, you'll be leaving here the same way the prisoners do.'

Bannon frowns, hearing the words, but not quite believing them. He was expecting Quill to carry out that final threat now - not give him another chance. He has no idea what's going on, but he's not going to argue. He nods, hoping that Quill can see he's genuinely sorry and mortified about what happened.

'You can't react like that, again - do you hear me? If any of the other inmates find out you're triggered by that scar, they'll use it against you. Fuckers will see it as a weakness and exploit it. That goes for some of the other guards too.

'I'll talk to the wolf. Make sure she keeps her mouth shut.' He scrutinises the scar again. 'That's fucking impressive. I'm guessing it was a life and death situation?'

Bannon nods slowly. He hadn't been expected to survive. If not for a neighbour hearing the attack and coming to help, he could have died along with the rest of his family. Some days he wishes things had played out differently. Wished his neighbour had arrived a few minutes later. Wished he hadn't survived the attack.

'Wear that scar with pride.'

He looks over at Quill, confused by his statement.

'You look ashamed. Dropped your eyes when I touched the scar. Fuck that! Be proud of the scar. It's proof you're a tough bastard who survived something that would kill most other people. If you cower when it's seen, someone in here will notice. You need to face them head-on and make them look away first.

'Don't let it be the reason you don't survive in here. Because that's what it'll come down to. Survival. Outside or inside, that's all most of us here can hope for.' Quill sighs as he drags his hand over his hair, brushing the loose strands off his face. That same sad look crosses his face, before Quill gets himself together again.

'I'm not taking you off that inmate. That would go against you with the Warden and the other guards. If they think you're not pulling your weight, you'll become a target. You don't want to start your time here with a mark on your record. Whether you like it or not you'll bring her meal to her tomorrow. You got that?'

He nods. It's not like he's in any position to argue. Quill is taking the whole thing a lot better than he could have hoped for.

With one last and strangely lingering look, Quill leaves the room. Bannon slumps back against the counter, trying to roll the tension from his shoulders. He needs to stop drawing attention to himself in all the wrong ways.

Bannon hurries to his room, desperate to find solace before someone else walks in on him. He locks his door and faces his reflection in the small mirror over the chest of drawers against the wall. His collar is still open, the repulsive scar clearly visible in the V at the neck of the shirt.

Bannon takes a deep breath, then lifts his hand, gingerly touching the scar, forcing himself to really feel it, instead of just brushing off it. Quill's words play in his head. Wear the scar with pride.

He'd never had one second of pride when it came to that night and his injury. Shame, regret, sorrow. They played a big part. Pride? Not once.

So why is he wavering now? Why are Quill's words striking him differently to everyone else who has ever tried to pull him out of that place in his head?

15

MURT

As they approach the castle, Murt's heart pounds faster in his chest. The last time he was here was when they helped take down the Raven King. They'd survived the battle, but he left the castle with a permanent limp and a price on his head. Being banished for helping the Blackjacks had been worth it. He doesn't regret what he did.

If the Elders can't get their heads out of the past, leave them to it. Nothing will change and the wolves can continue to hide in the shadows. Fucking great legacy for a species to leave behind - a dying species.

As if reliving the incident, the injury on his hip throbs, the damaged nerves protesting as they near the building.

'You good? Murt? Hey! Hello!'

He looks around at Garret. 'Sorry?'

'Just wondering if you're still with us. You have that serious clan leader face on. Like you're expecting trouble.'

'Trouble follows us, Garret. We'd do well to expect it at every turn. It's the only way we're going to stay alive.'

'Fuck!' Garret mutters. 'You're full of the joys of life today, aren't you?'

Murt doesn't bother responding. Garret is probably right. He is a bit doom and gloom, but with good reason. The Whelan clan has gone from shite situation to shite situation over the last few years. Just for once he'd like to have his clan all together and safe.

The car pulls up in the courtyard, the heavy gates sealing behind them like the doors to a prison cell. One by one, the brothers climb out of the car, waiting while Thea and Fletch walk around the front to meet them.

'It's a different castle,' Thea says, jarring him out of his thoughts.

'I'm sorry?'

She nods to the castle doors. 'Davyn had the same look on his face the first time he came back here. Fear, dread, unease. The vampires living here have tried to bring some life back to the building. It's got a long way to go, but it's getting there. I've even begun a garden around the far side of the castle in memory of Davyn's mother.'

'A garden? That's something I never thought I'd see here,' Murt says, some of the unease fading away.

'Small steps. Dav is doing what he can to leave his own mark on his family legacy. A better one.'

'Well, anything he does will be a damn sight better than what his father was doing. Is he here?'

Thea shakes her head as she walks towards the door, encouraging him to follow her. 'He'll be here in a few days. There was some Blackjacks work he had to see-to first. One of their contacts has disappeared. They're trying to find him.'

'A contact?'

'His name is Rhain. He works with The Order, or he did. But he's been secretly helping the Blackjacks by giving them sensitive information on The Order. His reasons are still unclear, but it seems he provided helpful intel at times.'

'And he's paid for that with his life?'

Thea shrugs. 'That's what they're trying to figure out. It looks like Rhain was taken by The Order because he betrayed them. The team are trying to find him, but they've had no luck so far. He could be dead by now. No one knows at the moment.'

Murt looks down at Thea, seeing something in her face. 'I'm guessing you don't care either way?'

She glances over at him. 'Well, he arranged to have me kidnapped, he's the reason my dad has no memory, and he gave Dav back to his father. So, no. I really couldn't care if he's ever found again.'

'I like your honesty. I'd feel the same in your shoes.'

'It's all about the bigger picture though. Besides, if he was taken by The Order there's no telling where he is, or even if he's alive. I'll cross that bridge if we get to it.'

'And how do you feel about this place?' he asks, nodding to the stone building in front of them.

'Better than I did,' she says, smiling as she gestures for them to follow her inside. 'It will take time, but I'm going to help Davyn repair what his father destroyed. Speaking of that, I've been working with Fergus to collate all the files Dav's father kept. I can show you what we've found on the prisons. If we can narrow down some locations it will make your work easier.'

'Our work?' Murt asks, following her into the huge reception hall. A fire is burning in the monstrous hearth, and tables are set up around it, providing an impressive banquet space. The last time he was here, it was filled with bloodthirsty vampires and blood. Lots of blood. Some of it his own.

'You and I both know that you and your brothers will tear each and every prison apart, freeing any wolves you find, while you search for

Sorcha.'

He smirks when she looks over her shoulder at him. 'You know me better than I thought. We need to figure out what's going on, then make our decision. I'm not going into anything blind.'

'That sounds like a great idea, especially with the whole banishment thing. You remember Fergus?' she says, gesturing to a vampire, dressed in an impeccable black suit with a crisp white tie. 'He's been appointed to run this place for Davyn while he's in Wales.'

The brothers shake his hand one by one, Garret and Con a little less enthusiastic than Fionn is. He doubts those two will ever be at ease with this new-found vampire tolerance.

'It's such a pleasure to see you again.'

'You too Fergus. You've done a hell of a job on this place.'

'I appreciate you saying that. I understand you'll be with us for a while. Can I show you to your rooms? I have four quarters ready on the third floor. They are alongside each other ,and each has a private bathroom. I hope you'll be comfortable.'

'Comfortable? Fergus, after living with these three idiots in a tin box for the last few months, what you just described sounds like heaven!'

QUILL

In all the years he's been head guard at the prison, Quill has lost count of the number of times he's had to *talk* to a prisoner. There had been too many interactions to count between his men and the inmates - both positive and negative. More often than not, on the negative side of the scale. A few times it had been because one of his men had taken things too far, but sometimes also because an inmate had attacked one of his men.

Whatever the reason, he was the one called in to sort out the issue. Usually, he'd have some private time with the inmate, and only one of them would be uninjured when he was done.

But in all that time he's never had to make sure a prisoner kept their mouth shut about one of his guards. Usually, it didn't matter what was said by either side. It's a prison. They're hardly going to be best mates or anything like that. Things are said. Allegations are made. It's part of life. As long as they didn't kill each other, Quill was happy.

But for some reason he can't quite figure out, he's about to ask the wolf to keep her mouth shut about what happened with Bannon. Ordinarily, it would be instant dismissal, at the least. The Warden would even allow him to kill Bannon if he wanted. His boss didn't take kindly to anyone hurting Quill. Hopefully the Warden won't call him up to his residence until the burn has healed.

This is a fucking nightmare!

When he went after Bannon, he was going to write him up. But when he found out the reason for the reaction, he'd done a complete U-Turn. The fact that Bannon was even able to set foot inside a prison housing nothing but wolves is a fucking miracle. He gets why Bannon freaked out. No question of that. It was bound to happen at some stage. At least he was the only witness - well apart from that irritating wolf.

But he still doesn't get why he's willing to give him such a big break by keeping the incident to himself.

He must be going soft in his old age.

Or he's attracted to Bannon and it's fucking with him.

Quill stops outside the wolf's cell as that thought hits him. That's what it boils down to. He's risking his job to cover for the male he's attracted to. He knows nothing about Bannon. Nothing except the brief details about the savaging, yet here he is, willing to do this because of an adolescent attraction that will come to nothing.

He'd spent the last hour trying to figure out why he's going to do this and is still no closer to finding an answer. He doesn't get into any personal shit with his men. It's not how he runs the prison. They're all big enough and bold enough to handle things themselves.

Then again, he's never had one of his men freak out the way

Bannon did. He flexes the fingers on his injured hand. It still hurts like hell. To hide the injury, he's wearing leather gloves. He does that from time-to-time, so it won't necessarily arouse suspicion.

He looks at the heavy metal door separating him from Sorcha. He can pick up on her scent. Like Bannon, it's a scent he easily recognises. He's not going to go for his usual heavy-handedness with the wolf in this situation. It's not going to work with her. But he's at a loss as to what will work. He's tortured her twice. Hurt her so badly, that the odds of her doing anything he asks her are slim to none. He can't blame her either. If the tables were turned, he'd be less than helpful.

'Is he okay?'

He frowns when he hears her voice, barely audible through the thick door. Why is she so worried about a vampire guard? Wolves don't give a shit about anything or anyone, except themselves and their clan. Upsetting a vampire guard shouldn't bother her in the slightest. If anything, it should give her a kick.

'I know I upset him, but I honestly didn't mean to. I let my inner bitch take the lead.'

He smiles in spite of himself, getting a hold on it quickly. Fuck! He might as well get this over and done with. Instead of ordering her to sit on the bed, and waiting while she did, he unlocks the door and steps inside, closing the door behind him. The wolf backs away, moving towards her bed. He can smell her fear. She's got too much attitude for her own good, but she still respects him. Still fears him.

Usually, he wouldn't care less how the prisoners feel about him, but knowing she's afraid of him just puts him in a worse mood. It was what he wanted, what the Warden wanted, so why is it troubling him more than pleasing him?

Unfortunately, that's the bad mood he unleashes on her. He walks right up to her, pushing her back until she drops down on the bed. Quill leans over her, one hand to either side, ignoring the pain from his palm as he puts pressure on it. Sorcha leans back, nearly lying on the bed to move away from him. Her eyes tighten as she lies back. She's obviously still in pain from the last flogging. That shouldn't bother him either... but it does.

She glances at the gloves covering his hands and he hears her heart rate increasing. She thinks he's wearing them because he's going to hurt her.

'You going to hurt me again Officer?' she asks, voicing his thoughts. 'My back isn't even healed yet. You could do some serious damage if you wanted to.'

Again, with the guilt hitting him. That doesn't happen to him. He needs to put some space between himself and this wolf before he has a complete personality alteration. But he doesn't move. He hadn't noticed before how green her eyes are. Why would he? It's not like he stares into prisoners' eyes on a daily basis.

She frowns, clearly as confused by his lack of reaction as he is. Fucking great show of his authority.

'I need you to keep your mouth shut about what happened between you and Bannon.'

'About what happened? What did he say I did?'

She swallows, and Quill feels his fangs growing when he focuses on her slim neck. *She's a fucking wolf Quill!*

He has to wait a minute before he can respond. His damn fangs are screwing with him. 'He freaked out. Weakness is exploited in here. His job shouldn't be at risk because of this incident.'

She turns her head towards his burnt hand as if she can see the injury. 'He burned you. I can smell it. Ouch! Karma's a bitch Officer.'

He ignores her attempt at having a go at him. 'It was an accident.' He should stop talking. Stop interrupting. He's here to command, not converse.

'You really are up your own ass, aren't you? You flog me, now come begging for me to do you a favour. How about I just get right to the ending? Fuck off, Officer! You don't get to ask me anything.'

He growls before he can stop himself. Getting angry at her won't help win her over. Not that he can. He lost that chance as soon as he tore her flesh.

He's lost. He's never had to do this before, so doesn't know how to handle it.

'Why?'

He turns his attention back to the wolf. 'Why what?'

'Why do you want to protect him?'

'It was an accident!'

She nods, then pushes herself up the bed, putting more distance between them. 'I know it was.'

'You do?'

'I pushed his buttons, and he reacted. I would imagine hurting you was as a result of that. Unless he is a total idiot, he's not going to intentionally hurt his boss.'

'I caught him off guard.' Just like his fucking mouth is doing right now.

'So Quillan,' she says, her smirk back as she uses his full name just to piss him off. 'There is actually a heart under all that asshole exterior. Who would have known?'

Fuck, she is pushing his buttons. But he likes it. Too much. 'If the Warden finds out, he's gone. If the other prisoners find out, they'll make his life hell. If the guards find out, he'll be even more isolated than he is. But, if you're really that much of a bitch, then forget this conversation and do what you want.'

'Oh, so we're back to that old tactic?'

'You're a prisoner. I can threaten you as much as I want. You know that. I can bring you back to that room right now and continue what I started last night. This isn't some friendly chat.'

'Ah but Officer, it's also not your usual prisoner/guard chat either. You're kind of blurring the lines here a little. Why does it matter to you so much? If he's fired, you'll just get another guard dog in to replace him. One vampire is the same as the other. What's the big deal?'

'He deserves a fair chance. That's all I'm saying.'

'He deserves a fair chance at what exactly? Deserves a chance to be corrupted by you and the other asshole guards in here? Deserves a chance to raise a whip to me himself? Or maybe he deserves a chance to torture some innocent wolf in another way? Come up with some inventive punishment so he can leave his mark on one of the prisoners.'

He curses to himself. How the hell does he answer that one?

'What's the real reason you want me to keep quiet?'

She doesn't buy his reasoning. He can tell instantly that his bullshit is seen as just that. A lie. Something he is trying to convince himself is true, even though it's far from that. Is the lie that obvious? If she can see through it, who else can?

'What the fuck does that mean?'

'I'm just saying that out of everyone here, I can see why *he* would deserve a fair chance.'

She shifts on the bed, brushing her leg against his groin. It was probably completely unintentional, but it wasn't entirely unpleasant. Fuck, she's right. He is blurring all kinds of lines with these thoughts.

He pushes off her bed, standing a few steps back from her. 'Should have known better than to try and reason with a wolf.'

'And I should have known better than to expect honesty from a vampire. Guess we're both disappointed.'

He resists the urge to bare his fangs at her. It won't do any good. She's one of the single most stubborn wolves he's ever had the misfortune of meeting. He'll just have to make sure no other guards deal with her. He can keep most of them away, but Duna will be more difficult. She's his eyes and ears on the floor when he's off duty. She checks on all the prisoners.

'You know what? Fuck this and fuck you!' Losing his temper won't help in the slightest, but this entire situation is testing his patience.

'Two conditions Officer.'

He stops at the door turning around to glare at her. 'What the fuck gives you the impression you can ask for anything?'

'You being here asking me for this, that's what.'

She's got him there. The wolf gets to her feet, wincing as she straightens. She takes a few steps towards him, facing up to him like she's got nothing to lose.

'Fine! What condition?'

'I said conditions. Two. First, I want some real food. I know I'm pushing my luck, but have you tried that crap I get? It might as well be just that - crap. It tastes as bad. Incinerating it was the best thing Bannon could have done. But the damn bacon didn't even burn. It was too far gone.'

It's a valid request. And she's right. If it tastes as bad as it looks, crap is putting it politely. The problem is getting the food to her. He can hardly walk around with a lump of steak in his pocket, or a bowl of pasta hidden up his sleeve.

'I'll see what I can do.'

Her face drops at his response. 'Right. Got you.'

'When I say I'll see what I can do, that's not a brush-off. I mean I'll see what I can do. I just need to figure out how to get the food to you. You keep your mouth shut, and I'll find a way to get you decent food.'

She nods, a small twinkle in her eye at the thought of potentially getting decent food.

Why does he want to do more for her, just to see that look on her face again? Why does the thought of hurting her again, as he will no doubt have to do, sicken him? 'You need to keep this between us.'

'Of course. Wolves have integrity. I'll keep my mouth shut.'

'I don't believe that for a minute. You haven't been able to keep it shut so far.'

Sorcha smirks, realising he's joking even though he manages to hide his own smile. 'On this point I will.'

'Two?'

'No more visits to that room.'

He should have been expecting that one, but it still catches him off guard. Food he can probably do. Not bringing her to the interrogation room so the Warden can watch him break her, will be a whole lot harder.

'I'll see.'

She nods, knowing as well as he does that it's not a definite. 'Then you have my word, Officer.'

'Thank you.' Where the fuck did that come from? The head guard does not thank a prisoner. Judging by the look on her face, she wasn't expecting him to say that either.

She nods, her green eyes showing no emotion at all.

The conversation has come to a natural end. He's done what he came here to do. Time to get back to work.

Quill opens the door, pausing as she calls out to him. 'Until later, Officer.'

He smiles to himself, making sure he keeps his back to her, before he closes and locks the cell.

SORCHA

Sorcha paces her small cell. It must nearly be time for her meal. Her food delivery is the highlight of her day, even though the food itself isn't anything to write home about.

But after Quill's unexpected conversation yesterday, she can barely contain her excitement, even though she knows there's every chance Quill won't be able to organise anything for today. It could take him a few days, but she hopes he'll do what he can. It's her reward for keeping quiet about what Bannon did, so it's not going to go in his favour if he doesn't deliver. Quill and Bannon had more to lose than she did.

But it's not just the prospect of having a real meal that's exciting her, although that's a big part of it. It was the memory of their interaction yesterday as a whole. His behaviour seemed completely out of character as head guard.

She saw something in him yesterday that she hadn't seen during their brief meetings. Except for the floggings, her interactions with him since she transferred from the other prison had been few and far between, but nothing like yesterday. He's confusing her. She detests him, yet is intrigued by him. It makes no sense whatsoever.

There's no denying Quill is efficient at his job. There's a coldness to him that you can't miss, and she should know, having been on the receiving end. But in his eyes, she saw something more. She saw sadness. It completely caught her off-guard. She assumed there would be nothing there - that he was just an emotionless brutal guard dog.

But there's more to him. He was willing to make a deal with a wolf to protect Bannon. Willing to risk his job to make sure no one heard about what happened.

That's what's thrown her. Being a heartless brute, she can accept. The conversation yesterday, not so much. It showed a side to him she didn't imagine could exist in someone like him. He intrigues her, as Bannon does - but for very different reasons.

Her excitement fades a little when she thinks about Bannon. There's a chance he won't come back in. If Quill wants to keep the drama to a minimum, he'll reassign Bannon. Move him to another area of the prison far away from her.

That thought isn't a welcome one.

Then she catches Bannon's scent. It's still faint, so he's not close to her cell yet. She sits on the edge of her cot, then gets to her feet, before sitting again. This is fucking ridiculous. Why does he excite her? Why is she letting this vampire get to her like she is? Boredom?

If only it were that simple. Deep down she's worried it might be more than that. Deep down, she's worried she might be attracted to both Quill and Bannon. Well, life had been boring over the last few years. Maybe she's just making up for lost time.

Sorcha sifts through the scents surrounding her. He's much closer now - either outside the door, or a few feet away. So why isn't he coming in? She sits on the edge of her bed and stares at the door, willing him to come inside.

Then she hears the locks disengage. The heavy door swings open and Bannon walks into her room. He doesn't look at her. Doesn't acknowledge that she's there at all. And that hurts.

He places a metal first aid box on the table, her dinner on a tray on top of the box, then leaves the room before she can say anything to him. She jumps when the door is slammed shut and locked again.

Sorcha stays where she is for another few minutes, just staring at the door. Why is his reaction getting to her so much? Maybe because, for the first time since she was taken, she thought she'd found someone who saw her as a person - not just a prisoner.

'Well good work there Sorcha. You messed that one up good, didn't you?'

She looks over at the first aid box he delivered along with her usual dry dinner. Why did he leave her a first aid box? Is she going to be hurt again? Then she's hit with another scent. So wrapped up in the fact that he had ignored her, Sorcha hadn't noticed the aroma coming from the box.

She gets to her feet, moving slowly in case any sudden movements would scare the food away. It's stupid, she knows that. But she's not taking any chances.

She lifts the tray off the box and slowly opens the lid. Tears form in her eyes when she sees the dinner Bannon delivered inside the first aid box.

Quill stuck to his word, and then some. She assumed he'd bring her some fresh bread. Maybe some fruit or cheese. Something simple like that.

Instead of that, he's managed to sneak a plate of fresh lasagne into her cell. It's straight from the oven, the sound of the bubbling cheese like the best music she's ever heard. It smells divine. It's been so long since she's had a proper, fresh, hot meal.

She takes a forkful, then closes her eyes as she opens her mouth. As soon as it hits her tongue she groans aloud. It's so much better than divine.

Sorcha takes her time enjoying each and every mouthful, chewing slowly to savour every bite. Then she licks the plate and fork clean. To hell with table manners. She'd even lick the floor clean if she'd dropped any of the food.

She sits back in the chair and looks at the door. He's still there. Now the food is gone, she can pick up his scent again. Was he watching her eat the food? Vampire eyesight is as good as a wolf's, so he could probably see her in the dim light from the window in the door.

She gets up and slowly approaches the door. 'I'm sorry if I upset you. I didn't mean to. I just let my mouth run away with me.'

Nothing from Bannon.

'Thank you for the food.'

He stays by her door another few seconds before walking away, his heavy footsteps fading as he leaves.

BANNON

After delivering the food to the wolf, Bannon heads back to the showers where he's meant to be supervising. There's no sign of Quill, but that's not unusual. Three other guards are helping him make sure the prisoners behave while Quill sees to his other duties.

He looks around him, almost as if he's afraid someone caught him giving the wolf proper food. Quill told him to bring the wolf a second dinner, and he knows why.

He knows it had something to do with what happened in the wolf's cell yesterday. Maybe it was his way of making sure she kept her mouth shut about it. Bribing her with food, so he could save his job.

Two of the prisoners start a scrap beside one of his colleagues, so he steps in to help. Bannon pulls one of the wolves off the guard, throwing him into a stall far away from the guard.

His colleague nods his thanks, then goes back to the other side of the room. Bannon is getting more respect from the other guards than he did when he first started.

He's earning that respect a day at a time. They're realising that just because he can't talk doesn't mean he is a push over. He's here because he isn't a pushover. He's here because, when provoked, he pushes back... hard.

He's here because, when he pushes back hard, he has killed.

It only happened once, but he's here because of that.

Here there are rules, a job to do, no time to think or dwell on the past and his mistakes, and that's it. Simple. Uncomplicated.

Or was, until he messed up again.

Quill.

Sorcha.

Him.

One complex and utterly avoidable situation he created by doing absurd things like releasing his power in anger, and running out of her cell when she saw his scar. Acting like an idiot. Losing control and hurting Quill. Because of that, he's now buying her silence by swapping her food.

Not that he's got a problem with that in the slightest. He'd swap out all the prisoners' food if he could. Just because they're in here doesn't mean they should have to eat whatever rubbish the prison is giving them.

Quill appears at the door. 'Bannon!'

He walks over to his boss, keeping his shoulders back and his eyes on Quill. He's already shown weakness in front of Quill. Never again.

But Quill doesn't seem to be pissed off at him. 'All good?'

Bannon takes a second to realise what Quill's asking him. He nods once.

'Good. Take inmate Sixty-Four out for exercise when you're done here. I'll check her cell.'

Bannon nods. *Check her cell*, as in *get rid of any evidence of the meal*. It's the first time he's been tasked with taking her out alone. After his pathetic display the last time, he wasn't expecting Quill to trust him again so soon.

'I reckon you're good to do it alone,' he says, as if hearing his thoughts. 'If she gives you any shit, click the call button on your radio twice. I'll know it's you and help you out. Just don't fry the bitch.'

He could swear Quill winks at him before he turns away, but it was probably just in his mind.

Quill slams his palm against the door to the room, startling everyone. 'This isn't a fucking pool party! Shower and get the fuck out of here. Move!'

After spurring on the inmates, Quill leaves, and Bannon restrains a smile. That male can flip between a hard ass and someone who gives a shit, in the space of a few seconds.

SORCHA

Sorcha smiles at him when he steps in to the cell, and it immediately cheers him up. 'Hi Bannon.'

She could be imagining it, but she could swear he smiles a little when he hears her say his name. He gestures towards the door, but still doesn't say anything.

'Exercise time? I thought I was being left to my own company for the rest of the day.'

Still nothing from him. Surely his silence is more than him following the rules. It's got to be something to do with the huge scar on his neck.

She leads the way out to the courtyard with Bannon following closely behind. She stops at the door to the yard, waiting while he unlocks it. There's something strangely soothing about being in his company. He doesn't push her around, or try to be all alpha male with her like most of the other guards. Well, except for Quill. He's all alpha male without having to try.

Bannon holds open the door for her, then joins her in the yard. It's raining, but she honestly couldn't care less. It could be blowing a gale out there with sleet and hailstones, and she'd still be desperate to get outside.

The rain quickly soaks through her jumpsuit, and it helps her feel alive. When she was able to shift into her wolf, she would love to go out in the rain and run for miles. She loved the feeling of the water soaking into her fur.

'Will you walk with me?'

Bannon glances around him as if expecting Quill or the Warden to jump out of a corner somewhere. 'It's just a walk. It'll make going around in circles a little less boring.'

She is convinced he's going to say no. Or shake his head. But he surprises her by nodding. Well, that's certainly unexpected, but welcome. 'Thank you.' She walks along the inner wall, the imposing form of Bannon beside her, keeping her company.

'You're getting wet. Sorry about that.'

He shrugs, not appearing to be bothered. His black uniform shirt clings to his skin, the material hugging his body as the rain soaks into it. Damn, she is clearly going through a particularly horny stage. She's never had these thoughts about anyone - fellow prisoner or guard. And she's certainly never looked at any of the guards with anything other than contempt.

Attraction and lust had been a distant memory for a hell of a long time. She must be making up for lost time with Quill and Bannon. But did she really have to be greedy and want both of them? Surely one was enough.

Hell, she's not in a position to even have one of them!

But a girl can dream, can't she? Especially in here. Dreaming is the only thing that keeps her sane.

And dreaming about Quill and Bannon won't be a hardship. Quite the opposite. She glances sideways at him. Not a hardship in the slightest. His dark hair is stuck to his forehead. It's longer than she had thought. Not nearly as long as Quill's, but there's certainly enough to grab on to.

She turns away quickly, blushing to herself.

It's not helping that he's staying silent. At least if he would talk to her, he could distract her from her thoughts.

As they finish their second circuit, she can't help herself and steals another quick look. Out of her gloomy cell she can clearly see the scar on his neck now. It's right at the front, over his Adam's apple. This will probably end badly, but she has to ask the question. What's the worst that can happen? He'll throw her back in her cell. That's where she'll be heading to after this walk anyway. She's got nothing to lose. 'You can't talk, can you?'

Instead of attacking her like he did when she mentioned his scar, he swallows deeply then looks down at her. Bannon doesn't do anything for a long time and she's afraid to interrupt him.

He finally shakes his head.

'Oh. I'm sorry.'

When his dark eyes meet hers, she hates the sorrow she can see.

'Have you never been able to speak?' She knows her attention moves to his neck, but she can't help looking.

Bannon leaves the question unanswered for a long time, then stops and slowly reaches up to unbutton the top of his shirt. He pulls the collar back and gives her a proper look at his scar. It stretches from under his chin to well below the base of his neck. 'Oh my God! What happened to you?'

He licks his lips, then points to her.

'Me? I don't understand?'

Bannon moves his hands, trying to tell her something using sign language. Realising it's a lost cause, he stops and drops his hands, resting them on his hips as he glares at the ground, clearly frustrated.

'Okay. Me?' What the hell could he mean by that? She'd never met him before she arrived in the prison. He's a vampire. She's a wolf. It's not like they would have mixed on the outside. Then it dawns on her what he's trying to say. 'Oh Bannon. You mean a wolf?'

He nods and her stomach tightens.

'You were attacked by a wolf?' She takes a step closer, ignoring the puzzled expression on his face. 'May I?'

He nods again, so she slowly reaches out to touch the scar, relieved when Bannon doesn't flinch under her touch. She traces a finger down the raised thick line of dark pink flesh. He wasn't attacked. He was savaged. There's evidence of teeth and claws cutting and slicing into him.

'How did you survive this?'

He takes hold of her wrist, moving her hand away from him. His grip is firm, but he doesn't hurt her. His touch is almost tender. His brown eyes glow softly as he stares down at her. He can't tell her what happened - that's the problem. Because of one of her species, he can never use his voice again.

'I'm not surprised you had the reaction you did when I asked you about it. I'm so sorry for asking a question you can't answer, and I'm sorry for what happened to you.'

He tilts his head to the side and frowns at her before releasing her wrist. He points to his mouth, waiting until he has her attention before he mouths one word. *'Why?'*

She can easily read his lips as he slowly asks the question. 'Because it must have been a horrible experience. I'm truly sorry you suffered like that.'

He seems confused by her answer. It must be incredibly difficult for him to be working in a wolf prison, let alone be placed on her guard duty. Perhaps the Warden arranged that deliberately. From the little she knows, it appears he gets a kick out of creating difficult situations for people living under his roof. No wonder Quill was so quick to step in and make sure no one found out about what happened to him.

'Can you communicate with anyone else here?'

He pauses for a moment, then shakes his head.

For some reason, she can't bear that for him. He's as alone as she is. Completely cut off from the world around him. 'Would you teach me sign language?'

Bannon stares at her for a long minute before smiling and shaking his head, as he turns away from her.

'Hey! I'm being serious,' she says, hurrying to catch up with him. 'I'd like to learn.'

Bannon stops, turning back around to look at her. *'Why?'* he mouths again.

'Why not? I have nothing else to do. Nothing. I'm stuck in here for the rest of my life. I'm bored. So much more than just bored. I'm dying in here,' she says, holding a hand to her chest. 'I just want to do something. Besides, wouldn't it be nice to be able to communicate with someone in this shithole? Please Bannon.'

She needs him to agree to this. Desperately needs him to. She meant everything she just said to him. She's dying in so many ways in this prison. Being able to use her brain for even a few minutes will help her feel alive again.

She keeps her eyes locked on Bannon's, silently willing him to agree to this. Then he does. It's the smallest of nods, but to her in that moment, it's as if he shouted it.

'Really? Thank you! That would be amazing.' She holds out her hand and, after the briefest of pauses, he shakes it. 'I'm so excited about this. It would be nice to get my brain going again.'

Bannon smiles. It makes the briefest of appearances, but it's truly beautiful. He gestures to her hand, pointing to the tattoo on the back. *'What does that mean?'*

Sorcha takes a second to draw her attention away from his mouth. Until she met Bannon, she'd never really looked at someone as they spoke. Not in the way she needs to look at him to *hear* what he's saying.

She holds out her hand, showing him the Celtic design tattooed over the back of it and up her arm. 'This is my clan crest. My four brothers have the same one. It tells the world who we are. Warns them not to mess with us,' she adds with a grin which doesn't last long. 'Guess it didn't work too well for me.'

Bannon leans over to get a proper look at the tattoo. *'It's beautiful,'* he mouths as he straightens again.

'Thanks. It helps me feel close to my brothers. I know that sounds stupid, but it's really the only connection to them I have in here.'

Bannon shakes his head. *'Makes sense.'*

Knowing that he understands makes her feel a little better. Not much, but for some reason, having him get what the tattoo means to her helps her feel a little less alone.

Bannon gestures to the yard ahead of them, his hands moving as he signs something.

'What was that?'

'Walk,' he mouths, smiling at her. *'First lesson.'*

Sorcha continues her laps, smiling to herself as they walk around the yard.

Bannon agreeing to teach her how to sign is a small thing. Nothing to get excited about. But when her world consists of darkness and loneliness, having something to look forward to, something to do to occupy herself, is its own kind of freedom.

QUILL

Quill wakes up in a dire mood, and it's only free-falling as the day drags on. He marches down the corridor towards the main body of the prison, Bannon trailing after him like a well-trained puppy. Any guards or prisoners in his way, rapidly step aside as he barrels past. He'd usually keep his emotions under wraps, but he doesn't have the energy to worry about it today.

He glances over his shoulder at Bannon. The male has his eyes down, his expression serious.

Quill looks away again. He had serious reservations about Bannon when he first started. How the fuck could he possibly keep the inmates in check if he couldn't speak? But Quill had been forced to reevaluate his initial opinion of the male. Bannon may come across as a little gentler than the other guards, but he has a strength and control that he respects. The silent guard is well able to hold his own against the rowdy inmates. One look from those hard brown eyes and the inmates got back in line fairly damn fast.

He can't blame them. There's something about Bannon's eyes that gets to him, too. He'd prefer they didn't get to him, but that's part of his bad mood.

Bannon is in his head more than he has any right to be, and it's beginning to piss him off. Assigning himself to work with the newbie every day isn't helping, but he doesn't want to give him to anyone else. He's being irrational and possessive with no good reason. Bannon isn't his. Fuck, he doesn't even know if he wants Bannon in that way.

Yeah right! That sounds no more convincing that time than it did every other time he's said it to himself.

He needs to get Bannon out of his head and get back to work. If he shows any weakness, any distractions, he'll be walked all over - by the guards, the inmates, and the Warden.

Lunch will be wrapping up in a few minutes, so they'll be needed to round up all the inmates and get them outside for exercise. That should keep everyone busy for a while. Keep his mind busy.

The noise increases as they near the cafeteria. He points to his left and Bannon leaves him, rounding up the inmates with another guard, ushering them outside in single file.

Quill brings up the rear, making sure no stragglers are left behind. It's not a warm day, but the inmates don't care. The inmates didn't ever seem to care what the weather was like. Being outside gave them a small break from the otherwise monotonous hours locked away. Fuck knows he gets that. It didn't matter if you were an inmate or a guard. This place killed a part of you as soon as you stepped onto the island.

Quill brushes his hair back from his face as he stands to the side of the yard watching from afar.

It's how he prefers to run things. He keeps his distance - from the

111

guards as well as the prisoners, only getting involved when there was no other choice. He's the big gun the other guards called in as a last resort. It's not something he likes or enjoys, but everyone has their place here. Their role to play.

He looks up at the top floor of the building, towering above the exercise yard. The Warden lives up there, squirrelled away in his tower, while the wolves and vampires he controlled lived in misery under his feet. Fucking psychopath!

Quill detests that vampire with every ounce of his being. Given the opportunity, he'd gut him and bathe in his blood. But that's a fantasy, nothing more. The Warden is untouchable. He's too powerful. Too high up the vampire hierarchy.

And Quill sits firmly at the other end of the food chain.

He looks over at Bannon, unable to hold back the warmth that spreads through him at the sight of the male. That vampire is stunning. Quill has never labelled himself. He likes what he likes. Male. Female. Human. Vampire. It doesn't matter as long as they hold his attention. And Bannon is doing that.

The vulnerability he saw from the male yesterday in the break room got to him. So did the overwhelming strength he sensed. The scar is fucking huge. He doesn't doubt it nearly killed Bannon. He's damn lucky to have just lost his voice. He could easily have lost his head. The fact he survived his injuries, and the accompanying trauma, shows how strong he is - how determined... and Quill appreciates that.

He sees the same strength in that damn wolf. Has done from the first day he met her. She hasn't given up. Fuck he has, and he's a guard. The fact she has the strength and conviction to stick her finger up at everything she's been put through is something to admire, something to respect. And she is absolutely someone else who has caught his attention in ways she shouldn't.

He scrubs his hand over his face, frustration and anger adding to his bad mood. Trust him to want what he can't have under any circumstances. Guards. Vampires. A wolf. A prisoner. His life is complicated enough without heading into a situation like that. It would be doomed from the start.

His phone vibrates, filling him with dread. Only the Warden and Duna have his number. Duna should be in bed so it's not going to be her. Resigned to the fact his day is about to get a hell of a lot worse, he answers the call, keeping his attention on the wall ahead of him instead of Bannon. It doesn't feel right talking to the Warden while Bannon is there. 'Yes, sir?'

'I'd like a meeting with you Quillan. Now.'

Before he can answer, the Warden ends the call, leaving Quill staring at the wall ahead of him, the phone still to his ear.

Well, isn't that fucking brilliant! Just what he needs right now.

Before he can stop himself, he looks over to Bannon. The male is already facing him. If he didn't know any better, he'd swear Bannon is worried.

Yeah, right. Wishful thinking. He's probably wondering why Quill is glaring at him as if that call was his fault.

I'd give anything to stay here with you.

He silently curses himself. He's just making this worse for himself.

Quill turns and leaves the yard, making his way through the prison to the Warden. The bad mood he woke with is becoming a distant memory, as the panic and dread building with each step far surpasses everything else he was feeling.

BANNON

Bannon walks along the corridor to the area of the building where the guards' dorms are housed. The shift had been long and tedious. Especially as he had to do most of the work with Duna instead of Quill. She makes him extremely uncomfortable. The female has a way of looking at him that makes him squirm. It's as if she can see inside his head, see his thoughts.

But with Quill gone, she's moved to the day shift, and she's the boss for now, so he just has to get on with it. No one had seen Quill since the exercise yard yesterday. He'd sent Duna a text leaving her in charge and there's been no word since.

One of the other guards mentioned that this isn't unusual. Quill goes MIA from time-to-time, but that doesn't mean Bannon isn't worried.

He saw something in Quill's face yesterday that chilled him to his bones. Quill was actually scared by that phone call. He presumes it was from the Warden, but it's not like anyone would tell him anything, even if he could ask. After being warned off by Duna, he's not going to ask any questions about Quill.

He stops when he picks up on the familiar earthy cologne through the closed door of Quill's room. Quill is in there. There's no mistaking that scent. He wasn't there last night or this morning when he passed by. There's a chance he had left the island entirely yesterday. He only gets one weekend off per month, but maybe Quill has more perks given his position.

He's about to walk on, but under Quill's cologne he can smell something else. Blood. Quill's blood.

Bannon is overstepping his boundaries, he knows that, but there's no way he can just walk by and not check on him. Something deep inside him won't let him just keep walking, without knowing everything is okay. He knocks on the door, then getting no response, tries again, pounding harder this time.

'I'm off duty. Go away!'

Hearing his muffled voice through the door is such a relief. At least he's alive in there. And seriously pissed off, if his tone is any indication. But Bannon isn't going anywhere. He's not leaving until he sees him.

He beats his fist on the door again. This time it works. The door is yanked open and Quill glares at him. Even though the room is in complete darkness, Bannon can see the dark shadows surrounding his bloodshot eyes. He pushes inside the room before Quill can stop him.

'What the hell do you think you're doing? Get the fuck out of my room!'

Bannon turns on the light, before facing Quill and examining his pale face. The guard looks exhausted and not at all his usual

115

composed self. His hair is out, the messy dark blonde locks framing his face. Then his attention is drawn to Quill's neck, and the teeth marks on his skin. *'What happened?'* he signs.

'I said get the fuck out of my room before I physically remove you!'

Quill shoves Bannon's hands down. 'Would you lay off with that! I haven't got a fucking clue what you're saying when you do that hand stuff.'

Anger and worry take charge, and Bannon pushes Quill back against the door. He puts his face right up to Quill's and points to his mouth. Quill fights, but after a minute, his eyes drop to Bannon's mouth.

'What happened?' He mouths the words slowly so there's no mistaking what he's trying to say.

Quill licks his lips, the piercing in his tongue momentarily catching Bannon's eye.

'It's none of your business.' Quill's voice drops, the hostility quickly leaving. 'The only thing you should be worried about is doing your fucking job.'

Bannon shakes his head and gestures between the two of them as he mouths, *'Partners.'*

Quill shoves Bannon off him, driving him back a step as he laughs. 'Partners? Are you fucking serious? I'm your boss, not your fucking partner! Don't go getting all close and personal with me. It won't work. We're here to do a job and that's it.'

He slumps onto his bed, wincing and holding his ribs. As well as the bite marks, his arms are covered in what look like knife cuts. He's healing fast thanks to his vampire blood, but there are so many of them.

Bannon fills a cup with water from the bathroom adjoining Quill's room and grabs a wad of toilet paper before kneeling on the ground in front of Quill.

'What are you doing?'

He gestures to Quill's top, then points up.

'I'm not taking my fucking top off.'

Quill pushes Bannon's hand away when Bannon gestures at Quill's top again, a bit more forcefully this time. Not taking any shit from Quill, he slams his hand on the bed, startling Quill.

He's angry, and that's what's powering him at the moment. Quill is his superior, but kneeling in front of him, looking at the blood and cuts, all he can feel is rage burning deep inside him.

Someone hurt Quill, and that really pisses him off.

Quill clenches his jaw but stops fighting against him. 'There's a first aid kit in the cupboard under the sink.'

Bannon finds the kit, noticing as soon as he opens it that it's been used quite a bit and needs replenishing. He kneels in front of Quill, watching as the male slowly take off his top, wincing when the movement hurts.

Bannon gasps at the sight of Quill's chest. The tattoos that cover his hands, arms, and neck are just the tip of the iceberg. The broad expanse of his toned chest is covered in the swirling Celtic designs.

Catching his reaction Quill glances down at his chest, then lifts his head again, his eyebrows raised. 'I guess I'm addicted.' Bannon leans to the side, trying to see if they continue around his back. Quill turns, showing him that they do.

Bannon had never really been a fan of tattoos, not seeing the attraction. Well, that was until Quill. A male can change his mind, given the right incentive.

But it's not just the tattoos that catch his attention. Quill's broad chest is covered in bite marks and cuts.

His knuckles are undamaged. No sign he fought anyone. And that makes no sense. Quill is more than capable of standing up for himself. Even if he were caught unawares, he'd still have some sort of injury on him. He wouldn't just sit back and let someone cut him like this.

His neck is torn, the skin ripped open as if he were savaged. The scar on Bannon's neck aches when he thinks about that word. He's only ever used it in relation to his own injury. Quill may have fed someone, which doesn't help quieten the jealousy coursing through Bannon, but it wasn't a gentle feed. Far from it.

Bannon turns on the bedside light so he can clearly see what he's doing and his eyes lock onto the thick marks around Quill's wrists. He runs his fingers over the deep red gouges. Not only was it a rough feed, but it also wasn't a voluntary one.

Quill pulls his arms back. 'Just clean the wounds,' Quill says before he can try to get any answers from him. Quill's voice is barely more than a whisper, loaded with exhaustion.

Bannon nods, desperate to know what's going on, but isn't stupid enough to push for an answer Quill isn't going to give him. He knows that much. All he can do for now is make sure Quill's wounds are taken care of.

Bannon can feel the fire raging inside himself, desperate to be unleashed. But he holds it in, concentrating on Quill instead. Pushing his rage down, he taps the inside of his wrist then points to Quill's mouth.

Quill frowns, then shakes his head when he understands what Bannon is saying. 'No fucking way! I'm not feeding from you.'

Bannon curses to himself. He wishes he could argue with Quill using his voice. It's exhausting trying to make an argument with single words and gestures. Quill opens the top drawer of his locker and takes out a pen and a scrap of paper. Seems they're on the same track.

Bannon quickly scribbles a note, then holds up the page to Quill. *'You need to feed. It will heal your wounds.'*

'Do you not think I know that! But I'm not feeding from you.'

'Why not?'

'Because... we're partners.'

Bannon smirks as he writes again. *'I thought we just worked together?'*

Quill holds up his middle finger. 'I think I preferred it when I didn't understand you.'

Bannon returns with the same gesture before writing again. *'I'm offering to do this, so what's the problem?'*

Quill sighs, but his eyes lock on Bannon's neck. He's tempted. 'Why are you even offering?'

'Because I want to help you.'

'Why? There's blood in the fridge in the kitchen. You don't have to do this.'

'I know I don't have to. I want to. You'll heal faster with fresh blood.'

'You haven't answered my question. Feeding me is a big fucking deal. I sure as hell wouldn't order you to do it, let alone expect you to offer.'

Because I'm worried sick about you and I need you to be okay. Instead of writing the truth he sticks to a believable lie. *'Because you gave me a break when I was freaked out with the wolf.'*

It's only a small part of the reason he's willing to let Quill feed from him, but it does the trick, stopping any further arguments.

Quill licks his lips again and his tongue brushes off the rings piercing each side of his bottom lip. He looks up at Bannon, his unusual eyes mesmerising his subordinate. Bannon has never seen eyes like Quill's.

He's never seen a vampire like Quill. Everything about him - how he looks, how he acts, the fact that he's a male - it all contradicts everything he thought he knew about himself. Quill throws his world on its head, and as much as it terrifies him, he doesn't want to walk away.

Offering to feed him is just as much for selfish reasons as it is meant to help. He wants to know what it feels like to have someone like Quill feed from him.

'Fuck. Fine! But this stays between the two of us. No one else finds out. I'm being fucking serious. No one can know. Especially the Warden. I'm not fucking with you, Bannon. He can't find out.'

Bannon nods. He has no idea what business it is of the Warden's who his guards feed from, or why it would be a problem, but he'll agree to anything if it means he gets to do this. He's terrified, and has no idea where these feelings are coming from, but he's running with it.

As soon as he agrees to the terms, Quill doesn't mess around. He grabs Bannon's arm, pulling his wrist towards him. Bannon gasps as Quill's fangs extend and he bites down, puncturing his skin. Bannon's eyes roll back in his head when Quill sucks, his pierced tongue caressing his skin, the sensation hitting all parts of his body at once.

Quill's hand is suddenly on his arm, holding his wrist tight to his mouth, his lips pressing firmly against Bannon's skin as he drinks deeper.

Quill's other hand tightens on his shirt, holding him in place as the world tilts on its axis. It's one of the most euphoric experiences Bannon has ever had - especially in the company of a male. He has no idea how long Quill feeds for, and he honestly couldn't care if he's drained dry.

When Quill slowly pulls his teeth out of Bannon's wrist, Bannon immediately misses the contact. Quill draws his tongue across his bite marks, and Bannon could swear he hears a growl deep from within Quill's chest.

He lingers against Bannon's wrist, his breath warm on his skin as the two of them recover from the feeding. Quill releases his hold on Bannon's arm and leans back, putting distance between them. He licks his lips as he keeps his attention on the bite marks he just created.

Neither of them moves for a few minutes and that suits Bannon just fine. His head is spinning, and his dick is embarrassingly harder than it should be. Quill closes his eyes, then brushes his hand through his long hair. His fangs slowly retract as he comes down from the feed.

Bannon would love to see him with his fangs and wings out. That would be one hell of a sight.

Quill opens his eyes again, but doesn't look at him. 'Thanks. You should go now.'

That's one way to bring him down from his rush. But it's something he should have expected. It was just a feed to help him regain his strength. It was only *more* in Bannon's delusional fantasies. He nods as he gets to his feet. He doesn't want to leave like this. Not without something else being said. But there's nothing.

He opens the door and steps outside. 'Bannon? Thank you.'

It's not quite what he would have liked, not that he knows what that would involve, but it's a start. He nods and smiles, then heads over to his room. As he turned away from Quill, he noticed something that confuses and excites him in equal measure.

Quill's green and blue eyes were glowing. Nothing about what happened between them would lead him to believe Quill was in any way angry. So, does that mean there's a chance Quill might have enjoyed their interaction as much as he did?

DAVYN

As soon as he turns off the main road, the knot in his stomach tightens, the rock-hard lump making him queasy. Davyn stops his Land Rover just inside the gate to the castle and stares into the darkness beyond the reach of the headlights.

Bastian had offered to bring him over in the helicopter, but he'd refused. He needed to come here under his own steam, in his own time. The ferry across from Wales to Ireland had given him time to work up to coming back here. The drive across Ireland should have taken about two hours less than it did. Stopping numerous times on the way to talk himself into just continuing down the road had wasted a few hours.

It helps that Thea is at the end of the driveway waiting for him. His mate is the one thing that's kept him alive the last few months - in more ways than one. Being a Prime vampire who is addicted to blood, trying to keep one step ahead of the Blood Fever that's chasing after him, means feeding is a life-and-death situation.

Too little, and he won't survive. Too much and Fever will take hold, turning him into a blood-crazed monster. Thea's blood is the key to keeping him strong, healthy, and sane. That woman is everything to him. He would kill for her. He would die for her.

But that doesn't mean he's in a hurry to continue down that driveway to see her. He pulls off his eye patch, massaging the skin surrounding his useless right eye. Just another part of his father's legacy. Most of the scars on his body are down to his father - directly or indirectly. Scars from countless beatings, or from his father's fighting pits. His childhood had been shite. Living in that castle had been fucking miserable.

He looks at his phone as it vibrates in the holder in front of him. It's a message from Thea. *You can do it, sexy. I'm waiting for you.*

He smiles as he sends back a response. *Just psyching myself up. I'll be there in a minute.*

Trust Thea to know why he's taking so long. He puts his Land Rover in gear, then drives down the potholed driveway. He doesn't know what he was expecting, but when he rounds the corner and the castle comes into view, he stops the car again. The stone monstrosity had always been in darkness. His father preferred to make the castle as miserable as possible.

But it seems Thea has begun working her magic on the place. Huge torches line the perimeter wall, matching the two that frame the entranceway. Most of the windows are also illuminated, giving the place a feeling of life for the first time in his one hundred and seventy years.

This is down to Thea with Fergus's help.

He pulls up in the courtyard, some of the dread fading when Thea opens the main door and stands at the top of the stairs, smiling at him. Dav gets out of his car, barely taking two steps before she launches herself at him, wrapping her legs around his waist as he lifts her from the ground.

'I missed you so much.'

'You've only been gone a few days.'

She kisses him, then unwraps her legs so he can put her back on the ground. 'It was a long few days. How are you doing?' she asks, taking his hand.

'I'm grand.' He's not, but she'll know without him having to tell her. He's still not convinced it was a good idea to leave the castle standing.

'Good effort, but miserable fail.'

'Are you two finished yet?'

Dav smiles at Fletch as the human doctor peers around the door. 'We're done.'

He steps out from behind the door, his bag slung over his shoulder. 'Welcome back sire.'

'Don't you fucking start!'

Fletch grins widely. 'You good?'

Dav nods. 'So far. You heading back now?'

'That I am. With you here, I'm sure Thea's safety is in good hands. I'll head back to the Compound. I want to get some more medical supplies boxed up. If you find these prisons, you might need a restock.'

Thea hugs the doctor, then kisses him on the cheek. 'Thanks for helping me to convince the Whelans to come back here.'

Fletch laughs at that. 'Did you see where they were living? Don't think much convincing was needed. 'Right. Well, I'm off. Can't leave Nix waiting. See you soon.'

He walks down the steps, then climbs into the BMW. Fletch beeps the horn as he drives away, the lights fading down the long driveway.

Thea gets up on her tiptoes and kisses Dav. 'Come on. Murt and his brothers are waiting for you.'

As he walks through the castle, the vampires who still call it home bow when he passes. He fucking hates that, but he'd been told many times by both Thea and Fergus that it's the way they want to show him respect. He's not going to be able to change that. Doesn't mean it's something he can ever accept.

'How did Murt handle the news about Sorcha?'

'He was surprised, but he's here, so he believes there's something in it. We've spent the last few days mapping out possible sites. Nothing is ringing a bell with the Whelans. How long can you stay for?'

He shrugs, earning a dig in the ribs from Thea.

'I didn't say *how long do you want to stay for?* I asked *how long is Nix letting you stay for?*'

He glances down at her and smirks. 'Apparently, as long as I need to. So ideally, I'll be back in my car in an hour.'

She laughs, and even though he's in his personal version of Hell, he can't help but smile. 'How the fuck do you do that?' he asks, pulling her to a stop just outside the great hall.

'Do what?'

'Make me smile even though I'm here.'

She shrugs, wrapping her arms around his waist. 'I guess I'm just downright amazing.'

'That's an understatement.' He wants to kiss her. Fuck that! He wants to throw her over his shoulder, bring her out to his car, and get the fuck out of here as fast as he can. But that's not what he does. He's never run from a fight in his life. He's not going to run from a fucking building.

'Where are the wolves?'

She nods to the great hall. 'They're camped out in the living area to the back of the hall. We've set up a nice little office space there. There's plenty of room for us to spread out all the files so we can go through them.'

'Better not keep them waiting then.' He takes her hand again, not in any way embarrassed by the strength she gives him. That's how they work. Both halves making the other whole. Or maybe it's just her that fixes him. Fuck knows she's a hell of a lot more put together than he is.

As soon as he steps into the back living room with her, any ill feeling about being back here disappears. This is Blackjack Davyn, not the abused version. This is where he shows he's fit to destroy everything his father created.

'Davyn!' Murt says, getting to his feet. 'It's been a while.'

Davyn accepts the embrace even though it catches him off-guard. 'Yeah. Thea told me what happened. Why didn't you get in touch?'

Murt drops back into the chair as the other three brothers greet Davyn. 'Now, you're not going to tell me a vampire such as yourself hasn't heard of stubborn male pride?'

Davyn laughs as he takes a seat at the table. He knows all about that. 'How did that go for you?'

Murt grimaces, before taking a drink from his pint of stout. 'Not so good. But in all seriousness. We are grateful for the roof over our heads. It's much appreciated.'

'It's a permanent thing if you want it,' Dav says, smiling at Thea when she passes him a drink. 'Fuck knows I won't be using this place. It's your home now. You won't have any trouble here. I couldn't give a fuck about the wolf/vampire feud. That's outside these walls. If anyone tries to take it inside, I'll deal with it.'

'I don't doubt that for a second. So, these notes of your father's make for interesting reading. Did you have any idea these prisons existed?'

He shakes his head. 'I was just in the cells below the castle and the fighting pits. Fucker kept the prisons a secret. But as far as I know, there were no wolves in the pits. He must have kept them in the prisons for some reason. No idea why he didn't mention the wolves. He liked to brag about what he was doing. Liked to get a reaction. You find out how he was funding the prisons?'

Con nods, taking over from Murt. 'From some of the records we found this morning, your old man was taking payment for keeping the prisons stocked. They're privately owned, but he was supplying the inmates.'

'How the fuck was he doing that? He didn't have a moral compass. Who decided these people committed crimes?'

'Not all did commit a crime. Some were convicted through either the Wolf Elders or Vampire Council. But not all of them. Some seem to have just been stuck in there, because someone wanted them in there.'

Davyn should be surprised, but he's not. He doubts anything his father did in his long life would take him by surprise. 'Did you find any mention of your sister?'

The silence that follows tells him everything he needs to know. It was probably too much to ask for there to be a clear-cut record of Sorcha in those files. It doesn't mean it's not there somewhere though. Centuries of records will take time to sort through - even with Thea, Shep's girlfriend Izzy, Ethan's team, and the Blackjacks working on it in Wales and Ireland.

Murt takes another swig of his stout before speaking again. 'We feel that she's still alive. We have a bond and it's fucking strong. We'd know if she was dead. We're sure of it. These prisons are the best lead we have. Just because we haven't found her name in black and white doesn't mean it's not in there somewhere. Either way, we're going down this route.'

He doesn't blame them. From what Ethan has told him, there aren't many other options to explore. 'My car is loaded with equipment Ethan thought could help us narrow down some possible locations. He's also on standby if we need help. I'll be fuck-all use to you going through the records because I can't read, but I'll help in any other ways I can.'

Thea had been trying to teach him how to read, but it's a slow and frustrating process. One he puts to the bottom of his list more than he should.

'Just giving us access to these notes is help enough, Davyn,' Murt says, slumping back in the chair. 'It's been eight years with nothing. At this stage, we'll take any slim possibility over that.'

'I'll get the equipment unloaded, then we can check out the locations.' Dav pushes up from the table, gesturing for Thea to stay put. He goes out to the car, not surprised to find Fergus there with a few other vampires unloading everything.

'Welcome back, sire... I do apologise - Davyn.'

He restrains his smile. The old vampire can't seem to drop the formalities no matter how many times Dav tells him to. 'Can all this be brought to the room where Thea and the wolves are working?'

'Of course, Davyn.'

He reaches into the back of the Land Rover, but Davyn stops him. 'I need a word.' Fergus nods and follows him to the far side of the courtyard away from any potential eavesdroppers.

'Is there something wrong, Davyn?'

'No, but I need your assurance it'll stay that way.'

'Of course. I'll do what I can.'

'Murt and his brothers are guests here. They're under my protection. Under the protection of the walls of this castle. If... when we find their sister, the same will go for her. Fuck, the same goes for any wolf they approve bringing in. I won't have any of this old-fashioned feud bullshit going on in here. There's been enough misery in these walls to last a lifetime. I won't have even one vampire or wolf under my protection getting shit from anyone else. You get what I'm saying?'

Fergus nods quickly. 'Of course, sire... sorry, Davyn. I share your thoughts on where the future of this castle lies. I assure you, every being who enters as a friend will be offered sanctuary. May I ask what we should do in the event of a less than savoury individual seeking entry?'

'Refuse. If they don't fuck off, call me immediately. I'll make sure they regret fucking with me.'

Fergus clears his throat, before nodding briskly. 'I believe they would find that particularly unpleasant.'

'You could say that. Was Thea okay the last few days?'

'Very much so. I find her welcome company. She has helped to transform the garden. It's nowhere near how your mother had it yet - but the task has just begun. I don't doubt she'll create a truly beautiful garden in memory of your mother.'

'Make sure she has anything and everything she needs. That goes for protection, too. She doesn't go outside the grounds alone.'

Fergus nods. 'That goes without saying. I will not let any harm come to her.'

Davyn knows Fergus means that, but he's not trained for the type of protection Davyn is talking about. That will change in time. Training has been put in place for some of the more capable vampires in the castle. He hopes that they'll be able to withstand any potential issues that might come knocking. Until then, he's not taking any chances.

'You okay if the Whelans hang around?'

'It's not my concern Davyn.'

'Drop all that, Fergus. This is your home. Are you okay with them being here?'

Fergus smiles at that. 'I appreciate you asking, but yes, I am more than okay about them being here. They add some... personality to the stone walls. I enjoy their company. Although, our food bill may increase somewhat. Garret and Conal have particularly healthy appetites.'

'I'll make sure you've got enough funds coming in. You need anything else?'

Fergus pauses, averting his eyes from Davyn for a moment before he answers. 'You are putting a lot of time, effort, and funds into the castle and all of us who live here. I was wondering if that means you plan to someday return and take your place as head of the house?'

He should have known that question would come up at some stage. He likes Fergus, and he can't say that about a lot of the people from this time in his life. He respects him too. For that reason, he's not going to be honest and risk offending him.

Dav would rather die than ever come back here full-time. His mother was murdered here. His father and brother tortured, brutalised, and abused him for years in these walls. He'll never call this place home. Never wants to be here with Thea.

But he's also not going to turn his back on all the good vampires that came before his father. That's the only reason he's hanging on to this place.

'The head of this house will have to sit in Wales for now. I'm not walking away from the Blackjacks.'

Fergus smiles, but it's with less enthusiasm. 'Of course. I understand.'

'I've put a good male in charge. I trust him to be my eyes and ears here.'

That brings back the smile. 'I appreciate you saying that, Davyn.'

He dismisses Fergus with a brisk nod. As the male goes back to help unload the equipment, Dav climbs the stone stairs to the top of the turret nearest him. When he gets to the roof he walks over to the edge, scanning the wild Atlantic Ocean stretching for miles in front of him. The sound of the sea still gets his heart racing for all the wrong reasons. He spent a good few decades in a flooded cell, entirely at the mercy of that very ocean.

He picks up on her scent before she even steps onto the roof. When she walks over to him, Dav pulls Thea into his arms, tucking her head under his chin as he listens to the sea.

Thea wraps her arms around him. 'The car is unpacked, and Fergus is getting some food prepared for you.'

'I need to help them find her.'

'I thought you were going to leave in a few days?'

'That was my plan. But she's only missing because of my father.

130

It's his fault.'

'But that doesn't mean it's your fault. Why do I get the feeling you're blaming yourself? You didn't do this, Dav.'

He releases her, then sits on the cold stone wall surrounding the roof. 'I should have stood up to him decades ago. I wasn't in that cage all the time. I could have fought back when they took me out. I should have—'

'Stop!' Her loud interruption startles him. 'Your father and brother were abusing you. The only thing you could have done was exactly what you did do.'

'What? Nothing?'

'You survived. You're here today because you fought for yourself. That's all you could have done. But not just that,' she says, sitting down beside him. 'You're still fighting. No one would have blamed you for levelling the castle and never setting foot in Ireland again. Yet here you are, trying to create something you can be proud of.'

'Too little too fucking late.'

'Not for Sorcha. Murt and his brothers are adamant she's still alive. They can feel her. We don't know how many others are with her, wherever she is.'

She's right. She usually is when it comes to things like this. She's told him numerous times he's being too hard on himself for feeling guilty that he survived, when so many others didn't. 'Fergus asked if I'd stay.'

Thea nods, her face telling him she knew this was coming.

'He'd mentioned it to you already?'

'It's a compliment. He likes having you around. God knows why,' she adds with a wink.

He shakes his head, looking back out over the sea. 'I can't stay here long term.'

'I know. All you can do is take one visit at a time. It might be different for Fergus having the Whelans around the place. They're certainly keeping him on his toes.'

'No doubt.'

'What's going to happen there?' she asks, brushing her dark hair behind her shoulder when a gust of wind blows it over her face.

'I've said they can stay if they want. There's plenty of room. It makes sense to have them here if they're under my protection. At least that way they're not hiding from their Elders in a caravan in a field.'

'I'd say they'd prefer this option to that one. I can't imagine how the four of them fit into the small caravan. It must have been cosy.'

'Yeah. Wouldn't say they'd be in a hurry to go back to that.' He stands and offers her his hand. 'We'll eat, then I'll keep you company while you read through reams of paper.'

Thea reaches up to kiss his cheek. 'So, does this mean you'll be more open to me teaching you how to read? I haven't broached the subject since you had that tantrum a few weeks ago and threw the book across the room.'

'It wasn't a tantrum!' He's fighting a losing battle, judging by her laugh.

He stops to let her climb down the narrow staircase before him. 'Oh, it was absolutely a tantrum.'

He growls at her, but she just laughs it off. 'Moving on from your tantrum my lord, did you have a chance to think about a new name for the castle?'

'Yeah,' he says reaching the bottom of the stairs where she's waiting for him. He'd put a lot of thought into that one. His father had renamed the castle Raven's Blood after his self-given title of the Raven King. It's a name that needed to die. There's no point in trying to fix what his father did without changing the name, too.

'My father decided on the name when he took over. I want to change the name back to what it was when my grandfather ruled.'

She smiles up at him as she takes his hand. 'That's a great idea Dav. What was it called?'

'Darkhaven. I think it works. It should be a haven, not a prison.'

She wraps her arms around his waist. 'It's perfect.'

SORCHA

Sorcha wakes with a start when the door to her cell locks with a bang. She rolls over and spots a few pieces of paper on the table. She wipes her eyes, trying to clear her vision as she picks them up and unfolds the top one.

Bannon had printed out the alphabet in sign language.

Homework. I'll be testing you.

She grins to herself as she scans the images on the pages, before rereading his words. It's strange reading something that came out of his head. She takes talking for granted. She can't imagine what it's like for Bannon to have to write what he wants to say. And it's not like he can convey emotions that way. He's as alone in here as she is. Trapped with no one to talk to.

She'll change that for him.

When the door opens a few hours later, Sorcha is confident she knows the pages by heart. She leans back against the wall as she watches Bannon walk over to the table and place the first aid kit down on it.

She slowly pushes to her feet and walks over to the table. She opens the box, excited to see what Quill has arranged for her today. Every day, she expects to get her old food again, but Quill is sticking to his word. 'Oh, hell no! You did not just give me that to eat?'

He frowns as he looks down at the food, then shrugs and mouths, *'What?'*

'That's a freaking Hawaiian pizza! A pizza! Is that for me?'

Bannon nods, then pulls out the chair for her. She has no idea how she doesn't actually burst into tears at this moment. The food and his out-of-the-blue gesture are so perfect, even in her current surroundings. Bannon steps around the side of the table and leans against the wall.

'Okay?' he mouths when she finally looks at him.

Unable to say anything she just nods, as she gingerly picks up a slice of pizza.

'Would you like some?' she asks before she takes a bite.

He shakes his head, but she holds out a slice anyway.

'I can't eat while you just stand there watching me. It's been a long time since I shared a meal with anyone. I've been in solitary for... well, I have no idea how long. Please. Just one slice.'

He slowly takes the slice from her, but waits until she tucks in before he eats.

Sorcha closes her eyes and groans loudly. 'Oh damn! That's the best pizza I've ever had! Hawaiian is my favourite. I like anchovies, too. Can't beat a pizza with ham, pineapple, and anchovies.'

He wrinkles his nose at that, and she can't help but laugh loudly at his expression. Her own laugh sounds so strange to her. Laughing hasn't been a regular occurrence since she was captured. Plus, he looks completely adorable, which is bizarre considering who he is. She needs to keep reminding herself he's here to make sure she can't escape. They're not friends or comrades.

'What's wrong? You're not a fan of fish on pizzas?'

Bannon briskly shakes his head.

'Weirdo!'

He smiles as she fires that adolescent retort back at him. Bannon finishes his slice of pizza, then lifts his hands, signing something as he raises his eyebrows.

'Oh, the pages? They're between the wall and the mattress.'

He slides his hand down behind her bed, pulling the pages of sign language free from their hiding place. He walks back over to her and places the pages on the table.

As a wolf, she's naturally graceful. Having the ability to use four legs from time-to-time helped. But she never thought of a vampire as graceful. Growing up, vampires were the enemy. They were cold, emotionless voids who attacked wolves. Bannon is not like that. She could watch his body move all day and never tire of it.

He taps the pages as he raises his eyebrows.

'Oh, I'm done with that,' she says around a mouthful of pizza. 'I've finished the homework you left me.'

He smirks, then he shakes his head.

'You doubt me now?'

Bannon leans against the wall, his arms crossed and that adorable smirk still on his face. He gestures to the pages and nods expectantly at her.

'Oh, testing time?'

He nods again.

She even impresses herself when she gets through the alphabet without making any mistakes. When she's finished, she steals a quick look at him to see his reaction. He's smiling. A full genuine smile and she loves it. 'Was that okay? I don't think I made a mistake. Did I?'

He gives her a thumbs up, then pulls the notebook from his pocket.

Bannon writes for a few seconds, then holds it up to her.

'I wasn't expecting you to have memorised all of it so fast.'

She shrugs. 'There's not a lot else to do down here. To be honest, I really enjoyed having something to get my brain working again. Are you teaching the other guards too?' She knows the answer, but she wants to keep talking to him. It's such a change to actually have a conversation with someone.

Bannon shakes his head, then points to her.

'Just me?'

He nods, then writes again. *'No need to teach them. We don't have anything to say to each other.'*

'Is there anyone here you can have a conversation with?'

A pause, followed by another shake of his head.

'I'm sorry.'

'Why?'

'I know what it's like not having anyone to talk to. It's lonely. But not being *able* to talk to anyone, even with people around, must be incredibly isolating. I don't like to hear of anyone in that situation.'

He frowns and then offers her a small smile. Bannon gestures to the door, then gets to his feet.

'You have to go? Can you not stay for another few minutes?'

He goes to write something but changes his mind, slipping the notebook back in his pocket. His hands move slowly, and Sorcha is thrilled when she recognises what he's signing.

'W. O. R. K.'

His smile is incredible and, even though he's a guard and she's a prisoner, she suddenly has the overwhelming urge to help him smile like that more often. She had made the effort to communicate with him and she has no doubts he appreciates it.

'Will I see you later?' She shouldn't want to see him again. His job is to keep her locked away from the rest of the world. To keep her from her family.

But something tells her he's in a similar position. He's also locked away from the rest of the world. Not being able to communicate with anyone else on this island is keeping him locked in his head.

Bannon pauses, then frowns and looks towards the door. His eyes widen and he gestures to the pages. Instantly understanding, she hides them down the back of her bed, stuffing them between the mattress and the wall.

She sits back on her chair just as Quill steps into her cell. He looks from Bannon to her, his broad body hidden in shadow. 'Problem Officer?'

Bannon shakes his head. Quill looks to her again and she just smiles. 'You want some pizza, Officer?'

Quill tilts his head to the side. 'You really don't give a fuck, do you?'

It's not a question, more of a statement, so she continues eating instead of responding.

'We all good in here?'

Bannon nods again, clearly uneasy around his boss. 'So,' Sorcha says, wiping her mouth. 'I guess I have you to thank for the food.'

'Just sticking to our agreement.'

'How about adding a third condition to our agreement, Officer?'

Quill visibly bristles at her question, while Bannon looks at the two of them in confusion.

'Your boss here is going to learn sign language too, aren't you Officer?'

Bannon's head whips around to face Quill who, much to her amusement, drops his eyes to avoid looking at Bannon. Seeing an opening she can't help but jump right into, Sorcha pulls the pages from behind her bed and holds them out to Quill. 'He printed these out for me. It took me a day to learn the alphabet. Let's see if you can do any better than I did.'

If she had a camera she'd take a picture of Quill's face. It's priceless, moving from shock to anger, then to resignation. Quill slowly walks over to her, taking the pages from her hand. He looks over the information, glancing up at Bannon every few seconds, who appears close to throwing up.

'You can borrow them if you want.'

Quill folds the pages and, eyes still on Bannon, slowly slips them into the back pocket of his combats. 'Finish your dinner. We're not warming that up for you.'

Smiling to herself, she grabs the last slice of pizza, eating it as she watches the seriously hilarious awkwardness between the two guards. Bannon is completely out of the loop, while Quill is hovering towards embarrassment being outed like he was.

He reaches up to tuck some hair behind his ear. She'd never noticed until that moment how long his hair actually is. If he let it out of the bun it would probably reach his shoulders. The more she looks at him, the more she realises he doesn't quite fit with the strict prison officer look that the rest of the guards have. Not at all.

His long hair, unusual eyes, piercings, and tattoos, shouldn't be hidden away in here with the rest of the stuffy guards she has to deal with.

Then she catches Bannon giving him what she would imagine is a similar look to the one she's giving Quill. Holy shit! Is Bannon attracted to the grumpy guard?

She wouldn't entirely blame him if he was. Quill is a dick, but she can absolutely see what the attraction is.

'Bannon. Out. Back to work.' Quill says, stirring her and Bannon out of their thoughts. Quill watches the other guard leave with a backward glance at her. Once he's gone Quill walks over to her. 'What were you doing?'

'About what?'

Quill crouches down, his huge body dwarfing hers. 'Don't fuck with me wolf! I promise my fangs are sharper than yours. What were you doing with him?'

'Why? Is someone jealous?'

He doesn't appreciate that, getting to his feet and crossing his arms. 'Watch it!'

'Oh, I was watching it Officer, and with great interest.'

Quill curses under his breath as he turns around to leave. 'Wait! We were just talking. What else could, or would we be doing?'

'You take me for a fool or something? He can't talk.'

'No Officer. You just can't hear him. That's why you need to learn sign language. I heard him today. It was only a few sentences, but he was able to talk to me. You haven't bothered to try yet.'

She is convinced Quill is going to strike her. The anger in his eyes is hard to miss.

'Why are you still fighting?'

His question completely throws her off guard. 'Fighting what?'

'This place,' he says, looking around her small cell. 'Everyone in here breaks at some stage, but you haven't. Why?'

'I doubt you'd understand.'

He absently turns the thick silver bracelet around his wrist. 'You'd be surprised. Try me.'

This entire situation is completely bizarre, but she gives in. Even talking to Quill is better than not talking to anyone. 'Fighting is all I have left. As soon as I let go, I'm as good as dead. I know I'll spend the rest of my life here, but that doesn't mean I'm going to give in. It's not what we do.'

'We?'

'Wolves.'

Quill's head tilts ever so slightly to the side, his eyes softening. Instead of answering, he just nods, then leaves the cell. As he locks the cell behind him, Sorcha lies down on her bed. What the hell was that? Quill was actually semi-decent with her. Even bordering on nice.

She thought she knew how things worked in these prisons. After so many years, she was convinced nothing could surprise her. But when Bannon walked into her cell, her stagnant life shifted. He fascinated her like no one has before. And now Quill is acting strangely around her, and she is fascinated by him, too.

Sorcha closes her eyes, curling into a ball to try to get warm. She shouldn't be looking at Quill differently either. After all, he's the one who has flogged her twice, hurting her so badly she lost consciousness. This unexpected attraction to Bannon is confusing things with Quill.

But is he really that bad?

Looks-wise he could be described as attractive - if not for the cold death glare of course. But there is something about him that intrigues her.

She turns to face the wall, angry at herself for letting these thoughts enter her mind.

What the hell is wrong with her? She's been locked away for too long, that's what. Alone for so long that even the company of two vampires is a better alternative to being on her own.

BANNON

Bannon looks up as Quill storms into the kitchen, completely ignoring him as there are two other guards in the room. The head guard makes himself a coffee, then instead of taking a seat or leaving the room, walks right around the table for no apparent reason. Bannon looks up, realising there was a method to his trip around the room. It was to put himself in Bannon's direct line of sight, but behind the two guards.

'Your room in five,' Quill mouths slowly, before storming off again.

Bannon stares after Quill for a few seconds, before he snaps out of his daze and clears away his dishes. This has to be about what happened in Sorcha's cell and the cryptic conversation they had.

Quill said his job here is safe, so what other reason would there be for needing a secret meeting? And why is the excitement building at the thought of spending a few moments alone with Quill - even if he is in trouble for something.

He's embarrassed to admit to himself that Quill is getting to him as much as he is. He's never been more confused in his life, and there had been some seriously confusing moments over the years.

After he was mauled, his life took a massive turn in a direction he never expected or planned. He went to bed that night with a family. He woke up to screaming, soaked in blood, in agonising pain, with a wolf savaging him, and his family dead around him.

Ever since that moment, he's been in a box, closed off from everyone he knew. The rest of the world continued as normal. Everyone around him got on with their lives, while he was left locked away with no voice, no way of communicating, no way of making himself heard, and utterly alone.

The possibility of being able to have brief talks with Sorcha is like a new lease of life to him. He's still floored by the fact she took the time to learn sign language. She's the first person since he was mauled who has taken the time to *hear* him. And that's worth more than he could ever express. It's foolish to get carried away with her, but he's enjoying her company. She's not like any of the other prisoners. There's still some life in her, still some fight. It also hasn't escaped his attention that she's beautiful.

Sorcha is just adding to his confusion. He's only been in love once in his life, and it hadn't ended well. Not being able to speak after the accident had put up a barrier in that relationship, and she had left.

He understands why, but it didn't help boost his confidence in any way. In fact, he'd been so low for a long time he'd contemplated whether it would be easier to just give up.

Maybe he was a coward and that's why he's still here. Maybe it was the other way around? Whatever the reason, he's still breathing, and working, and had now somehow found himself being drawn to two people.

Sorcha is the first person in too long who actually wants to *hear* what he has to say. He'll have a voice again, and he can't wait. She's doing that for him. In spite of everything else she's going through, she wants to do this for him.

Hearing that Quill might consider learning sign, as well was a shock. But he might have just been saying that to shut her up. His job is to run the prison. He only needs to give orders. What his guards have to say in return isn't on his radar. He's the voice of the Warden inside these walls.

As Bannon turns the corner leading to the bedrooms, he picks up on Quill's scent. He's waiting just down from Bannon's door, coffee cup still in his hand, his blue and green eyes glowing slightly. Bannon unlocks his bedroom door and steps into his room, leaving the door open behind him. He gets as far as his bed before the door closes behind him. Quill's scent fills his room, the woody cologne wrapping around him in a way he both loves and fears.

Quill places his cup of coffee on the small desk by the bed, then crosses his tattooed arms, his eyes focused on the carpet between Bannon's feet, instead of on him. 'I asked the wolf to keep quiet about you having that freak attack, and agreed to replace her meals, in exchange for her silence.'

Bannon had suspected Quill spoke to Sorcha, but wasn't expecting him to make a deal like that with one of the inmates. Bannon waves his hand, catching Quill's attention before he mouths, *'Why?'*

'Why the fuck do you think? I've got enough inmates and guards to babysit. I don't need another headache.'

Of course. Why would he think it was anything other than saving himself some trouble. Bannon smiles as he nods, then crosses his own arms, mirroring Quill's posture. Two can play that game.

'What's that look for?'

Bannon shrugs. He's off the clock so fuck him.

'You are so fucking infuriating you know that? I'm trying to help you. I could do with less of your attitude!'

There's attitude all right, but that's not coming from him. He's done with this. Bannon pushes past Quill, opening the door and gesturing for him to leave. Quill slams the door shut again.

'We're not done.'

Bannon angrily points to his mouth. *We are! Get out!*

'Is it true? She's actually learning how to sign?'

Quill's change of topic trips him for a few seconds. He nods. Then he sees it. A very slight narrowing of Quill's eyes. Bannon smiles to himself when he realises what he's seeing. Quill is jealous.

But that begs the question... jealous of whom? Is it his closeness to Sorcha? Or hers to him?

'I am so fucking tempted to wipe that smile off your face. You're here to make sure she doesn't escape. Nothing else!'

Bannon tries to walk away from him, not that there's anywhere to go with Quill blocking the door. All he can do is put some space between them. Give Quill a chance to either calm down or leave him alone.

This isn't an argument he's going to win. Even if he could talk, he still wouldn't win. Quill is just a hothead who would pick a fight with his own shadow given the mood. He fucked up. He knows that. But he's not going to spend the rest of his time here apologising, or kissing his damn feet, just because Quill gave him a break.

'Don't turn your back on me!'

Bannon clenches his fists, the flames springing to life before he can stop them. He slowly turns to face Quill, the flames travelling up his arms to his elbows.

Instead of laying into him for using his powers, Quill silently stares at him, his mouth open. Bannon moves towards Quill, stopping when he's right in front of him.

Don't you dare push me around.

The words are said in his head, but Quill gets his message loud and clear. The head guard holds up his hands, his fingers hovering inches from Bannon's flames.

'That's hot. You going to burn me again?'

Something in his tone suggests he's not merely talking about the temperature of the flames. Bannon pulls some of the heat back into his body, but leaves the flames coursing over his skin. Realising that the temperature has dropped, Quill reaches out again, this time his fingers brush against Bannon's.

Quill swallows deeply, his Adam's Apple bobbing in his thick neck.

'Fuck! That's freaky! How are you not burning me?'

'*Control,*' he mouths.

Quill smiles as he watches the slow-moving flames touching his skin. 'Impressive.' When his fingers lace with Bannon's, he has to fight to keep the flames under control. Burning Quill to a crisp would seriously ruin whatever mood is being created. 'This can't happen. I can't let it happen.' Quills voice is so low he can barely hear him.

Is he talking about this thing between them, or about his flames? Bannon squeezes his hand, the unfamiliar feelings he's experiencing giving him pause. He has no idea how to act in this situation. He's winging it.

Quill's thumb rubs against his skin, the rhythmic circles firm yet gentle, as the head guard keeps his attention on the flames travelling along Bannon's skin and over his own hand. 'I can't let it happen,' he says again, and Bannon is still no closer to figuring out what *this* he's referring to.

When Quill licks his lips, Bannon knows he's going to do something that could either be reciprocated or rejected by Quill.

Bannon leans forward and kisses him. Quill pauses for less than a second, then kisses him back. This time Bannon takes the lead, going with instinct instead of rational thought. With the warm flames still surrounding his hands, he pushes Quill back against the door, pressing him against the wood with his body. Quill's toned chest rubs against his as he kisses him, his hands combing through Quill's hair, pulling some locks free from their tie.

His tongue brushes against Quill's and he silently groans when he feels the barbell piercing. Unfortunately, it's not his body's only reaction to the contact. His dick hardens, pressing against Quill.

The contact seems to bring Quill to his senses. He stops the kiss, pushing Bannon back a step. 'Fuck! Sorry, I can't do this.'

Bannon's flames instantly die, along with his badly timed hard-on. He nods as he takes another step back from Quill. He wants to ask why Quill can't do this. Wants to ask if Quill is as drawn to him, as he is to Quill? Wants to know why he kissed him, then pushed him away? Wants to know if, like him, Quill wants more.

He watches as Quill brushes his hair back from his face, taking a deep breath as he stares up at the ceiling. 'Fuck! This can't happen.'

It's said more to himself than to Bannon, but it doesn't help him figure out what the hell is going on.

'I have to go,' Quill says suddenly, scrubbing a hand over his face. 'I have to go.'

He pulls open the door, but doesn't leave the room straight away. Instead, he turns back around. Bannon watches as he lifts his hands. *'Bye,'* he signs absolutely perfectly.

Bannon smiles at him but he's gone, the door clicking shut behind him.

Bannon lies back in his narrow bed and stares up at the ceiling. What the hell was that? Quill had actually learned to sign *bye*! It's such a massive deal to him. He's gone from having no one in his life willing to learn, to two strangers who want to help him.

Two strangers he's playing a dangerous game with. Not that he's *playing* at anything. That's not what he does. When it comes to relationships he's usually in the old-fashioned camp. He takes his time, getting to know the person he's with before he even kisses them.

Everything is getting turned on its head when he's near Quill. Sorcha too. He can't be attracted to both Quill and Sorcha? It makes no sense. A male vampire guard and a female wolf prisoner. Talk about picking two of the most unsuitable mates he could possibly find.

Clearly, he's going through some sort of vampire version of a midlife crisis. There's no other explanation. But whatever it is, he needs to get over it. Fast.

By giving Sorcha those notes, he's already crossed a line that could get him into a shitload of trouble with the Warden if he finds out. He doubts Quill will say anything about it. Sorcha too. She's no idiot, but that doesn't mean he's off the hook.

He checks his watch. It's barely four in the afternoon. His dinner break is ending in ten minutes. Then he's back at work for another two hours. Quill is finished for the day, so he won't see him again until tomorrow. Something he's grateful for. He needs time to breathe. Just to figure out what the hell is going on in his head.

He's your boss and she's a prisoner. Don't blur the lines.

MURT

As he drinks his coffee, Murt looks out the window at the wild Atlantic Ocean. If not for the history of this castle, it would be spectacular. If only the sea could wash away all the blood, pain, and death that took place inside these ancient walls. Buildings such as this should stand proud and strong, not hide secrets no one should know about.

He wasn't expecting to settle in here as fast as he has. He's well used to sleeping rough. They'd had to do it enough times over the years, both in wolf and human form. He and his brothers could sleep standing up in the middle of a field, if the occasion called for it. Garret had been known to sleep while Murt was talking to him, but that's another issue.

Stretching out last night in a huge bed in a vast bedroom is a first. It certainly beats sharing the caravan with his three brothers, who could snore loud enough to wake the dead. Having a bathroom to himself too is another extra bonus. They'd lived in that caravan for longer than any of them had been comfortable with.

If only their ancestors could see them now! Upgraded from a caravan in a field to a castle. But he's not getting carried away. There's nothing to say they won't be back in that damp caravan again before too long.

Although, he could get used to waking up in this room every day. He has no doubt that Thea has worked her charm on the room. He can see evidence of her sympathetic touches in the decor. It certainly helped give the cold stone walls some warmth, some personality. With enough time he could see Darkhaven being transformed into somewhere warm and inviting.

On the car ride to the castle, he'd been filled with dread at seeing the place again. But now he's here, witnessing the changes that Fergus, Thea, and the staff have implemented, he's not in a hurry to leave. And with their alternative home no doubt growing damper by the minute in its muddy field, anything would be a better alternative.

At least here he doesn't have to share one room and a tiny bathroom with his three brothers. He loves them to death, but fuck can they get on his nerves at times! They fought like fuckers over the years, but it was nearly a daily occurrence in that caravan.

He turns as someone knocks on the door. 'Yeah?'

Davyn opens the door, and Murt immediately stands a little straighter. It's a ridiculous reaction, but one he can't help. When he swore allegiance to Davyn, he'd put the vampire to the top of his *people I don't fuck with* list. There aren't many people on it. Barely a handful at most, but Davyn tops that.

He doesn't fear the male in any way. But he does respect him enough to know that he's a lethal bastard if pushed. He just has to make sure none of the Whelan clan are the ones to push him. Without his protection, they could find themselves in more trouble than they're currently in.

'You good?'

Davyn is clearly as uncomfortable with the situation as he is. Being lord of the manor wasn't part of his great life plan either. 'So far. I was just about to head downstairs. Bury myself in more of your father's files.'

Davyn walks over to him, taking a piece of paper from his pocket as he approaches. He hands it to Murt, who glances at it, before Davyn speaks again. 'Thea found the location of one of the prisons. The bastard had them classified as Level One, Two, and Three. Fuck knows if One is good, or if it's Hell? This prison is down as a Level One. It's in Offaly near Leap Castle.'

Murt grabs his sweatshirt from the end of the bed, hurriedly pulling it on, before grabbing his boots. He'd heard of the place from stories his father told them when he was young. 'Why the fuck would your father pick there for a prison?'

Davyn scratches the scar on his face just under the eye patch which hides his ruined eye. 'I stopped asking why he did things the way he did when he threw me in a cell for most of my life. He did whatever he wanted, when he wanted. Usually, it didn't go deeper than that.'

Murt can well believe that. He'd heard enough stories about the Raven King to rival most ghost stories from his childhood.

'They're still going through the records to see if they can find more of the prisons. Now Thea knows what she's looking for it shouldn't take too long. She's talked to Ethan and filled him in. He'll do the same from his side.'

'Sounds like a plan. I'll get my brothers ready. I want to check it out ASAP.'

'Thought you would.'

He follows Davyn from the room, knocking on his brothers' doors as he passes. 'Get your arses out of bed!'

Thea and Fergus are already downstairs when they enter the living area, a map of Ireland spread out in front of them. Technology is life-changing, but you can't beat an old-fashioned map when you're planning something like this.

He examines the coordinates on the map. Leap Castle is well known for its ghosts, but not for secret prisons. There's nothing on the map to hint that wolves are being kept there, but why would there be? It's not like Dav's father would register it on any official record.

His brothers finally stomp down the stairs, alert and ready to go.

'What's up Murt?' Garret asks as he looks down at the map.

'Thea found one of the prisons near Leap Castle.'

Garret slams his fist onto the table. 'About fucking time! We moving out?'

'Take a breath, Garret. We're not attacking a vampire prison without a fucking plan.' Garret crosses his arms, his glare saying more to Murt than his words could. He knows how his brother feels. He's itching to go, but there's no fucking way he's going to risk another member of his clan unless he's sure they can make it out the other side.

He looks over at Fionn. Sorcha's twin is barely holding back the tears.

'You good Fionn?'

His brother nods. 'I'm good. What's the plan, Murt?'

Murt runs his finger along the map, tracing the road from Darkhaven to Offaly. 'It'll take about two and a half, maybe three hours to get there. Unless of course you get special speed exemptions by being a lord and all?' he says to Davyn.

Davyn shakes his head. 'No, I don't, but we're not going by road. We're flying.'

'You mean like wings flying?' Con asks, not looking too thrilled about that. 'Eh no offence, but I'm not on board with that.'

'I'm not carrying you heavy fuckers anywhere,' Dav says. 'Ethan is sending us a helicopter. It'll be here soon. He's also stocking it with weapons in case we meet resistance.'

151

'You can always live in hope,' Garret says with a grin.

'You're a strange wolf, you know that?' Con says, pouring himself a large coffee from the pot on the table.

'Any idea of numbers we'll be facing?' Murt asks, trying to get the conversation back on track, and away from Garret's thirst for violence.

Davyn shakes his head. 'No idea. But we're not going in hard. We'll be going in through the front door.'

As one, the brothers look at Davyn. 'We're what? So... no big guns?' Garret asks, disappointment all over his face. 'Really?'

Davyn shakes his head. 'Not at first. But if anyone stops me, then the big guns will come out.'

Garret claps his hands, rubbing them together as he smiles. 'Now that's an idea I can absolutely get behind.'

Murt looks up at the vampire lord. 'Are you sure you want to get involved in this?'

'My father. My prisons. My fucking problem. That bastard owned and pay-rolled these places. Now I do. I'm going with you. I want to see the faces of the vampires in charge when I pull the fucking rug out from under their feet. Might even stick them in a cage for a bit. See how they like it.'

The most he had hoped for was for Davyn to offer them some weapons, or perhaps a vehicle. He wasn't expecting him to offer to come with them. 'We appreciate any help you can offer Davyn.' And he absolutely means it. He can only imagine how difficult it is for Davyn to have to deal with the aftermath of his father's reign.

'I just hope your sister is there.'

'Me too.'

The silence stretches on until the sound of the heavy thump of rotors increases, as the promised helicopter nears the castle.

'That sounds like our ride,' Davyn says. 'Fergus, can you take the Whelans to the ammunition room? Let them take what they want. Stick to whatever you can carry as human or wolf. Your choice. We'll take off as soon as you're ready.'

Murt nods as Davyn leaves them with Fergus. 'If you'll follow me. I think you'll be pleased with the selection of weapons Davyn brought from the Blackjack compound.'

Murt follows his brothers and the old vampire down to the basement of the castle, then through an archway with a weighty metal gate across it. The brothers' mouths drop open when they see the collection of toys the Blackjacks have laid out for them.

'Oh, I'm going to enjoy this,' Con says, running his hand along one of the guns on the wall. 'Not every day you get a room of weapons to choose from.'

'Do you think Sorcha is there?' Fionn asks Murt, as Garret and Con drool over the weapons.

He really feels for Fionn. Sorcha's twin is feeling her loss so much stronger than the rest of them. The bond between wolf twins is powerful. Without Sorcha, he's incomplete, and there's nothing Murt can do about it - no matter how badly he wants to. It's like some of Fionn's spark is gone. He's quieter, more reserved than he was before she disappeared. And he laughs a lot less. Fuck, they all do.

'If not at this one, then the next. We *will* find her Fionn. I swear.' It's a promise he hopes he can keep.

Garret claps his hands together startling Murt. 'What the fuck are we all standing around for? We've got a prison to storm.'

Murt can't help but smile at Garret's enthusiasm. At times like this it's exactly what they need. Emotion has no place in situations like this. That can and will come after. First, they need to do what they do best. 'Just waiting for you to get out of the way so I can see what's on offer.'

Garret steps to the side, gesturing dramatically at the wall of weapons. 'Go for it Murt. It's all yours.'

He picks what he needs, loading a few bags laid out for them. Once they've each filled a bag, they follow Fergus back through the castle to the waiting helicopter.

And this is no ordinary craft. It's the same model as the one the Blackjacks have in Wales. The huge aircraft is plenty big enough to take all the wolves, Davyn, and a shitload of weapons.

Murt takes his seat, smiling widely when he recognises the pilot and the two passengers already on board. Fletch waves over his shoulder from the cockpit as Murt fastens his harness. He waves back then greets his fellow passengers. 'Ethan! Fallon! I wasn't expecting to see you.'

The Blackjack co-founder leans over and shakes his hand. 'I'm sure Davyn has filled you in on the plan about going in softly instead of with all-guns-blazing,' Ethan says.

'Yeah, you here for support?'

Ethan nods. 'I've been making myself available to help Davyn when he needs legal or protocol assistance. This is my area. It's where I excel.'

'And how about you Fallon? Why are you here - not that I'm complaining.' Not in the least. The Blackjack is one of the most formidable fighters he's seen. She's downright lethal. 'I go where Ethan does. I'm on his protection detail.'

Murt keeps any comment about that to himself. When he was last with the Blackjacks, Bastian had that job. Why would Ethan change to Fallon? It makes no sense. Bastian was just as capable of protecting Ethan as Fallon is.

He catches someone looking at him. Davyn meets his eyes and discretely shakes his head. Clearly swapping Bastian for Fallon is a no-go area. Fair enough. He's got enough on his plate without even going there.

'So, Ethan, do you really think we can just walk in the door?'

Ethan looks up the craft to Davyn. The vampire lord is staring at the floor, deep in thought. 'Us not so much. But he can. He's the only living relative of the Raven King. Legally, everything his father owned is now his. More of a bad thing than a good thing in some areas, but it will work to our advantage with this situation.' He straightens his tie that he always seems to be wearing. 'We're hoping that paperwork will do the job of guns. But if not, I'll make sure my ass is safely behind something sturdy before the guns come out.'

Murt laughs as he leans back against the side of the craft. 'Not a fan of the gun part then, are you?'

He can't imagine well-spoken, smartly-dressed, aristocrat Ethan charging into battle.

'I can hold my own when the situation calls for it, but no. I leave that part of the proceedings to you lot. *The pen is mightier than the sword* and all that.'

'I hear you Ethan, but personally, I'm all for the sword.'

'Me too,' Fallon says, before lying back in her seat and closing her eyes.

Murt decides to take a leaf from her book. It won't be long before they get to the site. He trusts Ethan knows what he's talking about, but that doesn't mean he's not going to prepare for the worst. That's how they've all survived as long as they have.

He glances over at Fionn before he closes his eyes. His brother's face is blank, his hands clasped tightly on his knees. Murt doesn't doubt Fionn will hold his own if they do need to fight. But he dreads to think how he'll be if Sorcha isn't there when they go in.

SORCHA

Bannon gives her a double thumbs up as she finishes signing the page of text he had slipped under her door early that morning.

'*Five-star student,*' he signs, spelling out the last word for her. '*Good work.*'

She could watch his hands moving all day, as he talks to her. There's such a grace and fluidity to his movements that completely captivates her. It helps that the smile he gives her as they work together is simply beautiful.

'I'm not too bad at this.'

He nods enthusiastically. '*You're picking it up fast.*'

They fall into a comfortable silence for the next few minutes. They're both sitting on her bed, leaning back against the wall. Sorcha would guess Bannon has been in her cell for nearly half an hour at this stage.

'Where's Quill today?' she asks, curious as to why the head guard hasn't been around for a while.

'I don't know. I think he's doing something for the Warden.'

Bannon isn't happy about that in the slightest. His face hardened as he signed.

'Is that a bad thing?'

Bannon doesn't reply.

'I've never met the Warden, but I get the impression he's not a particularly nice guy.'

Bannon takes out his notebook. This must be a long reply. *'I've only met him once. He gives me the creeps, but Quill works closely with him. Has to, I guess. But I get a bad feeling. Quill is different when he's talking about the Warden.'*

'Different how?'

'Withdrawn.' He shakes his head and sighs. *'Forget it. It's nothing to do with me. None of my business.'* He closes the notebook, but she stops him from putting it away by placing her hand on his.

'It has something to do with you, if you care about him.'

The look he gives her is the worst attempt at innocence she's ever seen. Oh, he has a thing for Quill all right. She's never been more sure of anything in her life. 'Oh, you are not going to try to tell me you don't have a soft spot for him?'

Bannon shakes his head emphatically.

'Fair enough. But between you and me, I'd get it if you did. He's intriguing,' she says, deciding that's the best word to use to describe Quill. 'He intrigues me. You both do,' she says, looking across at him.

That gets his attention. *'We do? I do?'*

'Of course. Clearly, I've been in prison too long. I'm getting hooked by two vampires.' She smiles, shuffling a little closer to him. He's still frowning, trying to figure out what direction to take this conversation in. Admit he likes Quill, or keep denying it.

'Whatever you do, or don't feel for him, is your business. I just thought you might like to talk to someone about it. Or maybe not. Like I said, it's your business. It will stay between us.' She laughs as she looks around her cramped cell. 'Not that I'll be telling many people, considering I'm in here most of the time.'

He keeps the frown going for another minute before he relaxes somewhat. Then the pen is scribbling on the notebook again. *We both intrigue you?*'

'Absolutely. I know that probably makes me sound terrible, liking the two of you, but I can't help it. There's something about each of you. I've tried to ignore it, believe me. But I figure *what the hell?*. I'm here until I die. It's not like I can make things worse for myself, by liking my two vampire guards more than I should. In fact, you're both giving me a distraction. Can't complain about that.'

Bannon moves back from her and hits her with the most adorable confused look. His eyebrows are so scrunched they nearly hide his brown eyes. Leaving him to his thoughts, Sorcha reads through the page of work he gave her, giving him time to process everything.

She honestly didn't plan to come clean with him. But she meant what she said. Admitting her feelings, whatever those feelings are, isn't going to do her any additional harm. Bannon and Quill won't hold any of it against her. It's a compliment, nothing to get upset about. The only one who can truly come to harm because of how she feels, is herself. She's the only one who stands to get hurt by lusting after the two of them.

Wrong time and place is an understatement. But there is no other place for them. They only have now, and here.

Bannon's hand moves closer to hers, wrapping around it and squeezing it. Sorcha looks up to find his chocolate brown eyes locked on her. *'I think I like both of you too.'* He mouths the words slowly, each one helping her smile grow.

'You do?'

He nods, and smiles at her in return.

'Wow...' Her quiet reply isn't intentional. It just comes out as she breathes, releasing a breath she didn't know she was holding. 'This is unexpected.'

His smile widens, and she imagines she can hear him laugh as he nods.

'Well. Not quite how I planned the day, but I'm glad that's all out in the open. I'm just not quite sure what to do now? It's hardly your typical living arrangements around here. Not that I'm assuming anything would happen of course. Or maybe it would? I don't know. This is a first for me.'

Bannon points to himself, then holds up two fingers.

'You too? Glad I'm not alone on that one. So, is it the situation as a whole that's new to you, or being attracted to another male?'

He holds up two fingers again, indicating the second option.

'Ah. Well, this is all very new to you then, isn't it? Does Quill know how you feel about him?'

Bannon shakes his head. He takes out his notebook to write something then, thinking better of it, puts the notebook down again.

'This is between the two of us. Like I said - who am I going to tell?' she says, gesturing to her living quarters. 'The only other living beings I see are you, Quill, and that female vampire.'

'Duna.'

'Is that her name? I'm not a fan.'

'She's scary.'

Sorcha nods. 'Absolutely. But we're getting off-topic here. Apart from you lot I don't see anyone. I think they're scared of the big bad wolf,' she adds with a mischievous grin.

He smiles at that, shaking his head. She may be joking about her impact on the other guards, but she knows it's the truth. Deciding he probably doesn't have anything to lose, he jots down a few words. *'I'm just confused.'*

She reads the words, nodding slowly. 'That might be the case, but have you also considered that, maybe you're not confused? Not about the part you think you're confused about.'

He frowns and shrugs, her statement probably just adding to his confusion.

'Okay, so just hear me out. I'm a firm believer in the whole *if it's meant to be, it's meant to be*. I was in love once,' she says, her voice quieter now. 'Cian is... was,' she corrects herself. 'He was everything to me. When I was captured...' she pauses as the image plays over in her mind. 'The last thing I heard was a gunshot. He looked at me as he died. In that moment, I swore I'd never feel that way about anyone again.'

Bannon takes her hand, his strong firm hold comforting her. 'I was so convinced I'd never be interested in anyone that way again.'

She looks up at Bannon, his warm brown eyes holding such affection it nearly brings her to tears. 'I never imagined I'd find love again – especially in here. Finding two people... well, maybe someone is trying to tell me that I still have a life worth living. What does it matter who, or what, we are? Male, female, vampire, wolf. None of that truly matters. Quill is an attractive, intriguing, intensely irritating male. What's not to like about him?'

Bannon smiles as he shakes his head, and gives her a double thumbs up.

'Don't overthink any of it, Bannon. I'm trying not to. Just go with it and see what happens.'

'Even if it's impossible?'

She reads the words a few times before she answers. That word comes up a lot when she thinks about her pull towards Bannon and Quill. Everything about it is impossible. But does that mean it's not worth it? Not worth fighting for?

'If I can teach you one thing about my clan, it's that the Whelans do not go for the easy option. We fight for what we want - no matter how impossible it seems.'

QUILL

The wolf was right. Karma is a bitch.

He bites back a shout of pain as the Warden's leather belt hits his flesh, the burning sting pure agony. It's the Warden's favourite punishment. That's probably why he ordered Quill to do this to the wolf. He punishes Quill by flogging him, then orders him to do the same to someone else. It's some kind of sick twisted mind fuck.

And it's working.

The belt hits his raw flesh again. The Warden has been punishing him for a good half hour at this stage. The asshole had to keep taking breaks, because his arm was hurting him.

He knew this was on the cards when he was called to the Warden's office. He'd failed to break the wolf. One order, and he hadn't carried it out. The Warden expected him to beat her daily, until she was a quivering mess at his feet, or dead. He wasn't going to do that. He blames himself for this lapse. He should have kept trying, but he couldn't stomach it.

He doesn't want to hurt her. Not only that, but he also doesn't want to see that look on Bannon's face again. Doesn't want to see the disappointment he saw that first time he flogged her.

So here he is. Taking the punishment meant for her, because he's too weak to do his fucking job.

The Warden finishes, brushing his hair back from his damp forehead. 'Get up.'

Quill struggles to get up from his knees. He's strong, but even his Prime strength can't deal with this level of abuse.

'Have I convinced you to do your fucking job and break that wolf? Do I need to demote you and put Duna in charge? I'm sure she would have no hesitation tearing the flesh from that wolf.'

Quill knows that's the case. Duna would take pleasure from it. 'I can do it, sir.' He knows by now that compliance is the only way he's going to get out of this room, without more of his blood being spilled.

But the Warden is far from done. He picks up the ornate letter opener from his desk and walks back over to Quill. Instead of looking at the Warden, he focuses on the painting on the wall, as the knife slices into his upper chest.

The Warden draws his tongue along the line of blood, turning Quill's stomach. When the elder vampire groans in pleasure, Quill has to swallow back the bile. He makes another incision, drinking Quill's addictive purer Prime blood.

The Warden's teeth graze his skin, adding teeth marks to the cuts he's making. Quill concentrates on the painting, willing his legs to keep him upright. He desperately needs to feed.

After about a dozen cuts, the Warden slowly licks the knife, cleaning his blood from the blade before dropping it back on his desk. He's already feeling the effects of Quill's blood, his eyes glassy and slightly unfocused. 'Dismissed.'

So high on blood, he forgets the reason Quill was there in the first place. No doubt the Warden will discuss the wolf with him again once he comes down but, for now, Quill is going to take advantage. He picks up his shirt from the floor, hurrying from the room before the Warden changes his mind.

Quill waits until he's outside the door, before he pauses long enough to put on his shirt again. He stumbles down the staircase, his feet missing the last step sending him crashing in to the wall at the bottom.

He's desperate for some blood, but doesn't want to go back to his room. There's nothing there except dark thoughts. Nothing there except reliving what just happened over and over again.

So instead, he heads back to the prison. It's a stupid thing to do. Even through his blood starvation, he knows that much, but he's not thinking rationally right now. He's just acting on instinct.

SORCHA

Sorcha gets to her feet as her cell is unlocked. Bannon smiles when he steps inside, and it makes her day. He places the tray of food on the table and leans against the wall as she eats.

'It's so good to see you. How's your day going so far?'

He appears momentarily confused by her question. Maybe he's not used to being asked that. Living and working with the same people day in and day out must be tedious. She doubts any of them care at this stage how the other's day went. They all had the same day.

He gives her a quick, if not slightly unconvincing, thumbs up.

'Have you seen Quill today?'

'He's around. Just busy.'

He seems bothered by that for some reason. The stoic head guard is getting to Bannon. And after the conversation Quill had with her a few days ago, the feeling might be more than mutual.

'Does he vanish often?'

Bannon shrugs. 'You're worried though. Is everything okay?'

'I'm not worried.'

His hastily scribbled response tells her otherwise. 'You're allowed to be. If you think something is wrong, you absolutely are allowed to be concerned.

He smiles and shakes his head. *'He's my boss. He's been here a long time. I'm sure he's fine.'*

'Oh, Quill can more than handle himself. He's probably just torturing some poor prisoner to get some kicks.'

Her comment troubles him, the frown is back again. *'I didn't know he was going to do that to you.'*

She shrugs, not wanting to get into it with him, even though she's the one bringing it up. It's a part of her time here that she'd happily forget. Or at least try to until Quill decides to hang her up again.

'Why did he interrogate you?'

It figures Bannon would think that about his boss. God forbid the almighty Quill did it just because he wanted to. 'There was no interrogation. He didn't ask me anything. Just flogged me.'

The long silence that follows has nothing to do with Bannon's inability to speak. Even if he could, she doubts he would have known what to say to that.

'There was a camera in the corner of the room. Either he was recording it all so he could watch it later, or the Warden was keeping an eye on proceedings. Either way, it was Quill holding the whip.'

'I'm sorry.'

She's surprised to read his words. 'You have nothing to apologise to me for. Well, not on that front. And it's not like I'm holding my breath waiting for him to apologise either. As he keeps saying - I'm a prisoner and you're all guards. I know my place.'

Another long stretch of silence follows, before he scribbles in his notebook again. *'Can I ask you something?'*

'Go ahead.'

'What crime did you commit?'

'Crime? What are you talking about?'

He quickly jots down a few words before holding the page out to her again. *'You're in prison. What crime did you commit?'*

It's the first time any of the guards have ever asked her that. They didn't care what she did. All that mattered was that she was an inmate. How she ended up in the prison doesn't seem to be on anyone's radar.

'Nothing.'

He frowns and places his notebook on the bed beside him, using his hands to talk instead. *'What do you mean you did nothing?'*

'I mean I went out for a run with my boyfriend, Cian. We were both in wolf form,' she says, the tears filling her eyes. 'I can't explain what it's like to be so free like that. We can run for hours, the wind in our fur, the dirt under our paws. There's nothing like it Bannon. Nothing in the world.'

She falls silent as memories of what happened next come back to her. Not that she has ever truly forgotten about that day.

'Cian was the love of my life. We'd been together for two years and I adored him. We were on our way back home, making our way through a forest about an hour from the house. The shot came out of nowhere. I didn't hear anything before. There was no warning, no sound at all. One minute we were walking side by side, the next, he was dead.

'I froze. I should have run or tried to find whoever killed him, but I couldn't do anything. I just stood there and looked down at his body.'

Bannon moves closer to her, his large body touching hers, comforting her as she cries. 'I don't even know how I ended up here. I was knocked out shortly after that and woke up in a cell. No one would tell me anything. I begged. Screamed. Shouted. Pleaded. You

166

name it I tried it, but I've never got any answers.'

Bannon taps her on the leg to get her attention. *'How long ago?'*

'Eight years or so. I wasn't sure how long, until I was brought here and Quill mentioned it to me.'

Bannon signs, but his hands are moving too fast for her to decipher what he's trying to say. He grabs his notebook again and scribbles a few lines. *'Eight years for no crime? No reason? No explanation? Are you serious?'*

'I'm not going to make up something like that. I was out for a run with my boyfriend. That's it. I didn't do anything wrong.'

Bannon doesn't respond to that for a long time. Having him take it so seriously, to actually try and comfort her by moving closer, helps ease some of her pain. He believes what she's saying. She doesn't know why, but she's convinced he believes her story.

That doesn't mean he can do anything about it. She doubts even Quill would be able to. The Warden might be the only one with the power to do that.

As the silence stretches on, she watches Bannon's hands on his knees, but he doesn't make a move to sign anything. But just having him here with her is helping. His calming presence is just what she needs. He's too good for this place. He has compassion, decency, he listens. Most of the rest of the guards are bullies. Nothing more.

Quill could be different, but she's still not fully convinced.

Bannon draws her out of her thoughts when he writes her another note.

'Do you want some exercise?'

She peers up at him, not sure where he's going with this, but he points back to the page, and she continues reading.

'The training room is down the corridor. I can take you.'

'But I'm not allowed in there. It's just for guards. If the Warden finds out, you'll get into trouble.'

He scribbles on the paper again, then holds it out to her. *'He's gone for the day. All the guards are in the cafeteria. It will be empty.'*

'Then, what are we waiting for? Let's go!'

He holds open the door for her which is strangely sweet. She's never had her cell door held open for her before. She follows Bannon down the corridor, away from her dingy, dark cell, towards the main body of the prison.

The rest of the prison carries the same decor as the corridor where her cell is. The white paint on the walls is more dirty brown than anything resembling white. Not that there's much paint left on the concrete blocks. Most of it has either flaked off with time, or been chipped off thanks to too many grubby bodies brushing against it.

The only difference is the smell. It's so much worse out here. 'How do you stomach that stench all day?' she asks Bannon, keeping her voice low.

He wrinkles his nose when she looks back at him and pulls a disgusted face.

'That's a big understatement. I feel sorry for you.'

He smiles before nodding ahead, telling her to keep her eyes forward, so she does. If he's risking himself by doing this for her, she's going to make sure it goes as he wants it to.

A few minutes later he taps her on the left shoulder, so she turns that way down a corridor towards a double door at the end.

After the cramped dark confines of her cell, this vast room is incredible. The equipment is far from new, but there is a lot of it. The exercise and weightlifting equipment is placed around the edges of the room, the centre left clear for a large sparring and exercise mat. The heavy black rubber is cracked and well-used, but there's still plenty of life left in it.

She slowly walks around the room, a renewed energy coursing through her. It's almost as if her wolf is stirring inside her at the thought of some exercise that doesn't involve walking in circles around the yard. 'So, this is what I'm missing out on by breaking guards' fingers.'

She glances over at him, thrilled to see him smiling.

168

'Maybe I should behave from time to time. Do the other inmates get to use this stuff regularly?'

Bannon takes out his notebook, writes his answer, then holds it up to her. *They use the smaller inmate gym. It's up to Quill and Duna how often.'*

She grimaces at his response. 'I wouldn't want those two deciding when I have fun. So, I guess I'm in the posh guard gym? Lucky me!'

Sorcha picks up one of the sparring sticks, then smiles over at Bannon. 'So, Officer Bannon. Did your training include sparring?'

He nods and points to her, eyebrows raised.

'Me? Oh, I can handle myself. Four brothers. How about you? Are you any good?'

Bannon unbuttons his shirt and drops it to the floor at the side of the room. The black tank top hugs his broad chest as he kicks off his boots, then takes off his socks. With his shirt off the thick scar on his neck is completely on show. It's so much longer than she initially thought, stretching to just above the neck of his tank top.

He smirks as he pulls the stick from her hand and Sorcha watches transfixed as Bannon slowly paces along the side of the mat, spinning the stick around his body as if he was born with it in his hands. The thick chords of muscles ripple and shift under his skin as he twirls the stick around his body with a grace that captivates her.

For a vampire he's seriously hypnotic, his movements smooth and fluid.

He takes up position on the mat and winks at her before pointing to the mat in front of him.

'Oh, I'm going to enjoy this,' she says as she pulls another stick from the rack and takes her place in front of him. Wolves tended to be stronger than vampires, but it's been a long time since she could feel the strength of her wolf. Plus, Bannon is so much bigger than she is. But she's fast. Really fucking fast. Time to show this vampire what she can do.

For the first few minutes Bannon takes the lead, sending her to the mat time and time again. But it's part of her plan. She'd never fought a vampire like this. There's no hope of winning unless she gets to know his style - how he fights.

And he fights well. Clearly someone has been training him. But he's not the only one who's had training. When it came to hand-to-hand combat, her brother Murtagh is unbeatable. From a young age, he'd trained the four of them, making sure they could defend themselves in a world where wolves are hunted by vampires.

They may have used their fighting skills on each other from time-to-time, too, but that's all part of being in a clan. And Murt didn't refrain from beating the shite out of them from time to time. Living with four hot-headed male wolves brought its own level of fun to day-to-day life.

Before she gets dragged into her head, consumed by memories of her brothers, Sorcha pushes to her feet again, then paces the mat, looking across at the vampire she's fighting.

He's different to other vampires she's met over the years. It's easy to get carried away in generations of hatred. Wolves weren't to mix with vampires. It was drummed into her from as early as she can remember. But then again, it was probably the same for vampires.

Perhaps it was Bannon's silence that helped her see what was underneath. With him, there are no empty words aimed at hiding who he truly is. Everything he says when he writes is intentional, thought out, truthful.

Or maybe she's just seeing something that isn't there. He's a new addition to her otherwise tedious life. That's the only reason she's excited about seeing him, about spending time with him, about trying to help him by learning sign language. He's a new attraction in a world of the same old, same old. In time, he'll blend into the background like everyone else. Become a part of the furniture. Part of the boring hell she's somehow found herself in.

But until then, she'll take the distraction. She'll take any distraction. Even a vampire distraction. He nods, his eyebrows raised

170

expectantly. 'Oh, I'm ready,' she says. 'Are you?'

He grins, the flash of his fangs appealing instead of off-putting. Before that unwelcome thought grows arms and legs, she launches at him. Time to show this vampire exactly what she can do. After winning the last few rounds, Bannon isn't prepared when she turns the tables on him. She uses all the training Murt gave her to overpower this much larger vampire, sending him crashing to the mat, knocking the air out of him.

He lies on his back on the mat, his eyes closed as he tries to control his breathing again. Sorcha straddles him, pinning his arms to his sides under her legs, stopping him from getting up again. She stabs the end of the stick onto the mat right beside his head, smiling widely when he slowly turns his head to look at how close that was to him.

'Got you!'

She should get off him, help him to his feet, and get on with the fight. But instead, she peers down at him, both of them breathing heavily. 'You okay?'

He nods once as he frowns at her. He does that a lot, but after spending a little time with him, she's not so sure it's down to confusion. Thinking perhaps.

Bannon doesn't try to get up, and she's in no hurry to get off him. Acting completely on instinct, she reaches out to brush some hair off his forehead. She can hear his heart pounding rapidly in his chest.

As if having an out-of-body experience, she sees herself leaning over to kiss him. There's no reason for the kiss, nothing he did to hint that it's something he wants, but in this place, taking what you want seemed to be how things were done.

Initially he does nothing. Just lies there as she places her lips against his. Then something changes. Still with his arms pinned by his sides, he lifts his head off the mat, pressing his lips firmly against hers, so he can kiss her back.

She's never kissed a vampire. For some reason she thought she'd be able to feel his fangs a lot more than she can, but that's probably because he's not ready to feed.

That thought sends an unexpected shiver through her body, her tongue pushing into his mouth in response. And she's not the only one getting carried away in the strange moment. There's nothing timid or unsure about his kiss either.

She has no idea how long the kiss goes on for, but when she pulls back from him, she's as breathless as she was after the fight.

'Sorry about that. I have no idea where that came from.'

He pulls at his arms, so she climbs off him, getting up and taking a few steps back as he stands. There's nothing showing on his face. No anger. No pleasure either. Kissing him might just have been the worst decision she's ever made.

'I am sorry.'

But then he shakes his head as he steps closer to her. *Don't be sorry.*

He mouths the words slowly so she can understand. 'Really? I didn't plan that, I mean it.'

Bannon opens his mouth, then frowns and goes over to this shirt, pulling out the notebook and pen. *Did you kiss me because you're bored, or for another reason?*

'Considering the fact you're a vampire I probably should go for the first one... but I think that would be a lie. I can't explain further than that, because I don't know what's going on. All I know is that I don't regret it.'

He smiles widely as he writes. *Considering the fact you're a wolf I should go for the first one... but I think that would be a lie.*

She reads her own words repeated in his writing. 'I see. Interesting.'

He nods, placing the notebook back in his shirt pocket. Bannon picks up the two sticks again, passing one to her.

'Again?'

She smiles and launches herself at him.

29

QUILL

By the time he reaches the prison, he's barely able to put one foot in front of the other. But more than that, the frustration, the anger, the humiliation burns deep inside him, somehow giving him the strength to keep going, even though he's used up the last of his energy reserves. It's pure stubbornness that's keeping him going.

He's the head guard. It's his job to keep the prison running smoothly. This prison is all he has. He can't... won't let the Warden take it from him.

Maybe this is a bad idea. What the fuck is he saying? Of course it's a bad idea. He should have just gone back to his room. Stumbling along the corridors like he's drunk, isn't going to help him keep control of the men, or this prison.

He's not going to find the blood he needs in here either. That's back in his room, or the fridge in the kitchen. He's not going to feed from a wolf. Not that it would do any good. He needs vampire blood at the least - preferably Prime blood.

Maybe subconsciously, he's looking for a guard to feed from. Or one guard in particular.

Bannon.

Now he's thinking about how his body reacted to drinking his blood. Thinking about what he'd like to do to Bannon's body, given half the chance. Thinking about ripping the black uniform from his body and sinking his teeth and dick into the male. The thought of drinking from Bannon as he fucks him, has his dick springing to life. He stops in the corridor, taking a few deep breaths to try and get control of his body.

But it's not an easy task. Even thinking about the taste of Bannon's blood has him biting his bottom lip as a shudder runs through his body like an electric shock. He'd liked it, liked the taste, the feel of it on his tongue, the strength it gave him. But more than that, he was aroused by him.

These fucking ridiculous thoughts are due to blood starvation. He knows that, but that doesn't stop them from coming to his mind.

He'd fed from many vampires and people over the years, and none had turned him on in the slightest. Feeding was something he needed to do to survive, but not until that moment in his room had he actually enjoyed it. Got pleasure from it.

The difference is Bannon. He's sure of it. Quill had never considered himself gay, or bi, or whatever. There were enough labels in his life without trying to figure that one out, too. Whatever is going on with his head is just going to have to stay there. He has enough to deal with as it is.

Quill checks his watch. The other guards should be at lunch, so the training room will be his for a few hours. He won't be able to do much of a workout in this state, but that's where his feet are heading, so he keeps going that way.

Quill frowns as he nears the room. He can hear a female laughing. He slowly approaches the door and peers in the small window at Bannon and Sorcha sparring with each other. Seems he's seriously pissed off someone in a past life. Fuck, he wasn't expecting to find them together. Not like this.

While he's furious at Bannon for breaking the rules, a part of him is impressed by his defiance. It shows he's got balls, and he appreciates that, even though from a boss's point of view it's something that's going to give him serious headaches.

He should go in there, reprimand Bannon, then drag the wolf back to her cell. But he doesn't. Instead, he watches, both the wolf and the vampire holding his attention for different reasons.

The wolf is beyond graceful. Even after being locked in a cell for years, the fluidity of her moves is breathtaking. Her long, dark hair swirls around her as she spins, each move of the stick timed to perfection, hitting home with each strike.

But Bannon is giving as good as he gets. The tall male has taken off his uniform shirt, the tank top showing his impressive arms and chest.

After watching them for a few minutes, he realises Bannon isn't exactly holding back. They're well-matched which surprises him. Wolves are generally stronger than vampires, but she's the first one he's seen training in this way. He doesn't usually let his men train with the wolves.

Bannon is sweating, but as with Sorcha, each strike is making contact.

His thick dark hair is stuck to his forehead, his dark eyes focused as he fights. And he's not exactly clumsy either. Training with him over the last few weeks has turned Bannon into a competent fighter.

He's stunning.

Quill rests his head against the cool stone wall beside the door. What is he doing? He's the head guard. He should only be thinking about getting that prisoner back into her cell, then giving Bannon a warning.

He hears her laugh again from inside the training room. People don't laugh in this place. He can't remember the last time he laughed. It must be years, maybe decades.

Fuck this! Going soft at this stage won't help him in any way. It's all about keeping himself safe. He needs to stop perving on them and do his job. Quill bursts through the door, bringing the two of them to a sudden stop. Sorcha and Bannon freeze as he glares at them, putting all of his anger and frustration into his look as he storms over to them.

He grabs the sticks from their hands, throwing them across the room. 'What the fuck is going on?' he roars at Bannon.

It's a stupid thing to ask. It's not as if Bannon can reply. He turns his attention to the wolf who, as usual, isn't shrinking away from him. She's got attitude in bucket loads.

'Well?'

'It's called exercise, Officer Quillan.'

He clenches his jaw when she uses his title. It wasn't a mark of respect. It never is from her. It's said in a mocking tone that, on one hand irritates him, but on the other, amuses him.

Quill turns his irritation back to Bannon. Maybe because he's an easier target. That just makes him a bigger asshole, but he's tired and annoyed, so he barely gives it a thought. 'She's a dangerous prisoner. Why the fuck did she have a weapon in her hand?'

He hates the twinge of guilt he experiences when Bannon opens his mouth, then closes it again.

'I appreciate you considering me dangerous,' Sorcha says. 'That's made me one very happy wolf.'

He throws her a *shut the fuck up* look, which unsurprisingly, she ignores. As he tries to figure out how to handle this without letting his irrational emotions get in the way, she moves her hands.

Quill watches as she slowly and carefully says something to Bannon in sign language. Bannon shakes his head quickly, moving his attention back to Quill.

They can talk. Sorcha and Bannon can talk to each other.

Why does that bother him so much? Why does he suddenly feel more alone than he usually does?

'What did you say?' he asks Sorcha.

'Maybe you should have learned sign language as we discussed a while ago, and then you'd know. He works for you. Do you not think it's worth even spending a few minutes a day to learn sign language? You're his fucking boss, after all!'

He reacts before he can stop himself. Quill knocks her to the mat, holding her down as he growls loudly. 'I've had enough of your attitude wolf! Do not forget your place here. And for the record, I did learn a few words, so back the fuck off!'

Bannon touches his shoulder, trying to get his attention, but he unknowingly brushes against one of Quill's many cuts. Bannon recoils when Quill curses in pain.

It does the trick though. The pain knocks him out of his rage, shutting down his emotions before they get the better of him. He pushes off the wolf, taking a step back from her as he rubs his shoulder. The wound was one of the deeper ones, and hurts like a bitch. Bannon points to his shoulder and mouths, *'What's wrong?'*

Quill wants to tell him exactly where to go, but the concern he sees on both Bannon's and Sorcha's faces completely throws him. 'A prisoner cut me. Get her back to her cell.'

The lie sounds convincing in his own head, but the fact that neither of them moves tells a different story. So why isn't he pushing the point? Why isn't he ending whatever this is, and manhandling her back to where she should be?

Why is he standing there being looked at like he's suddenly the one with the problem?

Bannon leans over, his attention on Quill's shoulder. He points to his eyes, then to Quill's shoulder, asking him to show them the wound.

Move! Stop this! Don't show them! He screams to himself in his head, but he can't leave. Deep down, he doesn't want to leave. Deep down he needs to know someone, anyone, gives a shit about him and what's happening in his life. Moving on autopilot, Quill unbuttons his uniform shirt, then pushes the material over his shoulder so Bannon can see the wound.

Bannon probes the tender flesh, before gripping Quill's jaw so he can turn his face around. And he lets him. He lets his subordinate take control. He shouldn't be letting him do this. In his own mind Quill is a fucking joke. A tired, broken joke.

'What happened?' This time, he mouths the words more forcefully.

'I told you. Rowdy prisoner. It's healing, so stop poking it.' There are so many more cuts on his chest, but he keeps them hidden. There are three or four bite marks on top of the cut on his shoulder, so it's not so clear what happened to him. He doubts they'd be able to tell he was fed from. He's not showing them anything that will get him in trouble. It's just a cut. That's all they'll think it is.

Then Sorcha is by his side, pushing onto her tiptoes so she can see the wound. Quill curses himself and his lack of reaction. He's just done today. For some reason he's an emotional mess and can't be arsed putting on an act. He's so tired of pretending he's okay. So tired of putting on this front, acting like a hard-ass who can handle anything thrown at him.

'Did you clean this at all?'

'Yes,' he snaps. Of course he didn't. He never does. There's no point.

'Well, it's a good thing you're not one of the medics here,' she replies, walking over to the corner to get the first aid box.

'Get back here!'

Yeah, like that's going to work. This shambolic performance isn't going to help assert his authority. He's pretty much blown that.

Bannon brings over a chair, so he gives up entirely and sits, staring at a tear in the rubber mat in front of him. He can't look at them. He doesn't want to get used to these two people looking out for him like this. It's not what he deserves. But it's what he needs.

When Sorcha's small, warm hands touch his skin he closes his eyes. He wants to just feel this for a few seconds. Just to feel safe and cared for.

'Can you hold that there Bannon?'

Then Bannon's much larger hands are on him.

'It's a nasty wound,' Sorcha says as she cleans it. 'I'd hate to see the other guy.'

He opens his eyes, but doesn't respond. There's nothing to say without elaborating on a lie, and making himself feel so much worse.

'Bannon? Will you pass me that antiseptic and gauze? It looks clean, but it won't hurt to make sure.' He sucks in a breath as the antiseptic stings the raw wound. He usually ignores the wounds, not wanting to see them afterwards. He probably should clean them instead of leaving them to heal without any help.

'I've never seen wing ridges before,' she says, taping a bandage over the wound. 'I guess that makes you a Prime?'

'Yeah,' he says, answering her question, trying to keep his shirt covering his chest.

'What about you?' she presumably asks Bannon.

Quill peers over his shoulder to see how she reacts to his answer. Bannon shakes his head in response, surprising her.

'What? Really? I assumed you were Prime, too. You're built like one. I thought you might have had mad powers as a Prime.'

Bannon smiles at that. Quill can't blame him. It's a compliment he agrees with. Bannon could be a Prime with his build.

'If you're Prime you don't have powers,' Quill explains, giving up on the whole head guard persona he's desperately trying to keep in place. 'It's one or the other.'

'Ah. Well, there you go,' she says. 'You learn something new every day.' Her fingers trace down the side of the ridge to the left side of his spine and he shudders. 'Sorry. Did I hurt you?'

179

Fuck! That felt so good. 'No. Are you finished?' He needs to call an end to this madness, even if he doesn't want to.

'Nearly. Why are you scarring? I thought vampires healed fast and wouldn't scar.'

'We heal fast, but that doesn't mean we don't scar. If the wound is bad enough, or not cleaned properly, it will leave a mark.'

'Clearly you should have used my first aid skills before now.'

He smiles to himself. Wolf is a smart ass.

'You're done,' she says, tapping him on the shoulder.

Quill stands, but immediately drops back onto the plastic chair when his head swims. *Not now, please.* He needs to get her back to her cell, haul himself back to his room, then collapse. Not the other way around.

'Are you okay?'

He really wishes she'd stop being so nice to him. 'Time to go back to your cell.'

He stands again, slower this time. Apart from a small wobble, he manages to stay on his feet. Quill fastens his shirt, then points to the door. 'Move. If you're caught here, we're all in trouble.'

SORCHA

Walking back to her cell, between two huge vampires, Sorcha does her best to hide her tears. In those brief moments in the training room, she had been alive again. Working out with Bannon was like nothing she's experienced since she was brought here. For those few minutes, she was free again. Then Quill burst in, and instead of wishing he hadn't arrived, she was thrilled to see him.

Which makes no sense considering who he is. But a part of her gets excited when she sees the two guards together. Bannon definitely has a soft spot for Quill. Whether Quill reciprocates or not, she doesn't know.

But a part of her shares Bannon's concern for the head guard. She doesn't particularly like him. He's hurt her either on orders from above, or just because he wanted to.

So why are Quill's injuries affecting her so much?

She's pulled out of her thoughts when they reach her cell. Bannon unlocks the door and steps aside to let her in. As she's reluctantly stepping back inside, she hears a heavy thump from behind her. She turns to find Bannon holding Quill off the floor. The head guard is on his knees, his head hanging limply in front of him.

'Shit!' She helps Bannon support his dead weight, stopping Quill from landing face-first on the concrete.

Bannon nods towards her cell, so together they half carry, half drag the unconscious Quill into her cell. Bannon takes the lead, guiding them over to her small cot. Once they get Quill onto it, they step back to catch their breath. Her small bed is barely holding the size of Quill, but it's better than having him on the ground.

'What's wrong with him?' she asks, as Bannon crouches down beside the bed to check on him.

He searches in his pocket for his notebook, writing quickly before showing it to her. *'He's dehydrated. He needs to feed.'*

'Feed? Oh, you mean blood. Well, don't look at me!'

'He's Prime. He needs vampire blood.'

She nods at his words. 'There's just one of them in here. I guess that's you.'

He scribbles down some words. *'He can't feed while he's unconscious. We need to wake him somehow.'*

'How?'

Bannon slaps Quill hard on the face.

'Fuck, Bannon! You'll wake him and he'll be raging at you.'

Bannon slaps him again, then grabs him by the shirt and shakes him. After a good minute Quill is still out-for-the-count, and getting paler by the second. It shouldn't bother her, but she can't let this happen to him. While Bannon does his best slapping and shaking routine, she gets close to Quill, his cologne momentarily distracting her, before she shouts his name right in his ear.

She's not sure whose efforts work, but either way, Quill eventually groans before stilling again.

'I think that's the best you're going to do. Can you try to feed him now?'

Bannon lifts his wrist to his own mouth and bites it before offering it to Quill. But it doesn't matter how many times he adjusts his position, he can't quite get the angle right. He points to Quill and motions lifting him. Sorcha nods when she understands what he wants.

She grabs Quill's shirt in her hands, holding it tightly then lifts his upper body off the bed. Bannon shuffles himself into position on the bed, sitting back against the wall. Sorcha lowers Quill's head onto Bannon's lap, manoeuvring Quill's head so Bannon can place his wrist up against his mouth.

'Come on Quill. Feed!'

She's furious with herself for giving a damn about him, but right now she's worried. He's strict and unyielding, but out of most of the other guards here, and in spite of her floggings at his hands, weirdly, she feels safe with him. That's rare.

She strokes the side of his face, running her fingers over the tight stubble on his cheek. He stirs again, so she takes Bannon's wrist and rubs it over Quill's lips, hoping that he latches on, or whatever he needs to do.

She smiles when he opens his mouth, his two huge fangs dropping from his gums. Sorcha holds Bannon's wrist firmly against his mouth, watching in fascination as Quill sinks his teeth in.

'Are you okay?' she asks Bannon, as he winces. He nods, his relieved smile mirroring her own. She sits back on her legs but can't seem to stop herself from rubbing Quill's face.

'Will he be okay, now?'

Bannon shrugs, then looks back down at Quill, still feeding from his wrist. They fall into a comfortable silence for the next few minutes, until Bannon carefully unhooks Quill's fangs from his wrist.

'What's wrong?'

'I need a minute,' he mouths, resting his head back against the wall.

Sorcha cups the side of Bannon's face. His skin is cold and pale. 'He's taking too much from you. Can I feed him? Can vampires drink wolf blood?'

Bannon shrugs tiredly. 'I think so. Are you sure?'

'I don't think we have a choice. He needs more blood and you're about to pass out. I'd prefer not to have two unconscious vampires in my cell. I could do without the backlash from the other guards.'

Bannon nods, so Sorcha kneels down beside Quill's head and offers him her wrist. It takes less convincing this time. Quill must be coming around. After the initial pain of the bite fades, the sensation is far from unpleasant. Quite the opposite.

She gasps, grabbing onto the edge of the bed to steady herself. Seeing Quill feeding from her is such a turn on. Everything about what he's doing is turning her on – and she wasn't expecting that.

Bannon holds up his thumb, raising his eyebrows as he silently asks if she's okay.

'Yeah. I'm fine.' She leaves it at that, giving herself time to enjoy the experience while it lasts. If it feels this amazing having a vampire feeding from her wrist, what would her neck be like?

What if they were naked while the feeding was going on?

That thought gets pushed aside when Quill comes back to his senses, his eyes opening all of a sudden. He releases her wrist and looks around him.

'What the fuck happened?'

'You collapsed outside my cell,' Sorcha explains. 'Bannon had to feed you. Then you took blood from me. How do you feel?'

'Yeah. Fine.' He tries to push himself off Bannon's knee, but can't get himself upright. 'Fuck!'

'You're not fine, are you?'

He closes his eyes again and sighs. 'I just need a minute.'

'*Tell him to go slow,*' Bannon signs.

'He said just take it slow.'

'You fed me?' he asks her, his tone more like an accusation than a question.

'You'd taken a lot from Bannon, so I stepped in when he had to stop.'

Quill doesn't respond to that, throwing another question at her instead. 'You learned sign language so you can talk to him?'

Sorcha shakes her head. 'No. I learned it so I can hear what he has to say.'

She could swear he looks sad at that, but maybe he's just tired.

He shakes himself out of whatever thoughts had captured him, then slowly pushes upright, sitting back beside Bannon. He pulls his hair out of its tie, running his hands through it. She really wishes he hadn't done that. He looks so different like that. It's like a small glimpse into the off-the-clock Quill. His dark-blonde hair just reaches his shoulders as she had suspected.

The way Bannon is looking at him, he's thinking the same thing she is. He's intrigued by Quill as much as she is.

'Thank you for feeding me.'

Bannon nods, then points to his mouth. '*Are you okay?*' He gestures to Quill's shoulder. '*What happened?*'

'Just because you fed me doesn't mean anything. I told you. We're work colleagues, not mates. Leave it alone.'

'Wow!' Sorcha says, butting into a conversation she probably should stay out of. 'He just helped you. Stop being a dick about it. All he's done is try to help. Maybe you should take a leaf out of his book? Treat us prisoners like we matter. Like we're worth something. Maybe if you did that, people wouldn't think you're such an asshole.'

'This isn't a fucking holiday camp! It's a prison. You're all here because you deserve to be.'

'Deserve it? Is that what you were told?'

'Don't even go there okay! Bannon filled me in on your cosy chat.

You're innocent right? Just like everyone else in this place.'

'Wow! Back to asshole I guess.'

'Yeah. I'm an asshole.' Quill braces himself against the wall, using it to push himself upright. 'I have to go. And you need to get back to work,' he says to Bannon.

Bannon gets to his feet, and gives him some sign language Quill will more than understand, before he storms from the room.

Sorcha claps slowly. 'Well done, Officer. Your position as prison asshole has been reinstated.' She takes Bannon's place on her bed, glaring over at Quill as he stands in the centre of her cell. He's trying to come up with a suitable reaction to that, but seems to be struggling. He's not used to being stood up to. But fuck it! She's got nothing to lose.

She's not in the least bit surprised when, instead of answering, he decides to follow in Bannon's footsteps and storm from her cell, momentarily forgetting that he needs to lock the door after him. But he returns a few seconds later, then locks the door, leaving her alone and empty.

'You are such a messed-up idiot Sorcha.'

Watching Bannon feeding Quill had been one of the most erotic things she's seen. Which is absurd when she thinks about it. Everyone was dressed. There was nothing sexual about it, except for who was involved.

As opposite as they can be from each other, the dark-haired, quiet, gentle Bannon, perfectly complements the light-haired, brooding, coarse Quill. Bannon seems to calm Quill, while the head guard gives Bannon a confidence she doesn't see from him when he's alone.

They need each other. And she wants them to need her, too. Fantasies such as that won't do her any good, while she's locked in here. These bizarre encounters could come to an end any day. Quill is the head guard. He could wake up tomorrow and decide to assign someone else to her care. Bannon and Quill would then be gone from her life.

186

As much as she enjoys talking with Bannon and arguing with Quill, she can't afford to let herself get carried away, or attached to them.

In here, attachments mean nothing. They can be torn from you in the blink of an eye.

With nothing else to do, she lies down on her bed, tears coming to her eyes when she smells the two vampires on her thin sheet. Their scents even complement each other.

Inside, her wolf howls sadly as she cries herself to sleep.

BANNON

'Stop!'

The harsh roar brings him to a stop, mere steps from his room. He was hoping to get back to the safety of his space, before Quill caught up with him. No doubt he's going to get an earful. He turns to face Quill. The male is visibly furious at him. He storms over, giving Bannon a full-force shove in the chest, throwing him back against his bedroom door.

'What the fuck was that?'

'What?' he mouths.

'Don't pull that shit on me. You know exactly what I'm talking about! She doesn't leave her cell. The only exercise she gets is in the yard. Do you have any fucking idea how much trouble you'd be in if someone saw you in there with her? You'd be out of here before you knew what was happening. Or you'd be in the cell next to her. Who the fuck knows? Never disobey me again! Never!'

Bannon clenches his jaw. It's at times like this not being able to speak actually helps him. The mood he's in right now, he'd probably say something to land himself in a cell. He clenches his fists to his sides, struggling to hold back his power. He can feel the fire raging inside, ready to burst out if he lets his guard down.

He takes a deep breath, then looks at Quill.

Quill slams his hand on the door to the side of Bannon's head. 'Stop looking at me like that!'

Bannon just keeps looking at him. He hasn't got a clue how he's irritating Quill. The guard is clearly in his own shit mood.

Quill looks down at Bannon's hands, before turning his attention back to his face. 'You got a hold on that, or am I about to get burned again?'

Bannon releases his fists, holding his arms down by his side. As much as he would love to burn this dump to the ground, he's not going to let it win.

'Guess that means I'm safe. Open the door.'

Just perfect. So now Quill wants to give him a reprimand in private. Whatever. He might as well get it over with. Bannon digs his keys out of his pocket, but instead of letting him open the door, Quill grabs his keys from him, shoves open the door, then gestures for Bannon to go inside.

When Quill joins him and then locks the door, Bannon knows he's in a serious amount of trouble. He's heard about Quill's temper and how he reprimands guards who disobey him.

It results in the guards finding themselves in the infirmary.

'I'm trying really fucking hard to give you a break, but you can't keep pulling this shit on me. Where the fuck do you get off making up your own rules? You answer to me!'

He angrily scribbles a shortened version of what he wants to say, then holds out the notebook to Quill. *'She's innocent. Someone captured her after killing her boyfriend.'*

Quill reads the words, shaking his head as he looks back up at him. 'Who? The wolf?'

He nods.

'So what? That's none of your business. Your job is to keep her in the building. That's it.'

'So, it doesn't matter that she didn't do anything?'

'No.' The pause before he answers tells a different story. He shakes his head in frustration. 'Don't argue with me!'

Quill slams him back against the wall, adding more bruises to the ones he gave him a minute ago. 'Every single inmate in here has some sad fucking story. Most claim to be innocent. It's what they do. If you're going to believe all the stories, you're going to fuck yourself up. She's here for a reason. That's all you need to worry about.'

'How can you say that?' His writing is gradually becoming more illegible, but Quill gets the gist of what he's saying.

'What the fuck does it have to do with you? We don't run the prison. We don't have a say in who is, or isn't locked up here. Our *only* job it to make sure they stay put.'

He goes to write his reply, but Quill grabs the notebook, throwing it across the room.

'Stop arguing! You need to listen to me. Leave it alone!'

He opens his mouth, desperate to have his say, even though Quill won't listen. His notebook is across the room, and he needs Quill to pay attention if he's going to lip-read.

But Quill isn't in any mood to pay attention. He slams his fist against the wall to the side of Bannon's head, startling him. 'Do you want me to fire you?' He holds up his hand, his thumb and forefinger nearly touching. 'I'm this fucking close. Don't keep pushing me.'

Bannon rests his head back against the wall. Quill is right. He can fire him, and then he'll be back on the street, searching for scraps. He needs this job. He needs the bed that comes with it. The Warden is the only one who could look into why Sorcha is here. He doubts the Warden is going to be in the slightest bit interested in releasing her - innocent or not.

He unclenches his fists, keeping his hands flat against the wall to either side of him. His palms are hot, the heat already working up his arms to his elbows. If he sets Quill, or his room on fire, losing his job will be the least of his worries.

Quill's attention is drawn to Bannon's hands, but he doesn't comment. If anything, he seems to be intrigued instead of angry. Quill's brows drop, hiding his eyes from Bannon as he continues to look down at his hands.

Quill lifts his head, his eyebrows still down. 'Show me again.'

'*Show you what?*' he mouths.

'You know what. Your powers.'

He hasn't got a clue what's going on, but he's too confused and frustrated to try and figure it out. He lifts one hand, holding his palm up in front of Quill. The flames ignite on his fingertips, moving down his hand to his palm, until his whole hand is on fire.

'Fuck! You could do some serious damage with that.'

Bannon has never had anyone look at his powers the way Quill is right now. Just like his scar, people were wary of his powers, unsure how to act around him in case he freaks out. He's a liability on too many fronts. It's probably why he's spent the last few years isolating himself from the world. It was easier than being rejected.

He extinguishes the flames, then places his hand back down by his side as he waits for Quill to react in some way. The waiting is torturous.

'What the fuck are you doing to me?'

When he does speak, Quill's tone is far from hostile. It's more confused, which catches Bannon off guard.

Then the blow comes, but it's far from what Bannon was expecting. Quill leans forward and kisses him. It takes Bannon's brain too long to catch on. It's probably less than a second, but his first thought is

Quill is kissing me. But as soon as his brain catches on, he doesn't push Quill away. He kisses him back.

He thought the first time was a one-off. Was convinced it would never happen again, and they would both just carry on as if nothing happened.

Having Quill initiate it was something he never expected.

Quill's stubble feels amazing against him, the piercings in his lip and tongue turning him on more than he ever thought they would.

He's nervous about touching Quill, but lets himself get carried away in the moment. His long hair is still out, the thick locks sliding through his fingers as Bannon pulls him closer.

Quill growls, a low, almost predatory rumble from deep in his chest, his kiss growing more intense and desperate. He's far from gentle with him, his grip on Bannon's face firm and his kiss demanding. Bannon's head spins, the out-of-body sensation growing as Quill's tongue fucks his mouth.

His hair brushes against Bannon's face, his callused hands holding his head exactly where he wants it. He presses his body against Bannon's, trapping him against the wall. He can feel Quill's hard arousal against his own as their bodies grind against each other.

Quill is consuming him, fucking him in a way he's never been before. He never thought a kiss could be like this. Never imagined being kissed by someone like Quill would be so intense on every level. Never knew his own body would respond so strongly, that he would be turned on to this extent.

But he's never kissed anyone like Quill before.

He doesn't want this to stop. Wants more of Quill, even though he's scared. Scared how to take it further. Scared Quill won't want the same. Scared Quill wants the same. Scared he won't want to stop. It's all terrifying him.

Bannon moves his hand lower, cupping the side of Quill's face. His deep growl rumbles in his chest, vibrating against Bannon when Quill grinds against him, his solid body as all-consuming as his kiss.

All too soon, Quill stops kissing him, but doesn't move away. Both of them are breathless as they look at each other. 'Sorry. I didn't plan to do that.'

Bannon briskly shakes his head. *Please don't be sorry about that.* He says it over again in his head. He couldn't bear it if Quill regretted it.

'You just...' Quill licks his lips, the barbell in his tongue catching Bannon's attention. He wants that in his mouth again. 'I don't know.' His beautiful, eyes meet his again, the glow he thought he saw the other day back in full force. 'You confuse the fuck out of me Bannon,' he admits with a short laugh.

Without another word, Quill unlocks the door and disappears from Bannon's room. He's not the only one confused by what just happened. He liked it more than he thought he would. Damn, he loved it! Whatever unfamiliar attraction he had to Quill before, has moved into another new area, one he wants to explore again and again.

He had thought it was nothing more than silly lust or admiration, perhaps a crush that would fade in time. Now that they've kissed again, he realises it's so much more. This isn't a crush. Whatever he's feeling, it's real. He's attracted to Quill.

Which means he's in so much trouble.

What if Quill has now got it out of his system? What if Quill wants more? What if he wants to take it up a notch...whatever that would be? He's not so sure he's ready to even consider something like that.

What about Sorcha? Vampires hate wolves. It's been that way for generations. It was a hatred he was born into, only to be solidified decades later, when a rogue wolf decided to tear his family to pieces.

So why can't he stop thinking about the very thing he's forbidden to be near? The very creature he's detested since he was attacked. He should hate her. He has every justifiable right to hate her. But he doesn't.

When she kissed him, he hadn't disliked it. He welcomed it. It's something he didn't know he wanted to do, until she took the decision out of his hands. He's so grateful for that. He knows he wouldn't have initiated anything with her otherwise.

Even from that first moment when she arrived on the island, and he threw that wolf to the ground, holding her down so she couldn't escape, he knew he was in a world of trouble. Even in the dirty black prison jumpsuit, grime ingrained on her skin, her beauty had hit him.

It had screwed with him. When she smiled, she'd succeeded in distracting him. One minute he was in control of the prisoner, and the next he was the one on his back on the sand. He hoped Quill didn't see his pathetic effort. Thankfully his boss had taken to the air by then, so there's a strong chance he missed it.

He rubs his forehead. The cut Sorcha gave him when she arrived is gone, the scar fading quickly thanks to his vampire genes. It had been one hell of a punch she gave him, similar to the one she gave him when she threw him on his back in the training room.

Perhaps it's not as bad as he initially thought. So, she's attractive. She's certainly not the first woman he's been attracted to. But she's certainly the first wolf he had anything other than intense hostile thoughts about. And she's certainly a far cry from the image of any wolf he had in his mind.

Surely there are good and bad on both sides of the table.

He absently runs the tips of his fingers along the crude scar on his neck. He'd been unlucky to meet a particularly bad one. A feral wolf who changed his life for the worse.

Maybe she could alter his perception of her species? Maybe he's just a weak fool, who should stop letting her looks get in the way of sense and past experience. Maybe this place is getting to him? First, Quill catches his eye, and now he's thinking about a wolf in a positive way.

He's getting carried away imagining scenarios he has no business imagining. It was a meaningless kiss, not some big romantic relationship. He drops onto his bed, clasping his hands together tightly, as his mind goes through a whirlwind, with thoughts of Quill and of Sorcha confusing the hell out of him.

This is a mess. He lifts his arm, looking at the bite mark on his wrist from Quill. He doesn't want it to fade. He wants to remember the time the three of them shared in the cell. There was nothing intimate about it in the normal sense of the word, but feeding Quill, holding him like that while she was with them, was such an intense and alien experience.

He rolls over, burying his head in his pillow.

Now all he's left with is confusion and muddled feelings.

At the end of the day he's a guard, Quill is his boss, and she's a prisoner. Nothing is going to alter those positions no matter what.

32

DAVYN

The vast mansion at the end of the driveway in front of him isn't as imposing as Darkhaven, but it's far less inviting. Davyn never thought he'd say that about his father's castle.

He looks down the road, the silhouette of Leap Castle ominous in the dimming light. Thea's coordinates lead to the house, not the castle. Seems the castle was just the landmark his father used to pinpoint one of the prisons.

Fletch had brought the helicopter down in a field a few miles away, where two cars were waiting for them. Davyn wants to go in quiet. Landing a helicopter in front of the house wouldn't have helped.

Beside him, Murt peers out from behind a tree, his eyes glowing as he watches the house. Davyn has to hand it to the brothers. Their sister could be in there, but none of them have made a move towards the house. They know the plan and they're sticking to it. That's a rare quality and one he appreciates.

Although, right now, he'd prefer to go in with his guns out in front of him. All this fucking *lord of the manor* shit doesn't come naturally to him. He was raised in a damn cell, not with a fucking silver spoon in his mouth. That was reserved for his sadistic brother - may he rot in Hell.

Ethan taps him on the shoulder. 'Time to go. Lord Oldranson is needed.'

Davyn looks over at Murt. 'I want you to come too.'

'You do? Are you sure that's such a good idea? These places are run by vampires. If you show up with a wolf, it could fuck things up for your credibility."

Davyn pulls one of his guns out of its holster under his arm. 'Let me worry about my credibility. I want them to be thrown off when their boss comes in, with a wolf by his side as an equal.'

Murt grins and nods his head. 'Never thought you'd have an evil streak like that.'

'That's probably down to my upbringing.'

'If you're sure, I'm game.'

Davyn slides his gun back into its holster. 'Ready to be all demanding and bossy?'

Murt grins, taking his leather jacket from Con. 'Lead on, sire.'

Davyn flashes his big-ass fangs at him, before he turns and walks back over to the black Land Rover. He's got to arrive in style... apparently. He's just following Ethan's lead.

Murt gets into the back of the car beside him, leaving his brothers outside to keep watch. Fallon is driving, and Ethan is in the front passenger seat. Davyn checks his mic is in place, but hidden from view. 'You hear me?'

One by one, everyone checks in. In situations like this, Nix would usually run over the plan again, but that's not his style. He hasn't led a team often, but when he does, he gives his orders once, then trusts everyone was listening.

Ethan is going to take the lead when they get to the house, only letting Davyn step in if he's needed to apply a little of his style of pressure.

Fallon pulls the car to a stop at the bottom of the stone steps leading to the front door. Ethan turns in the passenger seat and looks at him. 'Are you ready?'

He keeps his response to a nod. He just wants to get this over with. Ethan, Fallon, and Murt get out of the car, but Davyn stays put until the door is opened for him. It's all about appearances, and you never know who's watching.

He climbs out when Fallon opens the door, making sure his guns are securely holstered, but not entirely hidden from view. He might be a lord, but he's also a Blackjack. There's no fucking way he's hiding that fact.

He's relieved when the vampire who opens the door, obediently ushers them inside, and asks them to wait in a drawing room to the left of the entrance hall. Davyn instantly gets flashbacks to Shep's owner's house when he had to go with Ethan to buy Shep back. He'd needed to throw his weight around with Shep's bitch of an owner, but it worked. Well, that and a hefty envelope full of money, so he could buy Shep for himself.

The door opens, stirring him back to the present. As soon as the vampire in the immaculate three-piece suit sees Murt, he snarls, pointing to the door. 'Get that dog out of here!'

So much for being all nice and polite. 'He's with me.'

'And you are?'

'This is Lord Oldranson,' Ethan says, taking over before Davyn is tempted to pull out his gun. 'I already told your man at the door.'

The vampire scoffs at Davyn, looking at him with disdain. Ethan and Thea had suggested he wear a suit to the meeting, but he had flat out dismissed that idea. He's a lord, whether he's wearing a three-

198

piece suit, or dressed as he is now in his fighting leathers, a black t-shirt, and black leather jacket. He's a Blackjack first - always will be.

'This is no lord,' scoffs the warden.

Ethan pushes in front of Davyn and thrusts the lineage paperwork in the vampire's face. 'This says otherwise.' The vampire grabs the paper from Ethan's hand, scowling as he reads it.

Davyn knows the moment the arrogant vampire realises his mistake. The cockiness fades, replaced by a look of fear. About fucking time! 'I killed my father. Cut his head from his body.'

The vampire nods as he looks over at Davyn. 'Yes. I heard he had passed. I wasn't aware it was by his son's hand.'

'Can you please confirm your name,' Ethan says, his tone soothing in the hostile environment.

'I am Dorian, the warden, my lord.'

That's good. So, he now recognises his station. One hurdle passed.

'As I'm sure you're aware,' Ethan says, getting back to the less aggressive formalities. 'The rule of succession means that what once belonged to the Raven King, now belongs to his sole heir, Davyn Oldranson. Is there somewhere we can talk?'

Dorian gestures to the couches at the far side of the room. He keeps his eyes and fangs on Murt as the wolf sits beside Davyn. Fallon takes up position between the couch and the chair, her attention on Dorian as it should be. She'll react if the vampire makes any move he shouldn't.

'I suggest you stop giving my friend here the evil eye.'

Dorian swallows thickly as he pulls his focus back from Murt to Davyn again. 'I apologise, my lord, but why do you work with one of these creatures?'

'You'd prefer he was locked in a cage?'

Dorian's face drops at the suggestion. 'Sire, of course not. I just meant—'

Bored with the pleasantries, Davyn pulls out his gun, holding it as he rests his arms along the back of the couch to either side of him.

'How about we move this along? We know about the prisons. Now what I don't know is, what exactly you've been doing with the money you're getting for keeping wolves imprisoned.'

'Money sire?'

'We have been thoroughly examining all his father's records,' Ethan says, taking over again. 'I suggest you don't waste his time by denying that you are stealing from him.'

'Stealing! No!'

'According to the files, you're being paid to keep the wolves incarcerated. Since his father was killed, no payments have been made to Davyn. What would you call that?'

Davyn gets up, irritation building with each second he's in the room with this vampire. Time to end this. He lifts his arm, pointing his gun at Dorian's head. No one else in the room moves. Even Ethan doesn't try to stop him. 'Where is the prison?'

Dorian gestures over to the door. 'Access is through the basement.'

Davyn lets his fangs drop before he smiles at Dorian. 'After you.'

SORCHA

She's had many memorable days in the prison - most for the wrong reasons. But today is different. Today she's eating her dinner in the company of two gorgeous vampires. She wasn't expecting either of them to stay with her while she ate. Bannon had brought her dinner as usual, but when Quill had stepped into the cell a few minutes later and leaned against the wall watching her, she'd nearly choked on her spaghetti.

Bannon had frozen too, clearly not expecting to see Quill either. As soon as he steps into the room, a strange awkwardness takes over. The last time she'd seen Bannon she'd kissed him. Every time she looks at Bannon he blushes slightly and looks away from her.

But she's not the only one bringing about that reaction from

Bannon. He had blushed when Quill walked in, and she's caught the two of them stealing sneaky glances at each other, each one turning away when the other catches them looking.

She hides her smile as she continues to eat. She's absolutely convinced the guards had shared a moment too. The obvious embarrassment and awkwardness between them is so cute. Then Bannon glances at Quill and licks his lips.

Oh shit! They kissed!

She's absolutely convinced of it.

She's a little surprised her first thought is that she wishes she could have been there to see that. The idea had never crossed her mind before. Being locked away with people whose personal hygiene levels no longer existed, didn't exactly inspire any warm and fuzzy thoughts. But looking at these two vampires in their crisp, and more importantly, clean uniforms, she can absolutely see the appeal.

But wanting both?

One of them isn't an option. Both of them is a greedy fantasy. One she needs to remove from her mind immediately.

'So,' she says, trying to get her head out of the gutter, and to ease some of their amusing discomfort. 'I've been practising the last page of sign language you gave me,' she says, looking over at Bannon. 'Do you fancy testing me?'

Bannon looks over at Quill, presumably asking for permission or approval, but the guard doesn't react in either way, so Bannon looks back at her and nods. Under Quill's quiet watchful eye, they spend the next few minutes running through the last page Bannon had given her, as she eats her dinner.

She's actually really pleased with herself. She gets them all right. Bannon is chuffed too, if his huge grin is anything to go by. It shouldn't make her happy too, but it does. She must be going soft in her old age.

Finished with her dinner she sits on the bed, leaning back against the stone wall. Quill and Bannon are still doing the awkward glances at each other.

'Are you two just going to stand there or sit?'

'We need to get back to work,' Quill says, doing his best to kill the mood.

No way, Officer. You're not getting out of this so easily. 'Surely you can spare me another few minutes. Please. Just sit for a minute.'

Bannon checks for a reaction from Quill but, getting none, slowly sits beside her, his attention still on Quill.

'What about you, Officer Quillan? I promise I won't bite. I've just eaten.' She pats the bed to her other side, but he keeps his distance, leaning on the table instead of going near her bed.

'This reminds me a little of home,' she says, desperate to give them a reason not to go back to work and lock the door, leaving her alone again. Even having Quill in her cell is a better option than being alone.

'How does this possibly remind you of home?' Quill asks, as Bannon mirrors his confused expression. 'Where the fuck did you grow up?'

She pulls her legs up, tucking them under her. 'It's more the company than the location,' she says, laughing at their reaction. 'I have four brothers,' she explains. 'I guess you two remind me of them a little.'

She's never mentioned her family aloud since she was captured. Not once, and it instantly makes her emotional. 'Sorry,' she says, quickly wiping away her tears. Bannon moves slightly closer to her, the side of his arm touching against hers. It's comforting.

'We used to sit down as often as possible and eat together. We'd argue, laugh, talk. My oldest brother, Murt, was all about family. All about our clan and making sure we got along as much as we could. Strength in numbers and all that. Our parents are dead, so he's sort of like a father figure. He's a major alpha wolf. You don't mess with him.

'Anyway, Murt never really said much at those meals. He'd just watch and listen. Took it all in. Well, unless he had to break us up.

Garret is a complete hothead and would usually try to start an argument with Con. They'd argue over the colour of the sky if they could.

'I think I miss my youngest brother, Fionn, the most. We're twins. I don't know what it's like for vampires, but wolves are connected to family members. We can sense them.'

'It can be the same for us,' Quill says. 'I've no siblings but I've heard it's the case.'

'Do you have any brothers or sisters?' she asks Bannon.

He shakes his head as he gestures to his scar. *'My sister was killed that night.'*

She translates for Quill, the words fading as she speaks. The room falls silent as Quill and Sorcha process that. 'I'm so sorry Bannon. Was she younger or older?'

He points up. *'Her name was Bree.'*

Quill looks at her, waiting for her to translate again. 'Her name was Bree.'

'I'm sorry,' he mutters, looking genuinely upset by the admission. Then Quill looks at her. 'Can you still sense your brothers?'

She rubs the band around her wrist. 'I've been away from them for so long I've lost that connection to them. My link to Fionn was strongest, but now that's gone, too. It's like a piece of me is missing. I've lost my wolf, lost Fionn, lost my family. I'd give anything to be at that table with them, listening to them argue about some ridiculous macho alpha male nonsense. I miss that so much.'

She didn't plan to be so open with them, but as soon as she mentioned her brothers, the dam just broke. She wanted Bannon and Quill to stay with her for another while, not to have a complete breakdown in front of them, and have them witness this pathetic show she's now giving them.

When Bannon wraps his arm around her, she doesn't hesitate for a moment. She lies against his side, the steady beat of his heart soothing her for the first time in years. She needed this. Needed to talk about Murt, Con, Garret, and Fionn. Needed to feel someone hold her again - even if it is a vampire guard.

'My father probably thinks I'm dead.'

Quill's voice is barely more than a whisper, but it startles both Bannon and her. 'Why?'

'I haven't spoken to him since I was brought here. We fought a lot. I like to get my own way. It caused friction between us. But even though we'd fight like cats and dogs, I miss that.'

'What do you mean you were brought here?'

'I meant *started here*.'

She doesn't believe he misspoke, but leaves it alone. She knows full well he'll clam up if she pries too much. 'Can you not get in touch with him?'

Quill shakes his head. 'It's better for both of us if he thinks I'm dead.' He takes a deep breath, then shrugs, ending that topic of conversation.

In that moment, the intimidating brute of a guard looks like a little lost boy. The sudden urge to get up and hug him takes her completely by surprise. But it's not something she acts on. It'll take more than a sad backstory to wipe his slate clean.

'I'm sorry about you and your father.'

He checks his watch and the dread builds. 'We better get back to work.'

She just blew it. By pushing things with Quill, she's scared him off. Which also means Bannon is going to leave. 'Of course. Wouldn't want the Warden getting on your back.'

'What the fuck does that mean?' Quill asks, his harsh tone cutting into her.

'Nothing! I just meant that I'm sure he gets on your back if things aren't done correctly around here. I didn't mean anything by it!'

He gives her a long hard look, before turning and storming out the door without another word.

'What the hell did I do?'

Bannon keeps his attention on the door as he shrugs. Quill's abrupt departure has confused him too.

He offers her a small smile before pulling a notebook and pen from his pocket. He quickly jots down some words which he shows to her. *'Ignore him. Keep working on your sign language. I'll test you again tomorrow.'*

'How long until you can come back?' She desperately wishes she didn't sound so clingy and pathetic. Maybe being alone for so long is finally getting to her. She's reached her limit and is now grabbing onto any company she can find.

'I'll be back as soon as I can.'

She nods, grateful he didn't give her a number. Realistically, it will be twenty-four hours before he's back.

'Watch your back out there, okay?'

He nods, then leaves, the dull clank of the lock slipping in place, helping to collapse the last of her hold on her tears. As his footsteps fade, she curls up on her bed, his handwritten sign language notes in her hand as she cries.

MURT

The smell is the first thing that hits him as he descends into the basement. When Dorian mentioned the prison was below the house, he never imagined the scale of it. From what he can make out, the tunnels had been dug under the structure above, going for miles in each direction.

The stench of sweat, blood, and bodily fluids envelopes him. 'How many wolves do you have down here?'

Dorian sneers over his shoulder at Murt, but doesn't answer his question. Or doesn't, until Davyn knocks his gun against the back of Dorian's head. 'He asked you a fucking question! Answer him.'

'I won't speak to a dog.'

Murt opens his mouth to reply, but Davyn gets there first. 'Answer him, or I will kill you.'

Murt wasn't expecting that response, but he lets it go. He's enjoying watching this pompous vampire get kicked around by Davyn.

'There are thirty-two here.'

Murt can barely believe it. It was well known that wolf numbers were in decline, but he assumed, as did others, that it was because vampires were killing them. Instead, they've been locked away, kept from their lives, from their loved ones. But at least they're alive.

He stumbles to a stop when they get to the end of the corridor, and a huge metal gate blocks their path. Murt peers through the gate down into the pit in front of them, and has to bite back the tears. Faces peer up at him from the gloomy pit, green eyes glowing brightly out of pale, dirty faces.

Tunnels lead away from the central area, presumably to the cells or living areas. 'My God...' He growls, turning to face the warden. The fucker is smiling down at his wolf prisoners. Actually smiling like he's proud of himself. Murt is usually restrained. He would be a lousy clan leader if he let his emotions get the better of him.

But right now, emotions consume him, taking over from any control he might have had. The wolf roars to the surface, his body shifting as it changes. It's forbidden to change in front of outsiders, but tell that to his wolf. It's furious and wants out.

Davyn, Ethan, Fallon, and Dorian watch in part horror, part shock, as his body twists into shape - bones, and muscles bending, snapping, and stretching, until his six-foot wolf stands in his place.

He should get pleasure from the fact Dorian has the good sense to piss himself in fear, but he's beyond caring about that.

Davyn places himself in front of him, his arms crossed, and a look of mild amusement on his face. 'You held back longer than I thought you would.'

He's not surprised that Davyn was hoping he'd shift. A few vampires facing a prison full of pissed-off wolves is a bad idea. But he can change that... hopefully.

'I'll get your brothers in here. The wolves down there are scared and angry. They'll need to see friendly faces.'

That's why Davyn wanted him here. It was a good call. Murt growls at Dorian, as Davyn uses his mic to call Fionn, Con, and Garret. He wants to kill Dorian, but he's not going to. He answers to Davyn. Wolf or not, his allegiance still stands. Besides, knowing the vampire as he does, Davyn isn't going to let Dorian live a long and happy life.

When his brothers arrive, all in their wolf form, Davyn turns back to Dorian. 'Open the door.'

'But sire... They'll get out.'

Davyn restrains himself to just slapping Dorian. 'Open the fucking door!'

Dorian keys in a code in the panel by the door then steps aside, trying to make his escape, before Fallon grabs him by the neck of his shirt. 'I think Lord Oldranson would like you to stick around for a bit.'

Davyn looks at the four brothers. 'I think you might need to do this bit alone. I reckon you'd have better luck down there than I would.'

Murt nods, turning to his brothers. *'Ready?'* he asks.

They nod as one, then follow him down the ramp to the open area filled with wolves. Thin gaunt faces turn towards him and his brothers as they reach the bottom level. He can feel his brothers' pain, their anger.

'I want blood Murt.' He hears Garret's voice in his head, the anger and frustration coming across clearly.

'I know Garret. So do I. But not yet.'

He turns as a tall man pushes through the crowds to stand in front of them. His dark hair is long and tied in a ponytail at the back. His green eyes shine brightly as he smiles at them. 'Fuck me! Murt Whelan.'

Murt changes back, keeping to a crouch to hide his now naked body. 'Rowan? What the fuck? I thought you were dead!'

'Get my cousin some clothes. I'm very glad to see him, but could do without seeing that much of him!' While Murt puts on a pair of trousers he's given by one of the prisoners, Rowan hugs Con, Garret, and Fionn, the three black wolves crowding him as they greet each other.

Once his modesty has been taken care of, Murt embraces the male, hugging him tightly. 'How long have you been here for?'

'Not long. I was moved here a few weeks ago from another prison. Apparently, I was a good *dog*, so got moved back to minimum security.' Rowan looks around the cave-like structure. 'Doesn't look like much, but believe me, it's a fucking palace compared to where I was.'

'Is Sorcha here with you?'

Rowan's smile fades. 'Sorcha? No. Was she taken too?'

He nods. 'Eight years ago. Well, we're hoping she was taken. Don't want to think about the alternative. Are you positive she's not here?'

'Not since I've been here, but that's not long. Hey!' he says, turning to the other wolves. 'Has anyone come or gone before me by the name of Sorcha?'

One of the females at the back pushes through the crowd. Her black jumpsuit is threadbare in places and in need of a good wash. 'Your sister.'

The flat statement brings a new lease of life to him. 'Yes. You've seen her?'

'Yes, I've seen her. She's the image of you. Spirited young woman.'

Murt laughs at that. 'Oh, she's that all right. Where is she?'

'Gone,' the woman explains. 'She was a handful at the best of times. Gave the guards a bit of bother. They moved her to the Level Two prison a few years back. Must be gone on four or five years now. I'm sorry.'

'Fuck!' So close. So fucking close to getting her back and they've missed her. Behind him, his brothers growl, each mirroring his own pain and frustration.

'I'm sorry Murt,' Rowan says. 'I had no idea she was here.'

'We only just found out about the prisons. We had no idea they existed until recently.'

Rowan looks up at the vampires, watching from the upper level. 'Can I ask what the hell you're doing with bloodsuckers?'

'The vampire with the eye-patch is Lord Davyn Oldranson. He's the son of the late Raven King.'

'Late? So, someone took that fucker down? About time.'

Murt nods. 'Yeah. Davyn did.'

Rowan glances up at the large vampire, still watching them, his lone green eye glowing slightly. 'Scary looking fucker. Still doesn't explain why you're here with him.'

'He's trying to fix what his father did.' Murt looks around at his brothers. 'We pledged our allegiance to him a few months ago.'

The silence that hits at that comment is almost tangible. Seems no one in the room was expecting that.

'By force?' Rowan asks.

'No. He's a Blackjack. We were called in to help take down his father. They did a lot of good for us Rowan. We wanted to put an end to the rift. We're only here today because of him.'

Rowan laughs loudly. 'Fuck me! Trust you lot to break all the rules. How did the Elders take that?'

'We were stripped of our land, our home, our funds, and banished to Mount Leinster.'

The silence comes back again. 'Mount Leinster,' Rowan eventually says. 'Fuckers didn't hold back, did they?'

'No. Wouldn't expect them to.'

Rowan nods. 'I guess there's just one question to be asked so. Any regrets bending a knee to him?' he asks, nodding towards Davyn.

'Not for a second,' Murt replies without hesitation.

'Do you agree?' Rowan asks Fionn, Con, and Garret. Each wolf nods their head.

'Well then,' Rowan says, rubbing his hands together. 'Looks like we're pals with the Blackjacks so.'

SORCHA

As soon as Duna and another male guard enter her cell, pulling her to her feet, she knows where she's being taken. So much for Quill keeping his word. She shouldn't have let herself get carried away. There are no rules in here. She has no control over anything that happens to her.

Sorcha struggles as she's dragged along the corridor and hauled into the interrogation room. She keeps struggling, even though she knows it's not going to do the slightest bit of good. This is happening. All she can do is get control of her fear and lock away the pain until she's back in her cell.

Her wrists are locked together, before she's lifted up and attached to the ring in the ceiling. Duna dismisses the other guard, then stands in front of Sorcha with her arms crossed. Maybe she's going to hang around and watch again. Maybe that's how this bitch gets her kicks.

Ignoring the guard, she takes the brief reprieve to get herself together, focusing on steadying her breathing before the fun kicks off.

The door opens and there he is. The blonde bastard shuts the door behind himself, then stands beside Duna. Sorcha spits on him, hitting the front of his shirt instead of his face, but it makes her feel a little better.

'What the fuck was that?' Duna asks, laughing at her feeble attempt to attack Quill.

She lifts her legs, kicking him where her spit had landed, but it's like hitting a wall. Duna and Quill grab her legs, shoving them down so they can secure them to the floor. The vampires stand again and Quill nods to the door.

'I've got this.'

'I can stay in case you need help.'

'I said I've got this Duna. Leave!'

Sorcha smiles at Duna as the female storms from the cell, clearly pissed off that her boss kicked her out.

Quill locks the door, then slowly drags the huge hunting knife along the counter at the side of the room, the metal scraping ominously against the wood.

'You bastard! Get the fuck away from me!' It's a useless waste of energy, but she's acting on instinct, not sense.

Quill rests the knife against the neck of her jumpsuit, his eyes on the knife as he cuts her clothes right down the middle, then tears the ruined material from her body.

'I knew you'd do this again! I knew it! Come on then Asshole! Go for it!'

Quill swaps the knife for the whip. As she continues her useless struggles, he steps closer, then wraps his hand around her neck, putting on just enough pressure that she stops her struggles.

'You need to stop and listen to me,' he whispers in her ear. 'It's important.'

She opens her mouth to try and speak, but he squeezes a little tighter.

'Just listen. We don't have much time. There's a camera behind me. I'm blocking it right now so he can't see. He'll see the bruising around your neck and that'll keep him happy. He wants you to suffer. I've been trying to put him off hurting you, but he's adamant he wants me to break you. He's ordered me to continue hurting you, or step aside and let Duna do it. I need you to break, Sorcha. I need you to break for me.'

Having Quill use her name helps a strange calm replace the panic.

'Fake it. Pretend. Put on a fucking Oscar-winning performance! I don't care. I just need him to think he's broken you. Do you understand?' He releases the pressure on her neck. 'Do you understand?'

'Yes,' she whispers back.

He pauses, his eyes dropping to the ground for a moment. 'I need to hurt you now. I can't just pretend to whip you. It needs to be real.'

'Okay.'

Her mind is racing, but for some reason, she believes what he's saying. This is down to the Warden. He wants his prison and his guards to be the ones to break the wolf that couldn't be broken elsewhere. Quill releases her neck, his eyes locked on hers as he steps back.

'Fight back. Spit and curse. Shout all you want, okay? He wants the sound on for this.'

She spits on him again and he grins. 'Showtime.' Quill turns and wipes his face as he switches on the sound. He snaps the whip in his hand as he walks around her. Keeping her attention off the camera she closes her eyes, bracing for the impact.

She'll break all right, but it can't happen straight away, or the Warden won't believe it. If the Warden suspects anything, she fully believes he'll replace Quill with Duna. That female vampire wouldn't be so interested in sparing her the pain.

The whip bites into her flesh, his strike hard and sure as it was every other time. He's not holding back, but with a camera on him, he can't take it easy.

Sorcha bites back a scream, biding her time before she submits to these vampires, even though it goes against everything that she is. But this isn't about beliefs, or sticking the finger up at anyone.

It's about her survival.

BANNON

He's just finishing his lunch when Quill appears at the doorway of the kitchen, gesturing for him to follow him outside. 'She needs you.'

Bannon doesn't understand what he's saying, but Quill doesn't wait for him to get clarification. 'I had no choice. I didn't. Take some first aid supplies and a spare jumpsuit with you. Don't let anyone see though. I'll cover you for an hour.'

Bannon reaches behind him to take his notebook out of his pocket, but Quill shakes his head. 'This isn't a discussion Bannon! It's an order. Just do what I'm telling you to do.'

Quill storms away, his heavy footsteps echoing through the corridor.

Without going after him, Bannon races to the supply closet,

stuffing his pockets full of anything he thinks he might need. Not that he has the first idea what he needs. Quill wasn't exactly generous with the information he gave him.

Once he's concealed everything, Bannon briskly walks to the prison, making his way down the levels to Sorcha's cell. Even from a few feet away he can smell her blood.

The bastard.

He forces himself to keep his pace steady, instead of racing over to the door. He unlocks it and steps inside, closing it behind him again.

Sorcha is huddled on her bed, her sobs reaching him from under her arms which are covering her head. He slowly approaches her, not wanting to startle her. With no way to tell her he's here, he pulls out her chair, dragging it across the floor.

She jumps, pushing back against the wall. Her face is streaked, the tears cutting tracks through the grime.

Bannon reins in the anger that threatens to set the room on fire. Quill flogged her. The bastard flogged her again! He gently helps her roll onto her front and glares at the blood coating her back.

'He said he had to do it,' she says, sniffing as she tries to control her tears. 'Said the Warden was watching, and he needed to break me.'

Bannon doesn't give a damn what reason Quill gave her. This was unnecessary. She hisses as he dabs disinfectant on one of the raw gouges.

'He asked me to pretend to break, Bannon. Said the Warden needed to think he'd broken me, or he'd get someone else to do it.'

He grinds his teeth together, as he cleans up after the Warden and Quill's handiwork.

Sorcha takes a hold of his hand, lifting her head off the bed so she can look at him. 'I don't think he wanted to do it. I really don't.'

But Bannon doesn't hear her words. All he can focus on is the hand mark he sees around her neck. He bares his fangs, the anger tearing to the surface. He gets to his feet, moving back from her as his hands erupt in flames.

'Bannon! Please don't do this. You need to calm down.' Sorcha agonisingly climbs to her feet, her face drawn tight in pain. She slowly approaches him, one hand out in front of her. 'It's okay.'

It's far from okay. Everything about this situation, and how he's reacting, is far from okay.

'I don't need you to fry me on top of everything else.'

He looks up at her, surprised that she's smiling at him. She winks and gestures to her hand again. 'I'd prefer you help clean my back than give me a suntan.'

What he wants to do is let his powers out and level this place. He usually has a hold on it. But, since coming to this island, the fire has been surging under the surface, waiting to break free whenever he drops his guard.

Bannon clenches his fists, the flames extinguishing instantly. Sorcha slowly takes his hands, blowing out a breath when she touches him. 'I honestly thought they'd be hot.'

She guides him back over to the bed and sits on the edge, her back facing him. 'If you could just clean off the blood that would be great. I'll heal in a few hours.'

Bannon fills the plastic cup with water, then kneels beside her bed. He dips the cloth he smuggled into her cell into the cup, wrings it out, then wipes dried blood from her skin.

'You know, it's funny what you miss the most being locked up in a place like this.'

He wrings out the cloth again. There's a lot of blood on her skin, but the wounds are beginning to heal, thankfully.

'I miss my freedom of course, but the part I really hate is being dirty.' She laughs once to herself. 'You're cleaning my torn back, and I'm complaining about being dirty. You probably think I'm mad.'

He shakes his head. He absolutely understands what she's saying. Being offered a shower once a week isn't something he'd be too happy about either. He rinses out the cloth again, cursing to himself when the water in the cup clouds with dried blood. This is ridiculous. He'll be here for hours cleaning her wounds this way.

Bannon checks his watch. It's nearly time for his shift to end, which means all the guards will be busy finishing up their duties.

He shouldn't even be thinking about doing this, but once the thought enters his mind, he can't shake it. Bannon stands, pulling her to her feet and passes her the jumpsuit he brought.

'What are you doing?'

With no time to write it down, he helps her get dressed, ignoring her questions, then opens the door and leads her out into the corridor. Moving quickly, he guides her down the corridor and up a flight of stairs to the next floor. After checking the room is empty, Bannon shoves her inside, closing the door behind them.

'Have you lost your...' her words fade away when she realises where they are. The shower block is empty. The inmates are only showered once a week, so no one will disturb them today.

Sorcha faces him, confusion all over her face. 'What's going on?'

Bannon turns on a shower in the right side of the room. It's far from private, but there's a wall partially hiding the stall. He points to the shower as he unlocks one of the storage cabinets, pulling out a fresh towel for her.

She's still standing in the middle of the room when he turns back around. If she doesn't get moving, they'll run out of time. He taps his watch then gestures to the shower, hoping she gets the message.

'Is this safe? For you I mean.'

Her concern for him is touching and unexpected. Bannon nods, gesturing to the shower again. Finally, Sorcha hurries over to the stall, stripping out of her clothes when he turns his back. Bannon stands near the stall, watching the door, straining to listen to everything going on around him. This could go wrong for both of them if they're caught.

He smells the antiseptic shampoo and soap offered by the prison. But in this case, it will help her wounds, cleaning them better than he could do with a cup of water and a rag. Her hisses of pain upset him, but he's given up figuring out his reactions to her. She's a wolf, but she's also more than that.

'Bannon? Can you please check my back?'

He turns around, realising ridiculously late that she's going to be completely naked in the shower. He blushes as she turns her back to him, giving him a clear view of her wounds, as well as her ass and legs.

After looking at the latter two a bit longer than he should, he mentally kicks himself, before focusing on her back. She looks over her shoulder at him, eyebrows raised as she waits for his answer.

'Is it okay?' He nods. It's a lot better than it was in her cell. 'Can you please pass me the towel?'

He averts his eyes, but not fast enough. Sorcha turns to face him, her naked body on full view to him. 'It's okay,' she says, taking the towel from his outstretched hand. 'There's no such thing as privacy in these places. I had to bottle up any modesty I used to have.' She wraps the towel around her torso, then picks up her blood-stained jumpsuit and well-worn underwear.

Bannon points to the storage cupboard, and Sorcha smiles when she sees clean underwear and jumpsuits. 'A shower and new... well, clean, underwear. You're really spoiling me.'

He leaves her to get dressed as he collects her old clothes, dumping them into the chute that leads to the laundry room in the basement. Just like the cleaner clothes she's putting on, her old ones will be disinfected and put back into circulation.

But seeing the sheer delight these clothes are giving her, he realises just how much the Warden takes from these wolves keeping them here like this. He can't imagine being so thrilled to wear someone else's well-worn underwear.

She spins around, her wet hair sticking to the back of her jumpsuit. 'Well? How do I look?'

He gives her a thumbs up, the smile she gives him in return having no place in a prison like this.

QUILL

Quill stares out at the horizon half tempted to walk into the sea and keep going. Float away from this place and his master.

But that would mean leaving them, and he can't do that. Not now.

He wasn't planning for this to happen. Why would he? He's the head guard in a wolf prison. The odds of meeting one person he's interested in are so small it's not worth mentioning.

But two?

Sorcha will never be able to forgive him for what he did to her. He's broken her. He'd whipped her into submission just like the Warden wanted. Some of her screams and protests had been an act, but he knows most were genuine. He could see it in her eyes.

Was that the case when she had finally given in? Were her tears of pain and anguish fake or genuine? Who the fuck is he trying to kid? They were real. Any fool could see that. Nothing that happened in that room was faked. The pain, the fear, the anger, the hurt. It was all coming from somewhere real. Just as his need to protect her.

He lost a part of himself when she finally broke. He should have been happy that the Warden will leave both of them alone now. But at what cost? She'll never be able to forgive him for hurting her, after he promised he wouldn't.

But just because she hates him, doesn't mean he won't continue to do everything he can to protect her. It won't be easy, but in his position, he can shield her from some of the horrors in the prison. Bannon clearly has feelings for her too, so he can help.

He closes his eyes as the invisible hand twists in his gut. He knows Bannon and Sorcha kissed. He's no idiot. But that's okay. He wishes he could be a part of what they have, but he fully understands why that can never happen.

The waves crash against the shore, a perfect partner to his foul mood. He stands with his eyes closed for a minute, the sound of the sea helping to calm the turmoil inside.

He's so sick of feeling like this. So tired of fighting every day against what he wants, and what he needs to do as a guard. He's always on duty, always watching his back, always watching everyone else's back. But he's never once had anyone watch his back. Never had anyone look forward to seeing him for just his company.

Every time he thinks about Bannon and Sorcha together in the training room, the jealousy eats away at him. He never felt anything like it before. Jealous at their relationship, at their ease and comfort with each other. Jealous that he wasn't a part of it.

He'd heard the wolf laughing from down the corridor. Not something she does often, but why would she? No one laughs in there. There's nothing to laugh about. But when he saw Bannon smiling too, it had really pissed him off.

He wasn't irritated that they were laughing, or smiling, or

whatever the fuck they were doing. He was irritated because he wasn't included.

He's not here to laugh. He's here to keep a firm control of the inmates and guards. What does it matter if some of them find companionship with each other? Fuck knows there's little chance of any other happiness in here. But is it so wrong that he wants to have a piece of that happiness with another vampire and a wolf?

Trust him to do things the hard way. He's heard of humans falling for two people at the same time. But not in their world. And if it did happen, it would never be between a vampire and a wolf. Being attracted to a male vampire isn't ideal either, but he'd never been one to conform to the old ways. Well, not when it came to matters of the heart.

He likes the two of them, likes them a lot, and he believes Bannon feels the same. Or at least he hopes Bannon does.

When he's with Bannon, all the pain and stress disappear. Even when he's just back from a meeting with the Warden, he can forget with him. The second he sees Bannon's deep brown eyes, it all vanishes. He's just Quill. Just someone who that fucking gorgeous vampire cares about - although he still has no idea why.

It can never come to anything though, and that's the part that's slowly killing him. Sorcha is a prisoner he's abused. Bannon is a guard under his command.

And he's a possession.

He opens his eyes as the wind changes, bringing with it the scent of the Warden. 'Quillan?'

A vice squeezes his chest, the dread escalating as he hears the footsteps cross the stones. Quill pushes the fear and the dread aside, and turns to face him.

As usual, the Warden is impeccably dressed, his tailored three-piece suit pressed to perfection. His greying hair scraped back from his face with far too much gel. 'I've been looking for you.'

'I just went for a run.'

The Warden stares at him for a few minutes, not saying anything. Quill gets the impression he's done something wrong, but can't think what.

'Aren't you forgetting something?'

He plays back his response and groans to himself. 'Sir. I apologise, sir.' But the apology is far too late. If the Warden demands anything it's respect.

'On your knees.'

Quill glances around him. The beach is empty. He can't see anyone in any of the dozens of windows in the huge house, but that doesn't mean someone isn't going to see him.

'If I have to ask again, I will not be happy.'

Quill swallows and drops to his knees, the rough stones digging into his legs. He lowers his chin, keeping his attention on the Warden's expensive loafers. The Warden walks up to him, grabbing a handful of his hair. Quill closes his eyes as his head is pulled back hard, his neck stretched painfully.

'I'm disappointed in you Quillan.'

He doesn't respond. He's not looking for a response. Quill closes his eyes, terrified that someone is going to see him like this. Terrified that his reputation, the only thing he has, will die.

'You disrespected me twice. Are you forgetting your place?' He releases him and Quill shakes his head. 'No, sir. I apologise, sir.'

The Warden grabs his chin, tilting his head back again. 'You've been distracted.'

'No. I'm sorry sir. I'm not distracted. I swear.' Speaking is difficult, thanks to the Warden's hand, but if he doesn't respond he'll make things so much worse for himself.

'I have been lenient with you the last few years. Perhaps that was a mistake. You are the head guard. You should not have to spend your day with the menial tasks others can complete.'

'It's not a problem sir. I can handle it.'

The Warden's hand leaves his jaw. 'It is I who decides what you can handle. I believe you should remove yourself from the day-to-day tasks of the prison. Stick to what you excel at. Let the others come to you, only if there is a situation suited to your firm hand.'

He doesn't want to take a step back. Working in the prison, doing those menial tasks is all that's keeping him sane. 'My firm hand, sir?'

'Punishment, of course. Be the one the others fear. Be the one the prisoners fear. I saw how you broke that wolf. Heard her howls of pain. It was poetic Quillan. Truly poetic. Do you have any idea how many have tried and failed where you succeeded? Where I succeeded? Your talents should not be wasted.'

The Warden can take all the credit he wants. He probably sat in his plush office, watching her scream and beg, while sipping some expensive drink.

'I like to make sure everyone is doing their job sir.' Fuck, he's a step away from begging for things to stay the same. It won't work though. Once the Warden has made up his mind, there's fuck-all he can do about it.

'No. You have trained them well. Take a step back and give them space to do their work. Duna can take over if needed.'

'I really don't think—'

The slap jars his teeth and stings like fuck. 'Inside the prison you are allowed to think. With me, you obey.'

'Sorry sir.'

The Warden sighs dramatically as he looks out at the sea. 'What is your relationship with the mute guard?'

'Sir?' Fear grips his heart, threatening to squeeze it until it pops.

'I've noticed you have arranged the roster so you are working together.'

'He's new sir. I always spend a lot of time with new recruits and personally train them. I need to make sure your prison is run correctly, and efficiently.'

The Warden runs his hand through Quill's hair, turning his stomach. *Please don't let anyone see this.* Quill couldn't bear the humiliation. He turns his attention back down to Quill and leans over. The Warden's fingers dig painfully into his scalp as he grabs a fistful of hair again. 'I only allow you the freedom I do, because I want you to be happy. I can easily take that from you again. I still have your cage...'

The sweat breaks out on Quill's back at the mention of that cage. He can't go back there. Not ever. 'I am happy, sir.'

'I hope so. You have some apologising to do for your recent lapse. You will come to my quarters tonight.'

'Yes, sir.'

The Warden runs his finger down the side of Quill's neck as he licks his lips. 'This is your last chance, Quillan.'

'Thank you, sir.'

Then he turns and walks away, leaving Quill on his knees on the rocks. He doesn't get up, until his master has disappeared back into the hulking house. Only then does he walk down the beach, screaming to himself when he's out of view of the house.

Davyn

When he rammed his talons into his father's neck, Davyn hadn't thought beyond saving his own life. They were in the sea, his father's talon buried deep in his sides, slowly tearing him apart. He had just wanted his father to stop. That was it.

He's not saying that, had he known about all this lord of the Manor shit, he would have done things differently. His father needed to die. But maybe he would have put something in place first, to free him from all this bullshit he's finding himself in time and time again, since he made the decision to kill his father.

He watches Murt and his brothers talking to the wolves below them in the prison. It looks as if the Whelans are working their magic on the wolves. Davyn doesn't want to have to keep them locked up, but if they're about to come after him, or any of the other vampires he's with, he might just have to give them time to cool off.

'Are you going to free them, sire?'

He nods, but doesn't look at Ethan. Yes, he's going to free them, but that didn't clear the slate where his father is concerned. He knows that first-hand. He'd spent decades either in a cage, or his underground cell. Spent decades wondering if he'd wake again, every time he lost consciousness. Spent too long hoping the darkness wouldn't let him go, once it claimed him.

'You can't free them.'

It takes him a good few seconds to realise that Dorian was the one to speak. He turns to glare at the male, cowering in the corner, his expensive trousers soaked in his own piss. 'What did you say?'

'You can't free them my lord. They have to stay.'

Davyn looks back at the wolves, taking a minute to get his temper under control. He needs Dorian breathing for another while. 'Where's your office?'

Dorian nods back the way they came.

Davyn talks to Murt through his radio. 'I'm going to look through the paperwork. You good?'

'We're good.'

He turns to Fallon. 'Stay here. Any trouble, make a run for it. Murt and his brothers can look after themselves.'

Davyn grabs Dorian by the collar, dragging him to his feet. He shoves him down the corridor ahead of him, his gun pressed against the back of the vampire's head.

'Please don't shoot me.'

'I don't shoot people in the back of the head. Now walk!'

Behind him, Ethan follows, ignoring the pleas for help from the prison warden. Davyn kicks in the door the warden directs him to, and dumps the vampire in the nearest chair. 'Call the guards.'

'But sire—'

'Now!'

Dorian pulls his phone from his pocket, and Davyn watches as he calls one of his contacts. 'It's me. Staff meeting in my office. Now.'

'Where are the records to do with the prison?'

He points to the filing cabinet against the wall. 'It's all in there sire. What... forgive me, but what are you doing?'

Davyn opens the door when someone knocks. The four guards are ushered into the room and Davyn relaxes slightly. He was expecting four well-built vampires, who could take on irate wolves without breaking into a sweat. The males he's facing, have spent more time in the breakroom, when they should have been in the gym. By the look on Ethan's face, he's thinking the same thing.

'Sit,' Davyn commands, using his gun to enforce his point. The four guards sit on the couch, each one concentrating on the gun.

Ethan gestures to Davyn. 'This is Lord Oldranson. The Raven King's rightful heir. And your new boss.'

The guards look from Davyn to Dorian, and back again. 'Is this true?' the larger of the males asks.

'He just said it is,' Davyn replies. 'Now the question is, where does your loyalty lie? With me, or with him?' he asks, nodding over to the warden, quivering in his chair.

'I've found the paperwork, sire,' Ethan says, using Davyn's title to highlight the point. 'It's all here.'

'And the money? Where did that go?'

'Money?'

'Stop asking me to repeat myself. It's not helping my mood. I know you're paid to keep the wolves here. I know that money should be coming to my father. And now me. And I know it's not.'

The vampire looks at his guards, maybe hoping they'll step in to help him. But no one moves or replies. 'It costs money to run the prison. It costs money to keep the prisoners boarded and fed.'

'Don't you fucking dare!' Davyn roars. 'Where is the fucking money?'

The warden pauses, so Davyn tries to hurry things along by

forcefully shoving his gun against Dorian's piss-soaked groin. Davyn lets his fangs drop, as he snarls at the vampire. 'It's in my account sire. I have the funds. I was holding them for—'

'You stole from me!'

'Your father—'

'Is dead! I'm in charge now. These prisons are mine. Which means you work for me.'

He wasn't expecting the asshole to jump up and down for joy, but he's on the verge of pissing himself again.

'Ethan. The warden would like to make a withdrawal.'

'But sire... please...'

Ethan gestures to the warden's phone. 'If you would be so kind as to log onto your banking, I can sort out that minor discretion immediately.'

When he delays again, Davyn pushes his gun harder against the warden. 'Last chance.'

Dorian finally does as he's told, and Ethan takes the phone from him and completes the transfer.

'And the wolves? What do you plan to do with them?'

'They are no longer your concern.'

'But sire. They're wolves. You can't...' His words fade away as Davyn growls at him.

'Where are the other prisons?'

'In the blue file sire. Top drawer. I only have the location of the next prison. The Level Two facility. We were never given all the locations.'

'How many are there?'

'Three sire.'

'Ethan?' He looks over at his boss as he searches the drawer. 'Did you find it?'

'I have it,' he says, opening the file to check the contents. 'The coordinates are here. We've got everything we need sire.'

He nods once, giving Davyn permission to end this the way he wants to. He straightens, keeping his gun pointed at the warden. 'I said earlier I don't shoot people in the back of the head. I prefer to look them in the eye.' He fires once, killing the bastard.

'I'm not usually one for violence,' Ethan says, joining him in front of the chair, 'But in some cases it's deserved.'

Davyn runs his hand over his gun, wiping off the warden's blood splatters. He then turns to the four guards, who are all looking in horror at the warden's body. 'I'm still waiting for an answer to my question. Where does your loyalty lie? With that dead, piss-covered fucker? Or with me?'

'With you,' they respond, each one standing to attention in front of him.

'Right. Now go to the prison and report to my team members Murt and Fallon.'

The guards hurry from the room, not giving their former boss even a fleeting glance as they walk away.

'Fallon and Murt?' Davyn says over his radio. 'Four guards heading your way. They've sworn allegiance to me. But if they cause any problems shoot them.'

'Now what sire?' Ethan asks, looking down at the body of the warden.

'First you can drop that fucking title. Then you can decide. I've done my bit.'

'Oh, is that so?' Ethan says, crossing his arms. 'How nice of you to leave me to clean up this mess. You know we can't just release the wolves? We need to know who they are, and why they were imprisoned here. There is a chance at least some of them are here for legitimate reasons.'

'You want to have that conversation with Murt? He won't take it well.'

Ethan nods as he straightens his red tie. 'I wouldn't expect him to. We'll figure something out.'

39

BANNON

He takes his cup from the coffee machine and sits at the back of the room, away from the other guards who are seated together, talking amongst themselves. Bannon sips his coffee, casually looking out for Quill, but there's no sign of the guard yet.

It's the first staff meeting that's been called since he began working here. He presumes Quill will hold the meeting, keeping it short, so they can catch the boat to the mainland and enjoy their time off.

One weekend a month isn't a lot, but the pay is so good he can't really complain. It's not like he has much to do when he is off or anything to spend his pay on. Lately, his thoughts revolve around Sorcha and Quill - not around any life he may have left behind.

The door opens and Quill stalks into the room. Bannon wishes his stomach didn't flip every time he sees the male, but it does. Every single time. He hasn't seen him for two days and he's a sight for sore eyes.

Or is, until Bannon gets a proper look at him. Quill looks exhausted. His black uniform is clean and pressed, his hair neatly tied back in a bun, but under the polish, he's pale and worn out.

He holds open the door for the Warden, then follows his boss to the front of the room. Bannon's concern grows with every step Quill takes. He's in pain. Quill is hiding it like an expert, but he sees it. The tightness around his eyes, the slight hitching of his breath as he walks, the stiffness of his usually fluid movements.

Without casting even the briefest of looks in his direction, Quill takes up position beside the Warden, his hands clasped behind him, his eyes straight ahead, intently focused on the bare wall opposite him.

Duna joins them at the front, mirroring Quill's stance. The Warden may appear weak and pompous, but with Duna and Quill standing to either side, he commands a level of authority he doesn't deserve.

'I understand the day shift are eager to finish so you can visit the mainland,' the Warden begins in his soft, well-spoken tone. He straightens his silk tie, glances at Quill then, getting no reaction, turns back to the room. 'I have a few points I wish to make before you leave. When you are on the mainland you are free to do as you wish. Enjoy your time off, but if you miss the boat back to the island, I will take that as your resignation. I am a fair but firm employer. You get one chance and only one. Isn't that right, Quillan?'

For the first time since he entered the room, Quill's eyes move from the wall, turning to the Warden as he answers. 'Yes sir.'

'Good.'

'Duna, I trust you and your team are ready to take Quillan's place while he is on the mainland?'

'Of course, sir.'

'Efficient as always. Thank you. Now, it's also been brought to my attention, that the division of work may not have been entirely fair over the last few months. That is in no way a reflection on you, Duna. I know Quillan isn't a fan of delegating. It's a quality I admire in him, but also one that is monopolising his time.

'From next week on, he will take a step back from day-to-day guard duties. I trust he has trained you all to an exceptional level. He will be available to assist if needed, but I expect the rest of you to pull your weight. Quillan will only intervene when it is absolutely necessary, and as a last resort. Duna, you will remain in charge of the night shift.'

'Yes, sir.'

For the briefest of moments, she doesn't seem happy with what the Warden just said, but like a well-trained guard, she hides it again.

'Is that clear with everyone?'

The guards nod, Bannon included, even though in his head he wants to scream at Quill. He stares at the guard, looking for some reaction to this news, but apart from a brief clenching of his jaw, he's motionless.

There's no valid reason for the Warden to make this change. The guards work well under Quill. Having him on the floor helps the prison to run smoothly. If he's to be locked away in a room sorting through paperwork, or whatever else the Warden has planned, it's a waste of his talent. He needs to oversee everything personally.

Bannon feels he knows the real reason for this change. He doesn't know why, or how, but that vampire has a hold on Quill. Something he's using to keep Quill on a tight leash. To keep him compliant. The Quill in front of him right now isn't the strong defiant male he's grown to care for. This version is timid.

Scared.

And that hits Bannon deep in his stomach. He forces his fists to unclench before the flames burst free.

'Does anyone have any questions for Quillan?'

Unsurprisingly there's nothing. No one is going to speak up.

'Good,' the Warden says with a satisfied smile on his face, which instantly stokes the fire inside Bannon again.

As if sensing something in the air, Quill looks at him. He looks down and to the right and Bannon catches him discreetly signing *no* as best he can, without drawing attention to what he's doing.

'Do you have anything to add Quillan?'

His attention leaves Bannon as he glances at the Warden again. 'I just want to reiterate what you said about missing the boat back to the island. Same goes for the one leaving here. It heads off in one hour, and won't wait for any latecomers.'

'Good point,' the Warden says, agreeing with Quill. 'I'll let you all clock off and prepare for your night.'

The Warden strides from the room. Quill follows after him, keeping his eyes on the Warden's back as he leaves the room.

BANNON

After the meeting, the guards he works with had dispersed back to their rooms to get ready for the night off the island before boarding the ferry chartered to take them to the mainland. The night shift will be holding the fort while they're gone. It will be their turn for freedom next weekend.

Quill had completely distanced himself from the group by that stage. He sat alone at the back of the boat, his blonde hair blowing around his face as he glared at the dark water.

He didn't speak to anyone on the trip to the mainland, or on the minibus to Wexford. No one had tried to engage him in conversation, leaving him to his silence.

When they get to the hotel, each of the guards check into their rooms, agreeing to meet in the downstairs club in an hour. Bannon's not in the mood to go out.

He's pissed off and isn't the only one. None of the guards will say it around Quill, but the general consensus isn't a happy one. Having Quill on the floor with them, added a level of security none of them wanted to lose. The prisoners respected him and, knowing they would be facing him if they played up, had helped keep them in line.

He'll still be there in that capacity, but it won't be the same.

And Bannon won't be working with him.

That's the part Bannon is most upset about. Well, one of the parts. Watching Quill with the Warden at the meeting had left a cold chill in his flesh. It was creepy. He doesn't know why that word keeps coming to his mind, but he can't shake it. There's something going on, and he can't figure it out.

He's also not thrilled about leaving Sorcha alone in that cell, while they are away. Walking away from her had been so much harder than he thought it would be. She's more than capable of looking after herself, he knows that. But that doesn't help to diminish his worry. It does help that, with such a small group of guards left running the prison, everyone will be on lockdown until Quill and his team return.

Between Quill and Sorcha, this night is going to be a disaster. He just wants to take the two of them somewhere safe, far away from the Warden and the prison. Since there's no chance of that ever happening, the only thing he can do is get this night over with, so he can go back and see her.

Quill is another matter.

He pulls on his jeans and a navy shirt, combs his fingers through his dark hair, smoothing any wayward locks, then closes his eyes. He can do this. He can go downstairs, stand in silence with the rest of the guards, have a few drinks, be ignored, then come back and crash.

Not the best plan for the night, but it's all he has. And that's before he even adds Quill to the mix. He has no idea how Quill is in a social situation when he's off the clock.

237

Does he drink? Dance? Talk?

Then more unhelpful thoughts join in the fun. What if he is with someone tonight? What if he takes someone back to his room with him?

He shakes his head, trying to dislodge those images from his mind.

Time to get this fun evening underway. He leaves his room, making sure the door is closed and locked, before turning to walk down the corridor.

But there he is.

Dressed in black jeans, black boots, and a fitted denim shirt that shows his incredible body, Quill stops him in his tracks. He turns to face him, his long hair out and framing his face. Neither of them moves for a moment, just taking time to look at each other.

He's probably mistaken, but he could swear Quill is looking at him the same way he's looking at Quill. Want. Need.

He opens his mouth to speak, but another door opens, and a tall woman walks out. She takes a second to look at Quill, then Bannon. 'Hello there. You both look lost.'

Quill locks eyes with him briefly, before turning to the woman and giving her a stunning smile. 'Not lost. I'm just heading downstairs.'

'Small world,' she says, walking closer to him. 'Do you want to walk together?'

Quill glances at him again. 'Yeah. Sure.'

'What about your friend?' she asks, smiling over at Bannon.

'He's waiting for someone,' Quill says, guiding the woman along the corridor towards the elevator, leaving Bannon standing outside his room.

He hasn't got a clue what just happened, but whatever it was, it hurt like hell.

QUILL

The woman is doing everything right. She's giving him attention, talking to him, laughing at the right times, listening when he's talking. So why can't he stop looking across the crowded club, desperately trying to catch even the smallest glimpse of Bannon through the crowds.

He's pathetic. Like some loved-up teenager trying to catch the eye of someone he likes. Which he actually is.

What makes him all the more pathetic, is the fact he had the chance to spend the evening with Bannon, but instead of doing what he should have done, he did the opposite.

The woman he's with isn't unattractive in any way. If not for the fact he's hung up on Bannon and stressing about Sorcha, he would have considered himself lucky to have caught her eye.

But he doesn't want her, or her attention.

'Are you in town for long?' she asks before sipping her Martini, her red lipstick leaving a blood-like stain on her glass. Trust him to compare it to blood, instead of something less gory.

'No. Just for the night. You?' He couldn't care less, but it's not her fault he's distracted. The least he can do is be polite.

'The same. I'm here with work.' Her hand lowers from the bar top to gently rest on his knee. 'I guess it was perfect timing bumping into you,' she says, smiling at him. She is beautiful. Her dark hair is a few shades lighter than Sorcha's, but nowhere near as long.

What the fuck is he doing?

'Would you agree?'

He nods absently. He can't remember what she asked. Whatever it was, his nod was the right answer. Her face lights up.

Then she leans across and kisses him. He probably should have been expecting it. They had been talking for nearly two hours. Her soft hand rests on the side of his face, her fingers combing through his hair.

He kisses her back, but again it's out of politeness instead of something he wants. He's such an asshole.

She smiles at him when she pulls back, her fingers still playing with his hair. 'I like your piercings.'

He subconsciously licks his lips, brushing his tongue off the two piercings. 'Thanks.'

'Do you have any more I should know about?'

The crowd parts and he sees Bannon. It looks like he's still nursing the same drink, sitting at a table with three of the other guards, but unable to join in. He looks downright miserable. Being somewhere like this must be seriously difficult for him. How the fuck do you meet anyone when you can't communicate with them?

'Quill?'

He turns his attention back to the woman. Fuck, he can't even remember her name. He's sure she told him. She must have if she knows his name. 'Sorry?'

'I asked about your piercings. How many do you have?'

'Just my lip, tongue, nose, and ears.'

She pouts a little. 'Drat. There was me thinking you might have been a little more adventurous.' She wiggles her eyebrows as she takes another sip of Martini.

'No. I might at some stage, but not yet.'

'Interesting.' She moves her chair closer, then runs her finger over the two rings in his lip. 'I really do like these.' She kisses him again, and this time he makes the mistake of glancing over at Bannon mid-kiss.

Bannon is looking at him. Straight at him as this woman is sticking her tongue in his mouth. The woman groans, shuffling closer to him, her fingers moving through his hair as she kisses him. 'How about we take this somewhere more private?' she asks between kissing his mouth, and nuzzling against his neck.

He looks over towards Bannon again, but he's gone. The rest of the guards are still at the table, drinking and socialising with a few women who have joined them. But no Bannon.

'Is that a yes, or a no?'

It should be a no. If he had seen Bannon sitting at the table where he was a minute before, he would have said no. No question.

But now he's pissed off. About what he doesn't know. Bannon caught him kissing someone else and left. That's his fucking problem! There's nothing between them. A kiss is fuck-all, no matter how much he might want to explore more.

And now Bannon has left.

Fuck him! 'Yeah,' he says, turning his attention back to the woman. 'I think that's a great idea.'

42

BANNON

The whiskey burns as it goes down his throat, the heat tracing down the line of the scar on his neck.

He should have stayed in the bar. Should have ignored the fact that Quill's tongue was down that woman's throat. Had they left just after he did, to go to one of their rooms?

Probably.

It's not like Quill owes him anything. Good luck to him.

Bannon climbs off the bed, grabs another bottle from the mini bar, twisting off the lid. He paces the room, bottle in his hand as that vivid image goes on a replay in his mind. This has to end. He'll drive himself crazy if he keeps going down this path.

What is he saying? He already feels like that ship has sailed.

He groans to himself when there's a knock on the door. It's probably one of his co-workers. He could do without a drunken slagging off, so ignores it. Then there's another knock, this one louder.

Bannon grabs the door handle, pulling the door open a little harder than necessary. It's one of his co-workers all right, but not the one he was expecting.

'Can I come in?'

He steps aside, giving Quill space to come into his room. As Quill pushes past him, Bannon quickly checks his watch. Less than twenty minutes have passed since he left the club. Barely enough time for Quill to have done much, if anything, with that woman.

Bannon hangs back by the door, completely unsure why Quill is here, or what he wants. Let Quill make the first move.

'I've been a dick.'

Bannon takes a few steps closer to Quill, sure he misheard him. He shakes his head, hoping that Quill understands what he means.

'Yeah, I said that. What I did tonight with that woman... it was a mistake. And I mean kissing her. That's all I did. I was just confused. Pissed off too. But that's not her fault. Or yours,' he adds looking at him.

'Things are... complicated in my life. That's no excuse for...' He sighs and shakes his head. 'I'm fucking this up big-time. Fuck! I don't even know what I'm trying to do. All I know is that when I was kissing her, I was wishing she was someone else.'

Bannon is nearly afraid to breathe. He doesn't want to interrupt Quill's train of thought. This is a very different Quill to the one he sees every day at work. He's usually so sure of himself. Seeing him vulnerable as he is right now, is knocking him off balance himself.

Quill turns to face him, his eyes glowing intensely. 'I wanted it to be you, Bannon.' He laughs harshly as he shakes his head. 'You've seriously fucked me up. I have a stunning woman ready and eager to be with me, but I can't get you out of my head. I've never felt...'

Clearly frustrated, Quill scrubs both hands over his hair, clenching them behind his head.

'You and Sorcha...you're both getting to me. In here,' he adds, tapping his temple. 'I don't know what to do, Bannon.'

But Bannon does. Acting on instinct or impulse, Bannon approaches Quill, stopping in front of him. He's never initiated anything with another male, before Quill, but he's not going to overthink this. He knows what he wants, and he's going to go after it.

When Quill lifts his eyes to meet his, Bannon kisses him. Momentarily caught off guard, Quill freezes, but it takes less than a few seconds for him to snap out of it, and kiss Bannon back. He takes control, pushing Bannon back against the wall. This time their kiss is less demanding, almost tender. His hand brushes against Bannon's, taking his hand firmly in his before guiding him over to the bed.

Oh shit!

He doesn't want to freak out, but this is all so new to him, he hasn't got a clue what to do. But Quill senses Bannon's uncertainty.

He sits beside him, their fingers still laced together. 'I want you, but I don't want to assume you feel the same. I know that sounds stupid after you just kissed me, but I want to make sure.'

Bannon looks around for some paper, and finds the complimentary hotel writing paper and pen on the bedside table. His hand is shaking slightly as he writes. Putting his feelings down on paper, seems so much more intense than merely telling him. Where does he even begin?

'Are you attracted to me?' Quill asks, helping him along, and Bannon couldn't be more grateful. He can do this if he's just asked questions. Pouring out his heart and soul on a piece of hotel writing paper doesn't feel right.

'Yes, I am.'

The smile that Quill gives him on reading the words, helps to quash some of his nerves.

'This one is a little more personal, but it's important. Am I the first male you've felt that way about?'

He scribbles the word, moving his hand aside so Quill can read it. 'I thought I was. That's not meant in a bad way at all.'

Bannon points his pen to Quill and raises his eyebrows.

'Me? No. I've been with both sexes. I'm attracted to individuals, not their sex. That's not how I work.'

Bannon nods. He doesn't know how he feels about that piece of information. He suspected Quill would be more experienced than he is, but hearing him say he's been with other males isn't pleasant. He doesn't want to think about Quill with anyone else. He's jealous, and they're not even together.

'I want to take this further,' Quill continues, turning on the bed to face him, his knee pressing against Bannon's thigh, 'But I don't want to rush anything. We have to work with each other at the end of the day. If we fuck this up and do something neither of us are ready for, work is going to be shit for both of us.'

'Go slow?'

'It's not a brush-off,' Quill says quickly. 'I'm going to be blunt here. I want to fuck you Bannon. I want you naked under me right now. I desperately want my dick inside you.'

Bannon blushes before he can stop himself. If anyone else had said that to him, he would have been tempted to punch them, or to make a quick exit from the room. But hearing this from Quill, his dick hardens, and his throat tightens, making swallowing difficult. His first thought is to undress and let him do just that.

'I'll take that blushing as a positive thing. I didn't just freak you out or scare you off then?' Bannon shakes his head *no,* and Quill laughs. 'I'll take that as a definite no. That's a fucking relief.' He cups the side of Bannon's face, drawing him closer, so he can kiss him again.

'I want to get into bed with you,' he says, when they finally draw breath. 'No sex I swear. I just want to be with you, if that's okay?'

Bannon nods again, relief flooding through him. He wants Quill. There are no doubts about that in the slightest. But he's not ready to take that step with him. Not yet.

245

Quill stands, unbuttoning his denim shirt and tossing it onto the chair by the bed. Then the black tank top joins the shirt. Quill kicks off his boots, then pulls off his socks before he unfastens his belt and takes off his black jeans. He leaves on his black fitted boxers, but nothing is going to hide, or disguise the impressive erection Quill has.

An erection Bannon has helped to bring on. The thought of being with him has given Quill a hard on.

Quill leaves him with that thought as he climbs into bed, lying back on the white pillows, his head propped up on his arm. 'You joining me or what?'

Bannon stands, his heart hammering loudly in his chest as he clumsily unbuttons his own shirt. His hands are sweating, which doesn't help the process. Excited nerves take over, turning the simple task of removing his own clothes into an embarrassing fumble. It doesn't help that Quill's eyes are locked on him for every single minute of his shoddy performance.

He finally frees himself from his clothes, leaving on his boxers as Quill did. He's been naked in front of males before, but that was in the gym. It wasn't in front of someone he wants, someone who is looking at him with such appreciation he feels himself blushing again. He's really going to have to get a grip on that annoying habit.

Quill pulls aside the duvet, inviting him into the bed. Bannon slides in beside him, leaving a gap between them as Quill throws the duvet over them again. He hasn't got a clue what to do now. So, instead of acting like a sixty-year-old male, he locks his body in place, terrified to even breathe.

Quill turns on his side, propping his head up on his hand as he smiles down at Bannon. 'You know I won't bite... well, unless you want me to.'

Bannon relaxes a little, but he's freaking out more than he thought he would.

'We're just lying down together. I won't touch you, if you don't want me to. I just...' Quill looks at the wall as he laughs briefly. 'I just want a bit of normal with you. Even just being like this is enough for me right now.' His mismatched eyes turn to him again. 'Things in the prison are so fucked up. Even having a meal with you is impossible with everyone else around, and *him* upstairs.'

Bannon doesn't have to ask who Quill means by *him*. He knows full well the Warden is the main reason Quill is constantly on edge, always worked up, or deeply depressed, and lost in his head. Bannon picks up the notebook from beside the bed, and quickly writes down the question he's been desperate to ask for too long.

'*What does he have on you?*'

Quill reads the words, then shakes his head. 'Nothing.'

'*Bullshit!*'

'What about you?' Quill asks, ignoring his mouthed reply and throwing the question back at him. 'Why are you working there?'

He considers not telling him, but he needs to prove to Quill that he trusts him. Maybe that way, Quill will trust him in return and open up. Maybe not. This is Quill. He rarely does what Bannon expects.

He sits up in the bed and writes out a brief and emotionless explanation. He's never told anyone about this before, but if he's going to tell anyone, Quill and Sorcha would be the only ones on the list.

Bannon passes the page to Quill and watches as the male reads what he wrote. '*I found the wolf who killed my family. I lost control of my powers and incinerated him. The Vampire Council didn't want to have it known that a vampire killed a wolf. They didn't care that the wolf killed my family in the first place. They just wanted the problem to go away. They wanted me to go away.*'

Quill curses under his breath as he scrunches up the page. 'And you were sent to the prison.'

Bannon nods. He's worried that Quill will get up and leave after reading that. Instead, Quill shuffles closer and places his hand over Bannon's. 'That's fucked up. What they did to you - not what you did. Sounds like the fucker who killed your family got off lightly. I'm sorry

Bannon.'

Bannon looks down at Quill's tattooed hand, wrapping around his on the bed. He closes his hand, gently squeezing Quill's. *You okay with me?* he mouths slowly, afraid of the reply.

Quill nods. 'Why wouldn't I be? Got to admit hearing that you've taken a life is a surprise, but I get it, and I don't blame you in the slightest.' He pauses again and takes a deep breath. 'I'm sorry for everything you've been through. You're a good person, Bannon. A rare, genuinely decent male, and you shouldn't be anywhere near the prison. It's toxic there. It ruins any good that is inside anyone who walks through the door.'

Bannon signs *thank you* and Quill smiles widely. 'Hey, I understood that one. I am trying to learn sign language, too, by the way. I know Sorcha twisted my arm to learn, but she shouldn't have had to.'

Bannon writes again, but this time Quill moves closer, and leans over him to read the words as he's writing them. His bare shoulder brushes against his own, and Bannon likes how it feels. *It's a big ask.*

'What? Learning sign language is a big ask?' Quill shakes his head, his blonde hair falling over his blue eye. 'No. It's not. I'll get the hang of it. It'll take time, but I will get it. You shouldn't have to go through all that writing to make yourself heard. I don't want that for you.'

Quill's voice is softer as he speaks. Very different to the harsh Quill he's used to back in the prison. Before he knows what he's doing, Bannon reaches out and moves Quill's hair back from his face, uncovering his blue eye again.

Quill doesn't do or say anything, just gives him time to get used to what's going on between them. Is it really that different being with Quill? He's attracted to Quill. He has no doubt in his mind about that. And kissing him is incredible. He didn't expect someone like Quill to be so gentle, but he keeps surprising him.

'You want to kiss me.'

He nods, even though Quill isn't asking a question.

'Go for it. You're in charge.'

Before he can let fear or doubt ruin this for both of them, he leans forward, resting his hand against the side of Quill's face as he kisses him. Quill kisses him back, but doesn't move in any other way. He just kisses him. When Bannon releases him, the stunning Prime smiles at him. 'You good?'

Bannon nods, sweeping his fingers through Quill's hair.

'I'm not usually a fan of having my hair touched, but I like it when you do it.'

'*Me too,*' he mouths, suddenly unable to stop touching Quill's long hair. Bannon shuffles back down the bed, lying on the pillow as he looks up at Quill. He wants him to lie down and hold him, but doesn't want to ask him to do it.

But Quill is on the same page as he is. He slides down beside him, lying on his side so close they're nearly nose-to-nose. 'Can I hold you?'

Bannon nods, holding his breath as Quill gathers him in his arms, pressing him against his chest. Bannon closes his eyes, losing himself in the warmth and intoxicating scent of this incredible male.

Since he lost his family, he's been wandering, lost and confused. He had no home, no friends or family, no voice. Life had been a day-to-day struggle for so long he can't remember what it's like to just be himself. Just to exist without watching his back, or being self-conscious about his disability.

But lying in Quill's arms, things begin to make sense again. He's safe and protected. And that's not him being weak or defenceless. He can stand up for himself if he needs to, but Quill *sees* him. *Really* sees him. And he's still here. Quill still wants him, even after hearing what he did. Quill hasn't opened up to him about his reason for being at the prison, but he's not taking that personally. It's how Quill is made. He keeps things close.

Bannon slides his arms around Quill's torso, holding on to the male as tight as he's being held himself.

43

QUILL

Thirty-five minutes left before this has to end. Quill pulls Bannon closer to him, loving the feel of his hard body against his. Bannon had slept for a few hours over the night, but Quill had stayed awake. He wasn't going to miss a single second like this with Bannon. As soon as they get back to the prison, he'll be lucky to get ten minutes alone with him. Holding him as he is right now, won't be on the cards.

He kisses the top of Bannon's head and the male releases a long, contented breath as he pulls Quill closer. The fact he's responding to him like that in his sleep, is more than he could have wished for.

He likes Bannon. Likes him a lot. And knowing that Bannon is exploring this new side of himself with Quill, means the world to him. He wants so much more with Bannon. He wants this powerful male on all fours in front of him, as he fucks him hard. He wants to taste him, as Bannon comes down his throat. Wants to feed from Bannon, while his dick is buried deep inside him. Wants their blood, sweat, and cum sliding on their skin, as they spend hours in bed together.

But what he has now will probably be it. And that's okay. If holding Bannon as he sleeps is all he gets to have, he'll be more than happy. It's not like his life is his own to command anyway. Quill knows exactly how he'll die. The only question is simply when it will happen.

Bannon wakes, hugging Quill tightly as he looks up at him. His deep brown eyes are sleepy and fucking gorgeous.

Fuck, this vampire is going to cause him nothing but trouble. 'Morning. You're fucking hot when you're asleep, you know that?'

When Bannon blushes, Quill beams. 'Then you go and blush? Fuck! Even hotter.'

Bannon kisses his chest before rolling off and lying back on the pillow, smiling over at him. *'Did you sleep?'*

He could read Bannon's lips all day and fucking night. 'A bit,' he lies. 'We'll have to go soon. We've already missed breakfast and lunch. We're going to have to come up with some convincing story why both of us went AWOL.'

Bannon reaches behind him, taking the notebook and pen from the bedside table. He props himself up on one elbow, and Quill watches as he writes. *'We both got lucky?'*

Quill laughs as he reads. 'Wouldn't be a lie.' He pulls Bannon down into his arms again. 'I really don't want to get up.'

Bannon nods. He holds the notebook up in front of him and writes quickly. *'Do you think Sorcha's okay?'*

He doesn't know why, but the fact Bannon is thinking about her is a bit of a relief. He wasn't sure how to broach that subject with Bannon. 'She's tough. She'll be fine. Duna will leave her alone. She sticks to the lockdown when they're covering the prison.'

Bannon licks his lips, frowning before he writes again. *'Is there something going on between you?'*

'Me and Sorcha? No. I...' he closes his eyes and curses under his breath. 'I did too much to her. Hurt her too much. How about you and her?'

Bannon frowns as he writes again. *'I like her. I think you like her too.'*

Quill reads the words as Bannon is writing. He tenses for a few seconds as he reads, but when he looks up at Bannon, he can't see any hostility. 'Yeah. I think we both have a soft spot for her. Is that going to be a problem?'

He writes again. *'She told me she likes both of us.'*

Quill reads the words over a few times. He thought that Sorcha might like Bannon, but not him. Not after everything he did to her. His introduction to her had been as bad as you can get. After he flogged her three times, he wouldn't have blamed her if she hated him.

That's okay with him, though. If she likes Bannon enough to accept that he'll be around too, that would be enough.

'You look surprised.'

Quill nods as he looks from the page to Bannon. 'I was jealous of you two. I saw you training together, she was learning sign language, and you were always in that cell with her. I just assumed you were the one she wanted. I've done some terrible things to her. I... ' What else can he say about that? It's something he can never take back, no matter how much he wants to.

'She understands how things work in the prison. She doesn't blame you.' Bannon smiles, then kisses him. When he releases him, Bannon gestures between the two of them. *'She likes both of us,'* he mouths.

'She should blame me. Should hate me.' Quill lies back on the pillow, his hands behind his head. 'Fuck! Is that even possible? Liking both of us? I mean... would you be okay with that? Fuck it! We can't really have this conversation without her. Scrap that. We shouldn't be having that conversation at all, full stop.'

He turns over on his side to face Bannon. 'This is an impossible situation. You know that as much as I do. The Warden is watching everything. You heard what he said at the meeting. I can't be as hands-on in the prison as I used to be. I won't even be working with you anymore, let alone have time to spend with you and her.'

'Why did he change things?'

Quill pauses, trying to figure out what to say. He can't tell him the Warden was jealous, and wanted to distance him from everyone who he could possibly get close to. He can't tell him his life is in the hands of that bastard, and he's powerless to do anything about it. He can't tell him that if he disobeys the rules, there's a strong chance Quill won't see any of them again.

'Who the fuck knows how that asshole thinks! But he's the boss. He's in charge.'

Bannon doodles on the corner of the page for a minute before writing again. *'I wasn't planning any of this. But I don't want to walk away.'*

Quill never thought he'd have someone say those things to him. It doesn't change anything though. 'We better get dressed. If we miss that boat, we're both in the shit.'

He pushes upright on the bed. It's time to get himself back into the real world, back to a world where Bannon and Sorcha are far away from him.

'So that's it?'

He looks at the words on the page Bannon holds up in front of him.

'I don't want it to be, but it's not going to be easy. I'll do what I can to see you and Sorcha, but I don't know how possible that will be.'

He gets out of bed and pulls on his clothes, trying to keep his eyes off Bannon, lying on the bed looking fucking gorgeous. At least they didn't have sex. If he had taken that step with him, Quill knows it would be so much harder to walk away. Even having those few hours holding him, kissing him...

He curses himself. Reminiscing about what happened will do fuck-all to help him move on.

'I'm going to get ready for dinner with the others, before we head back. See you down there in ten minutes?'

Bannon nods, but looks as miserable as Quill feels.

Quill opens Bannon's door, checking the corridor is clear before he leaves. He unlocks his own bedroom door, undresses quickly and showers, desperate to remove Bannon's scent from his skin, but also missing it the minute it washes down the drain.

44

QUILL

The trip back from the Wexford hotel to the boat, is the longest Quill has experienced. For each of those torturous minutes, he'd forced himself to avoid looking in Bannon's direction. It's painful enough being in the same minibus as him and not being able to talk to him. Not being able to touch him.

Bannon is avoiding him, too, staring blankly out the window of the bus. Dinner at the hotel before they left, had been awkward as fuck. Bannon was alone, trapped in silence as the others talked around him. Quill had tried to include him, but it wasn't easy. Especially when all he wanted to do was take him back upstairs.

He's such a fool. He shouldn't have called by Bannon's room last night. All it's done is make the pull to the male so much stronger.

Usually, it's a sexual attraction. A need to fuck someone, then move on, before he's back in the prison again.

He had that offered to him on a plate last night by that woman. Instead, he'd been more than content to hold Bannon, to touch him, to kiss him. He can't ever remember being in a bed with someone and not having sex.

He wants to take that step with Bannon, but last night wasn't the time for that. Bannon isn't someone you rush things with. If Bannon wants to have sex with him, it will be when he's entirely comfortable. It has to be on Bannon's terms.

The flat landscape of the peninsula stretches out in the darkness surrounding them. They're close. Then he sees it. In the distance, the imposing presence of the Warden's house stands out in stark contrast to the fields around it. Many of the dozens of windows in the side facing them are lit, like eyes in the darkness.

He doesn't doubt that the house was spectacular in its day. But knowing what goes on in there, gives the mansion a malevolence, a sinister air that only distance can help ease.

But as much as he hates the Warden's mansion, he needs to go back. It's got nothing to do with his job, or any obligation to the Warden. Sorcha is in there.

When Bannon had brought her name up when they were in bed together, it was like a piece of a puzzle had clicked into place. A puzzle he didn't know was missing a piece.

It's a complicated puzzle, but one he can't get out of his head. Knowing that Bannon is on the same page is just adding to his predicament. He likes Bannon and Sorcha. Bannon likes him and Sorcha. Sorcha likes Bannon. And it seems, by some miracle, that Sorcha likes him too. Or so he's been led to believe. He still can't quite accept that Sorcha could feel anything other than contempt for him.

He'd thought about being with both of them, but never contemplated it being anything other than some fantasy, that would play out when he's alone in his room.

A fantasy that could never become reality.

The minibus comes to a stop, knocking him out of his thoughts. He stirs himself back into the real world, getting to his feet and leaving the bus first. Bannon and the other guards follow, the silence as ominous as the house waiting for them across the water.

He feels Bannon looking at him and, unable to resist, glances at him. His mask is back in place, his handsome face showing no emotion, but his eyes betray him. Quill can see the sadness that's always present. It kills him that Bannon has this sadness in him.

He's proud of how far Bannon has come since he started working in the prison. He wouldn't have given him a day. He was convinced he'd be beaten down and would run for the hills at the first opportunity.

But he'd proven him wrong at every single stage. He's a strong, yet firm hand. A quiet threat that everyone recognises and obeys.

Was *he* the same when he'd started in the prison, all those decades ago? Had he been weak and seen as a pushover? He can't remember back to that male. It was a long time ago. But he knows the person he is today is all down to his time spent in the prison. He knows the coldness, the hardness, the unemotional side of himself that he used to threaten inmates and guards alike, was forged by surviving that place.

And now Bannon has been tarnished in the same way.

'Quill! Hey, Boss? You coming?'

He glares when someone nudges him in the arm but manages to hold back from decking the guard. 'What?'

'We're heading to the boat.'

'Right.' He follows after the others, all too aware he's been looked at like he's some fucking idiot. All except for Bannon, who flashes him a tight smile, before boarding the boat.

Once back on the island, everyone disappears off to their own rooms, Bannon included. Quill contemplates checking in with Duna and getting her report, but it can wait until his shift the next day.

He dumps his bag on his bed, then sits on the edge of the mattress staring at the bracelet around his wrist. Tomorrow will be different. The Warden had made that point crystal clear. He's to take a supervisory role from now on. It's not what he wants to do. The Warden is jealous. That's what it comes down to. He doesn't want Quill to do his job, because he wants him all to himself.

Greedy fucker!

Too bad Quill isn't as obedient as he would like. He'll do what's expected of him. He'll step back, let the other guards do the day-to-day stuff, while he oversees. It's going to be fucking boring, but he'll do what he's told. What he isn't going to do is stay away from Bannon and Sorcha. Not a fucking chance in hell!

He'll just have to be careful about when he visits her cell with Bannon. He can still roster Bannon to Sorcha, that won't be a problem. It's his own movements around the prison that he'll have to be careful about.

There are no cameras around the cells - something that had always annoyed him. Having no cameras there put his men at risk. But having no cameras there, also meant the Warden could turn his back on any incident between the guards and the inmates.

Until now, he had disagreed with the Warden's decision. Now he's going to use it to his advantage. He knows the location of every other camera, and knows this prison inside and out. He can make this work. He has to make this work. Whatever *this* is.

Quill lies back on his bed and closes his eyes. He's exhausted, his mind racing as it always does, going through different scenarios and weighing up the risks. He's not bothered about himself. The part that's giving him a headache is the Warden. If he even gets a sniff that there's something going on with the three of them, he'll put a stop to it.

That's what's scaring him - the Warden's potential reaction. There's every chance he'd kill Bannon and Sorcha. And that's if they were lucky.

MURT

Now back in his own clothes, Murt wanders through the underground prison lost in his thoughts. The prisoners had been taken up to the main residence, so they could get their first real meal in far too long. Faced with the option of a bullet or compliance, three of the original four guards were still on board. One hadn't been keen on the idea of releasing the wolves, so Davyn had taken care of him, adding another body to his count for the day.

If anyone had any lingering doubts about Davyn's seriousness, that final act had permanently quelled them. He stops at one of the cells. He's not even sure if they are cells, in the true sense of the word. There are no bars on the door. No locks either. The inmates could come and go as they pleased, choosing to stay in their cell-like rooms, or to stay in the communal hall. Neither option offered them freedom, but, according to Rowan, they had been left to their own devices for the most part.

He stops at Rowan's room, and leans against the door. Rowan is sitting on the edge of his bed, hands clasped on his legs as he looks around his space.

'You okay?'

Rowan jumps, startled by Murt's sudden appearance. 'Don't go sneaking up on me like that. You scared the life out of me!'

'Sorry.'

'And to answer your question, yes. I am okay. I'm sorry about Sorcha. Truly sorry. I had no idea.'

'How could you know? You've been here for years. Just like everyone else here.' He pauses as he looks around him. 'I can't believe our people are being kept like this.'

'Oh, this is nothing Murt,' Rowan says, getting to his feet. 'Level Two is worse. Far worse. So, cousin, what's the grand plan now?'

'Davyn owns this place now, and he's not planning on keeping it running, for obvious reasons. But he's also not keen on just opening the doors and letting everyone run free.'

'Worried about who exactly is locked away in here, huh?'

'Yeah. It'll take time to process everyone. Make sure you're all set up to carry on with your lives.'

'And you think a vampire can offer that to us? No offence Murt, but our dealings with vampires, of late, haven't been all too encouraging.'

'Davyn is different. He was raised in chains, so had no love for his father, or anything he was doing. He has now taken charge of his father's castle, and is turning it into somewhere wolves and vampires alike can be safe. Darkhaven is somewhere I think myself and my clan can call home. He'd like to open the doors to everyone here, too.'

Murt lets Rowan think about that for a minute or two. It's a lot to take in, and a lot to consider. He can't see they have much option though. The wolves here will need time to adjust to life again. Darkhaven is the perfect place to do that.

'And what would this vampire want in return?'

'Nothing. I swear to that. If you don't trust him, or the Blackjacks, I can accept that. In your position, I'd be hard pressed to trust them. But you know me, Rowan. Trust me. Darkhaven is somewhere you can be safe. Somewhere you can find your feet again. Plus, there are acres of land around the castle. Your wolf can run for miles in safety.'

That brings a huge smile to Rowan's face. 'Now you're talking Murt! You know how to win me over, don't you?'

He's relieved to hear that. He thought that final point might tip the scales in Darkhaven's favour. There wouldn't be many wolves who could resist all that space to run free. 'So, you'll come back with us?'

'Why not! Anything has to be better than here. I suppose you want me to help convince the others?'

'Do you think they'll agree?'

Rowan nods as he joins Murt at the door to his room. 'I think I can convince them. Are you coming back, too?'

'Not right now. We need to check through the records from the warden. There are two more prisons out there and Sorcha is in one of them. We're not going to stop until we find her.'

SORCHA

As time has no meaning in the prison, Sorcha has no idea how long it's been since she last saw Quill and Bannon. She knew they were going away for the weekend, but it felt a lot longer. Maybe the Warden had moved Quill to another job? Maybe Quill had moved Bannon to another job? Maybe she'll never see either of them again?

Maybe Duna will be tasked with her care from now on?

She quickly pushes that thought aside. She doesn't want to consider that she won't see Bannon again. Quill either, although she still can't quite figure out what's going on between her and that vampire. There are moments Quill acts like someone with independent thought, only to switch back to trained guard dog.

Perhaps he's been here too long, under the Warden's thumb, just taking his orders then passing them on. Perhaps, like so many of the other prisoners, he'd become institutionalised, unable to operate in *normal* conditions outside these walls and their rules.

If that's the case, her and Bannon are asking too much from him. He may not be able to accept anything they can offer him. Quill might just be a lost cause.

She doesn't want that future for Bannon. There's still hope for him. Still a chance for him to be untarnished by this place.

Sorcha jumps to her feet when the door opens but, instead of Bannon, it's Quill. For someone who's been away from here for a night, he still looks stressed and pissed off.

He dumps a uniform on the table, the sound of something hard hitting the surface confusing her. Quill gestures for her to get up and sit at the table.

'Where's Bannon?' she asks, settling in on the hard chair. She carefully unfolds the uniform, finding a plastic container hidden in the material. She wasn't expecting the head guard to continue replacing her usual meals with real food, but he surprises her every day by doing just that. Today he's spoiling her with roast beef, Yorkshire pudding, and vegetables.

'What did I do to deserve this?'

'You want out of the deal we made?'

'Of course not!' She knows there's nothing she can do if he decides to whip her again. He can kill her if the mood takes him, and no one would bat an eyelid. He's the muscle. The brains are upstairs somewhere, pulling his strings. 'I'm just not in the habit of trusting vampires. Especially ones who get off on torturing others for fun.'

His eyes narrow as she says that. 'It's my job. Shut up and eat.'

'Okay! Fine, I'll eat. What's crawled up your ass today?

'Look around you Wolf. You're in a fucking prison! It's all about rules. My rules and the Warden's rules. Now eat your fucking dinner!'

She does as she's told, instead of continuing the back-and-forth. There's something off with him today. He turns his attention to the floor, interrogating the concrete with his glare as she digs into her dinner.

'So, are you going to tell me where Bannon is, or is he on some big top-secret mission?' she asks around a mouthful of moist, succulent beef.

'I assigned him to another task. You're not the only prisoner here. Why are you so interested anyway? You worried about him?'

There's a note of jealousy in his tone that catches her off guard. 'I'm just curious Officer. So, how was your night off?'

He frowns at her. 'What?'

'Your night away from here. How was it? You hook up with anyone?'

'What the fuck does that have to do with you?'

She holds up her hands. 'Hey! I'm just making conversation. It's a perfectly reasonable thing to ask.'

His frown eases a little as he calms down. He's particularly stressed today for some reason.

'I've been ordered to distance myself.' He surprises her with the unexpected comment.

Sorcha finishes chewing as she processes that. Quill only takes orders from the Warden. Had Quill's boss seen the change in his demeanour over the last few weeks? Had he noticed some of the darkness had left Quill?

Probably. God forbid anyone should have even the smallest semblance of happiness in here.

'Distance yourself from who?'

'Everyone. He wants me to put my *skills* to better use.'

She lowers her fork at the venom in his voice. He's really pissed off, but thankfully, not at her. There's no need to ask what *skills* he's referring to. After what he did to try and put an end to her *interrogations*, she has no doubts he's not on board with this plan. 'What are you going to do?'

He lifts his head, his unusual eyes glowing softly. 'I don't have a choice.'

He's more than just pissed off. He's devastated, and not even trying to hide it.

'What do you want to do?'

He laughs bitterly as he shakes his head. 'What do I want? Have a look around you. Do you really think that matters?'

Sorcha turns around in her seat to face him. 'Forget where we are just for a minute. If you had a choice, what would you do? Just humour me. Please.'

Quill looks like he's about to argue, but sighs as if he has the weight of the world on his shoulders.

'I'd go for a run,' she says, taking the lead, to try and convince him to open up to her. For some reason, she had missed him while he was away. Her attraction and relationship with Bannon - whatever it is, makes sense. This pull to Quill doesn't. But just because it makes no sense, doesn't mean she's going to ignore it.

Yes, he'd hurt her badly. Yes, he'd been brutal and cruel. But he'd also saved her from more of the same. Deceived the Warden in order to help her, putting himself at risk.

She's drawn to him in a totally unexpected way. Over the last few weeks, he's become more than just the head guard who hurt her. Now he's Quill.

But that doesn't explain why she wants to kiss him.

Bannon is sweet, and kind, and gorgeous. Being attracted to him, being with him is easy. It makes sense. But she has to admit Quill is more attractive than she initially thought. She even finds his messy bun endearing, which is a new one for her. He may be the opposite of Bannon on the surface, but they're more alike than they probably realise.

And his eyes...

Those uniquely beautiful eyes were the first thing she noticed about him, but up close she was lost in them. Completely and utterly lost in spite of her best efforts to resist the pull.

'Not here,' she says, trying to get her train of thought back on track. 'I mean the mountains. Maybe along a headland. Somewhere without any boundaries or walls. Just open space where I could run free.'

He drops his arms to his side, before crossing them again. He's not being defensive. She can see that. It's more that he's not sure how to act right now. 'As a wolf?'

'Of course, as a wolf.' She twists one of the bands around her wrists as she smiles to herself, lost in the fantasy. 'I can't explain what it's like, Quill. Just to feel the grass beneath my paws, the wind through my fur, all the scents and sounds around me. It's the only time I feel truly alive. Truly at peace. Frequent hot showers, regular meals, and a comfy bed are all on the list, too, don't get me wrong. But to run with my wolf like that, would be the top of my list.'

When he doesn't say anything for a good minute, she goes back to her dinner. But she's lost her appetite. Thinking about her wolf always kills her appetite.

'I'd fly.'

When he speaks, his voice is barely above a whisper.

'But you can fly here, can't you?'

Quill shakes his head. 'Only if I really have to, as part of my job. I'm not allowed to fly just for the sake of it.'

'Where would you fly?' She never knew that about Quill. She assumed he could just release his wings and fly whenever he wanted. Not being allowed to fly is keeping a part of himself locked away - just like with her wolf.

When he smiles, she is speechless. He is stunning when he smiles. 'The place where I grew up has mile-after-mile of wild coastline. I used to fly over the cliffs, down to the ocean and soar over the waves. I fucking loved the feel of the spray on my wings. Nothing can compare to that.'

His smile fades, and he turns his attention back to the concrete. Quill stays where he is, the silence wrapping around both of them, neither willing to disturb it.

There's definitely more to this vampire than she originally thought. There's a sadness deep inside that she just caught a brief glimpse of. And for that she's grateful.

Then he lifts his head and looks at her and his glowing eyes lock on to her. Vampires' eyes glow when they're angry. She's seen it a few times when she's hurt one of the other guards.

Perfect! Has she just managed to piss him off, even more than he was when he first came in? That was, by no means, her intention. But she's quickly learning that there's no rhyme or reason when it comes to Quill.

No walk for her today so. Accepting that she's marked her cards with him, Sorcha turns towards her bed.

He pushes off the wall and slowly walks over to her, peering down at her with a strange look on his face. She has no idea what's going on, but she doesn't turn away, doesn't back down from whatever this is.

'Thank you, Sorcha.'

Now she's clearly hallucinating. 'Excuse me?'

He takes a step closer, bringing himself right in front of her. He's so close she can feel the heat coming off his body. 'I'd forgotten what it was like.'

'Forgotten what?'

'What it's like to be free.'

She has no idea what's going on, but whatever it is, she's curious to see where he's going with this. He's not angry. So why are his eyes still glowing? When he leans forward, Sorcha could swear her heart stops for a second, but then he backs away, putting distance between them again.

'Do you want to kiss me?'

He lifts his head so fast she wouldn't be surprised if he got whiplash. 'What?'

'Do you want to kiss me? I might be reading this all wrong, but I could swear that's where this is heading.'

He opens his mouth, then frowns, closing it again as he shakes his head. 'I'm not doing this with you.'

'Not doing what? Talking about this, or kissing me?'

'Either. Both.'

'Would it make a difference if I said I wouldn't stop you, if you did kiss me?'

'No.'

'It wouldn't? Why?'

'Not stopping me isn't the same as agreeing. I have a rule about guards and prisoners. I'm not going to blur the lines, unless you give me permission. I'm not that much of an asshole,' he adds with a shrug.

Having this massive guard ask her for permission to kiss her, is a pleasantly unexpected turn of events. One she appreciates, especially given her surroundings. 'I absolutely give you my permission to blur the lines.'

He seems a little surprised by her response, but recovers quickly. His hand grips the back of her head, holding her firmly against him as his lips crush against hers, the piercings to either side pressing against her.

Then he suddenly stops, taking a step back. 'Right.'

Sorcha laughs. She doesn't know why. It's completely the wrong reaction, but his confused comment just brings it out. 'Okay. Not quite sure what *right* means.'

Quill crosses his arms as he glares at the ground. 'Yeah.'

'Yeah? First *right* and now *yeah*. Do you want to try a full sentence?'

Nothing. Just a lot of frowning and staring at the floor. This isn't how she was expecting him to react after they kissed. Fair enough she hadn't thought about any post-kiss reactions from either side, but a *right* and a *yeah* wouldn't have been on the cards at any stage.

Quill nods to himself, then finally looks up at her. 'That felt right.' He smiles at her and nods again. 'Yeah, it felt right.'

'Oh,' she says by way of a reply. 'So that's what you meant by *right* and *yeah*. Just for future reference, it might come in handy if you actually finish, or even start the sentence, before you let it out.'

'Noted.' He places his hand against the keypad, and she hears the locks disengage.

'Hang on! Is that it? You're going?'

'I've got work to do.'

'So, you kiss me, say it felt right, then leave.'

'You'd prefer I said it felt wrong?'

'No! Of course not. And you know that's not what I mean. Can you not stay? Maybe talk for a bit?'

'About what?'

Frustrated, she waves her arms dramatically between the two of them. 'The kiss of course!'

'Right.'

'I swear you're the single most infuriating vampire I've ever met!' So, she may not have met many vampires, outside of the prison walls, but of the ones she had, Quill tops that particular chart. She doesn't think he's putting it on, either, to get a rise out of her. He's just not one for talking about what's going on in his head.

Without a reply, he opens the door, slipping out of her cell before locking it again. She goes back over to her bed, then lies down and closes her eyes.

It felt right.

He won't get an argument from her on that point. It *had* felt right. That fact had confused Quill too, but that confusion can only be a good thing. Perhaps he didn't expect to like kissing her? Perhaps for Quill, the idea of kissing a wolf was unpleasant? It wasn't necessarily something she would have given much thought to, until she met Quill and Bannon.

Now she can think of nothing else.

Sorcha smiles as she brushes her fingers over her lips. She still taste him, still feel his demanding kiss, still shivers at the memory of his pierced tongue probing her mouth.

It was one hell of a kiss. So was the one with Bannon. Both vampires had managed to remove her from her stagnant life for a few moments and make her feel like she mattered.

Both of them.

She groans, rolling over on the bed and burying her face in the pillow. Talk about your feast or famine situation. But if given the choice, could she pick one over the other?

It takes less than two seconds to make up her mind. No. If this was the outside world and she was in this situation, she'd want both males.

In here, a kiss from each may have been as far as this will go, but that changes nothing. Both Bannon and Quill are worth it.

BANNON

He wasn't expecting to see Quill today. After the Warden's staff meeting, he assumed Quill would be squirrelled away in his office watching proceedings on the security cameras. So, when he appeared in the break room while Bannon was having his coffee, he'd been both surprised and delighted, especially when Quill beckoned for him to come with him.

Bannon wants to ask what's going on, but Quill is marching along the corridors, not giving him a chance to make eye contact, let alone have the time to mouth any question.

His confusion grows when Quill stops at Sorcha's cell, looking both ways down the corridor, before opening the cell and ushering Bannon inside.

Sorcha gets to her feet, his own confusion mirrored on her face, when the two guards slip into her cell, Quill closing the door behind them.

'What's wrong?'

'I'm not good at this sort of stuff, so I'm just going to lay it out in black and white. A few truths came out while we were away from here.'

Bannon's heart speeds up as Quill speaks. He's going to tell Sorcha what they spoke about. It's not a bad thing in the slightest, just completely unexpected. He assumed after the way Quill left his room that it was done. Even though Quill had talked about taking things slowly, the way he abruptly left, had quashed any ideas of exploring their relationship further, and had killed any hope.

'What sort of truths?'

Quill looks from him to Sorcha as he nods to himself, maybe getting up the courage to speak the words. 'We all seem to be attracted to each other.'

The two males stare at Sorcha as she frowns. There's no response for a good minute, before she crosses her arms, facing them. 'You're attracted to each other?'

Bannon nods, his eyes on Quill as he responds.

'And to you,' Quill says quietly, almost like an afterthought.

Sorcha silently looks at the two of them, her arms still crossed and a frown on her face. There's another awkward silence as she continues to look at them, before finally smiling. 'Right.'

'That's it?' Quill says. '*Right*?'

'It worked for you, didn't it? I'm pretty sure that's what you said after you kissed me.'

Bannon didn't realise they'd kissed. He should have guessed they did, but it never crossed his mind for some reason. He gestures between the two of them.

'Yeah,' Quill says, answering his question. 'We kissed about an hour ago. You going to tell me you two didn't kiss?'

'Oh, we did,' Sorcha says, before he can reply. 'So, I've kissed the two of you. I guess the question is - have you two kissed?'

'Yes,' Bannon signs, trying to have at least a bit of a say in the conversation.

'Very interesting,' Sorcha says with a wicked smile. 'Very interesting indeed. Should I ask if you've gone further than that?'

'We slept together. While we were away. No sex though,' Quill says. He glances over at him. 'Not yet.'

Bannon swallows as his throat dries. Two small words, and he's getting excited. Thankfully, Sorcha speaks again, taking his mind off what Quill is planning with his *not yet* reply.

'Well, just to put my own cards on this delightful and unexpected table. Even taking into account the fact that one of you can be an asshole at times, I have to admit I'm rather fond of both of you. Incredibly fond of you.'

'I take it I'm the asshole,' Quill says.

'Well, it's hardly going to be Bannon now, is it?'

Quill flashes her a sarcastic smile. 'Thanks'

'My pleasure. So, now that we've got a table covered in a lot of cards, what next?'

Quill leans back against the wall, his tight posture relaxing, now they're all on the same slightly confusing page. 'I honestly don't know. What I do know is that I'm not willing to walk away from either of you. Even taking into account how irritating one of you is.'

Sorcha grins at him. 'I take it I'm the irritating one.'

'Well, it's hardly going to be Bannon now, is it?' he says, parroting her earlier comment.

'No,' Sorcha says, slipping her hand into Bannon's. Bannon tightens his grip on her hand. Nice to know he's not irritating, or an asshole. It just makes this situation all the more bizarre. Sorcha and Quill have clashed quite a few times. Maybe he's the calm in their storm.

'Things aren't straightforward in here,' Quill says, getting the conversation back on track. 'The Warden could throw a spanner in the works at any minute. He's already told me to take a step back from the day-to-day menial tasks.'

Quill's face changes, a cold anger taking over, much the same as it does for Bannon when that vampire is mentioned.

'I have to do what he says... to a certain degree. But there are no cameras outside of, or in the cells. I can still come here every day. I just have to be careful that I'm not caught. I'll leave the roster the same for you Bannon. If we do that, one or other of us - if not both - should be able to come here every day.' He shrugs, looking at them with a sadness in his eyes. 'It's all we can do.'

Sorcha reaches out, taking Quill's hand in hers. 'I'll take whatever I can get. I'm in the worst place on Earth,' she says with a short laugh. 'Yet I've somehow managed to find you two. How the hell does that happen?'

Bannon smiles at her words, then takes Quill's other hand in his, completing the circle.

'Wasn't expecting this either,' says Quill. 'But I'm not prepared to walk away from it.'

'Me too,' Bannon mouths when they look at him.

'Well, even if I wasn't locked in here, I wouldn't want to walk away either.' Sorcha laughs as she grips their hands. 'Two vampires and a wolf. What could possibly go wrong?'

48

QUILL

He's tired, hungry, and desperately wants his bed. He was called away just after lunch by the Warden and hadn't been allowed back to the prison until just now. He had thought about going to the prison to see Sorcha and Bannon but couldn't bear to be near them just yet.

He needed a shower first and something to eat. Quill groans as someone knocks on his door just as he steps out of the shower. Fuck! If it's Duna he's going to lose his temper. He's on the edge and could do without anyone pushing him. He quickly grabs a pair of boxers, slipping them on before he opens the door.

But it's not Duna. He steps aside as Bannon pushes into his room. He's still in his uniform so must have just finished his shift.

Bannon takes a moment to examine Quill's chest, no doubt noticing the new bite marks and cuts.

'How did the rest of the shift go?'

'Fine,' Bannon mouths.

Quill narrows his eyes. 'You're pissed off. Why?'

Bannon gestures to the visible teeth marks on his skin. *'That.'*

'It's nothing. Forget it.' He hates brushing off Bannon like that but it's not something he's going to discuss with the male. Not ever if he has his way.

Bannon reaches for his notebook, no doubt fully prepared to write a lengthy essay on why it's far from nothing, but Quill stops him by closing the distance between them.

'I said forget it. I don't want to waste time talking about it. I have a meeting with Duna in fifteen minutes. Did you come here to have a go at me, or did you want something?'

Bannon locks onto his eyes as he reaches for his notebook again. He writes a quick note then passes it to Quill.

'I can't stop thinking about you. Can't stop thinking about the hotel and sleeping with you like that. I can't get you out of my head, Quill.'

Quill doesn't know what to say. He wasn't expecting Bannon to be so forward with him. 'Is that right? I probably should admit I'm on the same page as you. It was a good night.'

Quill freezes as Bannon steps closer, his breath warm on Quill's flesh as he looks at Quill's lips. Bannon kisses him, gently pushing him back towards his bed.

Bannon moves back, waiting until Quill is looking at him before he mouths, *'I want you, Quill.'*

He swallows but his throat is dry. Bannon isn't even touching him and he's turning to putty. He doesn't know what Bannon wants to do or is planning on doing, but whatever it is, he'll let him take the lead. He *needs* Bannon to take the lead. It can't happen any other way – for himself and, more importantly, for Bannon.

'What do you want?'

Bannon glances down at Quill's groin before looking back at him, his eyebrows raised.

Fuck! Is Bannon asking if he can give him a blowjob? Hand job? Look at his dick? Whatever he feels ready to do, Quill has no problem letting him do it.

'Take what you want Bannon.' He not used to someone wanting him like this so Bannon isn't the only one venturing into new territory.

Bannon keeps his eyes away from him as he carefully pulls down Quill's boxers. He steps out of his underwear, then sits on the edge of the bed when Bannon points in that direction.

Ignoring Quill's very obvious hard-on, Bannon kneels in front of him then kisses him. It's almost as if Bannon is trying to put him at ease.

Quill leans back a little, resting his weight on his arms as Bannon turns his attention to his groin. He can't stop looking at Bannon. He has no idea what the male wants to do, but he can't wait to find out. He just needs to make sure he doesn't pass out from not breathing or has a heart attack while he's waiting. The anticipation is torturous.

Bannon reaches out, running his long fingers along Quill's length. It was barely a touch but Quill's dick twitches in response. When Bannon smiles at his reaction Quill bites back the curse. Bannon is fucking stunning.

He wraps his hand around Quill's dick, moving up and down his length, the pressure too fucking good. He knows exactly what he's doing.

Then Bannon crouches over, licking the tip of Quill's dick. 'Oh fuck! Jesus, Bannon.'

The gorgeous male glances at him as he does it again, his stunning brown eyes glowing when Quill curses in approval again.

'Suck me Bannon.' He didn't mean to say that aloud. The last thing he wants to do is put pressure on Bannon, but the male doesn't hesitate. His tongue explores every inch of Quill's dick, his confidence growing by the minute. Bannon is enjoying what he's doing. Really fucking enjoying it.

Quill gasps, leaning back on his arms when his dick slides into Bannon's mouth. 'Fuck, that is so hot Bannon.'

Clearly Bannon feels the same. One hand firmly grips the base of Quill's dick, the other massaging his balls as he devours every inch of Quill's dick. 'Fuck, Bannon!' The shout is barely contained when Bannon moves from his balls to massage just behind them, applying the right amount of pressure to have him on the verge of coming.

For his first time he's a fucking natural. Not only that – he's really getting into it, using his tongue, lips, and hands to drive Quill to the edge before slowing down again. Quill is transfixed watching Bannon sucking him off. Seeing him doing that to him makes the experience so much more intense. He can't keep his eyes off Bannon.

'Fuck! Who knew you'd be a tease.'

Bannon releases him long enough to flash him a quick but very sexy smile before devouring him again.

And the male takes it all, right up to his balls. Holding him firmly in place, Bannon keeps his eyes locked on Quill as he sucks him hard.

He's so close. Damn, he was close when Bannon got onto his knees in front of him. Quill slowly reaches out to touch Bannon's head. He brushes his fingers through Bannon's hair, gripping a handful at the back. He's going on instinct here and Bannon seems to be more than on board with that.

Quill's hips decide to take over, thrusting his dick into Bannon's mouth. Still looking up at him, Bannon's eyes burn brightly.

'I'm going to come Bannon.' He assumes Bannon will ease up, maybe let him finish himself by hand, but Bannon isn't done yet. He wasn't expecting to come in Bannon's mouth, but that's exactly what happens. Quill's orgasm rips through him, knocking the air from his lungs.

He's vaguely aware of Bannon's hand on his chest, supporting him as he rides it out. Bannon's mouth around his dick as he comes draws it out much longer than usual. The male doesn't let up, his mouth working Quill until he's got nothing left.

He didn't realise he'd closed his eyes, but when he eventually opens them, Bannon is crouched in front of him, smiling.

Quill blows out a long breath as he curses. 'Fuck me, Bannon. Where the hell did that come from?'

Bannon shrugs, looking a little embarrassed.

'That was fucking amazing Bannon. Thank you.' That was intense. So much more intense than any other blowjob he's ever had. The difference was Bannon.

Bannon fumbles in his pocket for his notebook. *'Thanks for letting me do that. It was amazing. I really loved it.'*

'Glad to hear it.' Quill leans forward to kiss him again. He's never kissed someone after they've swallowed his cum. Tasting himself on Bannon's tongue is so hot. He's sorely tempted to throw Bannon on his bed and fuck him right here and now.

But he'll have to wait. Small steps at Bannon's pace. Besides, he's run out of time. 'I'm sorry but I have to go. I've got a meeting.'

Bannon nods, pushing to his feet, then holding out his hand to help Quill up. He accepts the help. His damn body still feels like it's made of jelly after what Bannon did to him. He loved what just happened between them, but having to run off straight after, puts a dampener on his high.

'I'll do my best to see you and Sorcha tomorrow. It depends on what else I have to do.' Or what else the Warden demands he does.

Bannon nods, watching as Quill put his boxers back on again. He's upset and Quill can hardly blame him. He feels the exact same.

'Hey,' Quill says, stepping up to him. 'It's shite I know, but it's all we've got. You told me you don't want to walk away. I don't either. But if you can't handle this, or if it's too difficult for you, I'll back off.'

Bannon shakes his head. *'No!'* he writes quickly. *'I meant what I said. I want to stick with you. Sorcha too. I'm fine, really.'*

He's not, but Quill already has enough on his plate without adding his worries to the list.

Quill opens the door, quickly checking outside before he allows Bannon to walk out. 'Just for the record, you can do that again whenever you want.'

Bannon grins widely, then turns and walks along the corridor towards his own room. Quill closes and locks his bedroom door firmly behind him before collapsing back on his bed.

He can't quite believe that just happened. Bannon gave him a blowjob. Bannon. The part he can't quite believe is that it felt right – to both of them. They were both nervous about it, but for very different reasons. Bannon was nervous because Quill is the first male he's been with. Quill was nervous because it was Bannon.

The problem he's faced with is that, now Bannon has done that to him, he wants it again and again. He wants Bannon so much more than he did before Bannon entered his room today.

49

SORCHA

'This is fucking ridiculous! I can't get the hang of this.'

Sorcha laughs as Quill throws the page on the ground and gets to his feet. Bannon has been trying to teach him sign language for a good half hour, but the head guard is either too impatient to give it a chance, or too stubborn to let someone teach him.

'It's not that difficult.'

He glares over at her as he tucks some hair behind his ear. Even though his expression is stern, she can't help but smile. This hard-faced, no-nonsense guard is irritatingly attractive.

'Speak for yourself.'

'You just need to practice,' she says, as she hands him back the page he'd thrown on the floor.

'When the fuck do you expect me to do that? The Warden is keeping me busy. I don't have a lot of free time anymore.'

Bannon gives Quill a long hard look, before he turns his attention back to Sorcha, smiling slightly. They promised they wouldn't mention the Warden to Quill, in case he clams up and storms off. It's a promise both of them are struggling to keep.

Since they admitted their feelings for each other a week ago, she's seen Quill twice and each time he'd been distant with them, for the first few minutes. After a while he relaxed a little, but he's obviously dealing with something he's keeping from them. She's absolutely certain he is.

She'd discussed it with Bannon quite a bit, but he doesn't have any answers. Apart from sharing meals with Quill and the rest of the guards, he didn't see much of him either. The Warden is clearly keeping Quill all to himself.

'This is where wolves are far superior,' she says, trying to change the subject before Bannon ignites the place, as he's obviously worried about Quill, and whatever is going on with the Warden. She can feel the heat coming off his hands.

'You what?' Quill asks, his attention drawn from the pages in his hand. 'Wolves are what?'

'You heard me.'

'How the fuck do you figure that out?'

'Well, for one, we can hear each other in our heads when we're in wolf form.'

'So, you don't just yip and bark at each other then?' He winks, before looking back down at the page.

She likes that he's more comfortable with the two of them, letting a bit of the real him break free every now and again. 'No. We don't bark at each other. Well, not all the time. It's sort of like wolf telepathy.'

Bannon suddenly pushes to his feet, gesturing wildly.

'What the fuck are you saying?' Quill asks.

'He can feed from you,' Sorcha says translating for him. She has no idea why, but the image that jumps into her head is rather nice. 'What good would that do?' she asks, genuinely curious. The whole feeding thing vampires do is still something she's trying to get her head around.

'I'm Prime,' Quill explains. 'Sometimes - and it is only sometimes - if blood is shared between a Prime and another vampire, it can help them to communicate.'

That's news to her. 'How?' She gets to her feet, excitement taking over until Quill holds up his hand.

'It's not a vocal thing. It's like your wolf telepathy. I'd be able to hear him in my head. But it's not a foolproof plan. It usually only works between vampires with an emotional connection,' he adds quickly, looking at the ground instead of them.

'Does it work straight away?'

Quill shakes his head. 'I think it takes a few hours. Sometimes longer. There's no hard and fast rule.'

'But it's worth a shot, right?' she says, trying to move on from his awkwardness, when he mentioned the emotional connection. She's convinced it's there in some form or other. It's certainly there for her, for both Quill and Bannon.

Quill takes a good minute to convince himself to look over at Bannon. 'My blood is like a drug to Hybrid vampires. It's seriously addictive. Even a small amount can fuck with you.'

'Fuck with him how?' she asks. She'd never heard of that before.

'It can be like heroin is for a human. I don't think it's a good idea. Feeding from me is just going to fuck-up all of this. I'll work on learning sign.'

Bannon claps his hands, waiting until Quill looks up from the floor before he signs. *I won't hurt you. I promise.*

Quill laughs humourlessly. 'I'm not worried about that. I know you won't. But feeding from me is... My blood is... You can't drink it... This won't work anyway, so there's no point talking about it. Can we just leave it at that?'

'Your blood is what?' she asks, taking his arm in her hand, turning him around when he tries to walk away. 'What's going on?'

'I don't want my blood to fuck him up! Nothing good can come from drinking it! Nothing!'

His outburst takes them both by surprise. 'Why would it fuck him up?'

'I have to get back to work.'

'No!' Sorcha puts herself between Quill and the door, blocking his escape. The head guard crosses his arms, facing up to her as he always does when he's trying to enforce his authority. 'Why would your blood fuck him up? Humour me. I'm a wolf. I don't know much about the ins and outs of vampires.'

'Prime blood can be addictive for Hybrids. It's fucking lethal stuff.'

'So, Hybrids can't drink Prime blood?'

'They can, but only in small amounts. Same for Primes. We need Prime blood to survive, but if we drink too much, it can bring on Blood Fever.'

'That doesn't sound good,' she says.

'It's not. We become completely addicted, then we lose our minds and become crazy blood-thirsty killers.'

'Ah. Not nice at all.'

'No. It's not.'

'So, who feeds you?'

'I take a bag of Prime blood every few weeks. I really have to go.'

This time Bannon's hand shoots out, gripping Quill's arm to stop him escaping. He taps his finger against Quill's neck as he raises his eyebrows in a silent question.

'It's too much of a risk.'

Bannon shakes his head as he taps Quill's neck again. He wants to do this, and Sorcha can't blame him. If it works, it will open up such a whole new world for the two males. 'I think he's willing to take the risk.'

Quill curses to himself as he sweeps his hand over his hair. 'It's poison Bannon. I can't do it. I can't let you.

Bannon takes Quill's face in his hands, holding him firmly, so he can't look away. *'I want to do this. I want you to hear me, Quill.'*

Quill keeps his eyes locked on Bannon's mouth as he lip reads. 'I want that too. I do, but...'

His voice trails away as he closes his eyes.

Sorcha looks at Bannon, seeing that he's as worried about Quill's reaction as she is. This is so much more than just being concerned about this addiction thing. After seeing some of the wounds on his body, she has no doubts it's not just down to his Prime blood, and his fear that Bannon will become addicted. He's been fed from before and it wasn't voluntary.

'Okay, so I get that you're wary about this, but I'm here. I can keep an eye on what's going on. If Bannon looks like he's taking too much I can stop him. I'm strong enough to pull him away from you.'

Bannon nods enthusiastically at her suggestion.

'I think he wants to try. You don't have anything to worry about, Quill. I promise.

Bannon and Sorcha wait, while Quill continues whatever internal battle he's having with himself.

Deciding to help him feel more at ease, she takes his hand, gently pulling him towards her. Then she takes Bannon's hand in her other one, holding the vampires close to her.

'You don't have to do this if you don't want to,' she says, squeezing Quill's hand in hers. Her heart swells when Bannon takes Quill's free hand, and the large male doesn't pull back. Bannon faces Quill, waiting until the other male looks at him before he slowly mouths, *'I want you to hear me. But only if you're happy about this.'*

Quill nods. 'I want to hear you too. I want to do this.'

Bannon releases their hands, then slowly unbuttons Quill's shirt before dealing with his own, dumping both on the ground of Sorcha's cell. As soon as Quill's shirt is removed, the marks on his skin catches both of their attention. He's been bitten a lot. Most of the scars are fading, but some are still raw. He was fed from recently.

'Oh Quill...'

'Don't ask, Sorcha.'

He *will* tell her, but not today. Today is about being able to hear what Bannon is saying. She looks up at him and sees the same pain in his eyes. Bannon is just as worried about Quill as she is, but there's no point pushing the stubborn vampire.

Bannon gives Quill a thumbs up, his eyebrows raised in a silent question.

Quill nods. 'Yeah. I'm ready.'

But he doesn't look ready. This is a massive moment for him and Bannon. He shouldn't be filled with dread. Before she can talk herself out of it, she wraps her hand around the back of his head, pulling him down so she can kiss him.

Quill briefly hesitates, then kisses her back. It's very different to the last time he kissed her. Quill is less sure of himself now, his pierced tongue tentatively exploring every inch of her mouth.

Then Bannon joins in, his hair tickling her cheek as he kisses along Quill's neck. The groan of pleasure from deep in Quill's chest is the best thing she's heard for a long time. A hand combs through her hair, gently turning her head to the side. Quill breaks their kiss, allowing Bannon to take over. But Quill is still there, nuzzling against the side of her neck, his fangs grazing her skin sending shivers straight down to her toes.

'Bite me Bannon,' Quill says near her ear, his voice low and full of desperation.

Bannon pulls away from her mouth, his fangs growing as he looks at Quill. He is simply stunning. She never thought she'd say that about a vampire, but with his glowing brown eyes and huge fangs he takes her breath away. Keeping her positioned between them, Bannon gently tilts Quill's head to the side. He draws his tongue slowly along Quill's thick neck and Sorcha is transfixed.

She knew watching the men together would be intense, but this is way beyond mere intense. Intense doesn't even come close. Bannon looks down at her as he sinks his teeth into Quill's neck. He closes his eyes, his neck moving as he swallows Quill's blood.

'Fuck, Bannon...' Quill gasps.

He buries his hand in her hair, holding her against his chest as Bannon feeds. She watches in fascination as he slowly pulls out his teeth. So much for worrying about him taking too much. Bannon was clearly in control of what he was doing. Then, with a deep growl Quill, ignoring all build up, bites down on Bannon's neck.

She now fully understands why some people have commented that vampire feedings can become erotic in the right company. She never believed it for a second - until now. If she could, she'd transport them to a bedroom, remove all their clothes, and just enjoy being with these two surprisingly addictive vampires.

The fact that all three of them are turned on, doesn't help diminish any fantasy she might have playing in her head. The two males are aroused, and she loves that. She loves that both are attracted to each other. To her too, and she's certainly attracted to them.

Quill slowly draws his tongue along the side of Bannon's neck, then licks his lips as he pulls Sorcha closer. He tilts her head back and kisses her, before resting his forehead on Bannon's shoulder. He pulls Sorcha closer, the steady beat of his heart blocking out the sounds of the prison she's locked in.

Bannon's arm joins Quill's, wrapping around her back.

She has no idea what their relationship is, and she's in no hurry to decipher it. All she knows is that she can't remember feeling as content or happy as she does when she's in their company. With them she's more than a prisoner. More than just a number. She's Sorcha. A little piece of her true self comes out with Bannon and Quill. With her two vampire guards.

But she wants more. It's greedy and unrealistic given her circumstances. But that won't stop her wishing. It won't stop her imagining a life where the three of them can be together in some way.

If only life were that fair.

'I have to go.'

Quill's voice is full of such sadness it knocks her out of her happy thoughts. She looks up at him, seeing that sadness echoed in his eyes. 'Can't you stay for a bit?'

He brushes her hair behind her shoulder as he shakes his head. 'I've been here too long already.' He turns his attention to Bannon. 'You too.'

Bannon nods once, then kisses the top of her head as he steps back.

Unfair doesn't even come close to what's going on. This isn't a situation any of them can influence or change.

Bannon pulls some pages from his back pocket and passes them to her. She unfolds the paper, smiling when she sees more words for her to practice. 'Homework?'

He nods. *'I'll test you next time.'*

Sorcha smiles, grateful to be given some distraction from the loneliness that's building with every second. Usually, she'd be happy to be left to her own devices. These two vampires are throwing her world upside down.

Without a word or a backward glance, Quill leaves her cell, going back to whatever duties the Warden ordered him to do. Bannon smiles at her before he follows, quietly locking the cell behind him, sealing her alone in the dark gloom.

This isn't how it should be. Falling in love should be this incredible, euphoric time in your life. Instead, she's sitting alone in a dank, dark cell, deeply missing the two vampires who she is breaking all the rules with.

A wolf is forbidden from falling in love with a vampire. So, what does she do? She falls in love with two.

BANNON

The lunchtime rush goes painfully slowly for Bannon. All he wants to do is be alone with Quill and Sorcha. To hold them both again. To feed from Quill again.

But now all he can do is wait and hope. He doesn't know much about the connection between some vampires when they feed from each other. He's heard of it of course, but never known anyone who was able to do it.

If it does work between them, it opens up so many possibilities for the two of them. For the three of them. No matter what happens, there are three of them in this together. With Sorcha already able to understand what he's saying to a certain degree by sign language, if Quill can also hear him, he won't be so alone in the world. So trapped in his own mind.

He glances across the room, trying to catch Quill's attention, but as usual, he is all business when around other guards. He needs to be like that. Out here there has to be a wall between them, a professionalism, a lot of distance.

But alone, he lets that wall drop, and Bannon is rapidly becoming addicted to him. The way Quill is when he's alone with Sorcha and him gives a glimpse into a private, hidden Quill he doubts anyone else sees.

'Can you hear me?'

No reaction from Quill.

He tries to hide his disappointment, turning towards the far wall to check on another table of prisoners. Of the twenty-three wolves imprisoned here, he's only ever really interacted with Sorcha. Everyone else behaves for the most part, only needing a little shove every now and again to keep them in check.

Bannon still has no idea how the prison is operated. The Warden sits in his office on the top level of the house, but what he actually does Bannon doesn't know. He doubts even Duna knows. She seems to take her orders directly from Quill - not the Warden. All he does know about the relationship between the Warden and Quill, is that the head guard is called upstairs quite a lot, and when he comes down, he's withdrawn and distant.

He suspects the Warden is feeding from Quill. After tasting Quill's Prime blood, Bannon can already feel the strength of his pure blood running through him. He's not surprised others can become addicted to it. His head is buzzing, and he only took a few mouthfuls.

But then he thinks back to the raw scars on Quill's body, and the restraint marks around his wrists. Consensual feeding is one thing. Quill is entitled to feed anyone he wants. It's got nothing to do with Bannon. Being forced to feed someone else is another matter entirely.

'Quill?'

He glances over his shoulder, hoping to see something in Quill's face, but a hard mask meets him. Clearly, he didn't hear Bannon in his head.

How long does it take? Could he be talking to himself for the next week in the hopes Quill can hear him?

It's so frustrating.

Duna walks into the room and straight over to Quill. She talks to him for a moment, the head guard's eyes darkening as he listens. He licks one of the rings in his lip, before nodding and walking away from her. Something is wrong. Quill isn't happy about something.

His eyes meet Bannon's for a moment, before he leaves the room. He's probably going to the Warden. Maybe he's just been reminded by Duna to take a step back? Bannon has noticed he's pulling away from the daily duties of the prison as ordered.

Duna wouldn't overstep the mark like that. She's not that stupid. She's been promoted, spending a few hours overseeing the day shift as well as the night one. But Quill is still her boss and, unfortunately, she is also Bannon's boss.

Duna stalks around the room, coming to a stop beside him. 'All quiet?'

Bannon nods.

'Good.' She crosses her arms, standing beside him as she glares at the room of wolves. Something catches Bannon's attention. There's blood on the back of her hand. Duna notices what he's looking at, and wipes it on her trousers. 'The Warden wants Quill to discipline one of the wolves. He was caught stealing food from the bins after mealtime.'

The poor wolf must have been starving to take leftovers others threw away. That doesn't need to be punished by giving him time alone with Quill.

'You need to stop looking at him like that.'

He frowns at her.

'Quill is your boss. He answers to the Warden and no one else. What Quill does has nothing to do with you, so mind your fucking business and just do as you're told.'

Clearly, Duna has it in for him, and the feeling is more than mutual. He doesn't think she has any feelings for Quill, but she's not letting up giving him a hard time about him.

She turns around, getting right in his face. She's only a few centimetres shorter than him, but she's seriously intimidating. 'I'm no fool Bannon, so don't take me for one. If you get between the Warden and Quill you're signing your own death papers. And I mean that the Warden will order Quill to kill you. Do you want to have a guess how that will go?'

Bannon wishes he could tell her to fuck off and leave him alone, but he can't.

'How about I tell you? Quill will do as he's told. He'll kill you, because that's how things work in here. You follow orders, or people die. You follow orders, or you die.' She taps him on the cheek as she smiles. 'Just some friendly advice.'

Duna turns her back to him. 'On your feet dogs! Time for walkies!'

QUILL

Fucking Warden! He can't just give him a moment to himself. Can't just let him do his fucking job, without throwing something at him to put him back in his place.

Sending Duna to do his dirty work wasn't appreciated either. His orders usually came from the Warden directly. Having her deliver his order was another game he's playing with Quill. His way of showing his head guard who is in charge, and who can take his place if he fucks up.

He's wondered about that a few times when he'd disobeyed the Warden. Would he push back too hard one day and find himself as an inmate, with Duna kicking his ass on a daily basis?

She'd be the one to do it all right. There's no loyalty in this place - just survival of the fittest.

Quill shoves a prisoner out of the way, cutting off any protest with one look. Quill grabs the prisoner by the collar, pushing him back towards the cells. 'Get the fuck out of the way!'

The wolf picks up his pace, scurrying into his cell to get out of the way. He doesn't usually let his emotions affect his work, but the Warden is pushing his fucking buttons, and his bad mood is now in control. He was hoping the Warden would give him a week or so, before he enforced the new *take a step back* rule. Should have known better.

It doesn't help that he was already off his game thanks to what happened in Sorcha's cell. He doesn't know what the fuck to call it apart from intense. Having her with them when they shared something like that, made it so much more than a mere feeding. Stuff that! Having Bannon as the one to feed from him, made it so much more than just a feeding.

He'd been fed from countless times over the years, and he'd hated it. Detested it more than he could put into words. But that was because he can't remember the last time it had been by choice. He'd forgotten what feeding from, feeding with, someone you care about, feels like.

In another world, he would have given anything to have them both naked in his arms. He laughs to himself. It's painful enough knowing what they could have as it is. Adding that level of intimacy to their relationship would be impossible to walk away from.

As a Prime, he's bred to be stronger, bigger, purer than a Hybrid. But that's not the only part of him that's enhanced. His protectiveness, possessiveness, *touch them and die* side has all ramped up now. He didn't realise how badly he's fallen for them both, until what just happened in her cell. He would kill for either of them without question. Die for them, if it meant protecting them.

But in his current position, what can he really do to keep them safe? His authority is already on the line. It's only a matter of time before the Warden puts Duna in his place as the head guard. This new working arrangement is the first step.

When that happens, Bannon and Sorcha will have to fight for themselves.

'Quill? Sir? Quillan!'

His thoughts are interrupted by one of the guards, standing in front of him looking confused. That makes two of them. 'What?'

The guard points to the door he stopped beside. 'Duna told me to stay here until you arrived. The prisoner is inside. He's ready for you sir.'

'Dismissed.'

The guard nods before scuttling off, leaving him alone outside the interrogation room. As soon as he steps through the doors he'll be watched. Every move, every strike, every cut, every drop of blood spilled will be seen by the Warden. Quill's performance will be judged, and like the prisoner hanging inside waiting for him, if the Warden believes he could have done better, he'll be punished.

He needs to go inside. Needs to be entirely unemotional when he faces the prisoner. If the Warden is testing him, he needs to pass, or Sorcha and Bannon will be in trouble.

He opens the door, and looks over at the wolf. The blonde male is stripped to his underwear, his thin body quivering in fear.

Quill puts his back to the camera, closing his eyes as he gets into the right frame of mind for what he needs to do.

But every time he picks up the whip, he pictures Sorcha, hears her screams of agony as he struck her, over and over again.

The wolf whimpers, bringing him out of his head. He needs to do this, or he won't be able to protect Sorcha. He won't see her being hurt like this again.

Uttering a silent apology to the prisoner, Quill strikes him, the leather whip tearing into his flesh as the wolf screams.

SORCHA

Cursing, Sorcha dumps the page of sign language homework onto her bed. She can't concentrate. It must have been a few hours at least since the vampires left her cell, but she doubts even one or two words have been committed to memory.

Every time she tries to learn the words, her mind is taken back to the two males as they fed from each other. Had it worked? Were the two of them having conversations with each other?

She desperately hopes so. Bannon deserves to have his voice heard again. Someone in this stone prison needed to hear him. She's trying, really trying to learn how to hear him through signing, but if Quill could actually *hear* him, she doesn't doubt it would make the world of difference to Bannon.

It kills her that he's so sad all the time. He smiles a lot when he's in her company, but his eyes are filled with sorrow. It's not surprising given what he's been through, but losing his voice as he had was such a cruel twist.

She picks up the pages again, sighs, then drops them back on the bed. Her head keeps veering off to the feeding.

Watching Quill and Bannon feed from each other was ridiculously hot. And it shouldn't have been. They were drinking each other's blood. If anything, she should have been disgusted by the act and turned away. Instead, she had been inserted into the middle of their embrace, and didn't want to be anywhere else in the world.

In that moment, even if the cell door had been opened for her to leave, she doubts she would have moved from her place, right between the two beautiful vampires.

Vampires!

She's getting all hot and bothered over two vampires feeding. What is wrong with her? Vampires aren't meant to be hot. That's not what she was brought up to believe.

But that was before she met Bannon and Quill. Watching huge, gentle, stunning Bannon sinking his teeth into the equally huge, tattooed, pierced Quill, had been intense on so many levels. How could she not be turned on? She's been turned on since she saw them feed from each other. She's still turned on. No wonder she can't concentrate.

Sorcha jumps to her feet when the door unlocks and Bannon steps into her cell. 'What are you doing here?'

He hurries over to her, taking her face in his hands as he kisses her. But this isn't one of his usual kisses. His hands leave her face, gripping the back of her head as he crushes his lips to hers. He's upset. She doesn't know how she knows, but she's positive something has happened.

But she doesn't stop him, doesn't attempt to find out what's wrong. Because she knows how he feels. She needs this as much as he does.

Sorcha unfastens the top few buttons of her jumpsuit, and Bannon pushes it off her shoulders. He lifts up her bra top, tearing it over her head before he leans down, kissing and sucking each nipple in turn, one hand slipping down the back of her jumpsuit to slide over her ass.

'Touch me Bannon. Please.'

He shoves down her jumpsuit and underwear, then carries her over to the cot, lying her back on the thin blanket. He unbuttons his shirt, stripping it from his body, followed by his black tank top. His huge body covers her, his warm smooth skin sliding over hers as he kisses her. She runs her hands over his broad back as Bannon makes his way down her body, his hands and mouth exploring, tasting, touching.

'What's going on here?'

Bannon freezes when he hears Quill's voice behind him. Sorcha smiles over at the newcomer then up at Bannon. 'Looks like we've been caught.'

Quill closes the door, locking the two vampires in her cell. He leans against the door, his arms crossed and stunning eyes glowing brightly. 'Give her what she needs Bannon. I'll keep watch.'

Sorcha has no idea what's going on, but she's not going to argue. She turns Bannon's face back towards her. 'You heard him. Please Bannon.'

Bannon glances over at Quill again, clearly unsure how to proceed with Quill in the room. And Sorcha gets that. But it's what Quill wants. He wants to see them together.

'It's an order, Bannon. Give her what she needs,' he repeats. Bannon takes his comment at face value. He continues down her body, this time his movements slightly more frenzied, more predatory. Seems the male enjoys having Quill watching them.

It's not something she's against either. Having those glowing eyes watching everything Bannon is doing to her is more than merely a turn on. It's like someone lit a fire under what was already a heated moment.

Bannon lifts his head, hitting her with his glowing brown eyes as he hovers over her pussy, his breath warm and delicious against her.

'What do you think Quill? Should he lick my pussy? she asks.

The growl he releases is so much hotter than it should be. 'Yes. Spread your legs wide and let him in. I want to watch you lick her, Bannon.'

Bannon doesn't need to be told twice. He slides between her spread legs, his tongue lapping at her pussy, flicking against her clit, as Quill watches them, his deep rumbling growl driving both Sorcha and Bannon crazy. Sorcha writhes against Bannon's mouth, using him to help push her closer to the edge.

It's been so long since she orgasmed, it doesn't take more than a minute or two before she's coming. Sorcha stifles her screams of pleasure under her arm, riding out the waves as he continues to lick her, his tongue delving deep as she comes apart.

The animalistic growl that Quill releases has Bannon in a frenzy. His hands dig into her thighs as his tongue drives her closer to the edge again.

'What do you think Quill?' she asks, her breath coming in short gasps. 'Should he use his dick next?'

He growls in response and it's the sexiest thing Sorcha has ever heard. 'Fuck, yes...'

Bannon opens his trousers, sliding his thick dick out. He covers her with his body, his dick pressing against her, the anticipation of what's about to happen threatening to send her over the edge before he's even entered her.

He slides inside, stretching her, filling her. Bannon starts slowly, but with Quill's deep rumbling growls echoing around them, neither can keep hold for long. She wants Quill to join in, but having him watching them, having those glowing eyes on them is incredible.

'You like that, Quill?' she asks, grinding her hips against Bannon. 'You like seeing his dick sliding into me?'

He nods, his fangs bared. 'Yes.'

Why is she enjoying this as much as she is? It makes no sense, but not much about this prison does. 'Tell us what to do Quill. What do you want?'

'I want to see you both coming. Go harder Bannon.'

He does as Quill says, and Sorcha arches off the bed, pushing him deeper inside. 'So close Bannon.' He kisses her, his tongue matching the movements of his hips, each thrust keeping perfect time.

She's so close again. His tongue and dick sending her on a free-fall. Then Bannon's tongue leaves her mouth, and he turns her head to the side towards Quill. Both Bannon and Sorcha look at him as she comes, shouting out Bannon's name as she watches Quill's reaction.

He growls loudly, the sound deepening as Bannon comes a few seconds later. He doesn't say anything to either of them, but his growls tell them both enough. Quill enjoyed watching them like that.

Bannon kisses her, his touch almost tender as they both come down. He holds her, his eyes on Quill as he strokes the side of her face.

Sorcha doesn't understand what just happened. What she does know is that if it were to happen again, she wouldn't say no. Even having Quill watching her was something she enjoyed.

'You both better get dressed.'

Neither of them wants to move, but Quill is right. If they're found like this by Duna or any of the other guards, it would cause problems with the Warden and Quill.

Bannon stands up, holding out his hand to help Sorcha to her feet. Quill goes back over to the door to keep guard while they get dressed.

This isn't how she planned to come down from what just happened, but it's strangely comforting having Quill looking out for them. She's not an idiot. She knows it's Bannon he's looking out for − not her. But as long as Bannon is in her cell, she feel safer than she's felt for many years.

Sorcha fastens her jumpsuit, then pulls her thin mattress onto the floor. She lies on the cold floor, using the mattress as a pillow.

'What the fuck are you doing?' Quill asks as she pats the ground to either side of her.

'Lie with me for a few minutes. Both of you. Please.'

Bannon glances at Quill, before lowering to the ground, pulling her into his arms. They both look up at Quill, hoping that he joins them. Hoping that he can let go for even a moment and share this with them.

She's probably imagining it, but Sorcha could swear Bannon is holding his breath, waiting, like her, to see what he decides.

Then the huge guard walks over to them and lowers onto the dirty floor to her other side. She shuffles closer to Quill, Bannon doing the same until she's sandwiched between these two beautiful vampires.

QUILL

He can't remember a time in his life when he felt more at home, more relaxed, happier than he does at this exact moment. It doesn't matter that he's lying on the floor of Sorcha's dreary cell. It doesn't matter that the cold stone floor is digging into his back. It doesn't matter who he is, or what he's done in his life. Nothing else matters apart from the two people he's with.

Holding Bannon and Sorcha in his arms makes all the pain fade into insignificance. He's just Quill with them. Just a male they both, for reasons he'll never understand, seem to be drawn to.

Her smaller, perfect body is nestled between them, her back against his chest, her hand clutching his tight to her.

When he walked in on the two of them together, he hadn't been jealous. He probably should have been, but all he wanted was to see both of them come. He wanted to see both of them enjoying themselves, free from the burdens of the prison.

He wanted to join in, of course he did, but it's not his call. Bannon has never been with a male before. There is no way he's going to rush him into anything sexual. No fucking way. And as for Sorcha... He kisses her shoulder, right on top of a faint scar he left on her skin. How can he possibly ask her to trust him enough to take that step, after what he did to her?

He has no right to seek, or to expect, her forgiveness.

But what he can do is protect them. That's all he can do, and there's no fucking way he'll let her down again.

She grips his hand tighter, and he closes his eyes. Of course, he wishes he could do more with them, but he'll take whatever he can get. Holding their hands, holding them, just spending time with them. Every moment with them is precious. He knows that. If the Warden finds out, this could all come to a heartbreaking end.

It's his job to make sure that never happens. His job to make sure they're both safe. If he had his way, he'd free both of them. Get them far away from the Warden, and everything to do with the prison.

As each day passes, he's more sure of that than anything else. He needs to free them both. Bannon may not be a prisoner in the same sense that Sorcha is, but he is a prisoner all the same. Once the Warden gets his claws into someone, he won't let go.

He knows the Warden doesn't care about Sorcha either way. She's here because someone wanted her here. As soon as she was brought here, and he broke her, he lost interest in her. She became just another number.

She sighs contentedly, snuggling in against Bannon while pulling him closer behind her. He smiles to himself at the sight in front of him. Sorcha and Bannon are so different. The athletic, feisty wolf and the powerful, silent vampire.

Opposites, yet both are perfectly suited to him.

'I love the way you look at us like that.'

Quill frowns when he hears the voice. His first thought is that someone has found them, but then he realises the voice came from inside his head. The deep, fucking gorgeous voice came from his head.

He lifts his head so he can see Bannon clearly. 'Say that again?'

Bannon's eyes lift to look at him.

'In your head. Say it again!'

'You heard me?' he mouths.

'You said you love the way I look at you.'

When Bannon smiles at him, he could swear his fucking heart melts. He's not known for being over emotional, or even emotional at all if he can help it, but right now he has to stop himself from crying. He taps the side of his head as Sorcha pushes onto her elbows to look at both of them. 'I heard you in here,' Quill says.

'It worked?' Sorcha can't quite believe what he's saying.

'Talk again,' he says, kneeling up.

'I guess you're off the hook?'

'What do you mean?' he asks, not sure what Bannon means.

'You won't have to learn sign language now.'

Quill smiles as Bannon pulls him close for a hug, poor Sorcha getting squashed between them as they embrace.

'Watch the little wolf!'

Bannon releases him and Sorcha slides out from between them. 'Sorry,' Quill says, smiling at her.

'Hey, there are worse ways to go than getting squashed between you two.' She looks at the two of them, a huge smile on her face. 'You can really hear him?'

Quill nods. 'Not just hear him. I can hear your voice Bannon. Fuck, it's sexy as hell.' He didn't mean to say that last part, but it's the truth. Bannon's voice is incredible. Deep and smooth, something he could listen to all day. The thought hits him that he's the only one in the world who can hear Bannon's voice. The only one. That just makes it so much more meaningful to him. So much more special.

Sorcha grins widely. 'Sexy huh? I can absolutely believe that. But that doesn't get you off the hook in relation to sign language. You should still learn it, so I can be included in your conversations when needed.'

He can't argue with that. 'I said I would.'

'So can he hear you, or is it a one-way thing?'

'Can you hear me?' Quill asks, in his head, but Bannon looks blankly at him. 'I guess it's one way,' Quill says. 'It might change over time. Who knows? At least I can hear you. That's the most important thing.' His elation is quashed when his phone vibrates in his pocket. He doesn't want to take it out. Doesn't want to see what the Warden wants from him.

'It's him, isn't it?'

There's no need to answer Sorcha's question. They all know who it is. He gets up and pulls out his phone. *'My room.'*

Two words that fill him with dread. He stuffs the phone back in his pocket and smiles, trying to put Sorcha and Bannon at ease. It doesn't work, but it's worth a shot.

'I have to go. You better get back to work too,' he says to Bannon, hating that he has to leave Sorcha alone by giving that order.

Before Bannon can move, Quill opens the door and leaves the cell. He can't be with them for even a second longer. Every message, every call, every thought of the Warden taints his time with them. He can't do much for them, but he can protect them from knowing about what he has to do.

He's too far from Bannon to hear his voice and he misses it. But it's a good thing he's gone from his head. He doubts he'd be able to keep the wall up once he gets upstairs. He never wants them to know why the Warden has such a hold on him.

QUILL

Quill wakes with a jump when someone pounds on his door. His first thought is that it's the Warden, but then he hears Duna's voice.

'Sir? Are you awake?'

'I am now!' He climbs out of bed and throws on a t-shirt to hide the marks on his skin from the Warden's feed a few hours ago. He's still tired and weak. He knows his body is reaching its limit. It's taking longer to recover from each feed. His scars take days to heal, instead of hours. He's a Prime. He should heal fast, but lately it's closer to human healing times, than vampire ones.

'What?' he growls as he yanks open the door. He's not angry at her. She's just going to get the brunt of it. She's well used to it.

'We've had a death, Quill.'

'Who?' A vice clamps around his chest as he waits for her to answer. Please no. Not her.

'Fifty-three. Wolf was sick. Someone put him down.'

His instant relief at hearing that it's not Sorcha, is replaced by anger when she speaks so coldly about what happened.

'Who the fuck put him down?'

'I did. What's the matter? The Warden doesn't want to waste food and accommodation on one that can't be saved. It's been like that for years. What's the problem?'

He grabs the uniform trousers he threw on the floor when he got back to his room, puts them on, then laces up his boots. This is a fucking joke. He's sick to death of this crap happening in the prison, then being called to clean up the mess. Every fucking time.

'Hey Quill? What's up?'

He stands and shakes his head. 'Nothing. Just tired. Where's the body?'

'In the interrogation room. I can bury him myself if you're not up to it. I'm just following procedure by informing you.'

Quill locks his bedroom door, then turns to face her. 'I know. Ignore me. Just got out of the wrong side of the bed.'

She leans against the wall, her arms crossed as she examines him. 'What's going on with you?'

Just what he needs right now. Duna isn't someone he needs on his case. 'Do your job Duna. That's all I need from you.'

She straightens, a coldness coming over her features. 'Understood. Do you need help or not?'

'I've got it.'

She salutes, before turning and marching away from him. Great work. He's pissed her off big-time. That salute was as good as giving him the finger. Fuck it! He's too tired to worry about her feelings.

Quill makes his way to the interrogation room on autopilot, reaching the door without any recollection of how he got there. He opens the door, steps inside and closes it behind himself.

The old wolf is lying on a sheet of black plastic on the cracked and blood-stained concrete floor. His blood is pooling under him from the knife wound spanning his neck. At least she had the good sense to get the body ready for disposal.

Quill pulls his keys from his pocket, then crouches down beside the body. He unlocks the thick bands from around the wolf's wrists and ankles, placing them on the table beside him, before he wraps the body in the plastic sheet. Quill places his palm against the wall panel at the far end of the room and the door unlocks. He picks up the body, then carries it down the corridor and out the door at the end.

He curses and squints when the sun hits his eyes. He's not usually so sensitive, and can easily stay out for up to an hour without any problems. This increased sensitivity is probably thanks to the Warden's excessive feeding too.

Ignoring his stinging eyes, he carries the old wolf's body to the clearing around the back of the island, and places him on the ground. Quill grabs the shovel from its spot leaning against the tree, where he left it after he buried the last body, and jams it into the ground.

It takes a good hour to dig down far enough, his weak body doing fuck-all to help speed things along. He lowers the body into the ground, then stands beside the grave, looking down at the body, wrapped in plastic and put in an unmarked grave as if he was nothing.

No family to grieve him. No one to ever visit the grave, because no one even knew he was here. Who was he? How long had he been in the prison?

What did he do to deserve this life? What did that old wolf do to deserve having his throat slit, then his body thrown away like rubbish?

Nothing.

Quill hasn't read his file, but he knows that wolf was innocent. They all are. Before Sorcha he hadn't given it much thought. He blindly did his job, jumping through hoop after hoop for the Warden, turning off parts of his brain he should have been using.

These wolves are here, because rich vampires want them here. Maybe rich wolves too. It's not a prison for criminals. It's a prison for wolves whose only crime was to irritate someone with enough money to send them here.

He scrubs a hand over his face, not surprised that he's crying.

The only escape from this life for them is death.

He told Bannon that very thing when he arrived on the island. Quill picks up the shovel and begins the long task of burying the wolf.

He'll have to do this with Sorcha one day. If he's still alive when she dies in here, he'll have to bury her. Maybe he'll have to *put her down*?

The tears continue to trail down his face as he dumps shovelfuls of soil on the body. Bannon too. When guards die, they're buried alongside the inmates. Would he have to dig graves for both of them?

His tears turn from sadness to anger. No fucking way! Quill rams the shovel into the pile of soil with such force he nearly breaks the handle. No fucking way!

They won't spend the rest of their lives here. He won't allow it. He stops digging, resting his arms on the handle of the shovel as he catches his breath. A thought comes to him, one that takes root and grows.

A thought he can't shake, even though it had no place existing in the first place.

Both Sorcha and Bannon are too good for this place. Both need him to save them.

He needs to save them. But that will take time and planning.

With a renewed energy, he puts the old wolf to rest. He'll do this for them. He'll help them escape. No one knows the prison better than he does. No one knows the Warden better than he does. He can make this work.

It's the only thing he can do for them so he *will* make it work.

DAVYN

Over his nearly two centuries of life, Davyn had been at many banquets in the Great Hall of his father's castle. Most of those were spent chained to a stone pedestal at the head of the room. He was the entertainment his father brought out, to keep his cronies amused. He'd hoped for death more times than he could count. There were no memories of this room he wanted to hold on to.

But as Thea slips her hand into his, watching the Whelans and the newly freed wolves laughing and taking their fill of food and drink, he realises this might be the first positive one.

'It's amazing to hear, isn't it?'

'What?'

Thea smiles up at him. 'Laughter.'

'I can't remember the last time someone laughed in this room.'

'It's well overdue so. How are you doing?'

'I'm grand. Mostly. I wasn't expecting there to be so many wolves in there. Great fucking legacy I've been left with.'

'A legacy you're rewriting. That's a good thing.'

'There's little good about any of this. Yes, they're not prisoners anymore, but they've lost years of their lives for no fucking reason.' He knows first hand what that feels like. It's not something they'll recover from in a hurry. If at all.

She hugs his arm to her. 'True, but here they have a chance.'

He doesn't reply as Murt joins them. The wolf is smiling, something he hasn't seen him do too much. 'Thanks for the spread Davyn. It's appreciated.'

'It's all down to Fergus. He likes having people around to look after.' That's an understatement. Davyn didn't have much to do with Fergus while he lived here. The vampire was under his father's rule, so kept away from Davyn. He's come into his own since being freed from his father.

'Have you heard from Nix?' Murt asks, before taking a drink from his ale.

'I did. She's agreed that the funds the warden took for holding the wolves in that prison are now mine.' He takes a piece of paper from his back pocket and hands it to Murt. 'And I'm now giving it to you and Fergus. Use it to set these wolves up with new lives. I'll leave it to you two to sort it out for them.'

Murt looks down at the figures on the page and his face drains of colour. 'Davyn... no...'

'I'll make it a fucking order if I have to.' There had been just shy of ten million Euro in the dead warden's accounts. Davyn doesn't doubt the payments far exceeded that, but the warden had helped himself to most of it. Ten million would help give them a start. Anything else he finds in the other prisons would be added to the pot.

'Are you sure Davyn?'

'I don't want any of that money. Not one cent. It's blood money. Wolves bled to line his pocket. Line my father's pockets. Take the fucking money. Ethan will be in touch with the account details.'

Murt slides the piece of paper into his pocket, then holds out his hand. He grasps Davyn's hand firmly in his. 'Thank you. Not sure what else I can say.'

'You can stop going on about it.'

Murt laughs loudly and raises his glass to Davyn. 'As you command. So, any word on the next prison?'

'Ethan flew straight back to Wales. He's giving all the information to his people over there. He'll let us know when he has the location.'

Murt nods, clearly as eager as he is to go after the next one.

'How is your cousin?' Thea asks.

Murt looks over his shoulder at Rowan, stuffing his face with chicken and potatoes. 'Oh, I think he's good. Sounds like these wolves are some of the luckier ones. He was moved from the Level Two to this prison. It was rough in there. Dread to think what Level Three is like.'

'We'll find out soon enough,' Davyn says, taking quiet reassurance from Thea's tight grip on his hand.

Rowan hurries over to Murt and whispers in his ear, before nodding and rejoining the rest of the group.

'Is everything okay? Thea asks.

'It is. Would you and Davyn go to the walkway over the courtyard. We'd like to show you something.'

Murt smirks, before hurrying away to the rest of the wolves.

'What's he going on about?'

Thea shrugs, tugging on his arm. 'No idea. Come on. Let's go and see what they're up to.' Hand in hand, Davyn and Thea climb the stairs to the balcony running along the inside of the first floor, overlooking the courtyard.

He's not in the mood for all this socialising. The only thing on his mind is taking Thea back to their room and spending a few hours alone together. He wasn't built for holding court. He's a fighter. Always has been. He's at home in a firefight, not in a castle like this.

He takes hold of the railing as his head swims. 'What's wrong?'

'Nothing. Just tired.'

She turns his face towards her, then shakes her head. 'You need to feed. We'll see what Murt wants, then you are taking me back to your room and you'll have a good feed. You can't keep neglecting yourself like this. How many times have we had this conversation?'

'And how many times have I told you, I need to manage my intake.' He cups the side of her face, pulling her closer. 'I would die for you Thea. You are the only thing keeping me alive. But I will not put your life at risk to save my own. I love you.'

'I love you too. But I'm not going to let you starve yourself because you're afraid you'll become addicted to my blood. We're in this together. We're a team Davyn. You will feed, and I won't hear another word about it.' She kisses him, showing him yet again why she is the perfect mate for him. More than perfect.

'Whatever you say Thea.'

She smirks, looking incredibly pleased with herself. 'Oh Davyn...' Her voice trails away as something in the courtyard catches her attention.

He looks down into the courtyard, his breath catching in his throat. The inmates from the prison are gathered down there, each one in wolf form. He's never seen so many wolves in the same place before. He doubts vampires have and lived to tell the tale.

At the front, the four Whelan brothers look up at himself and Thea.

'What's going on?' Thea asks, her hand tightening in his.

'I don't know.' He's hoping it's not a hostile takeover, but he's not going to assume anything just yet.

Then something happens that shocks him more than a hostile takeover would. One by one, the wolves lower their heads, bowing to him.

'Davyn...'

Murt and his brothers have sworn allegiance to him. But he never thought the rest of the wolves would. It hadn't even entered his mind for one second. 'Fuck...' he can't think of anything else to say.

This doesn't have to happen. He won't have them kneeling to him because they feel indebted to him.

'You don't need to bow to me. You don't need to do this.' They all lift their heads as he shouts down at them, his voice carrying through the courtyard.

But it makes no difference. Not one wolf moves from their spot.

'I don't think they feel obliged to do this,' Thea says, leaning over to get a better look.

'Murt. Tell them they don't need to do this.'

But instead of backing him up, Murt lifts his head, howling up at the night sky. His fellow wolves join him, each voice adding to the deafening sound echoing around the courtyard.

'I don't think they're doing that because they feel they have to,' Thea says, smiling at him. 'I think they're doing that because they want to.'

She's right. He can barely believe it but, even after everything they've been through thanks to his father, they are choosing to kneel for a vampire - for him.

It's not what he wants, but he's not about to disrespect them by turning away from their gesture. All he can do is make sure this castle is somewhere safe for them to rebuild their lives.

BANNON

The second Bannon sees Quill at his door, he knows something is seriously wrong. Bannon steps aside to let Quill in, closing the door behind him. The male looks completely devastated. His uniform is soiled with dirt as are his hands. His blonde hair is loose, hanging over his face, hiding his eyes from Bannon.

Without uttering a word, Quill steps inside Bannon's room, coming to a stop in the centre. His shoulders are slouched making him appear so much smaller than he is.

Bannon walks around him, trying to get his attention, but Quill is miles away. With no other options available, Bannon wraps his arms around Quill, holding him, hoping that it will make a different.

For a long few moments, nothing happens, then Quill collapses in his arms. Bannon just holds him, letting him get himself together. Whatever happened it must be bad. He's never seen Quill like this before.

Quill takes a deep breath as he straightens, some of the strength coming back to his posture. His eyes are glassed over, almost as if he's been crying.

'I shouldn't have come here. I'm sorry.'

Bannon grabs his wrist, pulling Quill back to him as he tries to leave the room. He guides Quill into the bathroom and fills the sink with warm water. Quill remains silent as Bannon unbuttons his soiled uniform shirt, sliding it down Quill's arms. Moving slowly, he gently wipes a washcloth over Quill's arms and hands, removing the dirt from his skin.

When Quill is clean, Bannon takes the towel from the rack and dries him. Quill's head is still down, his hair hiding his face from Bannon. He brushes Quill's hair back and cups the side of Quill's face, desperate to figure out some way to help him deal with whatever he's going through.

He wishes he could ask him, but all he can do is be here and hope he opens up.

But instead of talking, Quill brushes his lips against Bannon's. He barely makes contact, but the fact he even made that small gesture is enough for Bannon to take over.

He kisses Quill, taking things slow until Quill comes out of his head.

Quill pushes against Bannon, guiding him back towards the bed. Bannon tears off his own shirt, desperate to feel Quill's hands on him.

But what really wants is to be with Quill. Really *be* with him.

'Be with me Bannon.'

After undressing quickly, Quill lies back on Bannon's bed, his well-built, tattooed body ready and waiting for Bannon to touch.

He's not nervous about this any longer. This isn't a fad or a phase

316

he's going through. The attraction to Quill is as real as his attraction to Sorcha. It doesn't matter that Quill is a male. What matters is that, having Quill naked on his bed turns him on more than he could have imagined possible.

Feeling confident and surer of himself than he's been for a long time, Bannon undresses then lowers onto the bed, straddling one of Quill's legs as he lowers to kiss him.

'I just want to forget for a while, Bannon.'

He's not sure what Quill wants to forget, but he's going to do what he can to help him. To distract him. To be with him in a way Bannon has never been with a male before.

He wants to do it for Quill – with him.

Bannon adjusts his position, momentarily holding his breath when his dick brushes against Quill's. He moves his hips again, this time putting more pressure against Quill. The male groans and it sounds so damn delicious. He wants to do whatever he can to hear that sound from Quill again.

Quill moves under him as they kiss, their dicks rubbing together, their movements becoming more frenzied by the second.

He wants to be with Quill like this. No question. He knows what he wants to do but that doesn't help with the nerves. He also doesn't want to hurt Quill by doing something he shouldn't.

He pushes up so Quill can see his mouth. *My first time.*

Quill nods. 'I know. Do you want me to help?'

Yes.

'I'd like you to fuck me. Is that what you want?'

He nods quickly, grateful that Quill is making this easier on him. The deep rumbling growl that Quill releases is like an invisible fist around his dick.

Quill turns around, getting on all fours in front of Bannon. He looks over his shoulder as he lowers his upper torso to the bed. 'Use your fingers first. I don't mind it rough, but your dick isn't small. Just go slow initially. I'm guessing you don't have any lube so just use spit.

Don't overthink it, Bannon. Just do what feels right.'

A few months ago, kneeling in front of another male's naked ass and wanting to get inside wouldn't have felt right. Now he can't think of anything else.

Doing as Quill suggested, he stops thinking. He wants to knows what it's like to be with Quill so what the hell is he waiting for. He slides his thumb into his mouth to lube it, while Quill purrs in appreciation. '

'Fuck that's hot.'

Bannon rubs his thumb over Quill's hole. The male groans and pushes back against him, desperate for more contact.

'Yes Bannon. More...'

He slides his thumb in, Quill's body clenching around him, pulling him in.

'Fuck...'

He takes Quill's curse positively so pushes his thumb right in. When he pulls out then back in again, Quill growls. He looks over his shoulder at Bannon, his fangs bared.

'More.'

His growled command spurs Bannon on. He replaces his thumb with two fingers, spreading Quill's ass until he's knuckle deep.

'Fuck, fuck, fuck! Bannon...'

He doesn't need any encouragement to keep going, to keep exploring. While his fingers pump into Quill, Bannon leans over, licking up from Quill's balls to where his fingers disappear into Quill's body.

Quill jerks as he moans. 'I want that inside me. I'm fucking begging you to eat my ass Bannon.'

Bannon growls silently as he replaces his fingers with his tongue. What begins as a few tentative licks and suck, quickly escalates. As soon as his tongue slides in, he can't get enough. Bannon grips Quill's ass cheeks, spreading him wide so he can get in further.

Quill grinds against him, his moans, groans, and growls of

pleasure fuelling Bannon's insatiable urge for more. He could do this all night, but his cock is throbbing, precum leaking from the tip.

'Yes,' Quill whimpers, rubbing his ass against Bannon's face. 'I want your cock in me, Bannon.'

With one last long swipe of his tongue. Bannon positions his aching cock against Quill's entrance. It's slick from all the attention Bannon just gave it. He spreads Quill's ass open, then pushes his cock inside. He nearly goes out of his mind with need as he watches his dick sliding inside Quill.

'Wait a sec. You're so fucking big. I just need... fuck you feel too damn good.'

He pauses, giving Quill time to adjust to him.

'Okay. I want all of you inside me.'

Bannon pushes his hips forward, marvelling at how Quill takes every inch of him.

'Oh, fuck Bannon...'

It is. So, so good. Bannon closes his eyes, the pressure of Quill squeezing him so tightly he can barely think straight. He loves the way his dick fills Quill's body so perfectly. Loves the way Quill is moving with him, making sure Bannon is as deep as possible. He's already addicted to being inside Quill. It's like nothing he's felt before.

'Fuck me Bannon,' he growls. 'I need you to fuck me.'

Bannon grips Quill's hips then does as Quill asked. He pounds into the male, Quill's groans of pleasure growing louder with each thrust.

'Harder, Bannon. Please...'

Bannon looks down at his dick sliding in and out of Quill. Damn that's so hot. He reaches around, taking Quill's thick cock in his hand, stroking it as Quill lets out a low moan.

'You feel so fucking good... Come in me,' he begs. 'Mark me, Bannon. Make me yours.'

Quill's spectacular inked body vibrates as he gets close. And he's not alone. Bannon is so damn close himself, but he wants Quill to come first. He wants to feel Quill orgasming while he's inside him.

Damn, he wants that so badly.

Bannon's fangs slide out of his gums, digging into his lip as he thrusts harder, the thought of coming deep inside Quill such an intense turn-on.

'I'm almost there.' Quill lets out a low rumble. 'Fuck I'm going to come.'

Bannon loses himself in the sounds and sensations for a moment. Their sweat-soaked skin slaps together as his frantic need to possess Quill takes over. Quill is his. He digs his fingers harder into Quill's hip as Bannon pumps into him, pushing him over the edge.

Quill comes with a loud curse, his dick spurting cum onto Bannon's hand and bed covers. But Bannon couldn't care less where Quill comes. Being inside him when he did was so intense. The way Quill's whole body tenses as it comes is more than Bannon can handle.

He silently curses as his own orgasm hits. His cum fills Quill as he continues to push into him, prolonging it for both of them as long as he can. He's not ready for this to end yet.

The next minute or two are spent just trying to breathe again as they both come down again. He's still inside Quill and is in no hurry to pull out. When he gets himself together enough to lift his head, he finds Quill looking back at him. His beautiful eyes are glowing softly, his hair tousled on the pillow around his head, his fangs still extended as he breathes heavily through his mouth.

Then their harsh reality hits back with a thump when Quill's mobile rings from the pocket of his trousers.

'Fuck it! Sorry Bannon. I have to get that.'

Bannon slides out, instantly missing the contact with Quill. The head guard rolls off Bannon's bed and searches for his phone as Bannon watches. Quill's wall is already going back up – even before he's answered the phone.

'Yes sir. I needed a shower and a change of clothes. I know sir.' Quill closes his eyes, his chin dropping to his chest as he listens to the

Warden. There's no one else in this place that Quill speaks to like that. 'Yes sir.'

He ends the call, dropping his phone onto his trousers on the floor. When he looks over at Bannon, his fangs are gone, and his eyes are back to normal. 'I have to go. Sorry.'

'It's okay,' he mouths. There's no point making Quill feel worse about leaving by telling him that it's far from okay.

'I better have a quick shower. Is that okay?'

Bannon nods, keeping the forced smile on his face until he hears the shower running. Quill is just going to leave without saying anything to him, and that will devastate Bannon. He could get off his bed and join Quill in the shower, but it would just make letting him go all the more difficult.

When Quill emerges a few minutes later, Bannon is still on his bed, the sweat chilling his skin. Without a word, Quill dresses, and Bannon could swear he deliberately keeps his eyes anywhere but on him.

As he slides his mobile back into his pocket, Quill finally looks over at him. 'Thank you.'

Of all the things Quill could have said, Bannon wasn't expecting that. *'For what?'* he mouths.

'For letting me be your first. For helping me forget for a while. For one intense fuck,' he adds with a sexy grin.

'I really enjoyed that.'

Quill nods. 'Yeah. Me too Bannon.' He shakes his head as he glares over at the door. 'I wish... I don't know. Do you think it would be like this outside these walls? I mean do you think we would have found each other. Found Sorcha?'

Bannon has wondered about that himself. *'I think so.'*

Quill raises his eyebrows. 'Yeah?'

Bannon nods enthusiastically.

'I'd have liked to know you away from all this,' he says, a sombre look on his face. 'Snatching these moments with the two of you...' He doesn't finish that sentence. He doesn't need to. Bannon knows how he feels.

Quill snaps out of his thoughts, gesturing towards the door. 'I'd better go.'

Bannon smiles as he nods, but inside he's desperate for Quill to stay. Quill opens the door, peering outside to make sure no one else is there. Before he leaves, he turns back to Bannon. *'Thank you for making me yours,'* Quill signs perfectly.

Before Bannon can comment on his use of sign language, Quill is gone. Bannon lies back on his bed, Quill's scent consuming him as he stares at the ceiling.

He should shower and get something to eat, but he can't find the energy or interest to do either. What he wants is to be far from here with Quill and Sorcha. He wants to be with them when they choose, not when someone else dictates it.

But unless something drastic changes, this is the way it will have to be.

SORCHA

'Are you out of your mind?' Sorcha lowers her voice in case the walls have ears. She wouldn't be surprised by anything in this place. Although, what just came out of Quill's mouth has knocked her for six. Bannon too, if his frown is anything to go by.

Bannon gestures wildly, his words rushing out faster than she can translate. 'Slow down a bit.'

He tries again, taking time to make sure she can understand him, but his movements are still a little abrupt.

'He says that you're crazy,' Sorcha translates, finally understanding what Bannon is signing.

Bannon gives her a thumbs up.

'Actually,' Quill says. 'He said I'm off my fucking head.'

'Ah,' Sorcha says. 'I missed the curse part. I'm just glad you two can *talk* to each other now.'

It has made things easier, but as her understanding of sign language isn't entirely fluent, Bannon and Quill are having more in-depth conversations than she can have. It's made the world of difference to Bannon, so she can't complain that she now feels a little excluded.

'I'm not crazy.' Quill gets up from her bed, pacing the small cell, while herself and Bannon watch. 'I've been thinking about this for a while. We're all trapped here. Bannon and I won't be allowed to quit any time in the near or distant future, and I don't need to tell you how things will end for you, Sorcha.'

He doesn't. She knows full well the only way she's getting out of here is when she's no longer breathing. 'Quill. Think about this.'

'I have! I won't dig a grave for either of you. I can't do that!'

She meets Bannon's eyes. *'What happened?'* he asks, his hands moving slowly so she can keep up.

'Nothing.'

'Quill. Talk to us.'

His eyes are so sad when he looks at her. 'I buried a wolf Duna killed. She killed him because he was sick, and the Warden couldn't be bothered to give him treatment. I've buried so many wolves, Sorcha. Too many. I know I sound crazy. I get that. But with a bit of planning, we can get out.'

She wants to hold him, but it's not the time. He's worked up, his mind clearly on this escape plan of his. Quill is beating himself up for what he had to do. He would appreciate being comforted. But in that moment, she sees how much of a toll being here has taken on him. He's broken in so many ways and it kills her. 'You're serious about this?'

'Yes. I've never been more serious about anything.'

'How can we get out?' Bannon asks. *'We're on an island. There's*

no way off.'

'The Warden has a private boat in a dock around the far side of the island. He uses it to bring other fat-cat vampires to his house so he can wine and dine them. He's throwing a party in three days time. He'll be entertaining until the early hours. That's when we make our move.'

Sorcha laughs as she leans back against Bannon, who seems just as amused by this conversation. 'Make our move? What move? There is no *move,* Quill.' She holds out her wrist, showing him the shackle.

'I can't leave while these bands around my wrist and ankles. The second I step outside the boundary, every alarm in the place will go off. And without the key, I'm stuck like this forever. I'll never be able to shift into my wolf form. I'm sorry, but unless you can figure out a way to get these off, this plan of yours isn't going anywhere.'

'Sorcha is right. And you know the Warden will come looking for you.'

Bannon has a point there. The Warden seems to have a special interest in Quill.

'Don't worry about that,' Quill says, sitting down beside her again. 'You've got to trust me on this. I know my way around this dump like the back of my hand. I have the key to your bands. I can get you to the boat. I can make sure all the alarms are taken care of.'

'You have the key?' She didn't know that.

'Of course I do. I'd have given anything to take them off you before now, but I wouldn't have been able to lock them back around your wrists again. I don't want them anywhere near you, but I only have permission to remove them from an inmate after death.'

She nods and smiles at his answer. She doubts she would have let him put them back on had he taken them off, even if he could.

'But he'll know it was you,' Bannon signs. *'He won't just sit back and let us escape.'*

'I know Bannon, but at that stage it won't matter. We'll be safe and far away from this hellhole.'

'If you're caught—'

'I won't be,' Quill says, trying to reassure both of them. 'I need to do this for us. I...' he pauses, suddenly seeming a little unsure of himself. 'I care about both of you more than I've cared about anyone else in my life. I can't stand seeing you locked up Sorcha. It's killing me a little more each day. I want nothing more than to see you running free. I know it's what Bannon wants too.'

Bannon nods, kissing the top of her head, then pulling her against his chest. *'My motorbike is in a storage facility on the mainland. I rode it to the dock on my first day and the guards who brought me over locked it away for me.'*

'Perfect,' Quill says. 'Would it fit three on it?'

Bannon nods. *'We'll make it work.'*

'See. You've got two very capable vampires ready to do what we need to do to get you out of here. Let us free you.'

'I know you're both capable,' Sorcha says, taking their hands in hers. 'I'm not doubting that for a moment. I just couldn't bear it if anything happened to either of you if this doesn't go to plan. I'll just be thrown back in here. You two are a different story.'

'It will go to plan,' Quill says with a confidence that gives her a little reassurance. 'We'll make sure it does.'

58

QUILL

Not for the first time in the last few hours, Quill drifts in and out of consciousness. Each time his world goes black, he doesn't fight it. Why would he? When he's conscious he can feel the fangs in his flesh, hear the vampires feeding from him, feel their hands as they grope him.

Over it all, the voice of the Warden can be heard, encouraging his guests to *take their fill*. He needs the Warden to feed from him tonight. Needs the Warden to take his fill. The more blood he takes, the more out of it he'll be. While he's lost to his blood-induced high, Quill will make sure Sorcha and Bannon escape.

He winces as another set of teeth bury into his body. The shackles around his wrists and ankles hold him down on the table, keeping him still, so the esteemed guests can do as the Warden suggested. He doubts he'd be able to move, even if the shackles weren't there. He can barely keep his eyes open. If they don't stop taking his blood, they'll kill him.

A few weeks ago, that wouldn't have been an issue. He wouldn't have cared if he lived or died. Now he *needs* to live. Now he has Bannon and Sorcha. Now they are depending on him to save them. No matter what else happens in his short life, that is something he's determined to do. He *will* see them free.

Just a few more hours and, if everything goes the way he's planned, they'll be far from here. If he's with them, that will be a bonus.

The next time he comes to his senses, the shackles have been removed. His limbs seem oddly lighter without the heavy restraints pinning him down. He slowly turns his head towards the seating area in the Warden's quarters. Through the thick velvet curtains draped across the archway, he can see the Warden sitting in his ridiculously ornate, and completely out of place chair by the fire, sipping a brandy.

He's alone, so presumably the feasting guests have fucked off back to their own ridiculously extravagant houses or apartments, where they'll spend the next few hours on a high, thanks to his Prime blood.

A new dread drags him further into the darkness in his head. He's not sure what's worse - being the buffet for the Warden's friends, or being alone with him. Sometimes the alone part is painful in a very different way.

'Finally back with us I see,' the Warden says without turning his attention from the crystal tumbler. 'Clean yourself Quillan. I am finished with you for tonight,' he says, his words slurring slightly. 'You can leave after you get dressed. I'll need you again in a few hours.'

He can barely move his head, but Quill still manages to drag his sorry ass off the table, landing in a heap on the plastic sheeting on the floor.

'Do not get blood on my carpet!'

Quill doubts there's any spare blood in his body to drip anywhere. 'Yes, sir.'

He's tired, sore, weak as a baby, and desperately hungry, but there's no time to dwell on that right now. Using the table as leverage, he pulls himself upright, taking a long time to get dressed, before finally exiting the Warden's suite without any further interaction with the bastard.

He must be spaced out, floating on his fill of Prime blood.

Quill shuffles from the room, pausing once he's closed the door, to give his head a chance to catch up with the rest of his body. The Warden isn't the only one floating. It doesn't feel like his body is his to control. Moving slowly, Quill climbs down the stairs to the bottom floor of the residence.

With one hand against the wall, he forces his feet to keep him heading in the right direction. The pull to Sorcha and Bannon is all he is aware of. The bond he has with them is the only thing keeping him going. He needs them.

As much as he doesn't want them to know anything about his relationship with the Warden, he needs to go to them. They'll ask questions when they see him. There's no way they won't, but the humiliation, the revulsion, the crippling shame is worth it.

He'll let them comfort him. Just this once he won't fight them.

Then he'll say goodbye to them forever.

BANNON

Something is wrong. Deep down he's convinced of it. No one has seen Quill for nearly three days. He missed work every now and again when the Warden needed him for something, but never for this long. Sorcha is uneasy too. She's stretched out on her uncomfortable bed, her head on his lap. He strokes his fingers through her long hair, trying to soothe her, but it's not going to work. Until they see Quill again, neither of them will be happy.

'Can you hear him?' she asks, turning her head to look up at him. Bannon shakes his head. He's been trying to focus on Quill, to concentrate on listening for any faint whisper of his voice in his head, but there's nothing.

'You're worried too, aren't you?' Sorcha lifts her hand, tracing her fingers down the side of his face.

There's no point lying to her. He nods, tilting his head towards her hand.

'Do you think he found out Quill is planning an escape?'

Bannon knows the *he* she's referring to is the Warden. He shakes his head. He very much doubts the Warden has a clue. Quill is far from stupid. He won't have mentioned it to any of the other guards, and certainly not to the Warden. He's sure they are the only three living beings in this prison who know anything of the plan.

'When do you have to get back to work?'

He looks at his watch. Fuck! He'll have to get back in a few minutes. With Quill missing, he has to pick up the slack. *'Five minutes,'* he mouths, hating the disappointment in her face. He hates leaving her. Hates that she has to stay in this cell, alone, in the dark for hour after hour.

Hates that he and Quill can't stay with her. Hopefully that will change soon. But if that's to happen, they need to find out what the fuck is going on with Quill.

As if he'd heard Bannon's thoughts, the door to Sorcha's cell bursts open and there he is. But something is wrong. Quill stumbles into the room, looking utterly destroyed. Leaving Bannon's lap, Sorcha jumps to her feet, hurrying over to Quill. The male stumbles as he crosses the floor, but Bannon catches him just as his legs give way, dragging him over to the bed.

'What happened?'

Quill slowly sits on the edge, wincing as he settles onto the mattress. He tiredly shakes his head. 'I can't...' he closes his eyes, dropping his head so low it touches his chest.

Bannon shakes his head at Sorcha. There's time to talk later. He helps Quill take off his t-shirt. Sorcha voices his silent curse when they see his exposed skin. He's covered in bite marks. Both arms, his neck, and torso. They're everywhere. Sorcha gently runs her fingers over the numerous bite marks on his flesh.

'Quill...'

He lifts his head to look at her. 'I just want to be here with you. Please. I just need you.'

'Of course.' She kisses his cheek, then climbs off the bed and goes to her small metal sink, filling her cup with water. She takes her spare t-shirt from the chair and dips the hem in the cup so she can clean his skin.

Bannon turns Quill's face around so he's looking at him. His eyes are sunken, the black rings so pronounced they seem to creep down his cheeks. This wasn't a mere feeding. Too much blood had been taken from him. Quill had been brought to the brink of death by the Warden and his feeding.

'What the fuck did he do?' He signs as well as speaking to Quill in his head. Sorcha needs to know what he's saying. He has no doubts it was the Warden. No one else had that kind of access to Quill. No guards or prisoners would have fed from him.

Quill shakes his head. 'Just leave it.'

Bannon grips Quill's jaw. He wants to scream at him, wants to tear his damaged voice from his throat and demand answers. But even if he could speak, there's no point having an argument with Quill about it. It's not going to do any good. Whatever is going on with the Warden it's not something Quill will talk about.

Bannon releases Quill. This isn't his fault. He tries to rein in his anger, but he's struggling to keep a hold on it. Right now, he just needs to help Quill. Bannon gently releases some of his power, holding him tight as he tries to warm his body. Quill is freezing. Bannon just hopes he's not going into shock.

Bannon desperately wants to go upstairs and kill the Warden. He has some sort of hold on Quill. He's absolutely convinced of it. Whatever it is, the urgency to escape has just been elevated. If that pompous asshole keeps feeding from Quill to this extent, he's going to end up killing him.

Attempting to take his thoughts off killing the Warden, Bannon taps the side of his own neck, over the vein.

Quill hisses when Sorcha dabs water on one of the wounds.

'Sorry. I'm trying not to hurt you.'

'I know. Everything is just a bit sensitive.'

'You need to feed,' she says, nodding towards Bannon. 'Let him help you.'

Quill nods, momentarily surprising both Bannon and Sorcha. He must feel terrible if he agreed without any argument.

Bannon lies down on the bed, pulling an exhausted Quill down with him. He leans over Quill, so his neck is against Quill's mouth, but the stubborn male then reverts to form by changing his mind and refusing to feed. 'I don't need this Bannon. I shouldn't have come here. I need to see to the cameras, then get you out of here.'

'Stop being stubborn,' Sorcha says, wringing the bloodied cloth out again. 'Feed or so help me I'll hold your head in place until you do. You're no good to us if you collapse halfway to the boat.'

Quill gives up fighting them. He wraps his hand around the back of Bannon's head, pulling him down to his mouth. The bite is like a shock that goes straight down his body to his dick. It's the same every single time he feeds Quill. Whether it's the earthy scent of the male, the feel of his hard body, the brush of Quill's pierced tongue against his skin, or just the simple fact that it's Quill, feeding him is something he can never get enough of.

He'll feed Quill every day if he can, but not like this. He's strong. Never shows weakness or backs away from a fight. To see him reduced to this kills Bannon.

Quill's hand falls from the back of Bannon's head, too weak to hold it in place any longer.

He meets Sorcha's eyes, seeing the same rage he's feeling. Her emerald eyes glow in the dim cell. He has no doubts she would get in line to kill the Warden. It would just be a race as to which one of them gets to the top of the line first.

They hold Quill for the next minute as he takes what he needs from Bannon. He'll have to stop Quill soon. Otherwise, he could take too much. Bannon would gladly give him his life, but that won't help to free him or Sorcha. He won't let the Warden do this to him again.

'*That's enough for now Quill.*'

The head guard releases Bannon, his eyes closed and his breathing heavy as he lies back on the bad.

'Is he okay?' Sorcha asks, combing her hands through Quill's loose hair.

'*This time. Next time he could kill him.*' He keeps to sign language, blocking Quill from hearing his thoughts, so he isn't aware of what he's saying.

'*There won't be a next time,*' she signs back in reply. '*He's leaving with us tonight.*'

'Quit talking about me behind my back.' Quill opens his eyes and smiles at them. 'I can hear your hands moving.'

'Sorry,' Sorcha says, kissing him on the forehead. 'You gave us a bit of a scare.'

He pushes upright, then brushes his hair back off his face. 'Yeah. Sorry about that.' He's still exhausted and far too pale - even for a vampire, but he's straight back to business as usual. 'It'll take about two hours for him to be incapacitated. Then we go.'

'Are you still planning to do this? Sorcha asks, sliding in between the two of them so they don't have to speak too loudly. 'We can wait a few days until you're stronger.'

He shakes his head briskly. 'No fucking way! If we don't do this today, it'll be another few weeks until we get the chance again. I have the keys to your restraints. I have the code to the boundary alarm. We're good to go.'

'What about you?'

'What about me?'

'*Are you strong enough to do this? You could barely walk a few minutes ago,*' Bannon says.

In true Quill bull-headed style, he gets to his feet and holds his arms out to the side. 'I'll take you right here and now if you want.'

Bannon doesn't doubt that. *'Relax. I believe you.'*

He may be putting on a macho act, but exhaustion is stronger than Quill's stubbornness. He sits down on the bed, trying to appear casual, but Bannon can see his limbs trembling.

His timing is off for so many reasons, but something inside is telling him to act. Something is telling him to kiss Quill, to be with him and Sorcha right here and now.

The plan is that all three of them will escape here tonight. But what if that doesn't happen? What if something goes wrong and they become separated? What if he doesn't see Quill or Sorcha again and they never know how he truly feels about them.

He takes Sorcha's hand, pulling her closer to Quill as he leans over to kiss the male.

'We can't do this now.'

'Yes, Quill. We can,' Sorcha says, pushing Quill back so he's lying on her thin mattress. 'Let us do this, Quill. Please. Let me do this.'

She rests her hand on his belt buckle, waiting for him to respond in some way other than frowning as he's doing right now.

'Do what exactly?'

'I want Bannon in me while I suck you. Unless or course you had something else in mind, Bannon?'

He quickly shakes his head. Damn that sounds too good to refuse.

Quill shakes his head. 'I'll keep watch if you two want to be together.'

Sorcha gently pushes him back on the bed. 'We don't want you to keep watch, Quill. We want to be with you. We want you here with us.'

'No. You don't. Not like that.'

Sorcha strips out of her jumpsuit then stands in front of him. 'I can absolutely guarantee that my body is fully on board with what I just said to you. I want you. I want Bannon. Call me greedy, but that's what

I want. If you don't want that, it's a different story. But don't tell me what's going on in my mind, Officer. I know it better than you do, believe me,' she adds with a smirk.

Quill's frown deepens as he keeps the silence dragging before he finally answers. 'You really want to do that - to me?'

'Yes,' she says, smiling widely. 'One-hundred-percent yes!'

His nod is barely there, but they both see it and react before he can talk himself out of it. Bannon pulls down his trousers, fisting his cock which is already hard and aching. Quill lifts his hips just enough to allow Sorcha to pull down his trousers, freeing his cock.

The male is still tired and weak, but his dick is ready.

Sorcha crouches over Quill, taking his dick in her hand. Quill is on the verge of hyperventilating. His chest is rising and falling rapidly as he watches what she's doing. 'Look at me.'

He looks at Sorcha, swallowing thickly. 'I'm not going to hurt you Quill.'

'I know. It's not you who hurts me.'

Bannon curses to himself. So that's what's holding him back.

'I want to do this to Quill - not Officer Quillan,' Sorcha says. 'He's a completely different person. I know that.'

Keeping her eyes on him, Sorcha slowly traces her tongue along his dick as she pushes her hips back, offering herself to Bannon.

Something changes in Quill's face. The doubt and hesitation are pushed aside. 'Oh fuck... Bannon, what are you waiting for?'

Seems Quill is recovering, his demanding tone doing nothing to calm Bannon. He presses his dick against Sorcha's pussy, taking it slow even though she's already wet.

'Fuck!' Quill shouts as Bannon slides inside Sorcha, who takes Quill deep into her mouth as Bannon fills her. Quill looks up at him, his unique eyes glowing, his fangs digging into his bottom lip as he tries to restrain his shouts.

'Fuck Sorcha! What the hell are you doing to me?'

She reaches up, caressing Quill's nipple with one hand while the other keeps a firm hold on his dick. The sounds she's making as she sucks Quill are the hottest thing he's heard. Mix them with Quill's moans of pleasure and the intense look in his eyes, Bannon has to slow down so he doesn't end this too soon.

Quill brushes Sorcha's hair back from her face, giving him a clear view of what she's doing to him. He doesn't say anything, but Bannon can see how much this means to him.

Her free hand claws at Quill's chest, her short nails marking his skin and sending the male into a frenzy.

'Finish me Sorcha. Please...'

Quill's hips lift from the bed, pushing himself further into Sorcha's mouth, his vicious fangs on show as he growls in pleasure.

'I'm so fucking close Bannon,' he says, his voice breathy and deep. 'Her first. Then you and me.'

Bannon grips Sorcha's hips, holding her firmly in place as he pushes into her, hard and fast. Her breathing increases, her moans growing louder as she nears. Then she comes, her pussy clenching him firmly as her orgasm hits. Bannon follows a few seconds later, thanks to Sorcha's own orgasm, and Quill's muffled curse as he comes too.

Seeing Sorcha and Quill coming, feeling their orgasms, hearing their moans and shouts, draws out his own release much longer than usual. When it ends, he's breathless, sweating, and more satisfied than he's ever been before.

In front of him, Sorcha has collapsed on Quill's chest, breathing rapidly, a fine sheen of sweat on her back. Quill's eyes are closed, his lips part as he too tries to control his breathing.

He wishes he could tell them how stunning they both are, wishes he could voice how he feels about them. All he can do is try to show them as best he can.

'Fuck!' He smiles at Sorcha's muffled curse from on top of Quill's chest. 'So, so fucked.'

Quill laughs briefly then opens his eyes. 'Yeah. What you said.

Fuck!' He looks up at Bannon and flashes him a quick smile. "I wasn't expecting that.'

Sorcha lifts her head, reaching back to rub the side of Bannon's face. 'To be honest, I wasn't either. Seems Bannon here is a horny vampire.'

He slowly pulls out of Sorcha, then climbs off them so he can crouch down beside them. *Can you blame me?'* he mouths.

'She is gorgeous,' Quill says, clearly surprising Sorcha.

'I am?'

'Of course you are. You both are.' He checks his watch and curses. 'Fuck. I have to go.'

Sorcha climbs off him, sitting back on her legs as he pushes upright. He's still a bit wobbly, but the colour has returned to his skin.

Bannon hates this. They have an incredible moment together, then Quill leaves, destroying the high. Sorcha feels it too. She reaches over and squeezes his hand, the smile on her face forced.

'As much as I love having you naked like that, you'd better get dressed.' Quill passes Sorcha her jumpsuit while Bannon sorts out his underwear and trousers.

'So, I'll take Sorcha from here at ten-thirty,' Quill says, back in guard mode again. 'I want you to wait on the beach,' he says, looking to Bannon. 'Wait at the end where the large boulders are. I'll knock out the boundary alarm so we can access his jetty.'

He pauses, closing his eyes for a moment before looking at them again. 'I'll head out now and leave some clothes there for you,' he says to Sorcha. 'They'll be male clothes, but I'll grab something in a small size. Don't change here though. Wait until we get off the island. The priority is putting distance between this place and you as fast as possible. How close do you have to be to your brothers until you can pick up on their scent?'

'It's hard to say. Usually a few miles, less if I'm in wolf form, but that was years ago. I don't know what my range is now.'

He nods slowly. 'We'll head into the midlands initially. Maybe they'll pick up on you. I think they're our best bet. I don't think the Warden has the balls to go up against four wolves - especially male ones.'

'But you think he will come after us, don't you?' Sorcha says, getting the question out before Bannon can.

If he had looked from Sorcha to Quill even one second later than he did, he would have missed the look that crossed his face.

Resignation.

The Warden will come, but Bannon believes it will have little to do with himself or Sorcha. If he does come after them, it will be Quill he'll be coming for.

'No,' Quill answers after a long pause. 'I seriously doubt it, but I'm not taking any chances.'

I'm not taking any chances. This is Quill rescuing them, not a team effort. While Bannon's first reaction is to insist Quill lets them take some of this burden from him, he knows it would be a wasted effort. Quill needs to take the lead.

Apart from being the only one who can access keys and alarms, Bannon knows part of what makes Quill the male he is, means that this is something he would have to control himself. And Bannon is happy to concede - until they're out of here.

After that Sorcha and himself will be making sure Quill is taken care of too. They'll protect him as much as he protects them.

Quill pushes off the table, wobbling slightly as he straightens. 'I'll get some clothes sorted for you now,' he tells Sorcha. 'Bannon, you go back to your room and pack anything you need to take with you. Hide the bag under your bed. I'll collect it and leave it at the rendezvous point with the clothes. Then you'd better get back to work. Show your face for an hour. When it's time, I'll come and get you Sorcha and we'll meet with Bannon.'

'That simple?' Sorcha says, her tone sceptical.

'Yeah,' Quill replies. 'If you both do exactly as I said, it will be that simple. Just stick to the plan.'

They both nod, but he still looks as if the weight of the world is on his shoulders and Bannon hates it. He wants to take this burden from Quill.

'Good. I'd better go.'

He walks towards the door, but Bannon stops him, pulling him into his arms before he can escape. Quill tenses, and he's convinced he's going to push away, but he lets Bannon hold him. Bannon releases Quill for a moment when Sorcha joins them, slipping between the two vampires exactly where she belongs.

'Another few hours,' Quill mutters quietly as he holds the both against him. 'We're nearly there.'

SORCHA

If she had a watch, Sorcha would have checked it numerous times over the last hour. Time has crawled by since Bannon and Quill left her cell. She only had to wait sixty minutes or so, but it feels like at least a day has passed.

Quill is methodical. He will have planned everything to perfection, but even so, nerves are getting the better of her. She needs this to go to plan - for Bannon and Quill more than for herself. The Warden can't keep feeding from him. The male who stumbled into her cell earlier had been weak and beaten.

She doesn't know why Quill is letting him feed from him, full stop, let alone to the extent he is. It's something she knows Quill isn't going to tell either her or Bannon about. Maybe when they're away from this place? Maybe when he learns to trust them, he'll be open and honest about whatever hold the Warden has on him? Or maybe he'll never tell them. It could go either way, knowing him.

She's seen a change in him over the last few days. He's more withdrawn, quieter, but also more tender and gentler with herself and Bannon. Each touch, each kiss, like it's the last.

He's thinking the worst. Already assuming they won't all get out. But they will. They have to. This place is killing each of them in different ways. But getting out isn't going to be as simple as Quill is pretending it's going to be. Too much can go wrong. She has no doubts Quill knows what he's doing, but he doesn't control all the other variables.

The part that's plaguing her are the repercussions if it does goes wrong. Repercussions on Quill and Bannon.

Her cell door finally opens and Quill steps inside. His face has a touch more colour to it, but he still looks tired and worn out. He smiles and holds out his hand. 'Ready to get the fuck out of here?'

Without hesitation, she grabs onto his hand. 'Where's Bannon?'

'He should be heading down to the beach as planned. I left his bag and a change of clothes for you at the boundary fence after I left here earlier.'

'Are you sure about this Quill?'

He cups her cheeks, his eyes locking on to hers with such intensity it's like he has a physical hold on her. 'Yes. I swore I'd get you out, and I stick to my word. But as soon as we set foot outside your cell door, you have to do exactly what I tell you to do. No arguments, do you understand? Inmate and guard, okay?'

She nods. 'Of course.'

'We're only going to get one chance at this. It has to go exactly as I planned.'

She squeezes his hand. 'Let's not keep Bannon waiting.'

He lets go of her hand, then steps back so she can exit her cell first. Until they leave the prison grounds, she needs to keep up the act.

She's a prisoner. He's head guard. If they're to get out, they have to keep up appearances. He shoves her in the back, forcing her to walk faster. She glares back at him, but his head guard mask is firmly in place.

Sorcha follows his lead, keeping her *pissed off inmate* mask on, even though her heart is racing with fear and excitement. She looks around her, hoping this is the last time she has to walk down this grotty corridor. Quill stops at the interrogation room and her feet stop moving her forward. She can't go in there again.

'It's the way out,' he mutters under his breath, sensing her trepidation at entering that space again. 'Trust me.'

He shoves her inside, closing and locking the door behind him.

Sorcha grimaces when the smell of blood, urine, and stale sweat surrounds her. The room is bare apart from two heavy chains hanging from the ceiling, the manacles at the end of each coated in dried blood. Some of that blood is probably hers.

She glances over her shoulder at the camera, but the light is off. No one is watching.

'We need to keep moving.' He walks to the other end of the room and Sorcha follows, images of what he did to her in here assaulting her as aggressively as the stench. How many more inmates has he hurt in here?

But Quill is the prison enforcer after all. All prisoners are threatened with one-on-one time with him if they step out of line, when they are first brought into the prison.

She knows he's capable of violence, but this level of brutality isn't something she can match with the parts of Quill she's seen over the last few weeks.

Quill opens the door at the far end of the room, holding out his hand to her. He knows she's been thrown by this room. She can see it in his eyes. 'It's not me Sorcha. None of this is. Give me a chance to show you.'

She takes his hand, nodding as he guides her through the door, locking it again behind him. The air is cleaner here, the faint salty notes instantly making her stomach tighten. Quill again uses a key to unlock the next door, but the view on the other side is a very different scene to the last one.

The moon is high in the sky, the stars visible in all directions. The sea crashes on the rocks at the other side of a small, forested area.

But again, something is wrong about this space. There are what look like graves dug out of the ground in the centre of the clearing.

The only way you're leaving here is in a body bag.

It seems the guard who checked her in wasn't being entirely truthful. Death didn't mean escape. If the prisoners are buried on the island, they'll never be free. Quill doesn't give her a chance to process any of that, grabbing her hand and guiding her through the trees and onto the beach. Her soft soled canvas shoes slip on the sand as he drags her along, trying to keep her moving.

Even though she should be worried about what they're doing, she can't help but marvel at her surroundings. After so many years, seeing water, feeling the sand under her feet, hearing the waves, it brings tears of joy to her eyes. The only other time she's been this close since she was taken, was when she tried to escape the day she was brought here. And now, here she is, trying to escape again. Maybe next time she sees the ocean, she'll be free to enjoy it.

'Nearly there,' Quill says, keeping his voice low. 'You okay?'

'Yeah,' she says, watching where she's putting her feet. There's no grip on her shoes, and the rocks bordering the beach and forest are slippery with evening dew. Freedom is so close. Just another few metres to Bannon and the boat. Just another few minutes until the three of them are away from here.

MURT

She's not here. Even before they had entered the prison, he knew they were too late. As with the Level One prison, the Level Two facility is situated a stones throw from a house known for its ghostly origins. The impressive Duckett's Grove in Co. Carlow, could be seen from the driveway of the house.

Murt walks along the corridor to the room the warden of this facility had used as his office. *Had* being the appropriate word. He can smell the blood before he gets to the door. The new lord of the manor is taking cleaning up his father's mess to a whole new level.

He leans on the door frame and looks at the bodies on the floor. Six guards and the warden. 'No one wanted to leave the Dark Side?'

Davyn frowns, not getting the reference. 'No,' Ethan replies when the confused silence drags on. 'No takers. They were more interested in the salary the warden was paying them, than doing the right thing.'

'No loss then,' Murt replies, stepping over a guard to stand beside Davyn. 'Did you get the location of the next prison from the warden?'

Davyn mutters a colourful curse under his breath. 'Fucker wasn't playing ball. All we could get from him was that it's in his files. Stubborn fucker lost three fingers and took a bullet to his leg, but still wouldn't open up.' Davyn looks up at Murt, blood splattered over his face and eye patch. 'I'm taking it she's not here?'

'No. She was moved to the Level Three facility a few weeks back.'

'Fuck!' Murt jumps when Davyn punches the wooden desk, splitting it in two. Ethan rests his hands on his hips as he peers down at the laptop now lying on the floor. 'Next time you do that, move the delicate computer first.'

'Fuck! Sorry. Is it okay?'

Ethan picks it up and examines it. 'It's faring better than its owner. No damage done.' He closes it and tucks it under his arm, as he gathers some files from the cabinet. 'I'll load up the car with what I need, then take it straight back to my premises. I'll have my people work on it until we find the location. I've called in extra transport to bring the wolves to Darkhaven. It should be here in about twenty minutes.'

Davyn nods, turning to glare at the bodies spilling blood all over the ornate and, no doubt, expensive rug.

'Thank you, Ethan,' Murt says, leaving Davyn to his glaring as he helps Ethan bring some files out to the car.

'How are the prisoners?' Ethan asks, placing the laptop and files on the back seat of the car.

'How you'd expect. Confused. Scared. Wary. Some have been hurt, so they'll need medical treatment. In time I hope they'll all be okay.'

'And how did they take to the idea of Davyn?'

Murt shakes his head. 'Not too well. They are a tougher, more hardened group than those in the Level One prison. It'll take time to win them around, and we'll need to keep a closer eye on this group until they're all processed. But they're willing to go to Darkhaven, so that's a good start. You can process them from there, and hopefully we won't have too many problems.'

Ethan pulls off his wool overcoat, laying it along the backseat. 'That's a good start. Hopefully seeing Rowan and the other wolves there will help them feel safe. I'll keep you and Davyn up to date with any information I find.' He looks around him. 'I don't suppose you've seen Fallon?'

'I think she's in the prison with Garret. So, what happened with Bastian?' he asks. The question had been at the back of his mind since he first saw Fallon arrive in Ireland with Ethan, instead of Bastian. But as soon as the question is out, he wishes he could take it back. Ethan's face pales, his hand lifting to straighten his already perfectly aligned tie.

'There was a difference of opinion that could not be resolved. Bastian is a formidable fighter and put my life before his own too many times to count, but it was a hurdle we could not overcome. Fallon is doing an exceptional job. I have no complaints.' He nods briskly before attempting a weak smile. 'It is what it is. I had better go and get Fallon.'

Ethan disappears back into the house, leaving Murt feeling like a prize asshole. He just poked his nose into Ethan's private life without meaning to. It's blatantly clear the difference of opinion has nothing to do with how Bastian was protecting him. It was on a deeply personal level. It was clear now that it had to do with a romantic relationship between the two.

Murt curses himself again as he walks into the house. He should have just kept his big mouth shut. Ethan nods at him as he passes on his way to the car, with Fallon following after him.

He goes back down the stairs to the prison, finding Garret, Fionn, and Con speaking to some of the inmates. 'We good?' Garret asks.

'Transport is on the way. Everyone ready to go?'

'Ready?' Garret replies. 'There's going to be a rush for the vans. How did it go with the warden and his guards?'

'They won't be joining us.'

Garret whistles. 'It appears Lord Oldranson isn't someone you mess with.'

'It seems not. Get everyone ready to move once the vans arrive. This place gives me the creeps.' Leaving Con and Garret to the newly freed wolves, Murt walks over to Fionn, waiting until he finishes talking to a male wolf, before he pulls him away. 'How are you holding up?'

Fionn nods quickly. 'Good. Well, fine. I'm fine.'

His youngest brother is far from fine, but Murt doesn't challenge him. He needs to hold it together. They all do. 'She was here a few weeks ago. She's alive and she was here.'

Fionn nods again, clenching his jaw to keep the emotions at bay. 'What did she do Murt? What did all these wolves do?'

Murt pulls Fionn close, hugging him tight to his side. 'Nothing. Wrong place at the wrong time? Maybe it was just the fact that they're wolves? There's a chance we'll never know why. All we can do is get them out of here and give them somewhere safe to live.'

'I can't feel her Murt. I thought I'd be able to, but there's nothing. What if she's still not—'

'Stop that!' he says, turning Fionn around to look at him. 'She's alive until we have proof otherwise, you hear me?'

Fionn nods, but he's struggling to keep the tears back. Murt hugs him, giving his brother privacy as he gets himself together.

'We'll find her Fionn. I swear we'll find her.'

BANNON

He checks his watch again. Quill isn't late. Not yet, but that doesn't mean Bannon is going to relax. That won't happen until the three of them are away from this place. He peers around the tree to the small boathouse. He can't sense anyone in the vicinity of the building, but that doesn't mean it's unguarded. Every walkway and path to and from the Warden's massive house, is monitored by security cameras. It had taken him a good twenty minutes to walk around the headland to the rendezvous point.

'You better be there Bannon.'

He smiles and turns when he hears Quill's voice in his head. *'I heard you in my head! I can hear you!'* Bannon hoped that he'd be able to communicate with Quill that way at some stage. The timing couldn't be better.

'This is going to be useful,' Quill says. 'You at the rendezvous spot?

'Yeah. I'm here. Where are you?'

'Five minutes from you. You alone?'

'Yes. I can't sense anyone.' Bannon says.

'Stick to the treeline and stay hidden. We're coming.'

The relief hits him like a wave. Quill is perfectly capable of carrying out his well researched plan, but it's too soon to become complacent. Hell, they might never be able to be complacent again. If the Warden comes after them, they'll be watching their backs for the rest of their lives. That's if he even lets them live.

Then he sees them rounding the headland, Quill clutching Sorcha's hand, keeping her moving fast on the unstable ground.

They don't stop to hug, or pat each other on the back for completing that phase of the plan. They're still on the prison grounds, so there's nothing to congratulate themselves for.

Quill releases Sorcha's hand, leaving her gasping for breath on a rock, while he searches in the undergrowth, pulling out two bags. He passes one to Bannon and the other to Sorcha. 'Hang on to those while I deal with all the alarms.'

While she's still catching her breath, Quill goes over to the control box attached to the fence surrounding the jetty. He taps in an eight-digit code, then seems to hold his breath, as he waits for the blinking light to extinguish.

As soon as it does, he unlocks the gate and ushers the two of them through the gate. Bannon leads the way down the jetty to the small powerboat sitting in the water. He throws his bag into the craft, then helps Sorcha climb in. Quill unties the boat as Bannon boards and starts the engine.

'Quill! What are you doing? Get in the damn boat,' Sorcha hisses.

He pulls a keyring from his pocket with a lone key hanging on it. He tosses it into the bottom of the boat. 'That's for your wrist and ankle bands.'

'Great. Now get in the boat!'

But he's backing away from them, putting more distance between himself and the boat. Bannon watches in horror as Quill engages the security fence again, locking them out and him in.

Sorcha scrambles to get out of the boat, but Quill shouts at them 'Get out of here!'

'Get in the boat!' Bannon quickly secures the boat, then chases after Sorcha, who's heading back down the jetty to Quill.

'Open the gate!' she shouts, but Bannon grabs her, holding her away from the fence before she accidentally sets off the alarm.

Quill steps back from the security fence, shaking his head slowly. 'I can't. I'm so sorry, but I can't come with you.'

'Yes, you can. Open the gate then get in the boat.'

'He'll just come after me if I leave. He's not going to let me go. He's never going to let me go. I won't put that target on the two of you. Bannon, get her to her brothers. Keep her safe. I'm trusting you to keep her safe.'

'I'm not leaving you here.'

'You don't have a choice Bannon.'

'Just get in the boat, Quill! Please!'

Quill shakes his head, taking another step back from them. He holds up his wrist, showing them the thick silver bracelet he always wears. 'This isn't a bracelet. It's a fucking ownership cuff that's locked on to me. The Warden bought me years ago. I'm his fucking property!'

Bannon hears the words, knowing instantly that Quill is speaking the truth. Everything makes sense now. No wonder the Warden could click his fingers and Quill would come running. He didn't have a choice.

'How is that even possible?' Sorcha glances over at Bannon. 'Is it?'

'Vampires can own other vampires. It's an old practice, one that they are trying to outlaw. It still happens though,' he signs.

Behind Quill the sirens come to life, a bright searchlight spearing through the darkness. 'Oh shit! Get the fuck out of here! Now!'

Bannon grabs her arm, dragging her kicking and screaming back to the boat. He shoves her in, then unties the craft again.

'Go Bannon. Please go.'

Quill's voice is firm and clear in his mind. Quill is right. He can't leave. Not if the Warden legally owns him.

With a heavy hand gripping his heart, he pulls away from the dock, the sound of Sorcha's quiet sobs giving his own silent tears a voice.

As they move away from the dock Quill steps back, disappearing into the trees. 'We can't leave him, Bannon,' she says, sobbing as she shuffles closer to him.

'We're not leaving him. I'll come back for him. I swear,' he signs.

The island fades into the night as they speed away, taking them to safety, but at too great a cost. They're both devastated. He can feel her despair. Her sense of loss. And it mirrors his. They've left the person they love in the hands of a monster.

Bannon looks down at the bags at his feet. Two bags. This whole escape plan went exactly the way Quill had imagined. He had never planned to get on the boat. He had never planned to have the freedom he arranged for Bannon and Sorcha.

Sorcha collapses back against Bannon as she continues to sob. Keeping one hand on the rudder, Bannon wraps the other around her, holding her close as they cross the water, moving away from the prison.

SORCHA

Bannon grips her hand firmly in his, pulling her along after him, keeping her moving through the trees. They'd changed out of their uniform and jumpsuit when they reached the mainland, putting on the clothes from the bags Quill left them.

Bannon then wrapped their old clothes in some rocks, dropping them into the water with her wrist and ankle bands, before setting the boat free of its moorings. He wanted to throw off their pursuers by not showing them where they made land.

He points to the storage shed just visible through the trees.

'How are we going to get in?'

Bannon pulls a key from his pocket, then smiles.

'That would help. Can you tell if there's anyone around? I can't smell anyone.'

He shakes his head. *'We're alone.'* He takes her hand and leads her out of the trees and down the track to the shed. Bannon looks around, then slips the key into the lock. He pulls open the door, dragging her inside, before shutting it again behind them.

Sorcha lets him guide her through the cars, motorbikes, and vans in the shed. These are too old to belong to the Warden. They must be the guards' vehicles. She looks around at the various different vehicles. Would Quill have a car or motorbike in here?

She doesn't get too long to think about that as Bannon stops by a black Harley. He runs a hand along the immaculate paint as he smiles. 'I presume this is yours,' she says.'

He nods. *'Didn't think I'd see her again. Can you open the door so I can wheel her out?"*

She hurries over to the door, holding it open while he pushes his bike out. Bannon relocks the door, then helps her onto the Harley. He opens the bag he had his clothes in and takes out a helmet. Without waiting for her to argue that he should wear it, he pulls it over her head, fastening the strap under her chin.

Bannon climbs onto the bike, waiting until she wraps her arms around his waist before he starts the engine and pulls away from the storage shed. Bannon doesn't hold the bike back, trying to put as much distance as he can between them and the prison before the Warden comes after them.

She has no idea how long Bannon keeps them moving. She just hangs on, lying against his back as he pushes the bike through the night. She's cold, tired, and can't stop crying.

This wasn't the way it was supposed to go. Quill was meant to be with them. All or nothing. Why hadn't he told them the Warden owns him? They could have found a way around it. Or could have at least tried. Bannon would have found a solution. They didn't have to leave him behind like they did.

But there's nothing either of them can do about that now. All they can do is run, regroup, then come back for him.

Sorcha gets lost in her thoughts until he turns off the road, guiding the bike around a barrier leading into a forest. He dims the lights as he follows the track through the trees, until they're clear of the road.

Bannon shuts off the bike, resting it on its stand, before helping her off the Harley. He holds her against his chest when her legs wobble. It's partly down to being on the bike for a while, but exhaustion and hunger aren't helping.

He turns to the left, guiding her through the undergrowth to an uprooted oak. Bannon gestures for her to crawl into the hollow left when it fell. Once she's under cover, he follows after, protecting her from the biting wind.

A shiver runs through her body. Bannon cups her chin, slowly turning her face towards him, then holding his hand in front of her face. She's about to ask what he's doing, when she notices his hand is glowing. Sorcha stares in amazement as the glow strengthens, until less than a minute later, his hand bursts into flame.

He opens his palm offering it to her.

'Are you serious?'

'It's safe. I promise I won't burn you. Trust me.'

Trying to understand sign language while the two hands signing are on fire, is difficult and more than a little distracting. 'I didn't get that. Sorry.'

He signs the words again, a little slower this time. *'Trust me.'*

She does. There's no question of that. Sorcha slowly reaches out, feeling the warmth from his hand the closer she gets to it. But it's not a burning heat. Her fingers brush off his, the warmth instantly hitting her cold skin.

'It's not burning. I still don't understand how you do this.'

He releases her hand, but shuffles closer so she can still feel the warmth from it. *'I don't know how it works. It's just my gift. You can touch me. I promise I won't burn you.'*

Sorcha turns around, shuffling back to sit between his legs. She leans against his chest, then groans as his body warms around her. 'I have no idea what you're doing, but thank you. That feels amazing.'

His hands move in front of her, the slight glow from his skin lighting the darkness in front of them. *I'll keep watch while you get some sleep.'*

She nods, exhaustion washing over her in waves. She needs sleep, but how can they possibly sleep while Quill is back in that place?

'Why didn't he tell us?'

Bannon tucks her head under his chin and continues to sign with his hands out in front of her. *'Pride. Embarrassment. Trying to protect himself and his reputation. I understand why he didn't tell us. It doesn't make things better, but I understand.'*

'I can't believe he stayed behind. The Warden is going to blame him for this Bannon. What will he do to him?'

Bannon doesn't say anything for a long time, but the way his body tenses around her, tells her he's as worried about that as she is. *'We'll get him back, but we can't do it alone. We need to find your brothers.'*

Bannon pulls her closer again, then runs his hand over the mark on her wrist left by the band. 'But I have no idea where they are,' she says. 'I can't smell them, or feel them near me. I haven't let my wolf out for so long I've lost their scent. I wouldn't even know where to start looking.'

'Are you afraid to shift?'

She nods against his chest. 'What if I can't do it? What if I try and nothing happens?'

'You are a wolf Sorcha. A beautiful, strong, feisty, wolf. Nothing will change that.' He leans over to the side, pulls his top lip back and she watches as his fangs drop. *'Don't think about it. Just let it happen. It's part of who you are, just like this is part of who I am. We can't stop being what we are. It's impossible.'*

'You know I never thought seeing a vampire release his fangs would be something I'd grow to like a great deal.'

'*And I never thought I'd want to be anywhere near a wolf again. I want to see you as a wolf Sorcha. I need to see you like that.*'

'But what if you freak out? I don't mean that in a bad way, Bannon. I just don't want to do anything to hurt you.'

He settles back in behind her again. '*I'll be fine. Don't use me as an excuse not to try.*'

He's right. It's unfair to put this off because she's worried about traumatising him. He'd suffered so horribly thanks to a wolf. She couldn't bear if he was scared of her.

'You're right. But I don't want to be alone while I do it. Will you stay with me?'

'*I'll never leave your side if that's what you want. But I thought wolves weren't allowed to shift in front of others?*'

'They're also forbidden from falling in love with a vampire. I'm already in trouble on that count. Twice. Do you think he's all right?'

'*Quill is the strongest male I've known. He'll survive. His priority was getting you back to your family. And that's my priority too.*'

'Are you absolutely sure you'll be okay if I shift? I don't want to upset you.'

He brushes his hand through her hair, then kisses the top of her head. '*I love you Sorcha. I want to see both sides of you. And I will love that side just as much.*'

'I love you too. I'll get some rest first, then try in a few hours.'

He wraps his arms around her, his warm hands holding her close as she closes her eyes.

Exhaustion pulls her into an uneasy sleep, her thoughts on Quill, hoping the three of them will be reunited again soon.

QUILL

The whip bites into his flesh again, but he barely feels the pain. His master has been hitting him for so long, he's moved past pain to numbness.

They escaped.

Through his punishment, that's the thing that keeps him going. Bannon and Sorcha are away from here.

He's alone again.

But they're safe. That's all that matters.

His master throws the whip on the ground in front of him, then grabs him by the chin forcing his head back. 'Why are you remaining silent? I don't like hurting you like this Quillan, but I have no choice.

I have treated you so much better than I needed to, and this is how you repay me? Speak!'

'You lost a prisoner and a mute guard. No one will care.'

His head swings to the side when he's struck. 'I care! And *I* did not lose anything. *You* released them. *You* planned their escape. *You* showed them to my private dock, then turned off the alarm. *You* did that Quillan! You disrespected me in the worst possible way. You are the head guard.

'Of all the pitiful creatures kept here, you were the one I treated the best. You had everything you ever wanted. The fact you turned on me like this, will have hit my standing in this facility. If I can't even control my head guard, how can I keep a hold on the prisoners? You have damaged my reputation more than you will ever know.'

If he wasn't up to his neck in a world of trouble, he'd probably get a kick out of that. The Warden doesn't get it. It doesn't matter what he does to him now. Bannon and Sorcha are safe. He'll happily die here knowing that.

Another sharp slap brings him back to the room. Quill sits back on his legs, the chains around his wrists digging into his flesh as he puts extra pressure on them. It's just more pain to add to the list. He barely feels it anymore.

The Warden unlocks him, then walks over to the door, gesturing for someone to come inside. Quill groans to himself as Duna steps into the room. If she's shocked to see him like this she doesn't show it. But that's why he picked her as his second. She's ruthless and barely lets emotion get to her.

'You leave me no choice, Quillan. I must set an example. Get him up.'

Duna pauses for a moment, then grabs Quill by the arm, hauling him to his feet. He wobbles, leaning on her as the room spins. She drags his sorry ass into the adjoining room, and Quill knows what's about to happen. Beside the Warden's ridiculously huge bed sits a metal cage. His cage.

He hasn't been in it for well over two years, but the Warden had kept it. Threatening him with it whenever he stepped out of line.

The black metal cage is just about tall enough to allow him to sit, but lying stretched out, or standing are out of the question. It's cramped and seriously claustrophobic in there.

'Duna, would you mind putting him inside. He needs some time to consider how much he's let me down.'

She isn't as rough as she usually is with prisoners, but she's far from gentle as she pushes him down and shoves him into the cage. He stays on all fours, desperate to keep pressure off his torn back. Duna meets his eyes as she locks the cage. He's probably imagining it, but he could swear she looks sad for a second.

The Warden crouches down in front of him, reaching through the bars to slowly wipe Quill's sweat-soaked hair from his face. 'I never thought I'd have to see you in here again. It upsets me Quillan. Truly it does. But this is where we are. Duna, you're in charge until I decide Quillan's future. You're dismissed.'

Quill looks over his shoulder at her as she walks to the door. Duna meets his eyes, nodding once, before she shuts the door. She won't say anything about what the Warden just made her do.

It won't make a difference to his future either way, but for some reason he still doesn't want the guards and prisoners under his command to know he's a slave. He worked so hard to distance himself from that, only to find himself right back where he started.

The Warden covers the cage with a heavy black velvet throw, blocking out the light and cool air.

'You should get comfortable Quillan. You'll be in there for a while.'

Quill hears the door opening and closing again, then he's alone. His blood drips onto the plastic covering the floor of the cage. Fuck his comfort. The Warden is only concerned that he doesn't get blood on the expensive carpet under the cage. That would never do.

The Warden hasn't treated him like this for years. It doesn't bode well for his future. His cards have been marked, and it's just a matter of time before the Warden pushes him to breaking point. He hates the fucking cage, but being put in here is like the light at the end of a very long and painful tunnel.

Years of being abused, of being fed from over and over again, will come to an end in the next few weeks. He'll be taken by either blood loss or starvation. Maybe the Warden will dump him in the prison, and let the inmates take him out.

While he was in charge of the prison, he wasn't unnecessarily cruel or harsh. Everyone knew where they stood with him. But he doubts they'd show him an ounce of compassion when he next sees them. They'll kill him. Maybe the guards will get him first. Or perhaps the prisoners will, while the guards watched. Whatever way it will end, he'll take it.

BANNON

It takes a great deal of effort to keep his eyes closed. Over the other sounds of the forest, the disturbing sounds of bones cracking and muscles stretching are too audible. Sorcha wanted him to stay with her, but wasn't keen on him watching the actual transformation. He's grateful for that - especially with the disturbing noises coming from her.

He'd never thought about what her body would have to go through, to change from her human form to the much larger wolf. It's fascinating to think about, but he's not keen to see it take place.

Then there's silence, the sounds of the forest around them taking over again.

His heart races as the growl brings him back to the night he lost his voice. His breathing quickens in time to his heart.

He's safe. It's Sorcha. She's not going to hurt him. But that doesn't stop the panic from building.

Then he hears her voice, but it's not out loud. It's in his head.

'It's me Bannon. It's okay. I'm not going to hurt you. Damn it! I wish I could talk to you. Please stop freaking out! It's killing me.'

He opens his eyes, backing away and hitting his head against the roots of the tree. The huge, black wolf is crouched in front of him, but shuffles away when he freaks out.

'You're safe Bannon.' Her voice is in his head again. He forces himself to breathe which, at that moment, is a big ask. He feels like he's having a panic attack.

'Please stop freaking out. Please!'

He finally gets his hands to do what he needs them to. *'How are you in my head?'*

'You can hear me! Oh my God! That's amazing! I don't think I can sign with these things,' she says, lifting her front paw.

Bannon watches as the huge paw is placed back on the ground by his feet. Damn, her claws are long. Her teeth too no doubt. He closes his eyes again, the phantom pain hitting his neck making swallowing difficult. *It's Sorcha. He's safe.*

Saying the words to himself isn't helping. He hasn't been this close to a wolf since he was attacked. He thought he'd be okay because it's her, but his brain isn't on the same page.

'Just listen to my voice Bannon. Forget everything else and just listen to me.'

He rests his head back against the tree roots and concentrates on just breathing, as he listens to her. It's her voice. It's Sorcha's voice in his head. It's the fact it's coming out of a wolf that's freaking him out.

'How are you doing that?' he signs back, trying to focus on anything other than the huge wolf in front of him.

'When we're in this form we can speak to those we have a special

bond with.'

He's honoured to know he made that list, and also more than a little relieved. If she wasn't able to communicate with him it would have made their predicament all the more difficult. *'Are you okay?'*

The wolf – Sorcha, tilts her head to the side. Seeing her like this is going to take some getting used to. *'That depends on you Bannon. Are you okay?"*

He takes a minute to just look at her. His heart is beating faster than usual, but other than that, he's okay. It's her. It's his Sorcha. *'You're beautiful.'*

'You really think so?'

Bannon smiles and nods his head. *'Yeah. I never thought I'd think a wolf is beautiful. But you are. Are you okay?'*

She nods her enormous head. *'Yes. More than okay. I can't tell you how much I missed this. I never thought I'd be able to be a wolf again. How about you? How are you dealing with this?'*

'I'm okay. Can I see you out in the open?'

She shuffles back, giving him room to climb out from under the tree. He gets to his feet and approaches her as she rises to her feet. Not only is she beautiful, but she's also huge, reaching half way up his chest. *'You're bigger than I thought you'd be. Can I... would you mind if I touched you?'*

'Why would I mind?'

Bannon slowly lifts his hand towards her, wishing his heart would calm down. Sorcha takes a step forward, nuzzling against his hand. He smiles widely as he runs his hand along her head, her soft fur sliding through his fingers. *'I'm touching a wolf.'*

'I'm so relieved you're okay. I was scared you'd be wary of me.'

He runs his hand over her head, whatever lingering nerves he had, fading quickly. This is Sorcha. This is the woman he loves. And she's a fucking huge wolf! *'I'm sorry. I'm not sure how to be with you.'*

'What you're doing is perfect.'

As much as he'd like to marvel at the transformation in Sorcha, time isn't on their side. There's every chance the Warden sent guards after them. They need to keep moving. The sooner they find her brothers, the sooner they can go back and get Quill. *'Can you pick up on your brothers?'*

Sorcha turns her head to the side and takes a few deep breaths. *'Not yet. I'm out of practice. I don't know if I'll even be able to sense them when they're close to me. All I can hope is that they sense me and come.'*

While that thought is encouraging, it also fills him with dread. He's not so sure her four wolf brothers will appreciate their sister bringing a vampire home with her.

'It's been a long time, but I hope the connection still remains. My twin Fionn should have the strongest bond with me. He'll find me. I'm sure of it.'

He picks up her clothes, stuffing them into the bag. She won't be able to stay as a wolf once daylight hits, but he's sure she'll want to be a wolf for as long as possible. At least on his bike, he should be able to keep up with her. *'Which way?'*

She nods towards the left. *'That way. Are you ready?'*

'I'll try to keep up.'

MURT

The feeling hits him before he's even opened his eyes. Almost like a tingle across his skin, like electricity travelling over his body. He gets up, throwing on shorts and a t-shirt before heading downstairs and out into the courtyard. The sensation only grows as he does his workout, distracting him so much he eventually calls it quits. He stands in the courtyard, the cold morning mist coating his bare arms as he looks around him.

What the fuck is going on? It's like his wolf is picking up on something, but isn't sure what. Maybe it's just unsettled after their recent move? There are still a lot of memories in the castle that could be pissing off his wolf. Fergus and Thea are trying their best, but it'll take more than some fresh curtains on the windows and flowers in the garden to erase what happened in these walls.

He grabs his towel from the steps where he left it, turning around to smile at Fionn as his brother walks down the steps. But then he sees the look on his younger brother's face.

'What is it?'

Fionn shakes his head. 'I don't know Murt. It just... there's something off. I can't describe it. My wolf wants to be set free.'

'Yeah,' Murt agrees. 'I'm getting the same thing myself.'

They both turn when they hear footsteps behind him. There must be something in the air today. Con and Garrett seem to be just as off form today as he is.

'What the fuck is wrong with you two?' he asks as they walk over to them.

'I've got this niggling feeling. Kind of like I've forgotten something,' Garrett says. 'Something is up Murt.'

'Fuck it! I'm going to shift. Something is going on and I'll get a better feel for it that way.' He ducks into the nearest doorway, stripping out of his shorts and t-shirt before letting his wolf take control. The second he shifts, the feeling hits him like a blow to the gut. *'Sorcha.'*

'What?' Fionn asks, hearing Murt in his head.

'It's Sorcha! I can feel her. Fuck! We need to go and find her!'

'Not like this Murt,' Con says. 'We need to talk to Davyn. Then we can shift and get Fergus and some of the other vampires to drive us in some of the vans. We get caught out in the open we're no good to Sorcha.'

Con is right. As much as it pisses off his wolf, he changes back, the transformation harder than usual thanks to his stubborn wolf. He crouches on the ground, trying to recover before getting dressed.

'Are you okay?' Fionn asks as Murt finally steps out from the doorway.

'My wolf didn't want me to change back. Put up a fight.'

'Is she okay Murt?'

'I can't sense any pain Fionn. Come on. Let's get Davyn.'

The brothers hurry inside, making their way to the living area behind the Great Hall. They find Davyn and Thea sitting on the couch, a book on Davyn's knee. Murt only realises after they've disturbed them, that Thea is teaching Davyn how to read. Fair play to her. It's not a job he'd fancy for himself.

'What?'

Davyn's gruff greeting isn't a surprise. He doubts the new lord enjoys his lessons. He can't see Davyn being a model student. 'Apologies for the interruption. We're sensing Sorcha. She's nearby.'

That brings Davyn out of his bad mood. He throws the book on the floor as he stands. 'Where?'

'We don't know. I shifted in the courtyard. My wolf picked her up much clearer than I can. What we need to do is shift and search for her that way. But we can't go wandering around in broad daylight as wolves. We need transport.'

'Fergus!' Davyn's roar brings the vampire scurrying from a side door. Before Fergus can catch his breath or utter a word, Davyn jumps in. 'We need two vans. I'll drive one. Find someone for the other one.'

'Is something wrong sire?'

Davyn doesn't bother correcting him on the use of his title. 'The Whelans need to go out as wolves, and they need to go now.'

'Of course. Give me two minutes.' He hurries away, but Davyn is already on the move. 'Thea, you stay here. Murt, with me.'

Murt glances over his shoulder at Thea. She holds up her hands, fingers crossed. He nods at her as he follows Davyn from the room. The human female is quickly becoming someone he considers a friend. For someone not of their world, she's taking to her role as Davyn's mate, with an enthusiasm he can't help but respect.

She reminds him a lot of his sister. Sorcha has the same inner strength he sees in Thea.

Garret, Fionn, and Con are waiting for him in the courtyard, the three huge black wolves pacing, eager to track their lost sibling.

'I'll stay in this form,' Murt says to Davyn as two black vans pull out of a side passageway, stopping in the courtyard. 'I can communicate with the others and give you directions.'

'They can do it without you?'

'Fionn is the key to all of this. He's Sorcha's twin. His connection to her is the strongest.'

'Whatever you say. Load up!' Davyn shouts, taking the van keys from Fergus. The old vampire opens the back doors of the van and steps aside as Fionn jumps in. His brother is on edge, the hair standing to attention along his back.

'You can find her Fionn. Concentrate on her. You can do it.'

Fionn nods before lying down, his wolf nearly filling the back of the van. Murt turns to his other two brothers. 'Fionn takes the lead, but you two keep sharp. There are a lot of emotions going around.' Con and Garret climb into the back of the other van, lying down as the doors are shut. One of Fergus' men takes the keys for the other van, climbing into the driver's seat.

'You getting in or what?" Davyn asks.

Murt climbs into the passenger seat as Davyn takes the wheel. 'Where to? Murt asks Fionn as he fastens his seatbelt.

'Head east,' Fionn says in Murt's head.

'East.'

Davyn pulls out of the gate and heads down the driveway. Murt tries to keep his wolf under control, but it's far from easy. It's desperate to break free and is fighting back.

'You okay?' Davyn asks, glancing over at him.

'My wolf is complaining.'

Davyn raises his eyebrow, before turning his attention back to the road, leaving Murt to deal with his wolf issue.

She's out there. He doesn't know why they can suddenly sense her again after so long. The only thing he can think of is that she's somehow been released from wherever she was being held, or has managed to escape and turns into a wolf again. He curses to himself as he squirms in his seat. His wolf is seriously kicking his ass.

'You going to shift in the passenger seat?'

Murt shakes his head. 'Don't think so.'

Davyn's eyebrow rises again. 'Don't think so?'

'I've got it Davyn. I'll let you know if that changes.'

'I'd appreciate that.' Even so, Davyn pushes down on the accelerator, forcing the van to go faster.

Murt glances over his shoulder at his brother. Fionn's eyes are closed so he leaves him alone. He's concentrating on finding his twin.

'We're going to find her Murt.'

'I know Fionn. I know.'

He keeps his other thoughts to himself. Keeps the thought that Sorcha being released now, could be a trap to lure them out of hiding. It doesn't matter. He'll make sure they get Sorcha and bring her back to Darkhaven.

Whatever else happens after that he'll address at a later stage.

BANNON

Exhaustion and hunger claw at him, but they need to keep pushing on. They'd stopped so she could have a walk around and hopefully feel, or sense her brothers. Beside him, back in human form, Sorcha grips his hand, lost in thought.

Whenever they stop, they keep to the fields along the roadside. The Warden didn't lose Quill, but that doesn't mean he's going to let them walk away. Bannon isn't going to take any chances.

He helps Sorcha over the gate, catching her when she nearly falls. 'Thanks.' He takes her hand again, holding her upright as she stumbles again. She's exhausted. Years in confinement has left her body weaker than it should be. She needs food and sleep more than he does.

'*Anything?*'

She shakes her head. 'I can feel something, but I'm not sure if it's them or not. I'm sorry about this Bannon. I thought... I was sure...' She stops talking as she breaks down. 'Why can't I feel them Bannon?'

He pulls her into his arms as she cries. He can't do anything to help her and that kills him. Quill was supposed to be here. She was supposed to be able to find her family. They can't keep riding around the Irish countryside hoping that something goes their way.

She suddenly pushes back from him. He frowns, but she's not looking at him. She lets go of his hand, turning around, examining their surroundings.

'*What is it?*' He signs the question again when she misses it the first time.

'Sorry. I thought... there's something...' Sorcha shakes her head, dismissing whatever she was about to say. 'Ignore me. I think I'm just overtired.' She takes his hand in hers again, but then turns back towards the road so fast, she nearly pulls him over.

He's about to ask what's wrong when she smiles. Not just any smile, this one is better than anything he's seen so far. 'Oh my God...'

'*What?*'

She pulls him back from the road, dragging him behind a large oak tree, shielding them both from oncoming traffic. He lifts his hands to ask what's going on, but she gently pushes them back down. 'Hang on a sec.'

Nothing happens for a few minutes, then he spots two black vans heading in their direction along the road. Beside him, Sorcha is frozen to the spot. Her heart is racing in her chest. He has no idea what's spooked her, but he's not going to put either of them at risk by pressuring her for an answer.

Vampires have exceptional senses, but since getting to know Sorcha, he understands wolves top vampires in some cases. She could very well have sensed something he has missed.

They crouch down as the vans suddenly pull off the road, following a dirt track that runs along the hedge bordering the highway.

He watches as they pull to a stop, and a huge male steps out of the first van. He knows instantly he's a vampire. There's no mistaking that. He turns his head towards them, his green eye narrowing on their hiding place. The eye patch hiding one of his eyes doesn't help to give him a friendly appearance.

Then another huge man climbs out of the passenger side and, without being told, Bannon knows he's related to Sorcha. The resemblance is impossible to miss.

But what happens next is something he wasn't expecting. The back doors open on the two vans and three huge black wolves jump out. They sniff the air, then, as one, turn to face them.

Before he can stop her, Sorcha breaks cover, racing towards the wolves. Bannon watches as she launches herself at them and the man, her smaller body instantly covered by theirs when they crowd her.

It doesn't take long for him to realise who he's looking at.

Sorcha's family have found her.

68

Sorcha

'Where are we going?'

Murt turns around in the passenger seat and smiles at her. 'Our temporary home. You'll be safe there.'

She smiles as Fionn pulls her closer. Apart from shifting back to human form and getting dressed, Fionn hasn't let go of her. And she's not complaining. Having him near her has brought back a part of herself she'd been missing for so long. They are both complete again.

In the driver's seat, the huge vampire stays silent as he drives. He's either leaving the family to get to know each other again, or he's not a fan of talking. Murt had made the introductions, before they loaded Bannon's bike into the other van, then all piled back into the second one.

She'd heard many stories of the Raven King while she was in the prisons, but had never met the vampire. Knowing he was the one to sell her to the prison is still something she can't quite figure out. Just like she can't figure out why her brothers are now working with his son. But she trusts Murt. He wouldn't do anything to put their family in danger. It's not what he does.

She smiles across at Bannon, hoping to put the vampire at ease. The poor guy has been like a deer in headlights since her brothers arrived. It's understandable. The four of them don't exactly give off warm and fuzzy vibes.

She'll have to talk to them about Bannon and Quill as soon as she can get them alone. It's not a talk she's looking forward to. She doubts her brothers will be thrilled that she's fallen in love with two vampires. But they are working with Davyn, so perhaps they won't be as against it as she thinks. Who is she kidding? One vampire they might be able to accept. Two? That could be pushing it.

The vans pull into a stone courtyard and come to a stop at the bottom of the impressive stone steps leading to the castle door. Davyn climbs out of the van, and opens the back doors so they can all get out.

A tall thin man hurries out through the vast doorway, handing her a blanket, before passing another one to Bannon. 'Welcome. Do come inside to get warm. You both look frozen.'

'This is Fergus,' Murt explains as he gets out of the passenger seat. 'He runs the place while Davyn is in Wales. You can trust him. Fergus, this is Sorcha and Bannon.'

He stops and smiles at both of them. 'I am so pleased to meet you. I have heard a great deal about you from your brothers. And welcome Bannon.'

'Bannon can't speak,' she explains to Fergus. 'But I can translate what he says. Or at least I can try to. I'm still learning.'

Fergus smiles and lifts his hands. *'It's very nice to meet you*

Bannon. *You are most welcome.'*

'You can sign?' Sorcha says, thrilled at the huge smile on Bannon's face. She instantly likes Fergus. There's something about him, something that reminds her of someone, but she can't place him. She feels like she's met him before somewhere, but has no idea where.

Fergus nods. 'Yes. One of the cooks is deaf. I learned it so she would not be at a disadvantage. I'm glad I can put it to more use.'

'Sorcha was the first person I met who was interested in learning,' Bannon signs to Fergus. *'I can't tell you how amazing it is to meet someone else who I can talk to.'*

'Well, I'm glad I can be of service Bannon. If you need me to speak for you, please let me know. It would be my pleasure.'

'How about we get these two inside,' Davyn says. 'They could probably do with some food Fergus.'

'Of course. I'll see to that.'

Feeling completely out of place, Sorcha follows Davyn and her brothers through the huge door and into the castle. She keeps a firm grip on Bannon's hand, grateful for his reassuring presence. Even with her brothers beside her, she's still a little uneasy.

It's been eight years since she last saw them, and so much has happened to all of them. It will take time to settle back in with them again, to feel like a part of the clan again.

Bannon follows after the pack, grateful that Sorcha has not let go of his hand. It's something her brothers have noticed, but thankfully not commented on. He's caught Murt looking at him a few too many times to be just mere curiosity.

They are led into a vast living area, filled with comfortable looking couches, surrounding an impressive fireplace. A long table sits in the centre of the room, covered in books and papers. A beautiful woman with long dark hair is glaring at a computer screen. She turns and smiles widely when she sees Davyn.

She gets to her feet and hurries over to the vampire, throwing her arms around his neck and kissing him. 'Welcome back.'

He takes her hand and nods to Sorcha. 'This is Sorcha and Bannon.'

Sorcha yelps when the woman hugs her tightly as if they've known each other for years. 'I can't believe you're here!' She releases Sorcha and smiles apologetically. 'Sorry about attacking you like that. I just feel like I know you, after all these weeks looking for you. I'm Thea. I'm Davyn's mate. Human mate. I feel that needs to be said around here,' she says, gesturing to her companions.

'Well, it's great to meet you too. And thank you for whatever part you played in locating the prisons. This is Bannon. He worked at the prison where I was held. He helped me get out.'

'Nice to meet you,' he signs as Sorcha translates.

'Hi,' Thea signs back. 'Sorry. That's all I know. I did a short course years ago, but I don't want to say more in case I get it wrong and insult you by mistake.'

'Sit down.' They do as Davyn commands, taking seats on the large couches surrounding the fire. 'Fergus will bring you some food. We'll give you time to talk. Shout if you need anything.'

Sorcha nods appreciatively at Davyn as he leaves the room, Thea's hand firmly in his. Less than a minute later, Fergus appears with bowls of stew for them, and Sorcha nearly groans aloud as the aroma hits her. 'This smells incredible. Thank you.'

'You're most welcome. I've made up some rooms in the guest quarters and took the liberty of arranging some clean clothes for you both.'

'You're a star,' Sorcha says around a mouthful of stew. 'I'm sorry. This is so good.'

He smiles warmly at her. 'I will make sure to pass your compliments to the cook.'

'How the fuck did you get out?' Murt asks as they eat. 'We found the Level One and Level Two prisons, but hadn't been able to find the Level Three one. It can't have been easy to get out of.'

She shakes her head as she swallows. She's truly never tasted anything as good as this meal. 'Bannon was one of the guards on the day shift. He looked out for me over the last few weeks.'

'Is that so?' Murt says, his eyes targeting Bannon who swallows deeply. 'How did he do that?'

'Oh back off Murt! Bannon is one of the good ones.' She reaches out and takes his hand. 'He's been incredible.'

Garret growls as he slumps back in the chair. 'Fuck Sorcha! Really?'

'Yes Garret. Really. What's the problem? We're sitting in a castle owned by a vampire!' she says, gesturing around her. 'Are you really going there?'

'I'll work with a vampire. Doesn't mean I'm going to fuck one.'

'Garret!' Murt's roar silences her brother. She loves Garret to bits, but he's an opinionated hothead at the best of times.

'Is it not good enough that our sister is back? What the fuck does it matter who she's with?' Murt looks over at Bannon. 'Ignore him. He's a dick. I'm the clan leader and I say you're welcome at our table any time. Is that understood?'

That last comment is directed at Garret, but Bannon nods too. The poor guy is going to need a stiff drink, after all this alpha male chest beating. She'd forgotten how stubborn her brothers are.

She smiles at Bannon, and he nods encouragingly. She'd taken the first step. She might as well go all the way. Having Murt defend them as he had, gives her a little hope he'll stay on that path, instead of joining Garret in his opinion.

But she's nervous.

Murt was always the one she would go to whenever she needed help. It was a given. Not once did she have to convince herself to speak to him.

Until now.

Asking for him to put himself and her brothers in danger to save Quill, might be a step too far. The idea of being in love with both Quill and Bannon is still so new to her. How does she tell him about the two vampires? Garret and Con will be a whole other problem, but if she gets Murt on side, they'll fall in line. That's the way their clan works.

And then there's Fionn. Out of her four brothers, she hopes he will be the most accepting of her relationship with the two vampires.

Bannon taps her knee, getting her attention. '*No matter what happens, I love you. We both do,*' he signs.

She smiles as she meets his eyes. Never has she believed someone more.

Murt rests his head on his hand as he stares at her. 'Out with it.'

'What?'

'There's something on your mind. Talk.'

'It's a bit sensitive.'

'You're in love with Bannon.' He laughs at the look on both of their faces. 'I may be a lone wolf and all that, but I'm not a complete fucking idiot. Anyone with half a brain can see how you two look at each other.'

'But there's more.'

Fionn takes over, clearly sensing the stress in his twin. 'What is it Sorcha?'

'We left someone behind. Someone we need to go back for.'

'Who?' Con asks.

'The head guard was actually the one to get both of us out. He couldn't leave because the Warden of the prison owns him. He stayed behind so we could escape. We need to rescue him.'

Her brothers are silent for a long time before Murt slowly shakes his head. 'Sorcha...'

It's a no. Saying her name in that tone is as good as a no. 'Please Murt. Don't say no. We need your help to get Quill out.'

'I get he helped you and you owe him, but I'm not risking our family to get him out. There are five of us and your vampire friend. How many guards do they have at the prison? Too fucking many for us to handle I'll bet. I'm sorry, but it's a no.'

'You don't understand! I can't leave him. Bannon and I can't leave

379

him.'

'What don't I understand? Explain it to me.'

'We're... Bannon, Quill and I... we're... together. The three of us. I love them both and they love me.'

It's like she flicked a switch, pausing time at that moment. He's not frowning, not showing any emotion on his face at all, which is nearly worse. Garret curses under his breath, but has the good sense to leave it at that. Con's face is blank, but that's normal for him.

But Fionn's reaction is the one that sticks with her. He's smiling. He understands how she feels, and that means the world to her.

The problem is, he won't speak out against Murt. Never has, and probably never will. He's not weak - far from it, but he does respect his eldest brother too much to argue against him.

'Please Murt. I'm asking my big brother and clan leader for help. I am begging you.'

She keeps her eyes locked on his as he mulls that over. They won't be able to get to Quill without his help. All that would happen is Bannon and herself would end up right back inside beside Quill. The Warden has too many guards. She needs the rest of the pack if they're to have even a slight chance of rescuing him.

But Murt is no fool. He wouldn't be in the position he's in if he were. Her eldest brother is a formidable leader and fighter. But he's also stubborn and will put the pack before anyone else. That's where she may hit a few problems.

And that was before she mentioned the fact she's in love with the two vampires. That won't have done her any favours.

'Sorcha...'

'I love him, Murt. I desperately need your help to rescue the male I love.'

'One of the two vampires you love.'

'Yes, I'm in love with both Bannon and Quill. And they are both in love with me and with each other. What does that matter? Quill sacrificed himself because he loves us.' She reaches across and takes

Murt's hand in hers, trying to get him to focus on her, and not the minor detail she's with two vampires.

'I spent too long alone in the dark. Then Bannon appeared in my life. And he changed it. I was still in Hell, but every time I saw him my life was made that little bit more bearable. When Quill finally opened up to us, it was like the final piece of our puzzle had clicked into place. Bannon got through his darkness too. We were in the worst place possible but somehow, when we were together, a little light shone through. I know it's unconventional and I am humiliating the pack.'

'Stop!' His sudden outburst surprises her. 'Now you listen to me Sorcha Whelan. Nothing you do will ever humiliate the pack. Your pack are your brothers, and we are nothing but proud of you. I haven't got the first fucking clue how you survived as long as you did in those prisons. But you did, and I am so, so, proud of you. We all are.'

'Too fucking right,' Garret says, surprising her.

'I'm proud to be your brother Sorcha,' Con says. 'Really fucking proud.'

'Me too Sis. You know that,' Fionn says smiling widely at her.

Murt squeezes her hand so hard it nearly hurts. 'I am so grateful you were able to find that light in the darkness. That you found something to fight for, to live for. We only saw Level One and Two of those prisons, and they were disturbing, so we can't even begin to imagine what Level Three was like, or what you have endured. I couldn't give a fuck if you're in love with an army of vampires, humans, wolves, or fucking leprechauns!'

'You mean that?'

'Of course I do,' he says, glancing at Bannon and nodding once. 'You seem decent enough Bannon.'

The vampire smiles, then nods, clearly in shock at Murt's acceptance of him.

'Love isn't something you turn your back on,' Murt continues. 'And if you've been lucky enough to find two guys who love you as much as you love them, you can't let that go.'

'So, will you help us? I know I'm asking a lot, and I know we'll be outnumbered, but we're going back either way. We will not abandon him.'

He blows out a breath as he rubs his jaw. 'I want to help you get him out, but what I said before stands. The numbers don't work.'

'I've seen you four fight. You can hold your own. And Bannon can handle himself.'

'If this warden fucker owns Quill, he won't let him go easily. From what I've heard, it costs a fair bit to own your own vampire - unlike us wolves who used to be picked up for free. We're going to need help. That's the part I'm not thrilled about. The Elders will be looking for us. If any of us are seen outside this protected area, we're dead. I'll take the lot of them down before I let that happen, but I've just got you back. I'm not willing to risk your life.'

'What help are you talking about?'

'Last year our pack swore allegiance to Davyn. It's a long story, but it's not something I regret...yet.'

She can't believe Murt of all people just said that. 'You did?'

'That's a big deal,' Bannon signs to Murt as she translates. *'Why would you do that?'*

'It was the right thing to do,' Murt explains. 'The past needs to be put behind us. It's just making us weaker. The alliance with Davyn and the Blackjacks will strengthen our pack. Besides, I kind of like Davyn. He's a no-nonsense vampire. Very black and white. It's refreshing.'

'But what does he ask for in return?'

Murt waits while Sorcha translates again. 'Nothing. We get to call this place home, and he gets us keeping an eye on things while he's away. It's a mutual back scratching arrangement.'

'But what can some stuffy well-fed lord do to help?' Sorcha asks. 'We need an army.'

Murt grins as her. 'Davyn is also a Blackjack. He's our army.'

QUILL

He bites back a shout as a hand grabs him by the wrist, dragging him from the cage. The plastic sheet is ripped from his back, the wounds opening again as the scabs are torn free. He looks up to find two of the Warden's bodyguards sneering down at him.

'Get up!'

There's no point in arguing. They're not going to give a fuck about him. Quill uses the cage bars to drag his ass off the floor, but doesn't make it further than his knees. His body has had enough. Being locked in the cramped cage for who knows how long, unable to stand or even lie down, hasn't done him any favours.

Realising they could be waiting a while, they take an arm each and lift him to his feet. He's brought downstairs in the Warden's private elevator. He's either being taken off the island, or into the prison.

This isn't going to end well for him. His gut feeling is proved right when he's dragged into the exercise yard. But the Warden has added a new piece of equipment to the centre of the yard. Quill works hard to steady his breathing, as he is brought over to the thick wooden post standing proud in the dirt. His arms are lifted above his head and heavy metal restraints locked around them, keeping him upright, his torn back pressed against the rough piece of wood.

Quill braces his legs, trying to stay up on his own feet. The cold rain and breeze coming off the Celtic Sea is strangely refreshing after the stifling cage. He looks around the yard, seeing Duna in the shadows at the far side, her blue eyes glowing as she watches proceedings. She's probably waiting until she can step in and permanently take his role.

She's welcome to it. Welcome to all the horrors that accompany the role. He looks up as the Warden approaches, a large black umbrella in his hand, keeping the rain from his perfect suit and groomed hair.

'Well, how are we doing?'

Quill doesn't bother responding. The Warden isn't looking for an answer. He forces his weak legs to hold him upright, taking some pressure from his wrists.

'Are you ready to talk yet Quillan?'

'About what sir?'

After everything he's taken over the last few days, the slap barely registers. He'll take a slap over having his back torn apart as soon as it heals.

'Where are the wolf and the mute guard? Where did you send them?'

'I didn't send them anywhere sir.'

'Don't lie to me! I own you Quillan. I can decide if you live or die. Do you understand that?'

'Yes, sir. But I can't tell you what I don't know.' He barely stops himself from screaming that at the Warden. He's been asked the same thing over and over again and given the same answer.

He's cold, sore, exhausted, hungry, and desperately worried about Bannon and Sorcha. But the fact the Warden is still asking him where they are is a good sign. If he had them, he wouldn't be wasting his time repeatedly asking the same question. Quill would still be getting this four-star treatment, but the Warden isn't one for wasting his time.

The Warden sighs loudly. 'I see. So that's how you want to play this.'

'I'm not... playing sir.' He can't stop his teeth chattering, no matter how hard he tries not to show weakness. He's never been so cold. 'I don't know where they are.'

'Very well. Perhaps some more time out here will help to jog your memory.' He turns to leave but stops, his smile sending a new shiver through Quill. 'I nearly forgot.' He reaches into his pocket and takes out a thick chain and padlock. 'No need to hide who you really are any longer. I believe after this incident your time as head guard might have come to an end.'

He unlocks the silver bracelet engraved with the Warden's crest, slipping it into his pocket. He had the bracelet made for Quill instead of the chain, while he worked as a guard in the prison. Looks like that privilege has been revoked.

He wraps the chain tightly around Quill's neck, snapping the padlock in place. 'Much better. Now we all know where we stand. Don't we Quillan? Duna, I'll leave him with you. Do not disappoint me.'

He glares at the Warden as he walks away, whistling to himself. Quill lets his head drop back against the post, staring up at the moon through the rain. It gives him some comfort to think that Bannon and Sorcha might be looking at the moon in that moment. That they're together and safe somewhere.

At least he hopes they're safe. Bannon would be doing everything he can to protect Sorcha. Maybe they've even managed to reach her brothers. That makes him smile. He'd love to have seen her running with her brothers. Five powerful wolves reunited again.

But that's not going to happen. He knows he won't see Bannon or Sorcha again.

Or his father.

He hadn't thought about him a lot over the last few years. There was no point. He was here and his father was far away. But since falling in love, his father has entered his thoughts often.

He thinks his father is still alive, but the odds are stacked against him. He'd overheard a new prisoner speaking about the death of the Raven King. No loss there. That bastard deserved to die in the worst way possible. But what did that mean for the vampires who served him?

What did that mean for his father?

Another shiver races through his body as the wind howls around the courtyard. Quill closes his eyes, picturing Sorcha and Bannon as he tries to get some sleep, or lose consciousness - whichever one comes first.

But he's not going to be that lucky. Duna walks over to him, her wet blonde hair plastered to her face. He hates the way she looks at him. Hates the pity he sees. 'Don't you fucking dare!'

She looks up at him, frowning.

'Do what you have to, but don't pity me. I didn't train you like that.'

'I don't want to do this to you.'

He wasn't expecting her to say that. Duna always did everything she was told. She's never once refused, or even hesitated when given an order. 'You don't have a choice.'

'It's not that simple.'

'It is. We do what we're told. It's how we survive.'

'But it's you Quill.'

He laughs at her response. He wishes he had known this side of

Duna while he was still the head guard. 'I'm just another prisoner now. Forget everything else.'

She clenches her jaw, looking at him in silence for a few seconds before she nods. 'He wants me to let the inmates loose on you. They get a minute each with you. He doesn't want them to kill you – just...'

'Beat the living shite out of me?'

She nods.

That doesn't surprise him. The Warden is seriously pissed off with him. He's going to do whatever he can to put Quill firmly back in his place 'Let them in. I'm fucking freezing. The sooner this is over with, the sooner I can go back to my nice comfy cage.'

'I'm sorry,' she mutters under her breath before she turns to another guard. 'Let them in!'

Quill nods at her when she gives the command. He doesn't hold this against her. They're all in the same situation. You do what you're told, or you die.

BANNON

Bannon paces the Great Hall, his boots echoing off the cold stone floor as he walks. He wanted to leave Sorcha alone with her brothers, but she insisted he stay. She wants him nearby, and he's not going to argue. In truth, he doesn't want to let her out of his sight. Even though they're surrounded by her family, and all of Davyn's people in the castle, he's uneasy. Incomplete.

All Quill and himself wanted was to keep Sorcha safe and help her get back to her family. They did that. But leaving him behind wasn't part of the deal. Given the choice, he would have given his life to save Quill as well as Sorcha. That male didn't deserve to be anyone's property, to be a *belonging* that the Warden can use and abuse as he sees fit.

He can't stop the dark thoughts that have plagued him since he heard Quill's words. The Warden was taking his blood. Using Quill to feed from. A constant supply of a heroin-like drug to feed his habit.

But what else was the Warden using Quill for? That's the part he can't pull his thoughts away from. Was he forcing himself on Quill? Forcing Quill to do things to him? He curses to himself. Thinking like that won't help him or Quill. Whatever the Warden is doing to Quill, he will die by Bannon's hand. If he knows Sorcha, her wolf will want to spend some time alone with the Warden too.

He goes back to the table, when Davyn comes back into the room with Thea and Fergus. Murt nods at Davyn as he walks past. Sorcha's brother is one intimidating man, but the fact he's so respectful of Davyn says a lot about the Blackjack. Bannon is not going to cross him no matter what.

'What's going on Murt?' Davyn asks as he takes a seat at the head of the table.

'We need to ask for your help. Sorcha and Bannon need to go back to the prison for a guard who helped them escape. He's important to them.'

'You don't need to ask for my help. I'll be giving it anyway. The plan was to take down all the prisons. I'm not about to walk away and leave the worst one operating. That was never going to happen.'

'Thank you, Davyn,' Sorcha says, taking Bannon's hand in hers.

'Hold on to your thanks. We still haven't got a fucking clue where it is. That's where I'll need your help, not the other way around,' he says to Sorcha and Bannon.

He nods to the map on the table. 'Any idea where to start?'

The prison is on the Hook Peninsula,' Bannon signs, with Sorcha translating. He points to an island just off the coastline. *This is it.*'

'That'll work,' Davyn says, adjusting the patch covering his eye. 'Can't get better than the exact location. Do you know where this guard will be in the house? Don't suppose either of you can sense him? Might help narrow down the search area.'

Bannon shakes his head along with Sorcha, who says, 'Bannon and Quill fed from each other a few days ago. Quill can hear Bannon in his head, but neither of us has sensed him since he got us out.'

They all turn as a loud crash comes from the doorway. Davyn gets to his feet along with Sorcha and Murt, hurrying over to Fergus. The vampire had dropped the tray of beverages he was holding, and is now propping himself up against the wall, looking as if he's about to pass out.

'Are you okay?' Davyn asks, helping him upright.

'I apologise sire. I'll clean it up.'

'No, you fucking won't. Sit down.'

'Forgive me for interrupting. I couldn't help but overhear... did you... what name did you mention just now?'

'Quill?' Sorcha says. 'His full name is—'

'Quillan,' Fergus finishes.

Bannon and Sorcha look at each other, before looking back at Fergus. 'Yes. How did you know?'

'Does Quillan have one blue and one green eye?'

'Yes.'

Fergus breaks into tears when he sees Bannon's response. Fergus laughs, then shouts and jumps in the air. 'I knew it! I knew he was alive. I've hoped he was. Every night I'd think of him, picturing his face in the hopes that it would bring him back to me.' He hugs Sorcha tightly, before surprising Bannon by doing the same to him. 'Thank you!'

'I'm confused,' Sorcha says.

'Quillan is my son,' Fergus explains, wiping his face with his sleeve. 'The King stole him from me decades ago. Is he well? Where is he? How is he?'

'How about you take a seat,' Sorcha says, guiding the vampire over to one of the couches. He settles into the seat, taking a brandy from Fionn with a grateful smile. 'I can see it now. Quill looks like you.

That's why you look familiar to me. I can't believe this!'

'I apologise for my behaviour.'

'Shut the fuck up,' Davyn says, cutting him off. 'Never apologise to me for something like that.'

The vampire takes a drink as he tries to compose himself.

Bannon can barely believe what he just heard.

Quill's father!

Of all the places to find him. Of all the vampires to be working with Sorcha's brothers. But even if he hadn't been told Fergus was related to Quill, he would have seen the resemblance sooner or later.

Fergus had spent his life in servitude under the vile Raven King, then he finds out his son was taken and is a slave himself.

'What happened to him?' Sorcha asks.

Fergus wipes a shaky hand over his face before he speaks. 'I'm afraid I do not know much about it. We...' he pauses and closes his eyes for a moment. 'Quillan and I did not always see eye to eye. He was a strong-willed boy, and it only grew in intensity along with him.'

He notices Sorcha smiling and nodding as he says. 'I see that hasn't changed.'

Both Sorcha and Bannon shake their heads. 'He's stubborn,' Sorcha says.

'I can well believe that,' Fergus continues. 'Unfortunately, it was something that came between us. In truth, it was my fault. I was working... forgive me, forced to work for the Raven King. Quill was unhappy about the situation. He wanted me to leave. To run away from that life and be free.'

Fergus pauses again and nods to Davyn. 'Escape isn't always an option, as you well know.'

'No,' Davyn mutters. 'It's not.'

'Quillan couldn't accept that, and I understand why. Perhaps he thought I was being weak by not fighting back, but I was trying to protect him. That's all I've ever wanted to do. I kept him away from the King. Or thought I had. But he noticed everything. When Quillan transitioned, he caught the King's attention. My son and I have the same blood in our veins, but Quillan had far surpassed me. He was strong, and so much larger than most of the other males in the area.

'One day when I arrived back from work, I found the house destroyed and Quillan gone. A representative of the Raven King was waiting for me. I was told that my son had been taken into the employ of the King elsewhere and, if I wished to keep him safe, I would do as I'm told.'

'Fuck!' Dav's angry curse is the only answer to all that. 'You should have told me when it happened.'

'You were in your own world of pain Davyn. There's nothing you could have done. Your father controlled everyone under this roof. We were all trying to survive in our own way.'

'And you never saw him again?' Sorcha asks.

Fergus shakes his head. 'Until you mentioned his name just now, I feared he was dead. I asked. I begged so many times for information on where my son was. But the only mention he made of him was that he was fighting well.'

Bannon turns as Davyn growls again. 'The fighting pits?'

Bannon had heard of them over the years, but thought that they were rumours or just stories. Or at least hoped they were. Sorcha's brother Fionn had filled them in on some of Davyn's background.

Learning that the fighting pits were so much worse than anything he could have imagined makes him feel sick. The thought that Quill could have been forced to fight for his life, until the Warden somehow got him, helps his fire burn deep inside. The more he hears about the Warden, the more he wants to see his flesh burn.

Davyn takes out his phone and turns on the video when the call is answered. 'Davyn. How can I help?'

'This is Ethan,' Davyn explains. 'He's the co-founder of the Blackjacks.'

Ethan lifts his hand, waving at everyone.

'I need you to search ownership records for a vampire called

Quillan,' Davyn says. 'His owner is some fucker on an island off the Hook Peninsula in Wexford. He's the final prison warden.'

'Of course. Just a moment.'

No one speaks as Ethan runs his search. Sorcha takes Bannon's hand in hers, rubbing her thumb over his skin as they wait. He loves that she keeps doing that. She touches him, takes his hand, rubs his arm. It's like she's reminding him that she's there with him. There for him. Maybe she needs the contact with him too. They're both desperately worried about Quill.

He looks over at Fergus, huddled in the corner of a couch by the fire. The vampire looks so much smaller than he was when they first met.

'Ah,' Ethan eventually says.

'Ah what?' Davyn asks before anyone else can speak.

'Quillan's owner is Anton Ormanson. There's not much about him online, but he's what you would call *new money*. His family hit it big about a century ago, and he's been living off the proceeds ever since. Ormanson is very much about appearances. He likes to splash his cash around. He throws lavish parties at his mansion where he shows off the artwork, furniture, etc he's purchased using his parents' funds.'

'While wolves suffer in the prison under his feet,' Murt says, glancing at his sister.

'Indeed,' Ethan says. 'He's a vile individual.'

'So, I go in and buy Quillan back?' Davyn asks.

'Buy him back,' Fergus asks, sitting up in the chair. 'You can do that? You can buy my son?'

Ethan shakes his head. 'I wish it were that simple. Quillan is your son?' he asks Fergus.

'He is.'

Ethan nods solemnly. 'In usual circumstances, Davyn would be able to do that. One of our team was owned. He had been for years. We found a loophole that allowed Davyn, as a lord, to go in and buy

Shep from his owner. That only worked because she couldn't refuse a lord. The problem in this situation is that Ormanson is a lord too.'

'What? How the fuck did he manage that?' Davyn asks.

'He bought the title. I know,' he continues as everyone in the room grumbles in response to that. 'Bought or not, legally his title is as valid as yours is Davyn. Which also means that legally, you have no claim on Quillan. There are only two ways you can get him back without him having to look over his shoulder for the rest of his life. One, the Warden willingly signs Quill over to you.'

Bannon shakes his head at that, the sudden appearance of a blue flame on his hands silencing the room.

Sorcha rubs his arm, drawing his attention back to her. 'Keep a hold on that. Quill will need every bit of your power to get him out.'

He nods, pulling the fire back inside, before taking her hand.

'You can take Bannon's response to that option as a *never going to happen*,' Sorcha says. 'The Warden is feeding from Quill. We think he might be addicted.'

'I didn't think he would just hand him over,' Ethan says, his smile helping to calm Bannon's rage. 'It's also not going to help that Ormanson is drinking Quill's blood. Hybrids can drink Prime blood, but not often, or in amounts of more than a mouthful or two. It is highly addictive. I would guess Ormanson is well past merely addicted to Quill's blood. I fear you are correct Bannon. He's not going to let Quill go.'

Fergus wipes the tears from his face. 'So, there is no hope? My son must stay with that bastard for the rest of his life?'

'I wouldn't go saying that just yet Fergus. What about option two?' Murt asks.

Ethan smirks. 'I think Davyn knows the answer to that question.'

Davyn leans back in his chair, stretching his legs out in front of him. 'Oh, that's easy. We take him by force.'

Sorcha

Bannon taps the table in front of her, drawing her attention from her plate. She hasn't eaten a bit of her dinner. She can't stomach it.

'You need to eat.'

'I've no appetite.' She nods towards his empty plate. The cooks in the castle are exceptional. Every meal she's had since she arrived was like something you'd get in the best pub anywhere in the country. It was tasty, homely, and filling. 'I see your appetite is just grand.'

He smiles as he wipes his mouth with his napkin before dropping it on his plate. *'I need my energy. And the food is amazing.'*

'You have a point there.' She pushes her plate away, then sits back in the wooden chair. 'What time is it?' She really needs to get a watch for herself. Having her own clothes at the moment would be a start. It's going to take a while to build up her belongings again.

'Murt wants to plan our attack in an hour.'

One hour. It could be a lifetime. Her brothers are going through the castle armoury, seeing if there's anything they can use to help rescue Quill. Even with all the weapons in the castle, the odds are against them. She knows that. Five wolves and one vampire won't be much of an army.

She has no doubt Davyn is a lethal fighter, but she can't see him tagging along. This isn't his battle.

Bannon frowns and points to his ear. Sorcha listens, finally hearing a dull whirring sound coming from outside. They walk over to the window, peering out into the darkness. Bannon points to the left and she sees a faint light far in the distance.

'Is that in the air?'

He nods, then turns, and makes his way over to the door, pulling her along after him. They hurry down the stairs to the courtyard, not surprised to see her brothers are already there. Davyn moves to the front of the crowd watching the huge black helicopter land just outside the gates to the courtyard.

'You have got to be kidding me,' Murt says as the door opens on the craft and a ramp lowers to the ground.

Sorcha's question never gets voiced, when what looks like a small army steps down from the craft. Eight people walk over to the castle, but not all of them are human. Six of the new arrivals are kitted out in matching uniforms and are carrying so many weapons she's surprised they can walk.

She squeezes Bannon's hand in hers when she realises exactly who she's looking at.

The rest of the Blackjacks have just arrived.

'What the fuck are you doing here, Nix?' Murt asks as the group stops in front of them.

The tall woman at the front smiles at Murt, shaking his hand. 'You honestly didn't think we'd let you have all the fun alone, did you?'

He looks to his brothers, then over at Sorcha and Bannon. 'You're going to help us?'

'Dav filled us in on what's going on. This isn't just a wolf problem. These prisons need to be dealt with. We're not here to step on anyone's toes, I promise. We'll take your lead on this, but we're going in with you. We'll have your back.'

Sorcha bursts into tears before she can stop herself. What seemed like a hopeless situation a few minutes ago, is now far from that. With the help of these fighters, they have a strong chance of getting Quill out.

Murt pulls her into a hug, giving her a chance to stop the tears, before releasing her again. Nix walks over to her and holds out her hand. 'I'm Phoenix, or Nix. I take it you're Sorcha. I can't tell you how pleased I am to meet you.'

'Nice to meet you Nix. I'm so embarrassed about crying. I'm just... this could work now. Thank you.'

'No need to thank us. We owe your brothers. Besides, this is what we do. So,' she says, addressing everyone else. 'How about we get a plan in place. Let's not leave Quill there a second longer than he has to be.'

72

QUILL

He fights against the hands, desperate to get away from them before he's hurt again. But these ones are different. Gentler somehow.

'Calm down, sir. It's Duna. I'm just trying to get you down.'

Down from where? He has no idea where he is, or what she needs to get him down from, but he's grateful for any help. He's so cold he can barely feel her hands on him.

He's lowered to the ground and a tube brushes against his lips. 'I got you some Prime blood. Drink it before someone catches me and we're both hanging from a post.'

He opens his mouth, groaning when the warm blood hits his tongue. After a few mouthfuls, he's able to open his eyes. Then he remembers why Duna had to get him down.

The rain has eased, but the biting wind is still swirling around the courtyard. He's surprised the prisoners didn't kill him. He was sure that when he was locked to the post, he wouldn't come to again.

'How bad?' he asks between mouthfuls of blood.

'You're still alive and in one piece for the most part,' Duna says, keeping her voice low. 'You're probably faring better than the Warden wanted. The prisoners weren't keen on laying into you as much as he hoped. Some didn't hold back, but most gave you a few slaps or punches and left it at that. Seems your *harsh but fair* way of running the prison made an impact on them. Spared you a serious beating.'

While he's grateful that they held back, he's also disappointed that he woke up. That wasn't what he wanted. Now he'll have to go back to the Warden and deal with more of his shit.

'Can you walk?' she asks, stuffing the empty blood bag into her jacket pocket. 'I can call in help to carry you, but I'm guessing you'd prefer I didn't.'

'I can walk.' With her help, he drags himself to his feet. If he's to go back up the Warden, he'll use his own fucking legs to carry himself.

Duna supports him as they silently and slowly walk from the exercise yard to the Warden's private elevator. Once inside, he examines himself in the mirrored walls. He barely recognises the male looking back at him. His soaking hair is plastered to his head, blood and mud coating one side of his head. His tattoos are barely visible through the bruises and cuts on his chest, and both arms are covered in blood from the shackles.

Maybe the Warden will just throw him in a corner somewhere and leave him to rot in peace. He's hardly going to want anything to do with him if he's in this state.

The *ping* as they get to the Warden's living quarters sends a chill over his already freezing skin. Duna takes his arm, leading him to the Warden's door.

He's fucking grateful she doesn't talk to him or ask him any questions. She's already done enough by giving him blood.

'Ah, Duna. Thank you,' the Warden says as she opens the door. 'Can you help him over to the sheeting on the floor and put him on his knees facing my desk.'

Duna lowers Quill onto the centre of the plastic sheeting protecting the Warden's flooring. Quill keeps his eyes away from Duna as she straightens, but her fingers linger on his arm for a few seconds before she walks away.

Quill holds his breath when the door closes, leaving him and the Warden alone again.

'How did your punishment go, Quillan? Are you ready to apologise?'

Quill doesn't bother engaging. The Warden usually hears what he wants to hear – no matter what you say to him.

'Crawl to me. Slowly.'

When Quill stays where he is, the Warden sighs dramatically. 'Get over here now, or I will order Duna to kill ten prisoners. There are plenty more where they came from. I'll have no problem refilling the cells again.'

Quill can be an asshole at times, but he's not about to sacrifice ten wolves for his life. Resigned to the fact this is going to happen, Quill does as instructed, crawling slowly to the Warden's chair, stopping on his knees between the Warden's legs.

His owner takes a thick metal open-mouth gag from his desk drawer and holds it up to Quill. 'Open.'

Quill doesn't move fast enough so the Warden grabs him by the jaw, digging his fingers into Quill's flesh. 'Now Quillan!'

Before he can fully open his mouth, the Warden jams the gag in, stretching Quill's jaw to painful limits. The Warden fastens the buckle behind Quill's head, securing it with a padlock.

He hates the fucking thing. The Warden always strapped it on when he wanted to use Quill. It had nothing to do with control or hurting Quill. He knows the Warden uses it because he's not quite sure that Quill won't bite his fucking dick off given half the chance.

He's probably right to worry.

The Warden opens his fly and offers Quill his limp dick. It's always limp. The vile thing is shoved into Quill's mouth, making him gag as it slides against his tongue. As much as he detests this, he knows by now that the only way it'll end is when the Warden comes.

The problem is, the bastard knows every trick in the book and can put it off as long as he wants. It doesn't matter what Quill tries, the vampire prolongs it, drawing it out until Quill nearly passes out from the pain in his jaw.

But this time is different. It seems this time the Warden does want to come. It's Quill who can't do what's necessary to bring an end to the humiliation.

He's so fucking tired he can barely move. Even when the Warden takes over, thrusting his hips, driving his flaccid dick into Quill's mouth, it's a futile effort. Unless the Warden is going to support Quill's weight too, this isn't going anywhere.

Irritated by the lack of enthusiasm from Quill, the Warden pulls out and shoves Quill back. 'Yet again you disappoint me. What do you expect me to do with you when you can't even apologise?'

He zips up his fly but leaves the gag on, which scares the fuck out of Quill. He needs it off – now!

'It seems you still have some thinking to do, Quillan. We'll try this again in a moment. Now get on the plastic.'

Quill crawls over to the sheet, leaning heavily on his arms to stop himself falling on his face. He can't remember ever being so tired or weak. Behind him, he hears the Warden unfastening his belt buckle. The first lash hits his ass, stinging like fuck even through his boxers. For a weak looking male, the Warden is strong.

The next strike is to his back, followed quickly by another to his ass. Quill gives up trying to stay upright. He slumps forward, resting his forehead against the cool plastic. The Warden doesn't care. This way he has full access to Quill's back and ass. He can go to town.

'I'll have to begin your training again Quill. I can't trust you until I know I have your full obedience.'

Even if the gag wasn't in his mouth, he wouldn't beg the Warden to stop. There's no point. The fucker is in the zone. Content to beat Quill into submission again, as he'd done so many times before.

And like all those times, Quill hides his face, letting his tears, snot, and saliva pool on the plastic below him. They're the perfect accompaniment to the suffocating shame and humiliation washing over him.

BANNON

As he stands in the Great Hall of the castle, surrounded by the most formidable fighters in the vampire world, Bannon feels completely out of his depth. Like Sorcha, he couldn't be more relieved or grateful for the help, but what form that help will take is still being worked out.

The two other humans who arrived with the team are with Thea. The doctor, Fletch, and Izzy, a human who is mated with the Blackjack Shep. He hadn't spent much time with the other human female apart from a brief introduction, but she seemed lovely. How a human can integrate into such a strange and chaotic world as the one the Blackjacks live in, he'll never know.

But it gives him hope there could be a future for him, Quill and Sorcha. If Davyn can be with Thea, and Shep can be with Izzy, then maybe a wolf can be with two vampires.

If they get Quill out.

Not that it solves the ownership issues, but one bridge at a time. At least if he's here, Bannon can protect him. Can protect both of them.

The humans are downstairs unloading medical supplies from the helicopter, to the new infirmary set up in the castle. Fletch was preparing for the worst. Apparently, after working with the team for years he knows what he's talking about. When the team went into a situation, they went in hard.

The leader Nix, examines the large map laid out on the table in front of them. The topographical map is of the south-east coast of Ireland, the Warden's house circled in red on its private island.

She rests her hands on her hips as she nods her head. 'That's an impressive setup he has for himself.' She looks over to Bannon. 'I believe Fergus can read sign language. Would it be okay if he translated for the rest of us?'

He'd assumed Nix would ask Sorcha for her opinion, not him. He nods quickly, smiling at Fergus as he comes to stand at the far side of the table, so he can see what Bannon is saying.

'Perfect,' Nix continues. 'So, Bannon. How many guards are we talking about?'

'Eight,' he signs. 'Two shifts. Three on the night shift, and five on days. But you can take myself and maybe Quill out of that count now. A female vampire called Duna is second to Quill. She's tough and mean.'

'Training?'

'Quill trained all of us. He's an exceptional fighter and an efficient teacher. He made sure we were all able to look after ourselves, control the prisoners.'

'I'm presuming that includes weapons training?'

He nods.

Nix smiles over at Fergus. 'I have to say, this causes a problem for us, but I like the sound of your son already. I'm looking forward to meeting him.'

'And I hope you get the chance to soon,' Fergus replies.

The tall, dark-haired vampire called Court moves over beside Nix. 'How do you get on and off the island?' he asks.

'There's only one road and it's guarded. Quill got us off the island by boat, but the Warden probably has the coastline under surveillance now. He's not going to let anyone off that way again.'

Court nods. 'Yeah. Once bitten - no pun intended. So, that leaves air. Does he watch the skies?'

Bannon shakes his head. *'Not that I'm aware of. Quill was the only one in charge of the actual prison guards. I left the prison a few times to go for a run on the beach. I didn't see anyone while I was outside. But I have no idea how many guards the Warden has himself up in the main residence.'*

Court looks at Nix and they raise their eyebrows in unison. 'Air it is,' Nix says.

Murt leans on the table and peers across at Nix. 'Air, as in flying? As in wings flying?'

'It's the best way to get across from the mainland. We can go in silence and drop down on the beach. Make our way into the prison from there.'

The wolves seem as happy about her suggestion as Bannon is.

'Are you suggesting the winged vampires carry the rest of us over to the island?' Sorcha asks. 'If so, how would that work? There are more of us without wings than there are with wings. It would take ages to get us all across.'

'If I may,' Fergus says, interrupting them. 'I know I am not a fighter in any way, nor do I pretend to be, but I am Prime. My wings work perfectly. As do the wings of many of the vampires in the castle.'

Nix shakes her head. 'We're not going to ask you to do that.'

'With all due respect, Phoenix, Quillan is my son. I would like to see you try to stop me from going. I assure you, I will not interfere. I know my limits. But if I can assist in getting the people over there who can help, I will do it.'

The Blackjack leader looks around the group of fighters, gauging their reaction to the offer, before turning back to Fergus. 'Very well. You won't hear any arguments from me Fergus. Get me a list of names, and we'll arrange who is giving who a lift. Are you going in as wolves Murt?'

The clan leader straightens, then crosses his arms. 'We'll have to go as far as the island in human form. Once we get closer, we can shift. We're going to be easier to sneak out of here and across the country if we're less noticeable. Sorcha will be able to pick up on Quillan's scent as a wolf. I'm sure Bannon will be able to as well.'

Bannon nods. *'Once I'm in the prison I should be able to talk to him as well.'* He doesn't add that it will only work if Quill is in a position to speak back. It doesn't need to be explained.

'Good. Bannon and Sorcha, I want you to draw me a map of the prison. I need as much detail as possible. While they're doing that, Bastian and Court, make sure the helicopter is loaded and ready to go. Willow, Shep, Fallon, and Dav, I want everyone kitted out and able to at least fire a gun. I'm not planning on getting Fergus or any of the staff involved in a firefight, but they need to be capable of at least holding their own.'

'Murt, I'll leave you to assign your clan where you feel they'd be most use. Okay so we'll aim to leave in two hours. We'll meet back here in an hour to go over the final details. Dismissed.'

SORCHA

Quill is in pain. She can feel it as soon as they get close to the island. She wasn't expecting the sensation to be so strong, but the nearer they get to the site of the prison, the stronger the feeling, the more it grows, and consumes her. Pain. Despair. Hopelessness.

'You can feel his pain too?' Bannon says, wiping rain-soaked hair back off his face as he climbs through the undergrowth.

She nods. 'Quill is in pain.'

'How do you know?' Murt asks from beside Bannon.

'I can feel it. We can feel it.'

The trees thin and there it is. The mansion sitting on its private island. An ominous monstrosity of a house, against the otherwise flat landscape.

'Fuck, that's gloomy,' Shep says, joining them at the water's edge. The wind is howling around them, driving the rain into their bones and sending waves crashing against the shore.

'It's worse inside.' Sorcha looks over at Bannon. 'Much worse.'

Davyn, Nix, and Murt come up beside them, looking across the water at the island. 'Where is the jetty?' Nix asks.

'To the right,' Bannon says, Sorcha translating for him. *'It's alarmed and guarded. Quill has the codes. I'd say Duna does too, along with the Warden and his personal bodyguards.'*

Nix turns to Shep. 'Are you sure you can handle that distance?'

The blonde-haired Blackjack considers that for a moment. 'I've been managing longer spans in the air. But I guess there's only one way to find out. If I end up in the water, then I can't handle the distance.'

'Fucking great!' Dav responds. 'Can't really talk myself. I could be following him in.'

'I've only just got wings,' Shep explains, when he catches them looking at him. 'Dav had to have one of his wings reset. We're both new to being up there.'

Sorcha doesn't care how new they are to flying. As long as they can get her remotely close, she'll swim the rest of the way there.

'Right!' Nix shouts, getting everyone's attention. 'You all know what to do. We'll land on the shore to the ocean side of the mansion. Unless you're a Blackjack, a wolf, or Bannon, you stay on that beach and keep out of sight. We're here for Quill and the Warden. The last thing we need are more bodies to rescue. Everyone clear?'

She looks around the group, waiting for everyone to nod in acknowledgement.

'Move out!'

Bannon quickly kisses Sorcha, before she disappears into the undergrowth with her brothers to shift in private. While still painful, the transformation is slightly easier than the last time. Standing next to her brothers, the five black wolves ready to be set free, she has never felt more alive.

She'd been waiting for this moment for eight years. Waiting to run with her brothers again.

It's just a shame this is to be their first outing together.

Nix stands beside her. 'You ready?'

Sorcha nods, sitting down and lifting a paw from the ground. Nix releases her wings, then takes hold of Sorcha's paw. She's not afraid of heights, but when Nix lifts her off the ground, she has to stop herself from using her claws to grab on to the vampire. Nix keeps low, Sorcha's back legs barely above the swell churning below her. Thankfully, they reach the beach within a few minutes, and she is lowered onto solid ground.

Around her, more vampires arrive, depositing their precious cargo on the beach. Shep and Davyn lower Fionn and Murt. Her brothers are still dry, so the males did themselves proud by making the journey on their new wings.

Nix takes out her gun as the rest of the Blackjacks arm themselves. 'Fergus? Take your people to safety. Trust us to get your son.'

He nods. 'Of course.' He looks at Bannon and Sorcha. 'Bring him home to me.'

Bannon nods, unwilling to drop the gun from his hand to sign a response.

'Let's go.'

Sorcha and Bannon take the lead, both of them acutely aware of Quill. It's like they've been reunited with a missing piece of themselves. She tries not to focus on his pain, but it's difficult to feel anything else from him.

The wolves and Blackjacks follow the beach around to the house, taking the same path she first did when she arrived here. She'd never thought for a moment that being moved to this place would give her two of the most incredible protectors she could ever wish for.

The group stop at the walls of the prison, beside the door that Quill led her through when he was helping her escape. They step aside as the tall dark-haired Blackjack Bastian moves to the front of the group. He removes his gloves, then places his hands on the door.

'There's an alarm,' he says in a Spanish accent. 'Complex, but I can disable it. Once I do that, the guards inside will be alerted.'

'How long to unlock the door?' Nix asks.

'Another thirty seconds.'

'Do it.'

Bastian closes his eyes, his hands moving over the door. 'Alarm is off... now!'

'Get ready,' Nix says as less than five seconds later, an alarm sounds from inside the house.

'Bastian! Whenever you're ready.'

Bastian mutters under his breath in Spanish, then steps aside as the door swings open. Without a word, they hurry inside and along the corridor. She can feel her brothers' anger when they pass through the interrogation room.

'I can smell your blood in here,' Garret says as the others growl.

'Not now!' She can't deal with them falling apart. Quill first, then she'll explain everything to them.

Nix opens the door leading into the prison, then stops when a blonde-haired female greets them, her gun levelled at them.

'Well, well, well. I'm surprised to see you again, Bannon. I presume one of these wolves is the inmate you took with you?'

'I presume you're Duna,' Nix says, her gun pointed at Duna's chest.

'I'm flattered you know who I am. And you are?'

'Nix. Leader of the Blackjacks.'

Duna nods slowly. 'Now I'm impressed, as well as flattered. It's not every day a Blackjack comes to call.' She peers around Nix and Bannon, seeing the rest of the team behind them. 'Or should I say all of the Blackjacks. Welcome to Hell.'

Sorcha braces herself, ready to pounce if she needs to take that bitch down. But instead of doing what Sorcha expects, Duna lowers her arm and takes a step back. 'You came back for him. Came back for Quill.'

Nix nods. 'We have, and we're more than willing to take him by force if necessary.'

Duna nods slowly. 'I guarantee you will have to use force. You won't be allowed to take him from the island without a fight. But that resistance won't come from me.'

Sorcha glances over at Bannon. *What the hell is going on?*

Bannon shakes his head. *I don't know.*

'I get that you don't trust me, Bannon,' she says. 'I can't blame you. But I'm sick to fucking death of the Warden, and what he does here. Quill is the only good thing about this place. He doesn't deserve to be here with the Warden. I'd very much like to help you get him out.'

She turns her gun around, holding it out to Bannon. 'If I do something you don't approve of, shoot me. But you need to make up your fucking mind. The Warden is with him right now, so I'd advise you don't leave him there much longer.'

Sorcha looks to Nix, waiting for her to make the decision. A part of her doesn't trust Duna as far as she could throw her. But another part can't help but believe her.

'Fine,' Nix eventually responds. 'My team will take you down if you step out of line. You should keep your gun too. You might need it.'

'Where is Quill?' Davyn asks, moving up beside Nix.

Duna gestures down the corridor to the left. 'In the Warden's private quarters.' She takes a keycard from her pocket and hands it to Bannon. 'Use that to get in. The Warden has private security. I have no idea how many vampires are with him. He looks after that himself. The prisoners and other guards should be in the canteen. I can help you all get through the security.'

Nix turns to Bannon and Sorcha. 'You go and get Quill. Shep and Bas with them. Everyone else with me.' Nix nods to Duna. 'After you.'

Bannon and Sorcha hang back with Shep and Bas, as the others follow Duna into the prison to get the rest of the prisoners.

'*Are you ready?*' Bannon asks her.

'*Yeah. I'm ready.*'

With the imposing forms of Bas and Shep following after them, Bannon and Sorcha hurry along the corridor, through the dorms, and up to the heavy metal door at the far end. Bannon places the card Duna gave him against the lock, and the light above the door turns green. Bannon pulls open the door, allowing her to pass through first, before following with the two Blackjacks.

They make it to the second floor before they hit resistance. Four huge vampires are waiting for them, each one armed and lethal.

'Fuck!' Shep mutters from behind them. 'I might just be a little impressed.'

'Shut up,' Bas says. 'How about you stop talking and start fighting.' Bas steps forward, putting himself between the guards and them. 'You go get Quill,' he says to Sorcha and Bannon. 'We'll take care of these guys.'

Bas shoves Bannon to the side when one of the guards shoots at him. 'Go!'

Without waiting to be told again, Bannon and Sorcha leave Bas and Shep with the guards. As she turns the far corner, Sorcha looks over her shoulder. The two Blackjacks are taking down the guards with scary efficiency.

But then a familiar scent draws her attention. It's blood. Quill's blood. It's coming from behind the door just ahead of them. Using the card again, Bannon unlocks it, kicking it open with such force, the door bangs against the wall.

Sorcha comes to a stop when she sees the sight in front of her. The Warden is leaning over a table of some sort, frantically feeding from a prone figure, lying on the surface.

She knows it's Quill, but it's not until the Warden straightens to glare at them, that she allows herself to accept that they've found him. But she's terrified they might be too late. There's so much blood. The air thick with the scent of it. And it's all Quill's.

BANNON

It's been a long time since he let rage control him. It happened once before. He had found the wolf responsible for killing his family, for tearing his voice from him. It was nearly a year later, but there was no mistaking that wolf when he bumped into him at a chance meeting in Dublin.

He hadn't planned on waiting for him outside the club at four in the morning. He hadn't planned on backing him into a corner in the alleyway. He certainly hadn't planned on letting his powers take control and burning the man to a crisp.

It's something he's regretted every day since then. That's not who he is. It's not who he wants to be and, since that day, he's worked hard to ensure he controlled his ability - not the other way around.

But watching the Warden bent over Quill's too still body, feeding from him like a crazed animal, that control slips. The flames ignite on his skin, racing over his fingers and up his arms. Beside him Sorcha growls menacingly, the rumble like thunder in the otherwise quiet room.

His attention is momentarily drawn from Quill to the huge bed beside the table Quill is lying on. The Warden's bed. Then he realises that Quill isn't actually on a table. He's lying on top of a cage. A fucking metal cage. Sorcha notices it too, the growl low and full of anger. They both know that's Quill's cage. They both know the Warden locks that stunning male in there like he's a pet.

The Warden lifts his head, then slowly licks his lips. 'Bannon. Dog. How nice to see you again. Although I'm not sure what you hope to achieve here.' He lifts the chain from around Quill's neck, shaking it, jostling Quill's head. But through it all, Quill doesn't react. Nothing at all.

'This marks him as my property. He has been mine for many years, and I have no intention of releasing him.' The Warden turns Quill's head to the side, facing them. He's deathly pale and far too still, his breath coming in short gasps.

'Leave now and I'll let you walk away without repercussions.'

Sorcha growls again, but the Warden is either too cocky, or too high on Quill's blood to take her seriously.

He laughs loudly as he runs his hand through Quill's hair. 'Oh, stop that, Dog! Do you really believe I'm worried about a mute vampire and a mangy mutt like you? I own him! Do you not understand? By law he is mine! If you take him, I will come and get him again. I can lock you up in here to rot, if you lay a finger on him. Now leave!'

'His pulse is weak Bannon. He's dying.'

Bannon doesn't need Sorcha's sense to tell him that. He can see Quill fading away in front of him.

'We're not leaving him behind.'

Beside him, Sorcha growls in agreement. Noticing that his unwanted guests aren't in any hurry to leave, he pulls a gun from his bedside table. The Warden walks away from Quill, around the end of the bed towards them. He points it towards the two of them and smiles. 'I really don't think Quillan would want either of you to die because of him. However, I have no ridiculous attachment to either of you. I *will* pull the trigger. Leave!'

Bannon lifts his hands, flames swirling over his flesh. The Warden shakes his head, directing the gun at Sorcha. 'Think about that Officer. If you unleash that fire, I'll kill her.'

He will. Bannon knows the Warden will do whatever he can to hold on to Quill.

But so will they.

The Warden holds the gun tighter in his hand. 'Don't even think about it, Mute. I will shoot her in the head. One less wolf in the world can only be a good thing.'

But before either of them can move, Quill launches himself at the Warden. He slams against the Warden's arm driving it down as he throws his owner onto the floor. Bannon and Sorcha hurry over to Quill who is struggling to hold the Warden down. Usually, that wouldn't be a problem, but he's so weak the Warden is going to get the upper hand again quickly.

Then a shot rings out and everyone freezes. The scent of blood and gunpowder fills the air.

The Warden shoves Quill off him, scrambling back, his pristine white shirt covered in blood.

But it's not his. Quill flops back on the ground, blood oozing from a wound in his stomach.

'No!' The Warden's scream echoes the one Bannon releases in his head. 'Look what you made me do!' He drops the gun and scrambles over to Quill. But he's not worried about the vampire. It's his blood he's concerned about. Instead of stemming the flow, the Warden gets down on all fours, licking the blood from Quill's side as it pours from the wound.

The Warden stops his frenzied feeding when he realises they're heading his way. He scrambles to his feet, hurrying from the room, but Bannon and Sorcha have other issues right now.

Bannon drops onto the ground beside Quill, quickly pressing down hard on the wound in his stomach. Next to him, Sorcha shifts back, her face tear-streaked and pale. She grabs the sheet from the bed, tearing it into strips and passing them to Bannon so he can press them over the wound.

Quill opens his eyes and smiles at them. 'Hey.'

Bannon smiles. *'Hey.'*

'You're naked,' he says, turning to look at Sorcha.

She laughs, wiping tears from her face. 'Yes. Very naked. Now stop perving and lie still.'

Bannon throws blood-soaked strips to the floor, grabbing some clean pieces and tying them firmly in place over the wound with more strips of sheet which he wraps around Quill's torso.

'Why... did you come back?'

'For you of course,' Bannon says, watching the blood already soaking into the fresh strips of sheet.

Quill smiles and closes his eyes. 'Didn't think... I'd... see you...' He's lost too much blood - both to the Warden and to his many wounds. The gunshot is by far the worst, but the Warden has beaten him badly.

Sorcha pulls the radio from Bannon's pocket. 'We need help! We found Quill, but he's been shot. He's bleeding out.'

'Sorcha,' Davyn says over the radio. 'I'm with Garret. We're heading your way. One minute.'

'They're coming Quill,' she says, running her hands through his hair. ''You need to hang on, okay? Just a few more minutes.'

'You look... really good with... no clothes on.' He gives her a weak smile.

Sorcha laughs. 'Oh, would you stop it. You've been shot.'

'I'm fine. It doesn't hurt.'

Bannon glances at Sorcha as he says that. That can't be a good thing. Before either of them can comment, Quill's head flops to the side as he loses consciousness. Bannon checks his pulse. It's still there. Weak, but still beating. But he's not going to last long.

Thankfully, Garret and Davyn arrive, the latter hurrying over to Quill, as Bannon instinctively hides Sorcha's body with his own. Davyn nods towards the door the Warden used to escape. 'Go after that fucker. We'll take care of him for you.'

Bannon hesitates, but Garret's deep growl gets his attention.

'He said we need to end this for us and for Quill,' Sorcha says from behind him. 'Are you sure you're okay with Quill?' she asks.

Garret's growl is loud and more than a little aggressive.

'Fine!' she says quickly. 'We need to go Bannon.'

Davyn and Garret move around to the other side of Quill, giving her privacy while she shifts back into wolf form.

Davyn turns on his radio. 'Fletch! Fallon! Quill is bleeding out. We're on our way to you.'

'Got that, Dav,' Fletch responds. With one last look at Quill, and the ever-growing pile of blood-soaked strips on the floor, Bannon and Sorcha hurry out through the opposite door, the scent of the Warden thick in the air.

It helps that they can both pick up on Quill's blood, too. The Warden reeks of it and it does nothing to calm either himself or Sorcha. He looks over at the stunning wolf beside him and smiles, his fangs elongating as the fire erupts to life on his hands.

It's time to go hunting.

QUILL

'Stop!'

He has no idea who is carrying him, or where they're taking him. All he knows is pain and anger. Both are fighting for control. He knows he's in a bad way, but he's not leaving here. Not yet.

'What the fuck are you talking about?' The huge vampire with an eyepatch glares over at him as he stops at the bottom of the stairs. There's a wolf a few steps ahead of him. He can only assume it's one of Sorcha's brothers, but he barely has the energy to talk, let alone have a chat with a wolf.

'I'm the... head guard. I can help.'

'Help? You've got a fucking hole in your stomach!'

'No! Bring me to the prison, or I'll drag my own ass there.'

The vampire growls at him, then curses under his breath. 'Fucking stubborn idiot. Fine! But if you die it's not my fault.'

Quill smiles weakly. 'No problem.'

They may not be on board with his plan, but neither the wolf nor the vampire argues with him. Each step is agony, each breath pulling against the wound in his stomach. If he makes it as far as the prison before he bleeds out, it'll be a fucking miracle.

He lost track of how long the Warden was feeding from him before Bannon and Sorcha came into the room. It must have been on and off for days after the prisoners had beaten him.

'Which way?'

He opens his eyes, not realising that he had closed them. He takes a few seconds to look around then nods tiredly to the left. 'When the alarms went off, the guards would have locked down the prison. They'll be in the canteen.'

He must zone out again, because the next thing he's aware of is shouting. He opens his eyes to find himself at the canteen door. Inside, it sounds like the guards are fighting back. He's proud that they would stand up to these vampires and do their job.

'You about to walk in there, or do you need help?'

Quill shakes his head. 'If you let go, I'll be on my ass.'

The vampire brings him forward, the wolf to the other side, Quill places his palm against the lock on the door, slightly surprised when his print still unlocks it. The wolf pushes open the door and the vampire half carries, half drags him into the canteen.

On one side, half of his guards are holding the prisoners back, and on the other side, the remaining guards have their weapons raised and directed at both the wolves and these new vampires. Duna is in the middle, trying to talk everyone down, but it's not working.

Quill takes a few deep breaths before he roars, stopping everyone in their tracks. 'Enough!'

The shout is nearly enough to knock him out, but thankfully it does the trick. The guards – his guards – look at him, their weapons still raised, but some of the assuredness gone.

Quill takes a few deep breaths, willing his body to hang on for another few minutes. He needs to make sure the prisoners and guards are safe. After that he'll happily lose consciousness.

'Stand down.'

His guards don't rush to lower their weapons, but they're not attacking either so that's a plus. Then the vampire supporting him speaks up. 'We're here to close down the prison. You can lower your weapons and join us, or you can be taken down. Your choice.'

When no one moves, Quill loses the little patience he has left. 'It's over. Lower your fucking guns and put an end to this.' He pauses, groaning as a wave of pain hits. 'We're still alive. We still have a chance to walk away. Please take it. Please.'

It's at that moment that his legs decide they're done. The eye-patched vampire holds him up, but without him, Quill would be on his face on the ground.

When he comes to again, he's lying on the ground with Duna crouched beside him. 'Welcome back. You passed out. I'd guess it might have something to do with blood loss.'

He winces when someone puts pressure against his stomach.

'Just lie still. They're trying to stop the bleeding.'

'I'm fine.'

She laughs at his ridiculous response. 'You did it, Quill. It's over.'

'What?'

'It seems that you have quite a few vampires here who respect you. They chose you over the Warden.'

He smiles as he closes his eyes. 'That's good. Have Bannon and Sorcha come back?'

'Not yet,' she says, her voice sounding like it's coming from far away. 'Just rest.'

He doesn't have a choice. His injuries finally catch up with him, drawing him into pain-free darkness.

SORCHA

With Bannon beside her, Sorcha prowls down the corridor, Quill's blood and the Warden's sweat thick in the air. She needs to add the Warden's blood to the mix. Sorcha glances over at Bannon. She's never seen him so angry, so much a vampire as he is right now. His fangs are enormous, his eyes glowing fiercely, the flames reaching to his elbows.

They reach the door at the end of the corridor and Sorcha comes to a stop. The door is closed and, no doubt, locked. It could be made of steel, but that's not going to stop him.

Bannon stalks towards the door, kicking it with all his strength. It takes three kicks before the lock breaks and a fourth to convince the door to slam open. Quill's scent is everywhere - not fresh, but he has been in this room at some stage.

She steps inside and looks around the room. It's the Warden's office. The asshole is hiding behind his desk, a silver letter opener in his hand. She growls when she sees the blood on the blade.

'It's Quill's blood,' she says, but Bannon already knows. He's growling deep in his chest. The thought of the male she loves being cut and fed from against his will, sickens her, and sends her wolf into a frenzy.

On the same page, Bannon lifts his arms, igniting the drapes to the side of the office, next to his desk.

'Stop it!' the Warden shouts. 'What the hell are you doing?'

Bannon slowly rounds the ornate desk, with Sorcha taking the other side, pinning the Warden against the wall. He glances at his curtains, his eyes widening as the flames spread along the wall and down to the carpet.

'I'm ordering you to cease immediately! Do you hear me! Stop this! I have done nothing I was not entitled to do. Quillan is my possession. Mine! What you are doing here is illegal. Not *my* actions. I've done nothing wrong.'

Even if either of them could respond verbally, neither would want to. There's nothing they could say that would change what's about to happen.

The Warden laughs, the panic entering his voice as he looks around his burning room. 'Killing me won't save him. You must know that. I have family. If anything happens to me, his ownership passes on to my next of kin. He will be passed on, just like all my other possessions. Nothing will change for him.'

Bannon glances over at her. He didn't know that either. It's not going to save the Warden's life, but it will give some doubt to Quill's future.

But that's something that they can deal with later.

They look at each other, words not needing to be spoken. Bannon nods, his hands out, controlling the fire so it doesn't spread too far. Sorcha growls, her wolf desperate for as much revenge as she wants. Not just revenge for the pain that Quill endured by the Warden's hands, but also for Bannon, for herself, and for each of her fellow wolves.

The arrogant smile leaves the Warden's face when he realises he might not be making it out of here in one piece. Sorcha howls loudly as she leaps over the desk, her teeth tearing into the Warden. She shakes him violently, snapping his neck. It's a quicker death than he deserved, but she held back to spare Bannon having to watch another wolf attack. He didn't need to see that.

Sorcha drops the body, her wolf slightly placated by the taste of his blood, the scent of it in the air.

'It's your turn.'

Bannon waits until she's clear of the body, then directs the fire from the walls where he's been holding it, to the floor and across the expensive carpet. Sorcha watches in satisfaction as Bannon's fire reaches the Warden. Then with a pop, the Warden ignites, the flame roaring as it consumes him. Bannon sends more power into the fire, the flame brightening as the temperature rises.

Sorcha turns to look at Bannon. He's truly spectacular with the flames racing over his skin. She doesn't want him to have to respond like this. Never wants him to have to take a life.

She looks up at him, seeing tears in his eyes as he incinerates the Warden's body. 'He's gone now Bannon. You can stop.'

He drops his hands and the flames vanish instantly. She brushes her head against his arm, trying to take his attention from the smouldering ashes of the Warden.

'Let's go to Quill.'

He eventually nods, turning away from the remains.

DAVYN

As Ethan and Shep get what they need from the Warden's office, Davyn glares down at the pile of ash on the charred carpet. He's got to give it to Bannon, the male is fucking lethal. He's never seen a power like that before.

'Have you found what you need?'

Shep steps over the ash, grimacing down at it. 'We have. Everything is on this dickhead's laptop and some paper files. It's fingerprint-protected, so it would have been handy if Bannon hadn't incinerated all of him, but we'll make it work.'

'What would you like to do with his remains?' Ethan asks Davyn as he slips the laptop into his case.

'Leave him where he is or sweep him up and throw him out the window. I couldn't give a fuck.'

'Right you are,' Shep says, moving back to the filing cabinet, this time dragging his boots through the ash. 'Oh woopsie! Sorry about that,' he says, his voice full of sarcasm.

'Quill is critical, but stable for now,' Nix says, joining them with Murt. 'Fletch, Fallon, Sorcha, Bannon, and Fergus have gone back to Darkhaven with him. He needs treatment urgently,' Nix says.

'Right,' Davyn replies. 'What about the inmates?'

Murt gives the ashes a brief look before dismissing them. 'That's where we might have an issue. I don't think we'll be able to just relocate them to Darkhaven, like we did with the other prisons. Some of the wolves have been here for decades. Been abused and beaten for decades. It won't be a case of just giving them freedom, and they'll be grand.'

'Fuck!' Davyn says, leaning back on the edge of the desk and crossing his arms. 'What do you want to do so?'

Murt glances at Nix before he responds. 'Well, that's where things might get interesting. The guard who helped us, Duna. She could be the answer.'

'How the fuck would she be the answer?' Shep asks, purposely walking through the ashes again. 'Wasn't she part of the problem?'

'She was,' Murt says, 'but after speaking to her and some of the other guards, everyone in this building was a prisoner. Even the guards. Bannon didn't want to be here, any more than Sorcha did. The Warden you're mushing into the carpet had something on everyone here - prisoners and guards. The guards did as ordered because, if they didn't, they'd find themselves behind bars too.'

'Are you saying that she is willing to help?' Ethan asks.

Murt nods. 'I'm saying that Duna and the other guards are eager to help. They only ask for their freedom too.' He pauses for a moment. 'Quill is very much respected and liked by all the guards. They'll swear allegiance to you, Davyn, if it means this ends.'

'Fuck!' he says again. He's had it up to his neck with all this allegiance crap. He just wants to be a regular fighter like everyone else.

'I know you're no happier about any of this than we are,' Murt says, clearly seeing how pissed off he is about the whole situation. 'We just have to do this, until we can figure out a better alternative.'

'Do what, exactly?' Shep asks.

Nix takes over when Murt glances at her. 'What Duna has suggested is that we leave the wolves here for the time being - in the house and dorms of course, not the prison. Murt will speak to Rowan to see if any of the less institutionalised wolves we already have at Darkhaven, would like to assist here.'

'You really think they'll want to stay here?' Davyn can't see why they'd want to, but this is far beyond his area of expertise. Fighting he can do. This, not so much.

'It'll be a slow process,' Murt says. 'Very fucking slow. But I'm thinking that if Rowan could find some wolves willing to help out over here, it could smooth the transition. I don't know,' he says, shrugging. 'I'm just making this up as I go along. Would some of your Darkhaven vampires be willing to help out?'

Davyn nods. 'I'll discuss it with Fergus.'

'Good idea,' says Nix. 'It wouldn't be a bad idea to make sure Duna and her men do as we expect them to. What do you want to do, Dav?'

'Where do you want me, Nix?'

'That's up to you,' she replies.

'Don't go doing that, Nix. I follow your lead. Give me some fucking orders!'

She represses a smile. 'Very well. Head back to Darkhaven. You do have the matter of Quill's ownership to take care of.'

'Fuck! Forgot about that.'

Shep slaps him on the back as he walks past. 'So, I might not be the only one wearing your crest around my neck?'

'You're more than enough.'

Shep grins at him. 'Oh, don't I know it! Seriously though. You thinking of claiming him like you did with me?'

Dav shrugs. He hadn't even thought of it, but it might be his only option. Having to buy Shep from his owner had been one of the low points of his life - and there were fucking loads of those to choose from. It doesn't seem to bother Shep in the slightest, but it doesn't sit well with him.

Potentially having to add Quill to that list isn't something he's too keen on, but it might be the male's only option.

'I'll get the necessary paperwork sorted, just in case,' Ethan says as he leaves the room with the laptop and paperwork in his hands. 'Give me a call if you need anything. I'm going to bring all this back to the office and get to work.'

'Thanks Ethan. Fallon is going to be busy with Fletch. You can take Bas with you as protection.'

'No!' Ethan's quick reply gets everyone's attention. 'I mean, I do not need protection. I have a helicopter waiting outside. I will be in the office - not walking around waiting to be captured.'

'Even so,' Nix says, either ignoring his discomfort at mentioning Bas, or unaware of it. 'You're not going alone.'

'Fine! Can you spare Court or Willow?'

She shrugs, already on her way out of the room. 'Take whoever you want. Just do not go alone. We've ruffled a lot of feathers by doing this. We need to watch our backs.'

Shep stands beside Murt and Davyn, now left alone in the Warden's office. 'We've got your back Dav,' Shep says. 'Let's get you back to Darkhaven. Sooner we get things sorted for you, the sooner we can all head back to Wales and get back to kicking the True Order's ass.'

SORCHA

Every fibre of her being is telling her to stay with Quill. To not let him out of her sight for a second. But as Quill is carried into the castle on a gurney, Sorcha sees Fergus, hanging back in the shadows as if he's afraid to interrupt what's going on with his son.

She holds out her hand to him, smiling when Fergus slips his hand into hers. Together they follow Fletch and Fallon as they wheel the gurney into one of the rooms they have been using as a medical centre.

She stands aside with Bannon and Fergus, as the human doctor shouts orders to Fallon and one of the vampires from the castle. Behind him, the Blackjacks and Whelans step inside the room, each one silent as they watch Fletch work.

She breaks down again, so Murt pulls her against his chest, holding her. 'Hey. Quill will be fine. From what I've heard about him, he's a tough bastard.'

She leans against her brother, watching as Fletch and Fallon work on Quill. He's too pale, too still and Sorcha hates it. He's always been so strong, like a rock she could lean on. The field dressing they had put over his wound is soaked with blood. Too much blood for someone who has been repeatedly fed from over the last few days.

'He's strong,' Bannon signs, catching her eye, almost as if he's reading her thoughts. 'He'll get through this.'

The Blackjack doctor leaves Quill with Fallon as he walks over to them. 'Right, so I'll give you the short version for now, then you're all going to leave me alone so I can see to him. Quillan is in a bad way, but I don't need to tell you that. The poor lad has been fed from to excess. Clearly, his owner has... apologies, *had* a serious blood addiction. There's evidence that asshole fed from all over his body. I'm thinking there may have been more than one feeding from him at any one time. This could be the reason for the restraint marks. I'd imagine it was extremely painful for the poor bloke.'

'Are you saying he was a fucking banquet?' Murt asks, getting the question out before she has a chance to.

'That's what I'm thinking.'

'Fuck! Sounds like you did the world a favour,' Murt says, nodding across to Bannon and Sorcha.

'I'm not usually one for violence, but I agree with you Murt,' Fletch says. 'I'm pumping Quillan full of blood. When he's more stable, I'll remove the bullet. That's really all I can do for now, apart from cleaning his other wounds and keeping him comfortable. The rest is up to him, I'm afraid. He's young and strong, so that's all in his favour.

'Now, I know you all want to be with Quill, but hanging around in here watching me, won't help him or me. Get out of my hair. I'll call you when he's set up in a room. '

Even though she doesn't want to leave she allows Murt to lead her from the room, Bannon and Fergus trailing after them into the waiting room set up in another of the bedrooms. Con, and Garret are already slumped on two of the chairs, waiting for her. 'How's Quillan?'

'He's not out of the woods yet,' Murt says. 'All we can do is wait.'

'More waiting!' Garret shouts, getting up to pace the room. 'I can't just sit by and wait. It'll drive me crazy.'

'Well, I might have something that'll help take all our minds off the waiting,' Murt says as he gets to his feet. 'There are a lot of prisoners who need to have a bed assigned to them. Sorcha, I want you and Rowan to work with Fergus on this. He runs the castle.' Murt smiles over at Quill's father. 'He knows everything about this place from what I'm told.'

'Indeed I do, Murtagh.'

'And you,' Murt says, looking back at Sorcha. 'You and Rowan know first-hand what these wolves have been through.'

'What do you think, Fergus? Are you up for it?' she asks, grateful that she's being given the chance to work closely with Quill's father.

'I can't think of a better use of our time. Unfortunately, some of the accommodation we have are the cells in the basement of the castle, but with some work, they could be transformed into comfortable living quarters.'

'Are you able to help?' she asks Bannon.

Try to stop me. Quill's in good hands. We can't do anything for him right now,' Fergus translates.

'Sounds like we have a plan,' Murt says walking over to the door. 'Might as well make ourselves useful.'

430

BANNON

Sorcha smiles and runs her thumb over his but doesn't say anything. There's nothing either of them can say. They've been sitting beside Quill's bed for the last four hours, but there's been no change.

The Blackjack doctor is giving him blood and fluids, but his colour hasn't improved. The bullet had been removed, and the wound sutured. The dozens of wounds and bruises on his flesh are still as prominent as they were hours ago. The restraint marks around his wrists are still red and raw. The bite marks are still visible, ugly tears in his skin that call to Bannon's powers.

'He's safe, Bannon. He's safe.'

Bannon closes his eyes, taking a deep breath as he gets a hold of his fire, before he can accidentally ignite her hand. He looks at her and smiles apologetically. *'Sorry,'* he mouths.

'What for? We both care about him. My wolf is seriously pissed off - believe me. We both need to keep control for him. Quill needs us.'

Bannon nods again. She's right, but that doesn't mean he's going to be able to restrain his anger. Quill is slowly dying in front of them, and there's nothing they can do about it. Nothing except wait and hope for the best.

Fergus already gave as much of his blood as he could to help his son. Bannon has no doubts that he would have given it all if it meant saving him. It's clear where Quill gets his strength from. Father and son are so similar to each other.

Sorcha reaches out, brushing her fingers over Quill's long hair. 'He should be healing by now, shouldn't he?'

He releases her hand. *'It might just take a little longer. He lost a lot of blood.'*

She nods, her hand still moving through his hair. 'He's beautiful. I think I was attracted to both of you when you ploughed into me on the beach that first night. You were both so different to each other, and to other vampires I'd met. I didn't stand a chance,' she says, smiling at him.

'It was the same for us.'

Sorcha laughs at that. 'I'm not sure Quill knew what he was thinking. Not for a while anyway.'

She has a point there. Quill had held back from both of them. *'Now we know why.'*

'Yeah. Fucking Warden!' She glances at the chain mark embedded around his neck. It was the first thing they cut off him when they got Quill back to the castle. The Warden, or his family may still own Quill but none of them wanted that thing around his neck.

'He was protecting us.' Bannon is sure that's part of it, but not the only reason Quill kept his ownership a secret. The truth is, Bannon isn't sure Quill knew *how* to tell them.

'Is there any change?' Fergus stands in the doorway, peering in at his son.

'Come in.'

'Would you mind?'

'Of course not!. Sit down, Fergus.'

'I just wanted to see if you needed anything.'

Sorcha gets up and guides him into the room, offering him her chair. 'Quill is your son. We won't have you wait on us.'

Fergus slowly sits, looking incredibly uncomfortable.

'You know,' Sorcha says, pulling up another chair and taking Quill's hand in hers. 'You and Quill look so alike. It's uncanny. You can absolutely tell you're related.'

Fergus smiles, hearing her words. 'Yes. It was always commented on. Although the piercings and tattoos are entirely his,' he adds with a small laugh.

'Oh, I don't know Fergus,' Sorcha says. 'They might suit you.'

He shakes his head as he laughs again. 'I believe I will pass. But thank you for making me laugh. There have not been many occasions of late to do that.'

Sorcha takes his hands in hers. 'Sometimes laughter is all you've got. How are you feeling after donating your blood?'

'Tired, but well enough - thank you for asking. The Blackjack doctor made sure I did not donate too much. I am being well cared for. We are all lucky Fletcher and Fallon are here to see to our needs.'

Bannon knows exactly whose needs he's talking about, and it's not his own. Fergus's eyes lock on the thick scars circling his son's wrists and neck, before travelling to the tubes and wires attached to him.

'He's one of the strongest men I have ever known,' Sorcha says, catching Fergus's attention. 'He'll pull through. I know he will.'

Bannon smiles when Fergus looks at him for confirmation that Quill will wake up. But it's not something he can promise. Quill is a Prime, but the blood loss, added to all of his injuries, might just be too much for this strong male to overcome.

QUILL

The first thing that hits him when he wakes up, is the smell of bacon and turf smoke. The first causes his stomach to rumble, the second reminds him of home.

He spent a lot of time in the kitchen of the castle, where his father used to work when he was a child. He used to sit by the huge open fire, while the cook prepared dinner for the asshole dictator who lived there.

Even though his father's boss wasn't the nicest of guys by any means, the time he spent in the castle with the other servants was the highlight of his childhood. The women would tell him stories as they cooked, offering him bowls of stew or soup and plates of homemade bread.

Since then, any time he caught the scent of turf smoke, he was instantly drawn back to that time in his life. An easier time, a happier time, a time when he was in charge of his own life.

He tries to roll over, but his body is weak and frail. The only things he can operate are his eyes. But when he opens them, he's more confused than ever.

The wall beside him is a heavy stone block, where tapestries hang with scenes of a hunter on a horse chasing after some deer. There's a fire in the hearth, a basket of turf beside it, providing the scent from his childhood.

Maybe blood loss is messing with his head, but he could swear he's seen tapestries like that before. There's no way he could be there. No way he could be back in that place.

It doesn't matter if his body is ready or not, he needs to figure out what the fuck is going on. As soon as he pushes himself off the mattress, strong hands hold him back down. *'Take it easy. You're safe.'*

He's not usually an emotional vampire, but as soon as he hears Bannon's voice in his head, he cries. 'You're here.'

'We both are,' Sorcha says from his other side.

The bed dips to each side as they join him. He doesn't bother holding back the tears. He's not crying for himself or whatever the fuck is going on with his body. He's crying because they're safe. Sorcha and Bannon are safe. Being back with them had never crossed his mind.

He'd hoped for it of course. Hoped too many times to count. But when he watched them disappear from his life on that boat, he assumed any happy future was sailing away with them.

Sorcha strokes the side of his face. 'You gave us one hell of a scare.'

'What happened?' His voice is as weak as the rest of his body feels.

'It's a very long story,' Sorcha says, her hand still on his face, the gentle rhythmic movements threatening to lull him off to sleep again.

'We'll give you the highlights for now. My brothers tracked us down as soon as I was able to shift. They're working with the Blackjacks, a team of vampires with a special skill set. One of them, Davyn, is the son of the Raven King.'

That gets Quill moving. So, he is exactly where he thinks he is. 'We have to leave! Now!'

Bannon holds him down which doesn't take a hell of a lot of effort. *'Let her finish.'*

'Davyn killed his father and is working with the staff in the castle to right what his father did. They helped to get you out of the prison. We killed the Warden, while my brothers and the Blackjacks secured the prison. You were shot, but the Blackjack doctor has removed the bullet, and has been treating you for severe blood loss, but he thinks you'll be okay. You just need some rest.'

Working with the staff? He wants to ask, but he's afraid of the answer. The Raven King was well known for killing whenever he fancied. His father worked for the King. Not by choice, but that was the way things were done back then. The King decided who he wanted where, and you couldn't do anything about it.

The King took the children of his servants to keep them under his control, to keep them submissive and obedient. He did that with him. That's how he ended up being sold to the Warden. He was the leash used to keep his father in line.

But he couldn't bear it if he was the reason his father lost his life.

Then some of Sorcha's words hit home. 'The Warden is dead? How? Who killed him?'

Bannon and Sorcha exchange a look that makes him nervous. 'What happened?'

'I killed him, and Bannon incinerated the body.'

Quill slumps back against the headboard, his body and mind struggling to keep up with everything. They killed his owner.

'We were so angry when we saw him feeding from you. We couldn't let that bastard lay one finger on you again.' Bannon lowers

his eyes, looking away from Quill. *'It was quicker than he deserved.'*

'The house is still standing,' Sorcha explains as she readjusts his pillows. 'Davyn and the Blackjacks are figuring out what to do with all the prisoners. It's going to take time to process all the records to see which ones are legitimate, and which ones are fabricated to keep the inmates there. Duna is going to work with Davyn and my brothers to make sure everyone gets sorted.'

'It's over...' The words are barely audible, said more to himself than Sorcha and Bannon. It doesn't mean he's free. Not yet. But he won't spend another minute on the Warden's dining table, or on his knees in front of him. That's worth celebrating in itself.

'May I enter?'

Sorcha looks over her shoulder, then smiles as she gets to her feet. Bannon joins her and Quill is confused, until he sees who they are moving out of the way for.

'You're alive!'

His father smiles as he nods. He rubs his hands together, the dry skin rasping in the suddenly eerily quiet room. 'I could say the same thing to you, son.'

Quill pushes himself up the bed, leaning heavily on his arm as he tries to keep himself upright.

'I knew you were alive, Quillan. I was sure of it. I looked. I swear to you I looked... but I couldn't find you. Not until Sorcha and Bannon mentioned your name when they arrived. I could barely believe it.'

Quill can't think of one thing to say to his father. His initial statement about the fact his father is still alive had exhausted his store. How do you put into words what happened over stolen decades? How does he tell his father how he was used, how he was treated? Fuck that, just telling him he's the Warden's property is bad enough. He doesn't know where to start. Doesn't know if he even wants to start.

'I'm tired. I better get some sleep.'

He didn't mean to sound so dismissive, so abrupt, so uncaring. The words come out and do their damage, before he can stop them.

His father nods briskly. 'Of course. You're still recovering. I won't keep you from your rest.' He nods again and Quill feels like a right asshole for pushing his father away after so long. He just can't deal with him now. Maybe not ever.

All he knows is that he's not ready to have the conversation his father will no doubt want to have.

Fergus stops at the doorway and turns around. 'If you need anything Quill, Bannon and Sorcha know where I can be found.' His father leaves and the silence returns. Ignoring the looks he's getting from Bannon and Sorcha, he shuffles back down under the covers and closes his eyes.

He wasn't lying to his father. Not really. He is tired — more like exhausted. He vaguely remembers being freed from the Warden's table, and being shot, but must have passed out after that.

He doesn't know how, but he roused himself in time to go to the canteen and talk to his guards. After that it was lights out for him.

It had been touch-and-go so many times in the past he had half expected not to wake up again at all.

He'll get some sleep. Try to regain some of his strength. He'll need it if he's going to deal with whatever his future holds. His ownership will pass to the Warden's next of kin. This is a brief break. Nothing more.

82

SORCHA

Quill is dozing when she peers into his room. Moving quietly, she tiptoes across the room, slowly lowering into the chair beside the bed. Each day his colour is returning. He's still sleeping most of the time, but at least when he's awake, he's talking a little more. Not much, but a few words are better than dismissing them as he did to his father when he first woke up two days ago.

Both she and Bannon had spent some time with Fergus, and they like him a lot. It's clear he's struggling as much as Quill is, but it will take time for both men to get used to the idea of being back in each other's lives.

Quill stirs and his beautiful green and navy eyes look across at her.

'Hey.'

'Hey.' She doesn't bother with the usual *you look better* pleasantries. Quill never appreciates them.

'Can you lie down with me for a bit?'

'Of course.' She lies beside him, cuddling up to his chest when he pulls her into a hug. Quill holds her, not saying anything for a minute or two, but she's more than content to stay in his arms for as long as he'll hold her.

He's still unsure about their relationship, about his place in their lives. He'd kept himself on the outside while they were in the prison, but that's not what she and Bannon want. They want Quill. Want all of him.

'I need to talk to you about something.'

Sorcha shuffles back so she can look at him. He's not happy about whatever he wants to say. If he keeps chewing on his lip rings he'll pull them out. 'What's wrong?'

'I need to apologise. Fuck, that's not even close to what I need to do.'

She gently brushes a lock of hair back from his face. 'Apologise for what?'

'Hurting you like I did.'

She frowns, not sure what he's talking about. But then she understands. 'Oh Quill. You don't—'

'Fuck that Sorcha! I need to say it. If I can ever be with you, I need to say this.' He pauses for a moment, his eyes drifting down to the bed instead of to her. 'I've done a lot of things I wish I could go back and undo. I tried to justify a lot of it by telling myself that I didn't have a choice. That the Warden was making me do it. That if I didn't do what I was told, I'd get the punishment myself. But that doesn't change anything. Not in here anyway,' he says, tapping his forehead. 'I'm sorry Sorcha.'

She slips her hand under his chin, gently lifting his head so he's looking at her again. 'What do you mean you'd get the punishment yourself?'

'It doesn't matter.'

'Don't do that, Quill. Talk to me. Please.'

She knows what he's going to say even before he says it. But a part of her still hopes it's not the case.

'After the first time I hurt you, I refused to do it again. I had to punish prisoners a lot. It was part of my job, but not unless they did something to deserve it. Not that any of them really did anything that would warrant that kind of punishment, but there had to be a reason.

'I think I could justify it more to myself, if there was a reason of some kind. But he just wanted me to break you. Just wanted to be the big fucking man you know. The vampire who broke the disobedient wolf. But I couldn't do it. Not after the first time. So, he showed me what would happen if I didn't do as I was told. He flogged me instead.'

She suspected as much, but hearing him say the words is upsetting. 'I'm sorry, Quill.'

'What the fuck are you apologising for?'

'I'm sorry that he hurt you, because you didn't want to punish me.'

'That's not on you,' he says, cupping the side of her face. 'Nothing that happened in there is on you. Well,' he adds with a small smile, 'Maybe me realising I wanted more from my life was on you. You and Bannon, both.'

His thumb strokes her cheek. 'It killed me doing that to you. I've always been able to lock away my feelings while I was punishing prisoners. I had to. It was the only way I could get through it. But I couldn't with you. I would have taken the lashes for you. I mean that. But it was either me or Duna, and I know what she's like. You'd have been torn to pieces.'

She kisses him, not in the least bit surprised when he hesitates before kissing her back. He's so guarded about being with Bannon and her. It's going to take time to convince him that he doesn't have to be the one standing by, protecting them.

Sorcha smiles at him as she combs her fingers through his hair.

She could do that forever if he let her. 'We were all surviving in there. I know that. Bannon knows that. You need to know that too. It was a struggle just to make it to the next day. I'm not going to say that I was particularly fond of you for the first few weeks, but I saw that it wasn't who you are. It took time, but you dropped that wall with Bannon and me every now and again, and we both fell in love with you.'

'I don't know how you can say that after what I did to you.'

Sorcha's breath sticks in her throat when she sees the tears in his eyes. This is really bothering him, and she loves him all the more for it. 'I can say that without any doubt in my mind, because I know you, Quill. Okay,' she says with a small laugh. 'I'm *getting* to know you. And the parts I know are incredible.

'You sacrificed yourself to save me and Bannon. You have protected both of us, looked out for us. You took so much abuse because of me. Because of us.' She runs her fingers over the faint restraint marks left on his wrists. They're not going to fade completely. The Warden had left his mark, and he will have to live with that reminder for the rest of his life. 'But that's in the past now Quill. We need to look to the future. To our future.'

He laughs harshly at that, angrily wiping his tears away. 'Future? I'm not sure we have one Sorcha. I'm a slave. That's not something that can be reversed.'

'I know.' She's still trying to get her head around how the ownership thing works within the vampire world. It happened from time to time with wolves, but again, it was usually a vampire who bought a wolf to keep as a pet. Wolves never owned other wolves.

'We'll figure something out. All of us, together.'

He looks back at her again, and this time his smile is genuine. 'You really think you can be with me, after what I did to you?'

Sorcha cups his face again, shuffling closer to kiss him. This time he doesn't hesitate, kissing her back. Her tongue brushes against his fangs and she groans. Kissing a vampire is so different, so intense.

Quill smirks at her when they pull back from each other. 'What was that groan about?'

'Fangs,' she replies, winking at him. 'That was a fang groan.'

'You like them?'

Sorcha nods enthusiastically. 'Hell yeah! I didn't think I'd like them so much. It's weird.'

Quill laughs, pulling her into a hug. '*Weird*. Thanks for that.'

'No, I mean liking your fangs.'

'I get what you're saying. I guess it'll be like you when you shift into a wolf. That'll be weird too.'

'Once you're up and about, I'll shift for you. It's better if I do it outside. My wolf likes space. She's not keen on being inside.'

Quill's hand takes hers, gripping it firmly. 'I can't wait. You should be free.'

'I am, thanks to you.' He smiles and nods tiredly. 'How about you get some rest. You look tired.'

'Will you stay with me?'

'Always.' She kisses his forehead, then strokes his hair as he closes his eyes and finally falls asleep.

Sorcha

As she takes a seat at the table, Sorcha can feel the tears threatening to fall. But they're not tears of sadness. These are happy tears. So happy. In all her years in the prison, she had thought about having dinner with her brothers too many times to count.

She wasn't sure about having this family dinner tonight, but Bannon had insisted. Quill is out of the woods, medically speaking. There's nothing she can do for him right now. He just needs rest.

And Bannon is right. She needs to do this, to get back some of her old life. It's been so long since she's been like this with her brothers, and she desperately missed it.

She takes her seat next to Fionn, smiling when he pulls her into a tight hug. 'I missed you so much.'

She laughs, slapping at his hands. 'You're squashing me! I need to breathe!'

He loosens his arms, smiling apologetically. 'Sorry. I have years of hugging to make up for. I never thought I'd be doing this with you again.'

'You're not the only one,' she says, picking up her glass and taking a mouthful of stout. 'Oh damn! That's amazing!'

'Lots of catching up on that too?'

She laughs at Fionn's comment. 'Oh yeah.'

It's just the five of them in a private study at the top of the castle. The room is cosy and homely compared to a lot of the rest of the castle. Fergus and the staff were doing their best to erase centuries of pain and death, rebuilding a legacy that everyone can be proud of.

She silently watches her brothers, laughing and joking with each other. This is what kept her going all those years. What she thought about when she was alone in her cell, staring at the ceiling.

'What the fuck are you smiling at?' Garret asks around a mouthful of stout.

'This. You guys. I missed this. Missed you all.'

Fionn pulls her into another tight hug, then kisses her on the forehead. 'We missed you too, sis. So much.'

Murt silences the banter by banging his palm against the table. 'If my siblings would shut the fuck up for a minute, I'd like to say something.'

'As long as you make it quick,' Garret says. 'I'm fucking starving.'

'You always are,' Con replies, grinning as he picks up his own glass.

'Anyway,' Murt says, ignoring the interruption. 'I never thought the five of us would be here again like this. I hoped we would, but for a long time it didn't seem like it would happen. But here we are. I could say a hell of a lot more, but I'm starving too.' He lifts up his glass. 'To Sorcha!'

'To Sorcha!'

She blows them all a kiss as they toast her. As if hearing how hungry the clan are, a team of cooks from the castle appear with trays of freshly baked bread and heaped plates of roast beef, potatoes, and fresh vegetables.

The smell is incredible, Sorcha's stomach growling loudly as the smell of the dinner fills the room. Over the next hour, she shares an incredible dinner with her family, listening to stories of what they've been up to for the last few years while she was missing.

They fill her in on their countless run-ins with the Elders, the Whelan clan's gradual fall from grace - not that there was much grace in the first place when it came to them.

They tell her about finding Cian's head mounted on the wall of the Great Hall. He's at rest now, buried with the rest of the wolves the Raven King killed over his reign.

The second he fell at her feet, she knew Cian was dead. But having that confirmed is both a blessing but still heartbreaking. She hates that he was put on display like that. He was such a kind gentle soul, and that image isn't one she wants in her head.

But it was the story of the day the Blackjacks contacted them to ask for help, that she finds the most bizarre. Everything that happened to her brothers after that initial contact, is all the more bizarre. Fighting alongside the Blackjacks, battling the Raven King and his men, taking a knee and swearing allegiance to Davyn, being banished by the Elders... it all sounds so surreal.

She doesn't want to think about her brothers living in a static home in a field, scraping together a few Euro to survive. It's not how things should have played out for their clan. The Whelan bloodline goes back for generations.

Murt may not be a fan of doing things the way her ancestors did, but that's not a bad thing. Sitting in this castle with her brothers, and with the two vampires she loves under the protection of the vampire lord Davyn, it appears her clan has already taken a path in a very different direction.

In that moment she could not be prouder.

At the head of the table, Murt is leaning back in the wooden chair, glass in his hand, as he watches his family together once more. He actually looks more relaxed than she's seen him over the last few days. He catches her watching him and winks, raising his glass to her. She lifts her own glass, her heart swelling and tears coming back to her eyes again.

She's home.

It's not their actual home from years ago. But does that really matter? They do say home is where the heart is. Having her four brothers, Bannon and Quill in this castle, it is very much her home. For how long that will be the case, is very much down to too many factors to think about right now.

Tonight is about her family. Tomorrow she'll worry about what comes next.

Or so she thinks, until Con decides to address one part right now.

'So,' he says, looking over at her. 'We going to address the elephant in the room? Or should I say vampires?' Con asks, his grin mischievous.

She was waiting for this. So far, they've kept their mouths shut and opinions to themselves, waiting for Quill to recover. Seems today is the day. 'Why don't you just come out and ask what you want to ask Con?'

He takes a drink of his stout, then gestures to Murt with his glass. 'He's the one who sticks his finger up at the rules. Not you. What the actual fuck are you playing at, sis?'

'I've become a fan of breaking those rules over the last few years. Rules don't mean much when you're fighting for survival.'

'No shit!' Garret says. 'There's breaking rules, and then there's pissing on them.'

'Jesus, Garret! Glad to see you haven't lost your way with words.'

'Fuck you Sorcha!' he replies, his grin softening his words. 'So, you going to spill the beans? Survival is one thing. We all get that.

Surviving by fucking two vampires is pushing that a bit.'

'Enough Garret!' Murt glares over at him, but Garret's grin stays in place. He's never listened to anyone except himself.

'Do we have to do this now?' Fionn asks, clearly uncomfortable with the entire conversation. 'We just got her back. I don't want us to fight so soon. Can we not just have dinner?'

Garret snorts. 'Who the fuck is fighting? Enquiring minds are just enquiring.'

'What the hell is the problem with them being vampires? You all took a knee in front of Davyn. You swore allegiance to a vampire.'

'And you're fucking two of them.'

'I said enough!' Murt roars as he rises to his feet, slamming both palms on the wooden table. 'You better shut your fucking mouth Garret, or I'll shut it for you!'

'Fine! Whatever. I'm just saying what she's doing is a big deal. It has a knock-on effect on all of us.'

'So, you fucking the waitress from the bar a few weeks ago impacts the clan too?'

'What? No! Of course not.'

'And neither does this. We took a knee to a vampire. That vampire is now keeping our necks off the chopping block. If you're going to hang on to the vampire bullshit the rest of the wolves do, then what the fuck are you doing taking protection from one?'

Sorcha bites her tongue, as Garret's face turns deep red. It's not often Garret will admit he's in the wrong. This might be one of those occasions. But instead of apologising, he just nods and shuts his mouth.

Murt slowly lowers onto his seat and crosses his arms. 'Sorcha, if you want to talk about them go for it. If you want to tell us to mind our own fucking business, that's grand.'

Opening up about her relationship with Bannon and Quill to her four over-protective brothers isn't something she's looking forward to, but it needs to be done.

'Of course I want to talk about them. I don't quite know how it happened. I was just trying to make it from day-to-day in there. I had been alone in solitary for so long. The only break I got was from a guard who delivered my one meal a day and then took me out for a few minutes of exercise. That was it. The rest of the day I was locked in the dark.

'Things changed when Bannon started as my guard. I knew there was something different about him. He was kind. When I figured out he couldn't talk, I offered to learn sign language. No one else in the prison knew sign. It hit me that he was as alone in there as I was.

'I'm not going to go into details. To be honest, I want to forget most of what happened in the prison. But over the weeks the three of us grew closer. They made me feel like I was someone again, instead of just number sixty-four. They cared about me, and I cared about them.

'So, is it the two of them and you, or do they have feelings for each other?' Fionn asks, genuinely trying to understand.

'We all have feelings for each other. Bannon and Quill are in love with each other and with me. And I love them both. I really do mean that. It wasn't planned.'

'It just happened, right?'

'Yes Garret. Believe it or not, it did just happen. It took time, but I do love them. I get you're not happy about it, but to be honest, I really don't care. I'd like you to be supportive, but I accept if you can't be.'

'I'm a dick.'

She looks over at Garret, frowning. 'I'm sorry? You're a what?'

'A dick,' he says a little louder.

'Oh, I heard you,' she replies. 'I just wanted you to say it again.'

He sticks up his middle finger as he smiles. 'I'm sorry. I'm still pissed off about the whole banishment shit, because of the vampires. And no!' he says loudly, looking over at Murt. 'I have no regrets about what we did. 'I don't have to be happy about the end result though.'

'Fair enough,' Murt says. 'Don't think any of us are.'

Fionn takes her hand, turning around to face her. 'You love them both?'

Sorcha nods. 'I do.'

The four brothers silently look at each other, leaving her hanging on for their response. Con has been unusually quiet during the exchange, which could mean all sorts of things. Con isn't fond of talking at the best of times.

'I like Bannon,' Murt says, surprising her. She looks up the table at her brother, seeing a huge smile on his face. 'Quill too.'

'You haven't even spoken to him.'

'I don't need to,' he tells her. 'He risked his life to save you. Bannon too. That's all I need to know.'

'I like Bannon too,' Fionn says.

Con nods. 'I've spent some time with Bannon. He's cool. Doesn't say much. My kind of guy.'

'Con!'

'What! I said he's cool!'

She looks over at Garret. 'Well? What smart comment are you going to grace us with?'

'If either of them hurt you, I'll kill them.'

She laughs, shaking her head. 'There we go. You know what? I'll take that.'

Murt holds up his hand, silencing the laughter. 'So, we're all good. You're back, Sorcha, and it's thanks to Bannon and Quill. We're not going to kill either of them.'

'Oh, great Murt. Thanks for that.'

QUILL

He comes awake just as the teeth sink into his flesh in his nightmare. Quill opens his eyes, wiping sweat from his face as he waits for the remnants of the nightmare to fade.

'Can I come in?'

The deep voice helps to bring him fully awake. He sits up and looks at the huge vampire filling the doorway to his room. There is no doubt he's about to have a one-on-one with Lord Oldranson himself. A thick leather patch covers his right eye, hiding some of the scarring on his face, the black jeans and t-shirt do nothing to mask the fighter's body underneath, but it's the coldness in his remaining green eye that chills Quill to his core.

'It's your house,' he replies, remembering that he was asked a question.

The Blackjack enters the room, lowering into the chair by the bed, the wood creaking under his weight.

Quill leaves the awkward silence to drag on. He's out of his depth on this one. He's not afraid of anyone, and can handle himself against the worst of the worst. He wouldn't have been able to do his job in the prison otherwise.

But Davyn is different. So is he. Now he's a nobody. A slave. A piece of property. Davyn is a highly trained fighter, a lord, the Raven King's son.

Davyn leans forward, resting his arms on his legs. He clenches his hands together, as he focuses on the floor instead of Quill. Something tells him this powerful lord is as uncomfortable about this conversation as he is.

'You okay?' he asks, finally looking up at Quill.

'Tired, weak as fuck, but yeah. Better than I was.'

Davyn nods. 'I'm not going to fuck around. The Warden has kin. Family who can take you as theirs. We've done some research. He was the only lord in his family. With him dead, they can claim you, unless another lord forces them to sell you.'

Quill nods slowly, unsure what Davyn is getting at. He knew the Warden had family, but hadn't thought beyond that. He always just assumed that he would die while the Warden owned him. Quill had never expected to outlive him.

'I can do that.'

'Do what?' Quill asks.

'I can force them to sell you to me. Fuck that! I can just claim you. I've done it before without any problems. I own another vampire, but it's just on paper. He does what the fuck he wants, whenever he wants. He's free to live his life his way - well, except on paper.'

He's surprised to hear Davyn say that. He didn't think a Blackjack would own another vampire. But this is the Raven King's son, so he should probably have expected to hear that. 'What are you saying? Do you want to own me too?'

Davyn adjusts his eye patch, his body language coming across as uncomfortable as Quill is about the whole conversation. 'Believe me, I don't like this any more than you do,' Davyn says, leaning back in the chair. 'We're both thrown into this and have no choice.'

'No choice? From where I'm sitting you have a lot more of a choice than I do.'

'I don't.' Davyn says, hitting him with his cold glare. 'If I refuse to claim you, I sentence you to a fucked-up life with that bastard's family. I'm as done with all this ownership shite as you are, but it's the way things work. For now, at least. Unless you want them to claim you, this is the only option.'

'Lesser of two evils, right?'

Davyn smiles briefly. 'Right. If you agree to this, you'll be free, except on paper. I don't give a fuck where you live, or what you do. You'll need to wear my seal to protect yourself, but that's as far as it goes.'

'What about you?'

'Me what?'

Quill adjusts himself on the bed. 'What does owning me mean to you?'

'Owning another vampire makes me fucking sick to my stomach, but if it means I can save even one vampire from going through the same thing, I'll do it. I was dead against owning any vampire, but it's working for the other male I bought. I reckon if he can handle it, maybe it's not a bad thing.' Davyn flashes him a quick smile. 'He's not one to keep his mouth shut if he's not happy about something.'

The two vampires fall into silence again, but not a comfortable one. Neither of them wants to be in the situation they're in - that much is clear, but that doesn't mean he's going to accept everything Davyn is saying and happily sign up for a lifetime of serving the vampire lord. It was a life his father had to endure. Maybe he still does.

'Is it my father? The other vampire that you own.'

Davyn shakes his head. 'No. Fergus is free. Believe me, I tried to get him to leave I don't know how many times, but he's a stubborn fucker. He runs the castle for me, but it's by choice. I swear to that.'

He doesn't know why, but he believes that. His father was always stubborn.

Davyn suddenly pushes to his feet. 'I'll let you get some rest. Think about it. There's no rush. You're under my protection while you're here.'

'Thank you. I mean that Davyn. Whatever else happens, I do appreciate that.'

'No need for your thanks.'

Without another word, the vampire lord leaves him, closing the door behind him. Quill collapses back against the pillow, suddenly feeling drained. Davyn is one intimidating vampire.

But that doesn't help him decide what he should do.

He needs to speak to his father. That's top of the list, even though it's something he's dreading. Growing up, his father had been his rock, the male he looked up to. When he had refused to leave the employ of the Raven King, Quill had been furious with him. He'd tried so many times to get him to leave, to run. But his father had refused.

It took his own capture for him to realise why. The King took Quill to keep his father in line. He was the reason his father wouldn't leave. But he was also the reason his father was forced to stay.

His father may be free now, but *he* never can be. He could very well die being the property of the Raven King's son.

Maybe running would be the better option.

BANNON

The castle may have an ominous history, but there's no denying the beauty of the location. With the vast Atlantic Ocean to one side, and miles of unspoiled land to the other, Darkhaven could not be situated in a more breathtaking location.

Bannon closes his eyes, letting the sound of the sea calm him. He hasn't been able to sleep since they first left Quill with the Warden. Every time he closes his eyes, he sees Quill stretched out on top of the cage, with that monster feeding off him.

He tries to relax, but he's so wound up it's nearly impossible. The flames are licking up his hands to his arms. He may not have killed the Warden himself, but he stood by and did nothing, as Sorcha did.

Hell, he had enjoyed watching it and enjoyed burning him to ash once he was dead. After everything the vampire did to Sorcha and Quill, he needed to die.

That doesn't mean the decision isn't bothering him. The day taking a life doesn't affect him in some way, is the day he needs to be seriously concerned.

But killing the Warden hadn't solved their problems. Yes, Sorcha is free and so is he, but Quill is still a slave. He opens his eyes when he senses her nearby. Sorcha is in wolf form with her brothers below him, running along the headland. He loves seeing her like that. Loves seeing her running free with her brothers.

'It's quite a sight, isn't it?'

Bannon jumps when Fergus appears by his side on the turret.

'I didn't mean to startle you. I thought you would have heard me coming?'

'I was concentrating on Sorcha,' he signs.

Fergus nods and smiles as he peers down at the wolves. 'Ah. That would explain how I could sneak up on you like that. She appears happy.'

'She is. She's free.'

'Yes. How are you doing Bannon? Everyone is concerned about Quill and Sorcha. But you have been through the wars yourself.'

Bannon touches his scar before he can stop himself, then drops his hand again.

'I wasn't referring to your scar. I was referring to what happened when you went to rescue my son. I understand the owner of the prison needed to die, but that doesn't mean it was an easy task for either you or Sorcha.'

He shakes his head. *'I knew how it would play out, but that doesn't mean I'm happy about what happened. When I saw what he was doing to Quill...'* He doesn't want to speak to Quill's father about how he was being kept. That's Quill's decision to make when he wakes up.

Fergus nods sadly. 'Quill hasn't told me anything about his time there, but I hope he'll share it with me when he's ready. I fear he gets his stubbornness from me. I just hope he gives me the opportunity to tell him I stayed here to keep him safe. It was nothing to do with my weakness. It was that stubbornness I passed on to him.'

'But that's what kept him alive,' Bannon signs. *'I've never met someone with such resilience. Well, apart from Sorcha.'*

Fergus laughs as he watches the wolf play-fighting with her brothers. 'I see that resilience in all of you. I cannot be more grateful that my son found you. Found both of you.'

'You're okay with that? With Sorcha and me? I know it's not—'

'Conventional? What is nowadays? After everything we have all endured, do we not deserve happiness in whatever form it comes into our lives? My son is alive, Bannon. He's downstairs and he will recover. I know he will, because that's who he is. But he's only here because of you and Sorcha. You could have walked away and left him.'

'Davyn was going to find the prison.'

'True, but maybe not in time. You got us there in time to save my son. And you were going back for Quill, not because of the prison. Do you love him?'

Bannon wasn't expecting Quill's father to be so upfront. *'Yes.'*

'And Sorcha? Do you love her too?'

'Yes.'

Fergus smiles widely at his answer. 'Well Bannon. To hell with convention then. It sounds like you have found your happiness. Not many find one person to love in their life. Finding two is exceptionally lucky. I only hope he accepts Davyn's offer to claim him.'

'Do you think he will?'

Fergus sighs loudly as he turns to face Bannon. 'I honestly can't say. The son I knew years ago would not agree. He detests the Raven King and everything to do with him - Davyn included. It will take quite some convincing to get him to change his mind. If he doesn't agree, we could all lose him again.'

QUILL

He pushes up the bed, wishing that his body would heal already. Everything hurts and he's as weak as a baby. He glares over at the tube attached to his arm. He needs the blood, but the tube is irritating the fuck out of him. Everything is.

He's sore, tired, and worried sick about what's heading his way. He's also pissed off at being stuck in this fucking bed all the time. His mood is taking a serious nosedive. He's actually kicked Sorcha and Bannon out for a while. The last thing he needs is to take out his bad mood on the two of them.

There's a knock on his door which comes at the wrong time in his *feeling sorry for himself* hour. 'What!'

The door opens and a head peeks inside. 'Hey. Is it safe to come in, or should I fuck off?'

He doesn't recognise the male, but that could be said about a lot of the people in this castle. 'Sure. Come in.'

The tall vampire comes in and gestures to the chair near the bed. 'Mind if I take a load off?'

Quill nods and waits while the male takes a seat. He knows this vampire is a Blackjack. Apart from his size, he carries himself differently to other vampires he's met. The confidence is hard to miss.

He stretches out his legs, then scratches his dark blonde hair before he speaks again. 'Right. So, introductions first, I guess. I'm Shep. You're Quillan right?'

'Yeah, but I prefer Quill.'

'Got you. Officially, I'm Shepherd but I only go by Shep. Anyway, I thought you might want to offload about your current situation.'

Quill laughs as he brushes his hair away from his face. 'My current situation? Fucking nice way of putting it.' He didn't mean to go all aggressive with the Blackjack, but he can't help himself. He's lost and doesn't know how to deal with any of this.

Shep holds up his hands. 'Hey, I get the attitude, but I'm on your side.'

'What the fuck do you know about me?'

Shep pulls a silver chain out from under the neck of his t-shirt, holding it in his hand as he looks at it. 'I know a lot more than you think I do. This little chain here marks me as the property of Davyn.'

Quill stares at the pendant twirling on the chain. He recognises the crest on the back of the demon-like head. It's a vampire family crest. 'Fuck! It's you?'

'It's me what?'

'Davyn said that he owned a vampire. He never mentioned it was one of the Blackjacks.'

Shep grins, dropping the pendant back onto his t-shirt. 'It's not something either of us are too keen on shouting about. It is what it is though.'

'How are you a slave? You're a Blackjack. It doesn't make sense.'

'It's a long and not-so-fun story, but I'll give you the shortened version. My delightful mother sold me to pay off a debt.' Shep lifts up his t-shirt, pointing to a line of scars running up his side. 'One cut for every hour of my time in bed with well-to-do vampires.'

'Fuck...'

'Yeah,' Shep says with a nod. 'Big time. Seven-hundred and fifty-three scars before they lost interest in keeping count of how many hours I had been used for. I was in that place for twelve years. But then I escaped, and found myself with the Blackjacks. I've worked fucking hard to move past all that shit, but it's still there in the background. Always will be. But I've got a life now, Quill. A fucking good one.'

'But one of the Blackjacks owns you? One of your friends.'

Shep brushes that comment away. 'Yeah, but it's not like you think. My first owner came back for me. I was heading back to that fucking bedroom for the rest of my life, but Dav got me out. He's a lord. He outranked my bitch of an owner. We couldn't figure out a way of getting around the contract, so to save my life, Dav agreed to take me as his.'

'He agreed?' He didn't realise his tone was sarcastic, until Shep snorts loudly.

'Hey now, don't go assuming he was jumping at the chance to own me. Far from it.' He picks up the chain again, the crest on the end catching the light as it spins. 'Like it or not, this chain protects me for the rest of my life. Dav hates me wearing this, more than I hate having it around my neck. It's not so bad though. Beats that fucking heavy chain and padlock any day. Kind of forget it's there most of the time.'

'What does he want from you in return?'

'Nothing at all. Apart from a teeny piece of paper Ethan is keeping locked away, I'm a free male. He did this to save me. There was no ulterior motive. If you accept his offer, you'll be free Quill. That's what his crest means. Freedom for vampires like us.

'Dav is working on a way of scrapping all this ownership bullshit, but until then, I'll take him as my owner any day of the week.'

Shep pulls his chair closer to the bed. 'Listen, I get how you feel about this. You can believe me on that. My owner was a total bitch, who chained me to a bed, and used me to pleasure herself and anyone else who would pay her. I hate her Quill. Really fucking despise her. I don't want to be owned by anyone.' He looks down at the chain hanging around his neck. 'Given the choice, I don't want this on me. But if I have to be owned by anyone, I want Dav.'

Shep tucks the chain back under his t-shirt. 'Take the chain from Dav. As a fellow slave, I'm begging you to take the fucking chain. Let him protect you.' Shep claps his hands together, then gets to his feet. 'Right! Enough of this heavy shit for one day. Seriously depressing stuff. Think I need to go and beat the shit out of something.'

'I know that feeling.'

'Oh, I'll bet. How about I show you how a true fighting master works once you're up to it?'

'I take it you're talking about yourself?'

Shep grins widely as he pushes his shoulders back. 'Too fucking right I am! So, tell me to mind my own and all that, but Fergus is wandering around like he's lost. I don't know your dad well, but the guy is seriously hyped to have you back. Never seen him so full of life. But I reckon you two need to have a bit of a chin wag. Clear the air.'

If only it were that easy. He wants to see his father, but after everything that's happened since the Warden bought him, he doesn't think he can face him. 'I don't know.'

'Okay... Mind me asking what's holding you back?'

'I just can't. I'll have to tell him what happened. I don't want him to know about any of that.'

Shep sits down again. 'Ah. I get you. Well, speaking as someone who was used and abused a lot, it's nothing to be embarrassed or ashamed about. I thought that way for a good while too. Fucking years, in fact. Can't say it's something that ever comes up in day-to-day conversation now.'

Shep stops talking, then smiles widely. 'Then I met the most amazing woman in the world. And she fell for me. Fuck knows why, but Izzy loves me, warts and all. I don't have warts,' he adds quickly. 'Figure of speech. Anyway, I was told by a very wise vampire that if someone loves you, all that past stuff doesn't matter. That was Dav, by the way. Every now and again he comes out with this deep and meaningful stuff.

'So, I told Izzy everything. All the crap I've been hiding for years. And she got it. It wasn't easy for me to get out, or for her to hear, but she understood. That's how I knew Izzy was the one for me.' He looks down at the ground for a moment. 'She's taking things slow with me. We're going at my pace when I'm ready. You don't find someone like that every day of the week.

'I'm guessing since Sorcha and Bannon risked their lives to save you, they feel the same way about you. They know what happened to you, and they still put their necks on the line to get you out. I'm not an expert on this, but I reckon if they had a problem with you, because of what the Warden made you do, they'd have left you there.'

Shep probably has a point. Maybe this Blackjack knows more about his situation than he thought?

Shep stands up again, stretching and yawning loudly. 'I can see some of my wisdom is sinking in. Anyway, I'll leave you to it. Loads to think about and all. I'll be around for a bit if you need to offload. Dav and Thea have my number. Call me anytime.'

'Thanks, Shep.'

He grins as he opens the door. 'Not a problem. One last bit of wisdom.'

'Go on.'

'Take your life back Quill. It's just a necklace.'

QUILL

It's great to be out of bed, but he's weak as fuck which isn't helping his mood. Quill leans on the dresser, trying to catch his breath after getting dressed. That's it. Putting on a pair of joggers, a t-shirt, and trainers had wiped him out. He hasn't even left his fucking room yet.

He lifts his head, looking at his reflection in the mirror. He barely recognises himself. His hair is out and badly needs some attention. The same goes for his beard which has grown since the Warden locked him up again. His body is smaller too, and he hates that.

He'll get it back. Get his body back to where it was. Or at least he hopes he will. With his future still undecided, he might not get the chance.

Everything Shep said to him makes sense. Every word went in, but that doesn't mean he's ready to accept it. Maybe the best thing for him would be to disappear in the night. Leave here, and leave his father again. But that also means leaving Bannon and Sorcha.

He curses, dropping his head to his chest.

Run like a coward? Spend the rest of his life running? Hiding? Watching his back, and living in the shadows?

But could he really have a life with Sorcha and Bannon by agreeing to let Davyn own him? How would it even work? Fair enough, Davyn might be on the level now. But a part of him is scared he'll be going from the frying pan into the fire, and then Sorcha and Bannon would get hurt.

There's a knock at his door, drawing him out of his head. 'Yeah.'

The door opens and there he is. His father.

He wants to rush over and embrace him, but he can't. Too much had happened. Too much time has passed. He doesn't know what to do, or how to react. His father is the same for the most part. He has some scars on his face which are a new addition. He doesn't doubt that was down to the Raven King. Another reason to keep distance between himself and the ruling family.

'Hello Quillan.'

His throat constricts at the sound of his full name, but he can't correct his father. He's not ready for that. 'Hey Dad.'

It feels strange saying that after so long. It's not something he ever thought he'd say again. But that's as far as they get. Neither male gets any further. Both stuck and unable to figure out what to say next.

After a few uncomfortable moments, Fergus gestures to the door. 'Do you have the energy to go for a walk?'

Quill doesn't think he does, but the idea of getting out of here for even a few minutes is too appealing to refuse. 'Yeah.'

They walk in silence down the stairs, his father taking it slowly so Quill can keep up. Fergus stops at a metal door, then pulls a key from his pocket. 'I need to show you something.'

He unlocks the door, and Quill is hit with the smell of the ocean as he opens the door. His father stops at the top of the stairs to offer his help, but he waves him away. 'The steps are steep. I don't want you to fall.'

'I won't fall.'

He slowly makes his way into the underbelly of the castle, the air turning damp, cold, and salty. As soon as they reach the bottom of the steps, he sees why. He knew the castle was built at the edge of a cliff, but he had no idea the sea had penetrated the lower levels.

The caves under the castle are vast, the space laid out with walkways suspended from the rock ceiling. Below the walkways, the ocean covers the floor, swirling as the waves send the water through any gaps in the rocks.

Then he spots the cages. There are dozens of them buried in the alcoves to each side of the cave. Thick metal grids seal off each of the half-submerged cages, creating horrific cells in which a prisoner could easily drown.

'What is this place?'

'This is one of the Raven King's prisons. The main one is on the floor above us. This was reserved for his special guests. He kept many vampires in here over the years. Far too many. When the tide is in, the cells further along fill with water.'

Quill shuffles further along the walkways, bracing himself against the damp rock to keep his balance. The walkway is wet and slippery. The last thing he needs is to fall into the water. 'Why are you showing me this?'

He was expecting his father to want a heart-to-heart, not to show him another prison.

'Trust me.' Without asking, his father takes his arm, supporting him as the walkway veers to the right around an outcropping. He leads him to a cell at the far end. The water is filling the cage, leaving a few inches of space between it and the metal grid serving as a roof.

'What is this?' Quill asks.

'I brought you here because you mistrust Davyn. You think he is like his father.'

'This place isn't helping to change my mind.'

Fergus points to the cell in front of them. 'This was Davyn's home for fifty-odd years. His father locked him in there, and when he wasn't ignoring him, he beat him. It took time, but he eventually escaped and joined the Blackjacks.

'Davyn is nothing like his father. He is a good man, Quillan. He killed his father. He's trying to kill the legacy his father left. He is trying to put things right.'

Quill watches the water swelling under his feet into the cage. How could anyone survive in there for even an hour, let alone fifty years? It says a lot about Davyn and the kind of vampire he is.

'If Davyn has given you the option to wear his crest around your neck, it is not the life sentence you believe it to be. You can claim your life back Quillan. You, Sorcha, and Bannon.'

Quill looks at his father, surprised by his comment. 'You don't mind that? Sorcha and Bannon probably aren't what you had in mind for me. A male vampire and a female wolf can't be the mates you saw in my future?'

His father smiles warmly. 'Why would I disapprove? All I've ever wanted for you was freedom and happiness. Why would I mind in the slightest? Quillan, you are alive. The fact you found happiness, in spite of everything you have endured, is quite remarkable. It's clearly evident that Sorcha and Bannon care a great deal for you. Neither would leave your bedside until you woke.'

'I don't know how I found them. None of it was planned. I just fell for both of them.' This isn't a conversation he was planning to have with his father when he came down here, but he needs to talk to someone about it.

'And I can tell they feel the same about you. But you cannot be with them unless you let Davyn take ownership. It brings a sour taste to my mouth to say this, but once you have been claimed by another member of the Warden's family, you cannot be freed again. Not until something drastic changes in the laws. Davyn can give you that freedom.'

'I'm scared.' He didn't mean to admit that. Being down here in this depressing place is getting to him. He thought his life had been hard, but even standing above the water is making him uneasy.

'Scared of what?'

'Everything. Fuck, I need to sit down.' His father helps him back to the steps and lowers him onto the bottom one. He's tired of being so weak. This isn't him. He's the strong one. Always has been. He can't bear having to be helped to even walk.

'What are you scared of son? Talk to me.'

His father sits beside him as Quill closes his eyes. With his eyes closed, he can almost imagine he's outside by the sea, instead of in an underwater prison.

'Not being in the prison. Being out here. Being with them. Like I said - everything.'

'It will take some adjustment. You are still recovering.'

'But being *that* Quill is all I know. I've been him for so long. I've been controlled, been told what to do nearly every moment of the last few decades. How do I get past that?'

His father smiles sadly at him. 'I don't know. What happened after the Raven King took you?'

'I spent some time in one of his fighting pits. I didn't want to kill... I didn't want any of it. I had no choice though. I don't know how long I was there. Time means nothing in the pits. One day I was taken from there and shipped to the prison. The Warden had been at one of my fights and took a fancy to me, or to my blood, or both.'

He pauses, nausea twisting at his gut at the memory of that day. 'I was actually happy. How fucked up is that? I was happy someone had bought me.' He laughs harshly to himself. 'That relief didn't last long.'

'He fed from you?'

'Mostly.'

467

'What do you mean by *mostly*?'

'He'd make me see to his needs occasionally. Not have sex with him. I was his slave. He'd never allow me to be with him like that. He'd sit in his chair behind his desk, make me kneel in front of him, then suck his...' He doesn't finish the sentence. He doubts he needs to. 'He'd hang on for ages. I think he did that on purpose. To draw out the humiliation as long as possible. I don't know which part was worse. The feeding hurt so much, but the time alone with him hurt in a different way.'

'Oh son...'

'It is what it is. Can't change what happened.' His father is lost in horrified silence for a minute. He's not surprised by his reaction. It's hardly a happy story, but the last thing he needs is pity.

His father finally composes himself. 'Sorcha said you were in a position of power. That you were in charge of the other guards.'

He nods, closing his eyes so he can focus on the sound of the water. It always calmed him when he was on the island. 'Eventually. He kept me locked in a cage at first, taking me out when he wanted to feed from me or... use me.' He's glad his eyes are closed. There's no way he wants to see his father's face.

'I don't know why, but after a few years he decided to let me do some jobs around the prison. Maybe he thought I was getting too withdrawn. I don't know. Whatever the reason, he continued to let me work there. It was a horrible job, but anything was better than being in that room alone all day. I enjoyed it. Enjoyed working.

'But mostly enjoyed having that bit of freedom. I think he realised I was more useful to him in the prison, than locked away. He was grooming me, gradually turning me into something he could use. I was his guard dog, his enforcer, his eyes and ears in the prison.'

'Is that why he put you in charge?'

'Maybe. I hope that wasn't the only reason though. He didn't want anyone to know he owned me. He thought if the other guards knew that, they wouldn't trust me and the Warden wouldn't have a link to the inside. I moved up the ranks myself. I made head guard myself. And as long as I came to him without argument whenever he called me, he left me to it.'

He pauses for a moment before speaking again. 'I did a lot of disgusting things while I was there. I fought against my orders initially, but every time I refused, he'd punish me instead. I couldn't take it. I was a coward – I know that. I should have fought harder, but I just wanted the pain to stop. I think I justified some of what I was doing by telling myself the wolves had done something to deserve whatever punishment I was told to give them. It was all a lie, but I convinced myself it was the truth.

'It's no excuse, but I needed to stay out of his room. If I did as I was told, he left me running the prison. If I disobeyed, I was back in his room with him. I hated that, Dad. I fucking hated it.'

His father nods. 'I'm not judging anything you did Quill. Was he addicted to your blood?'

Quill rests his forehead against the wall, squeezing his eyes shut as the emotional wrench forms a tight knot in his stomach. 'Yeah. He didn't feed much at first, but he couldn't resist the addiction in the end. He had this ornate dining table in his living quarters. He'd make me strip to my underwear, sometimes fully naked, and lie on it. Then he'd feed.

'When he was feeling really generous, he'd have these dinner parties, and I was the main course. He'd bring some pompous friends over from the mainland and they'd... they didn't care where they bit me, what part of my body they fed from. After a while he'd have to chain me down every time. It hurt so much. They'd tear at me, rip my flesh, just to get a taste of my blood. Then when they were finished, they'd leave me there for hours while they chatted and drank expensive wine.

'He'd eventually let me go. I'd have to stand on a plastic sheet he'd lay on the floor and clean the blood off myself. If I got any on his carpet he'd beat me. So, I usually just got dressed and went back to my room, before taking a shower. Try to forget what happened, then get back to my life.'

'I do not know what to say. I doubt there is anything I can say to help erase even a moment of your time there. Can you please look at me?'

He looks at his father, terrified about what he was going to see in his face. But he's not ashamed of his son. He's sad, but there's also anger there.

'I like Bannon and Sorcha. I like them a great deal. It would be a shame to lose such life-changing relationships because you won't take Davyn's offer.'

'I don't want to be owned! I don't want to be with them as a fucking slave. They deserve better than that.'

'And what about what you deserve Quillan?'

He can't hear that name any longer. 'Please don't call me that.'

'Call you what?'

'Quillan. That's what he always called me. He was the only one who did for the last few years.'

His father nods briskly. 'Forgive me. I did not realise.'

'No problem. It's just another thing he fucked up.'

'So it seems. As I was saying Quill, what do you think you deserve?'

He doesn't know. He hasn't known that for years. 'All I know is that I'm not right for them. Bannon is... he's lost so much. Had so much pain in his life. And Sorcha was locked away for no reason. Being lumped with a slave like me isn't fair.'

'Surely that's their decision to make?' His father shuffles closer to him. 'They risked their lives to rescue you. It's all they were thinking about, all they wanted since before I met them. Their sole purpose was you and you alone. I believe they've already made their decision about you.

'All you need to do is let them love you the way they want to. Davyn's seal will make that happen. He outranks all of the Warden's relatives. Once he claims you, you will be safe. You, Sorcha, and

470

Bannon can make a life for yourselves. I, for one, truly believe it is what you all want and deserve.'

'I'm sorry.' He doesn't know what he's apologising for. He just feels like it's needed. Maybe he's apologising for being taken? Maybe for being sold? Or maybe because he feels like he let his father down by doing every single disgusting thing he was made to do under the Warden's ownership - both in the prison and alone with his owner.

'Oh, Quill. You have nothing to apologise for. I love you. Nothing will change that. Our lives were not our own for so long. We had no control or say in any moment of it. But we have survived. We are both here and being given a second chance to have the life we both deserve. Wouldn't it be foolish not to grab that chance with both hands?'

Hearing his father say those words finally hits the wall he built around himself a long time ago. A wall that protected him from being consumed by everything he'd felt in the fighting pit and under the Warden's ownership. He breaks down, not caring that he's sobbing like a helpless baby.

His father hesitates, unsure if he would accept contact from him, but Quill takes that decision out of his hands. Right now, he needs his father. He moves closer to his father, collapsing into his arms when Fergus holds him close.

Once he lets the tears out, he can't stop. All the sorrow, the pain, the shame, the loneliness, comes out, but it's okay. His father has him, his embrace comforting him like it used to years ago when he was a child.

'I will protect you, Quill. I swear. I will not let anyone take you from me again.'

SORCHA

As she tidies away their lunch things, Sorcha can't keep the smile off her face. Life is good. It's still uncertain, but compared to how it was a few weeks ago, it's incredible.

Quill is still tired, but he's spending more time out of bed. He actually got dressed today which is great. It's a little strange to see both Quill and Bannon in everyday clothes. They look very different in jeans and t-shirts compared to their black uniforms. She never wants to see her old prison uniform again.

Sorcha climbs onto the bed next to Quill, taking his hand in hers. He's still distancing himself from her. He'll hold her hand and kiss her, but she usually has to initiate the contact. She understands why, but she needs him to move on from what happened. Accept it's part of their past and look ahead.

His hand trembles in hers, something that Bannon notices too when he joins them on the bed. 'Time to feed.'

Quill nods instead of arguing which surprises her. He's all about being tough and uncooperative whenever possible. Quill moves to the edge of the bed, but Sorcha has an idea.

She's seen Bannon feed Quill a few times now, and each time it was unbelievably hot. It was something she wanted to be a part of, but with Quill being so weak, the feed was purely to help him recover.

'What?' he asks when she scrambles over him, stopping him from pushing off the bed.

'Okay, I'm not going to beat around the bush here. I want you to include me in this.'

'How the fuck do we include you in a feed?' Quill asks.

'I was thinking that if we were naked, it would be a great starting point.'

Quill and Bannon glance at each other. They're probably having an internal conversation. But when Bannon hits her with his sexy, mischievous smile, she knows he's game.

Quill scrubs his hand over his hair, releasing most of it from the tie. 'You want that? Really?'

'What? You two sexy vampires naked in bed with me. No. Not at all. Why in the world would I want that?'

'Mouthy wolf.'

She grins at Quill as she takes Bannon's hand, pulling him over to the bed. 'I take it by his grin that Bannon is ready to get naked with me. How about you Quill?'

Quill slowly pushes to his feet, using the headboard to steady himself when he wobbles. 'I'll give anything to see you two naked in bed together.'

Three of us, Bannon signs, hitting Quill with a serious look. *'Always three.'*

Before Quill can come back with one of his many arguments, Bannon pulls off his own t-shirt, then unbuckles his jeans, removing them, his boxers, and his socks. He pulls back the covers then sits back on the bed, one leg raised looking all kinds of sexy as he waits for Sorcha and Quill to join him.

She loves this confidence that's breaking through over the last few weeks. He's coming out of his shell. Finding himself again after being lost for so long.

Sorcha quickly undresses before jumping on the bed with a giggle and crawling over to Bannon. She pats the bed beside her. 'room for one more.'

Quill stands and looks at them for a long moment, clearly having a serious argument with himself about it. But when he pulls his t-shirt over his head, Sorcha can't help but smile.

Still unsure about this, Quill sticks to the edge of the bed, but Sorcha grabs him by the arm, tugging him over to them. Sensing Quill's trepidation about this, Bannon pulls him down for a kiss. Sorcha lies back and just watches the two vampires kissing. Her body is responding to what they're doing. Her pussy is pulsing in time to Quill and Bannon's tongues as they invade each others' mouths.

Bannon breaks away from Quill, turning his attention to her. Quill doesn't stay on the sidelines for long, leaning down to kiss her when Bannon moves aside. She wants to be with Quill. Wants to feel him inside her while he feeds from Bannon. His hard dick is barely touching her, but when it brushes against her side, she nearly moans aloud.

'It's your turn, Quill.' Sorcha moves to the side, lifting her hips so he brushes against her pussy instead of her leg. She takes their dicks in her hands, loving the way both vampires look down, their fangs peeking out from between their parted lips. 'Fuck me while you feed from Bannon. Please Quill.'

When his unique eyes begin to glow, she knows he's not going to say no. Quill's large body covers hers as Bannon lies beside her so

Quill can reach his neck. Sorcha gasps as Quill's dick presses against her entrance, teasing her and driving her crazy. 'More Quill. Please...'

Little by little, he slides into her, slowly stretching, filling her. She reaches out, taking Bannon's dick in her hand, stroking him as Quill slides out then pushes in again.

'I'm going to feed.' Quill's voice is so much deeper than usual. His fangs are fully extended, his glowing eyes focused on Bannon's neck. When Bannon grabs a handful of Quill's hair, pulling him against his neck Sorcha can barely breathe. When Quill's fangs sink into the side of Bannon's neck the energy in the room shifts up a few gears.

Quill's body shudders as he feeds, his thick neck moving as he swallows Bannon's blood. Reenergised by the blood, Quill's hips roll back and forth, driving his dick deep into her, harder and faster until she's sure he's going to move the bed across the floor.

Bannon moves beside her as she strokes him, his dick sliding through her closed fist. To ground herself, she digs her fingers into Quill's ass, but that does nothing to calm the situation.

He pulls his fangs out of Bannon's neck, licking the puncture wounds before leaning down to brush his fangs against her neck. The sensation sends a spasm through her.

'Finish Bannon in your mouth.'

No need to make the suggestion. That's exactly what Sorcha was planning. Bannon kneels up and she takes him in her mouth without hesitation.

While Quill fucks her hard, she sucks Bannon.

'Fuck!' Quill says through clenched teeth. 'So fucking hot. I love watching you two together.'

Her orgasm is building, and she knows Bannon is close too. His whole body is vibrating, the thick muscles in his stomach rolling as he tries to hold back. She wants to keep her eyes open, wants to keep watching Bannon and Quill, but she can't. It's all too much. Quill. Bannon. The sounds of their bodies as they slap and slide against each other. Bannon's thick dick in her mouth. Quill's body pressed against hers as he pushes her over the edge.

She screams against Bannon's dick as she comes, riding out the waves as he takes over. He suddenly grips the headboard, the wood creaking under his hand as he comes. While she's still coming down, Bannon pulls his dick out of her mouth.

She opens her eyes when Quill pulls out of her. Then she realises why. Bannon takes Quill in his mouth.

'Oh fuck.' It's all she can say. There are no words to describe the scene in front of her. Bannon is on his hands and knees with Quill's dick in his mouth. It's obscenely hot.

Then Bannon slides Quill out of his mouth, and Quill comes all over her stomach and chest. Before she can comment, both males lean over her, licking and sucking his cum off her skin.

'Oh God...' They kiss their way up her body, licking her clean. They stop at her neck, Bannon to one side and Quill to the other.

'Bite me.'

The three of them freeze as the words come out of her mouth without any warning.

Quill pushes upright so he can look at her. 'What?'

'Okay, I didn't plan to say that. But now it's out there, is it such a strange request? I've fed you before and nothing disastrous happened.'

'That was for necessity, not pleasure. Are you sure you really want this?'

She nods. The more she thinks about it, the more she wants it. They both look over at Bannon and she's relieved to see he's smiling. 'Is that a yes from you?'

'I'd like that,' he mouths, and she can't help but notice the way his dick hardens against her leg.

'Yeah. I can feel that.'

'You want us to bite you now?' Quill asks, leaning down to tease her by scraping his fangs against the side of her neck.

'Fuck yes. Sorry. I mean yes please,' she adds with a laugh which turns to a groan when Bannon licks the other side of her neck.

'We'll be gentle,' Quill mutters as he nips at her ear, his fangs sending an involuntary shiver through her.

'I trust you both.'

She braces for the bites, but that's not the contact she feels. It's their hands and lips on her body. They kiss and nip at her neck while their hands explore her, both of them moving in complete unison, touching and caressing her all the way down to her pussy.

She didn't think she'd be ready to go again. But that's never going to be a problem with Bannon and Quill touching her.

Their hands grip her thighs, spreading her legs wide. Sorcha moans as their fingers brush against her pussy, teasing her clit until she's arching off the bed.

But when they bite her, their fangs sinking deep at the exact same time, she has to hold back the scream.

One of them slides a finger inside while the other massages her clit. Bannon and Quill take it in turns to tease her, working in perfect harmony to continuously hit all the right spots at the same time.

They're consuming her in every way. Their bodies pressed firmly against hers as they feed and tease her with the promise of one hell of an orgasm.

'Oh fuck...' There's no holding back the shout as she comes apart.

She must zone out for a moment. When she comes to, she's tucked under the covers, Quill and Bannon holding her, their naked bodies pressed firmly against hers.

'You okay?'

She sighs contentedly. 'I can't move. What the hell was that? Fuck me that was intense.'

Quill rubs his nose against the side of her face. 'You taste amazing. So fucking strong.'

'Really?'

Bannon nods, then licks his bite marks, the slow sensual swipes of his tongue doing nothing to help her recover.

'We could get used to drinking your blood.'

She never thought a statement like that would be such a turn on. 'You two are corrupting me.'

'I didn't think feeding could be like that,' Quill says. 'I think this should be the norm from now on.'

'So, we'll all be naked in bed whenever either of you feeds. I like that rule.'

Bannon gives them both an enthusiastic thumbs up before draping his arm across her, hugging her close.

She doesn't know if it was the out of this world orgasms these stunning vampires have just given her, or the intense feeding, but she can barely keep her eyes open.

'Sleep,' Quill says, kissing her cheek.

He doesn't need to tell her twice. Safe in the arms of her protectors, Sorcha falls into a dreamless, peaceful sleep.

QUILL

He doesn't know why he called Davyn and Shep back into his room. He's still no closer to deciding his future. But it's a decision he needs to make sooner rather than later. The longer he puts it off, the more chance there is of the Warden's family finding him and claiming him. If that happens, he could be placing Sorcha, Bannon, and everyone else at Darkhaven in danger.

He needs to make this decision now. Yes, or leave. Those are his only options. If he's going for the latter, he's going to have to disappear for good. Leave no trace. Nothing to connect him with Sorcha or Bannon.

But that's not what he wants. He needs them. Even if it's just to protect them he'll take that role in their lives.

But he thinks he can have more with Bannon and Sorcha. After what happened earlier between the three of them, he's beginning to believe that maybe the three of them can try to have a life together.

That won't be possible unless he makes a decision about his ownership.

He sits up when there's a heavy knock at the door 'Yeah.'

Davyn and Shep come into his room, their huge bodies instantly dwarfing everything around them. Quill is a big male but these two put even him to shame.

'You wanted to talk?'

He nods, gesturing to the chairs by his bed waiting until the two fighters have taken a seat, before he continues.

'I'm sorry I'm dragging my feet on this.'

Shep answers while Davyn continues his unnerving staring. 'Fuck that, Quill! It's a tough decision. I get that. Dav does too, don't you buddy?' he says, nudging the vampire lord on the arm.

'Yeah.'

'Vampire of many words,' Shep says with a grin. He leans forward, clasping his hands together on his knees. 'I'm going to be all serious now. Speaking as one slave to another, take his fucking offer. Take the freedom it brings. Be with Sorcha and Bannon. You might not trust this guy,' he says, nodding over at Davyn.

'But what reason would I have to sugarcoat any of this?' he continues. 'You saw my scars. I told you the truth about my time with my mistress. I now have a beautiful mate and a life I can live, without always having to look over my shoulder.'

Shep hits him with an intense look. No joking. No bullshitting. He's laying it all on the table. Being honest with him.

'We didn't deserve what happened to us, Quill. We've been abused and beaten. Been used, or made to do things we didn't want. I reckon out of everyone, we deserve a chance to live our lives the way we want for a change. Say *fuck you* to our previous owners and find out who we really are.'

'I accept your offer, Davyn.' The words come out in a rush without any conscious thought, but it's the right decision. At least if Davyn owns him, there's a chance he can spend some of his time with Bannon and Sorcha. Well, if her brothers allow it. That's another hurdle to cross. Something else to look forward to.

Davyn looks up at him. 'You sure?'

'I want to keep Sorcha and Bannon safe. I need to be with them.'

'Fuck yes!' Shep says, slapping him hard on the shoulder. 'Welcome to the family Quill. Hey, does that make you a step-brother or something like that?'

'I'm not your fucking father!' Davyn says, glaring over at Shep.

'Ah don't be like that. This is a good thing.'

'Don't you mind old Grumpy here,' Shep says, grinning at Quill. 'We'll be like Oldranson extended family members or something. I'll have to have a think about what to call us.'

'Don't you fucking dare! I am this close to flattening you Shep,' Davyn says, growling at his teammate.

Shep snorts at his growl. 'Whatever. So, are you going to make this official or what?

Davyn nods, then reaches into his pocket. He places a box on the bedside table. 'I brought this just in case you agreed.'

Quill can't help but be put at ease by Shep's carefree enthusiasm. If someone like Shep can be so relaxed with his new owner, maybe it's not going to be as bad as Quill thinks it is. The way Shep and Davyn are with each other gives him hope that he can have a somewhat normal life with Davyn as his owner.

Quill opens the box and has to bite the inside of his cheek when he sees the silver chain with a horned demon pendent.

'It's a damn sight better than that fucking heavy chain we both had to wear before.' Shep says, as if reading Quill's mind. 'Fits in more with my wardrobe style too,' he adds with a wink.

Davyn throws another glare at Shep, before looking back at Quill.

'That chain is to protect you, not to mark you as my property. I need you to understand that. I am only your owner on paper.'

'I understand. Thank you.' He places the box back on the table, already feeling as if a weight has been lifted from his shoulders. Or from around his neck.

'I'll ask Ethan to prepare the paperwork,' Dav says as he crosses his arms.

'It's that easy?'

'The Warden's family might put up a fight, but I don't back down. My title will make sure I get the final say. They fight and I'll fight harder. I reckon when I've paid for you, they'll back off. It's not anything you need to worry about. Me and Ethan will take care of it. From now on, you're free. That's all you need to know.'

'And how long do I get to pay you back?'

Davyn's green eye glows slightly. 'Fuck that! You don't pay me back. Ever. My father had plenty of funds. Most of that was earned by throwing me in the fighting pit. It's time that blood money was put to good use. No debt.'

Without waiting for a reply, his new owner gets to his feet and leaves, closing the door behind him. Quill collapses back onto the pillows and closes his eyes. That's a hell of a lot to process, but overall, it went surprisingly well.

'He's a fan of the dramatic,' Shep says.

Quill opens his eyes and focuses on the faint bite marks on his arms. No more being forced to feed others. No more cages or chains. No more on his knees in front of the Warden, being used however the bastard saw fit.

He'll be free.

'Feels fucking great, doesn't it?'

Quill nods, the smile he's been holding back finally being set free. 'Yeah. It does.'

Shep holds out his hand, nearly crushing Quill's hand when he shakes it. 'Welcome to the fucked-up family.'

90

BANNON

He's tired, hungry, and wound like a spring. Sorcha and Quill are safe. They're with friends, with Sorcha's family, but that doesn't mean Bannon is going to relax any time soon.

In the chair next to his, Sorcha is curled up in front of the fire, a mug of cocoa in her hands. She's in the same head space he is.

Until Quill's ownership is decided, they're all in limbo.

Bannon's canines slide down from his gums as the anger rises. He'd heard of vampires owning other vampires, but he thought the practice had died a death years ago. It doesn't matter how long he mulls it over, he's still struggling to see what exactly the messed-up dynamic was between the Warden and Quill.

'Do you think he'll agree to Davyn's proposal?'

Bannon shrugs, wishing he had a more certain response for her. *'I hope so.'*

'Me too.' She shuffles around in the chair to face him. 'I spoke to Shep. He's really pushing for Quill to agree. He said having Davyn holding his contract is just a formality.'

He smiles and nods. Quill is stubborn, hot-headed, and closed off. There's no way to know how he's going to approach this. There's nothing to say he won't just disappear into the night, and deal with the situation alone.

That's what he's most worried about. He's hoping Shep's own experiences with having Davyn as an owner, will convince Quill that a life is possible. But who knows what's going on in that male's head. Only Quill has the answer to that one.

He looks up as Davyn opens the door. 'He's made his decision.' Instead of letting them know what that decision is, he leaves again.

'Well, he could take some conversation classes from Shep. I couldn't shut him up and Davyn barely talks.'

Bannon pushes to his feet. *'Let's see what Quill has decided.'*

They walk up the spiral staircase and along the corridor to the guest room, where Quill has been recovering. As usual, the stunning vampire's face is completely unreadable as they join him by his bed. Bannon gestures for Sorcha to take the chair, while he remains standing. He's too wound up to sit.

'You look so much brighter,' Sorcha says as she reaches out to take Quill's hand. 'How are you feeling?'

'I'm grand. So, I made a decision on Davyn's offer. I'm sorry it took so long. I've just been trying to get my head around everything. A few days ago, I knew who I was. I was in a shite position, but it's all I've known for so long. I worked so hard to claw back what little bit of my life I could. Being the head guard of the prison was my way of taking back that control. And I know how fucking pathetic that sounds, but...' his voice trails away as he shakes his head.

Sorcha opens her mouth to speak but Quill holds up his hand, silencing her. 'I need to get this out in one go, or I won't say it at all.'

'Of course. Go on.'

'I love you. I love you both. I wasn't planning, or expecting, anything like this to happen. But it has, and I wouldn't have it any other way. Davyn will be my new owner. It will just be on paper, though. I believe that much. This is my chance to be as free as I can be, at the moment.'

Bannon feels like he's floating. He hears Quill's words, but their meaning is so immense he can't quite process it. After hearing what Shep had to say, he knows that Davyn will leave Quill to live his life the way he wants.

But if that's the case, why does Quill still look like he's waiting for the noose to tighten?

'What's on your mind?' Sorcha asks, seeing the same resignation in Quill's face that Bannon does.

Quill chews on his lip rings for a few seconds before he answers, his voice a lot quieter than it was a moment ago. 'When the Warden owned me, I did... the Warden... he made me do things. Things I didn't want to do. And I get if that means neither of you can accept me, or what I am.'

'What things?' Sorcha asks, her voice trembling slightly.

'Sexual things... to him. He never did anything like that to me, but I'd have to... suck him off. Fuck! I hate even saying it. But I didn't want to do it. I fucking hated every single second of it.'

Sorcha takes his hand and squeezes it in hers. 'I'm not going to speak for Bannon, but I will say that, for some reason I still can't quite figure out, I have fallen in love with you.' Quill breaks into a small smile when she says that. 'And believe me, I tried hard not to. I don't care about what happened with the Warden. Well, I care. I don't mean it like that. I would gladly kill him again if I could. I meant that it doesn't change how I feel about you. Not for a second.'

Then Quill looks over at Bannon. He might have heard Sorcha's words, but she's only half of the equation. He needs them both. Bannon can see it in his stunning eyes. *'I am deeply in love with you, Quill. Nothing will change that.'*

Quill's smile grows, and Bannon could swear there are tears in his eyes. 'Fuck!'

Sorcha laughs at his response. 'If that's not the most romantic thing I've ever heard, I don't know what is!'

'I don't know what else to say,' Quill admits, wiping his eyes before the tears break free. 'Thank you?'

She nods. 'Better. Could still do with more work.'

'How about I'm crazy in love with you both? Is that better?'

Bannon smiles when she launches herself at Quill, hugging him tightly. 'So much better!'

He hugs her back, a little hesitant but quickly losing himself to her embrace. 'Get your ass over here, Bannon, before she squashes me!'

Bannon sits beside Quill, instantly being pulled into the embrace by both Quill and Sorcha. Bannon closes his eyes, letting himself just enjoy the feeling of being with these two incredible people, who have got to him on a level he never knew existed.

He loves them, and they love him.

Quill releases them both, then picks up the box from the bedside table. He opens it, showing them the necklace inside. 'I'll have to wear this for the rest of my life. I love you both, but I will walk away, if all that is too much for either of you.'

Bannon takes it out of the box and hands it to Sorcha. She fastens it around Quill's neck, placing a kiss over the crest. Bannon does the same, hoping that it proves to Quill that it doesn't change anything between them.

'I have no fucking clue what I did to deserve having you two in my life. But whatever I did, I'm so fucking grateful.'

He's not the only one. Bannon feels exactly the same. With Sorcha to one side and Bannon on the other, Quill holds them both close, his grip never loosening as they fall asleep together.

91

QUILL

Over his century and a half of life, Quill can count on one hand the number of times he's woken up with someone in his bed. It wasn't how he did things. Maybe that was down to the Warden owning him? Maybe it was just his need to keep everyone away from him? Whatever the reason, it was something he avoided whenever possible.

But waking up with Sorcha's hand on his dick, and Bannon's fangs scraping along the side of his neck, he might just change his mind. He can see some definite pros.

'Morning,' Sorcha murmurs, before kissing him. 'Did you sleep well?'

'Yeah. Waking up isn't going too badly either.'

He gasps as Bannon nips his neck before kissing the mark he just left. He never thought he'd be comfortable being bitten after what the Warden did, but Bannon could bite him all over his body and he's just ask for more.

There's no comparison to what the Warden did and what Bannon does. And he really fucking likes what Bannon does. 'If you're hungry just go for it.'

Quill curses as both Sorcha and Bannon latch on – Bannon's fangs sinking into his neck while Sorcha slides his dick into her mouth.

'Fuck! I didn't mean the two of you.'

Sorcha stops, brushing her dark hair back from her face as she looks up at him. 'Oh, sorry. Should I stop?'

'No, you shouldn't. Ignore me. As you were. If you want to...fuck!' Whatever else he was going to say doesn't make it out as Sorcha swallows him again. Buried under him, Quill groans as Bannon's solid body holds him down, keeping him in place as he feeds.

'I love the sound of you sucking my neck like that,' Quill says, gasping as Sorcha's tongue circles the tip of his dick. Bannon pulls out of his neck and Quill groans when Bannon's tongue drags along his skin. Fuck he loves when he does that.

'I want my tongue in your ass, Bannon.'

The male looks down at him to see if he was being serious.

'Please.'

Sorcha moans aloud when Bannon nods. 'Oh my God! I need to see that right now!'

'Get on all fours.'

When Bannon rises off his body, Quill shuffles down the bed, wedging his face between Bannon's legs. He licks Bannon's ass, hearing the male growl in his head.

'Do that again.'

Bannon's breathy begging in his head is sexy as hell. He licks Bannon's ass again, this time a deep predatory growl rumbling deep in Quill's chest. 'You like that,' Quill asks, already knowing the answer.'

'I think he really does,' Sorcha says, leaning over to kiss Bannon as Quill slowly slides his tongue along Bannon's flesh again.

'Do you have any idea how hot you two look?'

Quill can only imagine how Bannon looks. He'd love to see his face right now, but there's no way he's going to stop what he's doing. He wants more. Wants to go deeper.

Bannon's ass and balls press against Quill's nose and mouth, but who needs to breathe? He sucks, nips, and licks any flesh he can reach with his tongue and lips. Then Bannon lurches forward, his moan of pleasure echoing in Quill's head, but Quill holds him in place. His hands are digging into Bannon's hips, firmly keeping him exactly where he wants him.

SORCHA

Every time she sees Quill and Bannon together it is so beyond a mere turn-on. She could watch their bodies like this hour after hour and never tire of it.

She loves the way these two males are with each other. Loves the way they can be such strong protective alphas, yet can also be with each other like this. Loves how they can share her.

Sorcha shuffles down the bed, watching Quill tease Bannon, flicking his tongue over Bannon's rim. Bannon fists the sheet in his hands, his fingers tightly gripping the material as Quill continues to drive him insane.

He looks over his shoulder at her, his glowing eyes sexy as hell. He bites his bottom lip, his fangs digging into his flesh. Fuck, he is incredible. They both are. A shiver runs through her as she watches the piercing in Quill's tongue disappearing inside Bannon.

Time to join in the fun.

She straddles Quill's legs, holding his cock upright as she slowly slides him inside. He growls loudly against Bannon's ass. Quill lets go of Bannon's legs, fisting the covers to either side of him as she takes him balls-deep. Sorcha closes her eyes as she sits back on him. He's breathing heavily, his fingers digging into the bed as his chest rises and falls.

Quill lifts Bannon off him. 'Turn around. Face her.'

Bannon adjusts his position, settling back on Quill's face, helped by Quill himself when he grabs onto Bannon's muscular thighs, holding him down again.

'I don't hear you licking Bannon's ass.'

Quill groans at Sorcha's comment, then his throat moves as he gets back to work. Bannon looks up at her then to Quill's cock buried deep inside her pussy. His brown eyes glow as he draws his lips back from his fangs.

The sight of him like that sends her into a frenzy. 'You like Quill doing that to you?' she asks breathlessly as she rides Quill, his thick cock hitting all the right spots.

Bannon nods, his arms straining to hold him upright. She grips Bannon's dick, stroking him as they both use Quill, grinding against him, faster and faster until they're both gasping for breath. Under them, Quill doesn't take it easy either. His dick thrusts into her in perfect timing with her as his mouth and tongue plough into Bannon.

Sorcha rubs two fingers against her pussy and Quill's dick, coating them with her juices as he continues to fuck her. Reaching behind her, Sorcha moves her hand lower, past Quill's balls to his ass. He instantly spreads his legs as much as he can. She rubs her fingers against his hole, his growls vibrating through his chest as he devours Bannon.

Sorcha easily slides one finger inside, helped by her juices coating it. Quill moves against her hand, forcing her finger deeper. Clearly desperate for more, she pulls out, then pushes two fingers into his body, tightness gripping her fingers while she sits back on his cock.

'Oh God...' she hisses. 'Fuck me... Fuck me, fuck me, fuck me,' she gasps as Quill thrusts into her, his ass squeezing her fingers, his entire body quivering as she teases him.

Face to face with Bannon, watching the variety of expressions crossing his beautiful face ramps up the intensity for her.

'Bite me Bannon. Please bite me.'

Bannon leans over, then without pausing, his fangs sink into her neck, the sensation shooting through her body from her toes to her scalp.

'I'm coming!'

Her orgasm hits like a tidal wave all over her body. Bannon releases her neck, kissing and licking the bite marks until he comes. Streams of hot cum shoot out from his dick all over Quill and her. Then it's Quill's turn. His roar is muffled by Bannon's ass, his hips jerking off the bed as he comes, burying himself deep in her.

Sorcha can't breathe. Whatever oxygen there was in the room seems to have disappeared. Bannon is quivering in front of her, Quill gasping for breath under them.

It takes a few minutes for them to recover, the sound of their breathing the only sound in the room. Bannon climbs off Quill, toppling over onto his side, lying on the bed with an arm over his face. Quill grunts as she tugs her fingers out of his ass before flopping to his other side, quivering all over.

BANNON

He's fucked. Bannon has heard people say that on TV and in films. But until this moment, he doesn't think he's ever been *truly* fucked. Doesn't think he's been so spent he can barely move. But he's not done.

He has no idea where this insatiable appetite is coming from. It could be Sorcha's wolf blood. It could be what Quill just did to him with his mouth and tongue. It could just be Sorcha and Quill.

Whatever is charging him, he's not going to fight back or resist.

Bannon climbs over Quill to flip Sorcha onto her back. Instantly, they're crawling over her, mouths going for her breasts. With Bannon on her left, Quill on her right, they lick up all Bannon's cum from her body. Sorcha lifts her hips from the bed, seeking any friction she can.

Bannon came a few minutes ago but tell that to his body. He's so wound up, his dick hard and ready to be buried deep inside Sorcha.

'One of you better move lower,' she says, gasping as Quill nips at her nipple.

'We're running the show now,' Quill says, with a wicked smile. 'You just need to lie there and keep making those fucking sexy moans.'

Bannon slowly and deliberately licks along the slit of her pussy. Sorcha spreads her legs for him, her beautiful body writhing under him as he licks her again.

Bannon clutches Quill's jaw, sliding his tongue into Quill's mouth so he can taste her.

'So good,' Quill murmurs, then goes down himself, swiping his pierced tongue along Sorcha's pussy.

'That tongue piercing Quill...' Sorcha whimpers.

Bannon knows exactly what she means. He can't get enough of that seriously hot addition.

He spreads Sorcha's legs wide enough so both of them can taste her at the same time, sucking at her pussy as she moans.

'Three is a dangerous number,' Quill growls as he laps at Sorcha's pussy, his pierced tongue brushing against Bannon's. 'I have an idea...' Quill's tone is devious as he licks Sorcha one last time before sitting back on his legs.

'You two lie side by side.' Once Bannon is lying beside Sorcha, Quill grips Sorcha's calf, then lifts her leg, positioning himself between them. Bannon kisses her as Quill slowly slides into her, his thick dick sinking into her pussy.

'Quill…' Sorcha murmurs as her eyes roll back in her head.

Bannon's thumb slides over her clit, rubbing in circles before he brushes his fingers against where Quill's cock slides in and out of Sorcha.

'Wings…' Sorcha gasps, as himself and Quill tease her. 'Release your wings, Quill.'

Bannon nods enthusiastically before speaking to Quill in his head. *'Please! We want you to do this with your wings out.'*

Quill straightens, his dick still buried deep in Sorcha. 'I can't say no to either of you.' Bannon watches, transfixed as the enormous wings slide out of Quill's broad back. The bones reshape until his wings spread to either side, the green and blue limbs absolutely stunning as he gently flaps them.

'Wow!' Sorcha says as Quill lowers, grabbing Bannon's face and kissing him, before doing the same to her.

Quill pushes back on his arms, pumping into Sorcha faster and faster, his wings coming forward to wrap around the sides of the bed, cocooning them.

Sorcha's next orgasm is fast approaching. He can feel her body shuddering under his fingers.

'More Quill! I'm going to come!' Quill curses as she comes, her body gripping him as she comes apart. But that doesn't mean Bannon is going to stop what he's doing. He's going to draw this out for her as long as possible. He could watch her coming all day. She is beautiful stretched out naked for them to admire and pleasure.

As she whimpers, Quill pulls out and hits Bannon with a sexy grin. 'Your turn.' It takes Bannon a second to realise exactly what Quill means.

'Oh God… yes!'

Sorcha's response is like she took the words from his own brain.

'It'll be easier if you're on all-fours again,' Quill says.

'If you're doing this, I want you in me,' Sorcha says, tugging on Bannon's arm. 'Quill inside you and you inside me.'

Quill growls at her suggestion. 'Fuck yes!'

Bannon has barely climbed between Sorcha's legs before Quill licks his finger and presses it against Bannon's hole.

'Ready?'

Bannon nods, desperate to feel Quill inside him. Initially, he tenses against the unfamiliar pressure, but that doesn't last long. Unfamiliar quickly turns to pleasure. Quill slides his finger in and out, giving him time to get used to the new sensation.

More. He doesn't realise he's uttered the words to Quill's mind until he responds.

'Oh, you want more?' A second finger joins the first, stretching him like never before. Under him, Sorcha writhes and grinds against him.

'You're being greedy now Bannon,' Sorcha jokes as Quill's fingers slide in and out of his ass. Then Bannon bucks against him as Quill hits his G-spot. Sorcha groans as he thrusts into her in response to what Quill is doing. If he had a voice, he'd be moaning his head off right about now.

Sorcha smiles at him as he struggles to think straight. 'I think you've corrupted him, Quill.'

Quill's deep sexy laugh doesn't help get his head back on track.

'I'm not going to apologise for that. I want to be inside you Bannon. I want to fuck you.'

Bannon nods, licking his lips to try and get some moisture back. Quill swaps his fingers for his thick, hard dick, the tip teasing as Quill pushes against him.

'Relax and let me in.' Quill groans out loud as he sinks deep into Bannon's ass.

Bannon's head spins as Quill's dick stretches him, fills him. It's so good he can barely believe it.

'I love watching you both like this,' Sorcha says, her fingers rubbing against his dick as it slides into her body. The growl that Quill releases as he buries himself in Bannon, reverberates through his body to his dick, snuggly buried in Bannon.

Bannon isn't sure he can hold himself together if Quill moves. He's ridiculously close to coming already.

Quill starts slow, but it doesn't stay that way. He bares his teeth, his fangs dropping from his gums as he moves, his pace increasing. Quill's dick inside him, Sorcha's pussy gripping him firmly, her fingers teasing him as she massages her clit – it's all too much.

'You look so gorgeous together,' she murmurs as she stretches out under him. 'Fuck me Bannon. Please...'

Easier said than done. Thrusting into Sorcha while Quill is doing the same to him is so powerful. The sensations take over. Right now, it's all about the raw need that's consuming him.

'Are you close?' Quill asks, his hand gripping Bannon's shoulders, holding him as he pumps his hips faster and harder.

Bannon nods quickly. *'Please...'* He has no idea what he's begging Quill for. He just knows he wants more. He *needs* more.

'You feel so fucking perfect,' Quill says, his wings lifting away from the bed to flap behind him. 'So fucking close too.'

Sorcha moans. 'Nearly there Bannon...'

Bannon's head feels like it's going to explode. He's so close, but he holds himself back. He wants to experience Quill coming inside him. Needs to feel Sorcha squeezing him as she falls apart. Then he'll come.

Sorcha's groans come one after the other as she massages her clit. Quill growls behind him, his body quivering as he draws closer.

'I'm coming!' Sorcha mutters as she works her clit harder. *'Come in me, Quill.'*

'Fuck yes!' Then Quill's grip on his shoulder tightens as he comes deep in Bannon's ass. Sorcha's pussy clenches around him as she comes, her loud moans of pleasure mixing perfectly with Quill's deep growls.

The sensation is enough to fracture the last of Bannon's fragile hold. His orgasm tears through his body, every nerve ending exploding as Quill's dick continues to throb inside him while Sorcha's pussy milks him.

By the time his brain comes back online, he's being supported by Quill who has wrapped an arm around Bannon's chest, keeping him from falling on Sorcha.

Quill slowly pulls out of Bannon's ass, as Sorcha ducks under Bannon's arm before flopping back on the bed again. Quill lowers Bannon beside her then drops onto his front beside them, one wing stretched over Bannon and Sorcha.

'Fuck…' Quill says, his voice low and rough. 'You both good?'

'Fucked, but so so good,' Sorcha answers. 'We are doing all that again many, many times.'

Quill laughs. 'Too fucking right. What about you Bannon?'

'Wow!'

Quill laughs. 'What's so funny?' Sorcha asks.

'He said it was wow.'

'Oh, it was absolutely wow.'

Bannon's brain is still mush after what just happened, but he does know one thing. What just happened between them was so much more than wow. It was perfect. Everything about himself, Sorcha, Quill is perfect.

SORCHA

As she takes a seat on the couch between Quill and Bannon, her two beautiful males each take one of her hands in theirs. Finding even one of them alone would have been something to be grateful for. Finding both of them is a miracle - especially considering how they found each other.

Her brothers and the Blackjacks join them in the living room. Nix called the meeting, but she has no idea what's going on. Whatever it is, it's big.

She watches in silence as each of the Blackjacks take up position on any free seats around the room, along with Thea, Izzy, and Fletch. Her brothers are on the other side of the room, filling another couch and two armchairs.

She's never seen so many wolves and vampires in the same room as each other. Never thought she'd ever see the two species side-by-side like this. Friends, lovers, comrades. It's such an achievement - one that should be celebrated, not hidden behind closed doors. But that will come in time.

Nix gets to her feet and walks over to stand beside Davyn, the huge lord of the castle as intimidating as ever, even sitting down.

'I'm sure you're all wondering why I've called you together. I'll get straight to the point. As you know, Davyn is going to keep ownership of the castle and try to bring it back to its former glory. There are a lot of vampires and wolves who need sanctuary. Darkhaven might be the place to offer that. But it's vulnerable. Fergus and his team are eager and capable, but they need training, which is the reason for this meeting. We have a proposition that could help everyone in this room.'

She looks to Davyn who isn't exactly chomping at the bit to take over the talking, but he steps up. 'If you're up for it, I want all the wolves to stay here. Call Darkhaven their home. That goes for Bannon, Quill, and the Whelans, too.'

'We can train everyone,' Nix says, continuing before anyone can interrupt. 'What we would like to suggest is that you all come to Wales to the compound, for a few weeks of training. Then the Blackjacks will spend some time here with you, implementing any changes or improvements you want to make. At that stage, if any of the wolves that have been freed would like training, you'll be able to offer that. There is a salary included, and all expenses will be covered.'

The room falls silent as everyone takes in what Nix and Davyn just threw at them. Sorcha wasn't expecting this. Clearly Murt and her brothers weren't either. This is a massive offer. It's life-changing for all of them. It will give them something to work for, something to belong to. But it's also a lot to agree to. By agreeing, this would be so much more than taking a knee to a vampire.

'You want us to become Blackjacks?' Murt asks, voicing the basic question that's probably on all their lips.

Nix nods slowly. 'That's up to you. If you want to become official Blackjacks, we'll go that way. If you want to stay independent and live here, that's fine too. We'll still train you either way.'

'There is one condition,' Davyn says. 'Darkhaven is not a wolf or a vampire settlement. It's my house, but everyone will be equal here. I won't have us heading the same way my father did. Any vampire or wolf who causes problems will be kicked out. Zero tolerance.'

'Can't say fairer than that,' Murt says.

'Quill. It's your decision what you want to do,' Davyn says. 'That chain around your neck doesn't come into this. Do what you want. Either way Darkhaven can be your home.'

Nix nods to her team, who stand and move over to the door. 'We'll let you have some time alone to discuss this.' As one, the Blackjacks leave the room, and Sorcha waits until they're alone before she speaks.

'That was unexpected.'

'You're telling me,' Murt says, scrubbing his hand over his face. 'I thought Davyn might let us kip here for a bit, but not all that.'

'Can they be taken at their word?' Quill asks. 'I know fuck all about the Blackjacks.'

Con nods as he steps in. 'They can. Nix and Davyn haven't done us wrong. Not once. If they're making this offer, it's genuine.'

'What do you think Murt?' Fionn asks.

'I'm interested. Fuck knows we haven't had any other offers. And it's a damn good one, too. We're lethal when we fight. Add a bit of Blackjack training and funding to that, and we'd be able to hold our own in any situation. Not sure about joining the Blackjacks officially, but I'm tempted by the rest. What are you thinking?' he asks Bannon. 'You and Quill could easily join the Blackjacks. I doubt they're ready for a pack of wolves to stir things up, but you two would make decent additions.'

'I've got no home, no family. no job, and apart from Sorcha and Quill, nothing else in my life. I'm interested.'

Murt smiles when Sorcha finishes translating. 'Exactly. I can't see that any of us have anything to lose.'

'I wouldn't say no to playing with their weapons,' Garret says, rubbing his hands together. 'I could do some damage with their kit.'

'That's supposed to convince me to agree?'

'You know you'd be right there beside me Murt.'

'Yeah,' Murt says with a grin. 'You have a point. How about you Con?'

He shrugs. 'Nothing better planned for the moment.'

'Wolf of many words as usual. Sorcha?'

She looks at Bannon, then at Quill, before answering. This could give them all a future where they could be safe together. But not only that, they would have a purpose, something to fight for. They're thinking the same thing. She can see it in their eyes.

'The wolves Davyn helped to release, need a home. Darkhaven could be it. But they're right. We're unprotected here. We need to train so we can keep them safe.'

'We,' Murt says, smiling as he sits back in his seat. 'You thinking of hanging around little sister?'

'You can't get rid of me that easily. But it does depend on Bannon and Quill.' She smiles at the two males. 'I'm not keen on letting go of either of them.'

'Oh, give me a fucking bucket,' Garret says, pretending to retch.

Sorcha holds up her middle finger. 'You know, prison did have its plus side. I didn't have to deal with you.'

'Right back at you sis. And I reckon there's little chance either of them are going to say no to this.'

Quill looks over at Bannon as he smiles. 'Sounds like we're all on the same page. I trained all the guards from the prison. I'm not saying I'm the best, but I know how to handle myself. So can they. I doubt any of them would turn up the chance of putting those skills to better use.'

Murt looks around the room as the silence falls. Each one waiting for their leader to make a decision. It's strange how Bannon and Quill seem to look to Murt for approval. It's probably just because he's her big brother, and they're trying to get onside with him, but it could be because they are actually looking to him for leadership.

If they do decide to join the Blackjacks, Nix would presumably be giving the orders but, until then, it looks like Murt will be in charge.

'Right. I guess we're going to Wales.'

BANNON

He's the first one to wake, the light streaming through the window bringing him out of one of the best night's sleep he's ever had. He looks to the side, smiling when he sees the spectacular male he's lying next to. On Quill's other side, Sorcha is draped across him, her arm stretching across Quill's chest to hold Bannon's hand.

Quill's blonde hair is tickling the side of his face, but he doesn't want to move. He doesn't want to disturb this moment. Quill mutters in his sleep, pulling the two of them closer to him. Even in his sleep he's still protecting them.

Bannon never thought he'd be happy about another male looking out for him in that way, but with Quill it's different. He has no idea what to call their relationship. But does it really matter how it's labelled? He loves Sorcha and Quill equally. He would give his life for both of them without question. Wants to spend the rest of his life loving them, being with them. Waking up with them like this every day.

He looks at the necklace around Quill's neck. They can have that future now. Quill will never be fed from again against his will. He'll never be used or hurt for someone else's pleasure. He'll never have someone else tell him how he should live his life.

Quill would make an outstanding Blackjack. The few training sessions Bannon had with Quill showed that much. He's meticulous. Disciplined. Strong. Protective. He could easily see him fighting alongside Davyn and Shep.

He'd like to think he could hold his own with the vampire fighters too. When he lost his voice, he thought his life would come down to mere survival. Any plans he had for his future were destroyed when he was injured. If he could prove himself to Nix, and demonstrate to her that he could be a valuable member of the team, it would give him back that purpose he thought he had lost.

'Good morning sexy.'

He looks over the vast expanse of Quill's chest to find Sorcha smiling sleepily at him. *'Morning,'* he mouths, desperate not to wake Quill. He still needs his rest.

She squeezes his hand. 'Morning to you too. You know, I could get used to this.'

He nods in agreement. He already has.

She pushes to her elbow to look down at Quill. 'He has more colour in his face.'

'*He* is awake, so stop talking about him.' Quill opens one eye then closes it again, groaning as he pulls them both close.

'How are you feeling?'

Quill sighs contentedly. 'Better. I need to get out of bed today. I've been here too long.'

'That might not be a bad idea,' Sorcha says. 'Get up and stretch those wings of yours.'

'Unless your brothers shoot me down first.'

She laughs and playfully slaps him on the shoulder. 'They're not going to shoot you. If they were going to do that, they would have done it already.'

He laughs, and it's a sound Bannon loves. He didn't realise how little Quill had laughed. But he didn't have anything to laugh about before, so he can't blame him. None of them did.

'So,' she says, climbing over Quill to lie in between them. 'Are you both excited about training with the Blackjacks?'

Quill rolls onto his side, facing them both. 'Yeah. I really am. I know the prison was fucked up, but I loved being head guard. I loved the training, and the teamwork. It'll be tough, but I reckon we'll both hold our own.'

Bannon holds up his hand, his fingers crossed.

Sorcha laughs at his response. 'You'll both kick ass. I know you will.' She twists a lock of Quill's hair around her finger. 'I'm going to miss you two when you go to Wales.'

'It won't be for long. You need time with your brothers to help with the other wolves,' Quill says, running his fingers up her arm. 'We'll train with the Blackjacks for a few weeks, try not to get killed, then come back to you.'

'Why would you get killed?'

They train hard,' Bannon signs.

'I hope so,' she says. 'They're the best. Then you come back and pass on all that training to the wolves and vampires here. With you and my brothers protecting the castle, Darkhaven will be safe. It can be home to vampires and wolves who have nothing else. Nowhere else to call home.'

'Do you think it's somewhere we could call home? The three of us I mean.'

Yes,' Bannon signs before Quill can answer. *'I think it can be.'*

'Yeah,' Quill says. 'I think so too. I lived a stone's throw from here growing up, and couldn't wait to get as far from here as possible. But there's a different feel to it now. Davyn, Thea, and my dad have made sure of that. I want to be a part of what they're doing here. I want all of us to be a part of that.'

Sorcha pushes onto her knees, so she can look down at both of them. 'It sounds like we have a plan so. This is so exciting! I can't believe a few weeks ago we were all prisoners on that island. Now look at us.'

'Naked in bed together?'

She playfully slaps Quill on the chest. 'No. Well yes, but not just that. We can make a real difference here. Be part of making sure the wolves get some of their old lives back and maybe help them track down their clans.'

'And the guards,' Quill says. 'Duna and the other guards deserve a second chance.'

'True,' Sorcha says. 'Do you think she'll come here too, once all the prisoners are brought back here?'

Quill nods. 'She should. There's the making of a Blackjack in her, too. I guess it depends on how the transition goes for her. I don't know what the Warden had on her. It'll be down to her what she wants to do.'

Quill pauses for a moment before he speaks again. 'I have to go back there.'

'Back where?'

'To the prison.'

'Why?' Sorcha asks.

'I need to see it again. Need to see Duna again, before I head off to Wales. I guess it's sort of like a closure of some sort. This castle haunted me for most of my life. All the things that happened here stayed with me. I don't want to add another fucking building to everything else that's in my head. I need to go back, stick my finger up at the place, then move on. I'm not expecting either of you to come with me, but it's something I have to do.'

Sorcha nods, then leans over and kisses him. 'I get that. I don't think I can go back though. I never want to see that place again.'

Quill grabs her hand, squeezing it firmly. 'I don't want you anywhere near that island again. If you'd asked, I probably would have tried to put my foot down.'

'I'll go with you.' Bannon doesn't want to see that place again, but he understands why Quill needs to go back. Quill is strong and tough, but there's no way in hell he's letting him go near that island alone. He'll be there for him.

When Quill nods, Bannon nearly falls off the bed. He was sure Quill would argue with him.

'Thanks.'

'So,' Sorcha says as she snuggles back in between them. 'I guess we'd better get up.'

Quill rolls over, caging them both under his body. 'Neither of you are going anywhere yet.'

QUILL

He'd spent so many years on the island he had grown accustomed to the place. The island itself never bothered him, it was what happened here that made him sick.

But stepping onto the jetty again, all that fear he thought he had a handle on, comes to the front with a bang.

'Are you okay?'

He nods at Bannon, not trusting his voice to remain strong if he vocalises his answer. He looks down as Bannon takes his hand, squeezing it firmly in his. He'll never know how Bannon can read him so well. How this male can get into his head without having to try. He squeezes Bannon's hand, keeping hold of it as they walk along the jetty.

Behind him, his father and Davyn follow along the jetty, keeping some distance between them.

He didn't want his father to come with them, but there was no talking him out of it. He understands why, but that doesn't help put him at ease. He doesn't want his father to see this place.

It was his whole world for so long. It was a world he fought hard to excel in, to survive in. But that doesn't mean he's proud of what he achieved while he was here. His status was built on blood and pain. His own, and that of the other prisoners he had to hurt.

Coming back here today is something he needed to do. Bannon wasn't on board with it. Neither was Sorcha. They both thought it would pick the scab off a wound that had just begun to heal. It's not a wound he wants to heal just yet. He has unfinished business here, and until he deals with that, he's not going to be able to move on.

As they round the corner and approach the door, Bannon releases Quill's hand. He appreciates the gesture. Inside those walls, he needs to be strong - or at least pretend that he is. Walking in holding Bannon's hand isn't going to help him.

'Welcome back.'

He comes to a stop as Duna steps out of the building, holding the door open for them. 'Good to see you again.' And it is. Anything that happened with Duna isn't on her.

'I'm surprised you came back.'

'I needed to.'

Duna nods, stepping aside to let them in. She nods at Davyn as he joins them inside. 'Welcome back sire.'

Davyn nods. 'Just need to make sure everyone is sticking to the plan.'

'Of course. The wolves are coming along, but it's a slow process. I'm not sure if all of them will be able to be rehabilitated.'

'Do what you can. We'll take any you feel are ready back with us to Darkhaven when we leave. Give you more time with the ones who need extra help.'

'I'll get them ready.'

'Can I get a minute with Duna first?' Quill asks the others.

'We'll go and check on the wolves,' Davyn says. Call when you're ready.'

'Thanks.'

'Are you going to be okay?' Bannon asks, keeping it to themselves instead of signing.

'Go and check on everyone. I'll be fine.'

Bannon, Davyn, and Fergus head towards the dorms where most of the prisoners have been moved, while Duna and Quill walk to the Warden's living area. It's probably just his imagination but there's a different feel to the place now the Warden is dead. It's just a building after all. It was the Warden and his practices that tarnished the old mansion.

They walk in silence into the Warden's office. Fuck! Bannon had gone to town in here. He knew Bannon had unleashed his power here, but the obvious control and intensity of the attack both impresses and scares him. He walks over to the desk and looks down at the charred patch on the carpet where the Warden had met his death.

For some reason, the first thought that hits him is that the Warden's main concern through all the feedings was that Quill didn't get any blood on his expensive carpet. It's kind of fitting that his charred remains have destroyed some of that carpet. Fuck him!

'I'm glad I get to see you again,' Duna says, sitting on the edge of the desk and peering down at the blackened carpet. 'I owe you an apology.'

'What for?'

'I knew what he was doing to you, and I did nothing to stop it. That day when I unleashed the prisoners on you... I should have stopped it. I should have done something'

Quill lowers onto the desk beside her. 'What could you have done? Everyone in this shithole was a prisoner for different reasons. We all

509

did what we did to survive.'

'I had no idea he owned you.'

'You weren't supposed to know. No one was. Being the head guard was the only thing that was mine. I wasn't going to risk that.'

'It's fucked up, isn't it?' she says, laughing hollowly.

'Yeah.' He looks over at her. She is more relaxed than he's ever seen her before. It wasn't just him that was being crushed under the Warden's rule. 'Can I ask you something?'

'Of course.'

'Why were you here? What did he have on you?'

Duna blows out a long breath as she shakes her head. 'Well, that's a question.'

'You don't have to answer it.'

She turns to face him. 'I'm going to answer it. I haven't spoken about it for years. To be honest, I assumed you'd know. Do you not have access to our records?'

'Just basic information. Nothing about why you were here.'

'Ah. That makes sense. The Warden liked to keep a firm control on things. Well, my brother got himself into some trouble with a local drug dealer. I lost... he died a few years ago. Overdose.'

'Fuck! I'm sorry.'

'I went after the dealer and killed him. The Council caught me and gave me two options - in front of, or behind the bars. It wasn't much of an option.

'But you were one of the good guys, Quill. I mean that,' she adds when he laughs. 'You could have pushed a lot harder than you did. You could have been downright cruel if you'd wanted to. I know you did things that hurt you - and I mean emotionally. But you never took pleasure from it. All of us could see that. If I had to answer to anyone, I'm so glad it was you. You made being here bearable. Thank you.'

He's completely floored by that. He hoped he had the respect of the guards under him, but wasn't expecting her to come out with something like that. 'Thanks. So, what's the plan with you?'

She shrugs as she looks out the window. 'Stay here for as long as Davyn needs me. There are still at least ten wolves who are struggling with the new regime here. I guess I need to make sure they make it. Kind of like a little salvation for everything I did while under this roof. It won't wipe my slate clean, but it's a start. After that, who knows? I hear you might be signing on with the Blackjacks?'

'It's on the cards, yeah.'

'Can't think of a better candidate. You'd make one hell of a Blackjack. Bannon too.'

'Yeah. He's stronger than he's given credit for.'

She smirks at him. 'And you're with both him and the wolf?'

'I'm not sure how it happened, but I am.'

'You are one lucky male, you know that! Not content with one, you have to grab two. Why the fuck not?'

He laughs at that. 'Yeah. Why the fuck not! They're amazing people Duna.'

'And you're okay?' she asks, glancing down at the necklace around his neck. 'With the ownership thing I mean.'

He nods. 'Yeah. I didn't think I would be, but so far, so good. Davyn isn't like the Warden. It's on paper only. The ownership doesn't matter anywhere else. I have to wear this chain, but I can handle that.'

'I'm glad Quill. I mean that. I just hope I get to work with you again in the future.'

He takes her offered hand, shaking it. 'We will. I'll make sure of it.'

SORCHA

As she watches Quill and Bannon oohing and aahing over Bannon's motorbike, she can't quite believe how things have worked out for her. Two of the most stunning vampires she has ever met. Complete polar opposites to each other in every way, the two vampires love her as much as they love each other. It shouldn't work. Nothing about their relationship should work. But not only does it work, it's fucking awesome! No jealousy. No fighting for attention. Just pure love.

Every minute with Bannon and Quill is like nothing she's experienced before. After growing up with four over-protective brothers, she never thought the idea of having two men in her life would be so appealing. And while she has no doubt both Bannon and Quill would kill, or die for her, she still feels so free with them. Perhaps meeting them in the situation she did, they are all too aware that, it's that very freedom she needs and craves.

Bannon gestures at Quill, presumably arguing with him in his head about something bike related. Frustrated, Quill brushes his hair back from his face, quickly tying it in a bun before he gets back to the argument. She could watch the two of them like this forever.

A week has passed since Quill was rescued and his strength has returned. Bannon and Fergus's blood has helped, but so did spending time with his father.

It wasn't going to be a quick fix. The decades were filled with pain - for both of them, but they are rediscovering their father/son relationship. Knowing that his father understands, to a certain degree, what the Warden did to Quill is such a weight off his mind. The thin necklace around his neck with Davyn's crest on it, seals the deal for him. He's safe.

For the first time in too many years, he's safe.

They all are.

And it's not just Quill who has taken advantage of the change in their circumstances.

Bannon has come into his own since leaving the prison, looking after Quill while he recovered, and being there for her like a rock. And it wasn't an easy job for him on either count - especially when it came to looking after Quill.

He was irritable, gruff, rude, and downright impossible. Typical alpha male shit that she's more than able to deal with, but it was Bannon's never-ending patience that won out. Seeing the shift in the dynamic had been interesting. The protector had become the protected.

Even though Quill has now recovered, the power struggle is still very much in play. Bannon isn't keen to hand over the reins to Quill who, unsurprisingly, isn't keen on letting anyone have his back.

Or at least that's what he likes to let on. Both Bannon and Sorcha know that's not really the case. He spent so many years with no one looking out for him, he's enjoying having people in his life who care about him - even if he pretends otherwise.

While she waits for them to finish whatever they're discussing, Sorcha wanders around the garden outside the castle wall. It's a stunning spring evening. The sun is still out, but it won't be for long. Quill can't stay out in the sun for longer than an hour or so. His sensitive Prime eyes aren't keen on the light, but he seems to be coping right now.

'What are you smiling about?' he asks, crossing his arms as he looks over at her.

'Me? Oh nothing. Just waiting for my two alpha males to stop beating their chests over a motorbike.'

'Thanks,' Bannon signs.

'What are you thanking me for? That wasn't a compliment.'

Bannon grins as he signs back. *'You called us alpha males.'*

She groans. 'Oh right. Trust you two to focus on that part. Anyway! Are we going to drool over Bannon's bike all day, or do what we planned to do?'

'We're waiting for you to get yourself sorted,' Quill replies, leaning back against the castle wall.

'I sincerely apologise. Turn around then. I don't play by all the rules, but I'd prefer you didn't watch me do this.'

Sorcha shifts into her wolf, keeping away from the two vampires for the moment. Bannon might be fine with her in this form. But Quill hasn't seen her as a wolf. She has no idea how he's going to handle it.

'You can open your eyes.' She's mainly talking to Bannon, but there's a chance Quill will be able to hear her too. She has the same connection with him as she does with Bannon.

'Fuck!' Quill says, his eyes still closed. 'I can hear you in my head.'

'Really!' Sorcha says. *'That's great! I hoped you'd be able to. Are you going to open your eyes now?'*

He does, and stares at the wolf in front of him. 'Fuck!'

'She's stunning, isn't she?'

He nods. 'Yeah Bannon. She's fucking gorgeous. Never thought I'd say that about a wolf.'

Bannon takes his hand, walking with him over to Sorcha. He looks a little nervous, which she wasn't expecting. *'Are you okay?'* she asks as he steps closer.

He nods. 'Yeah. Sorry. Just never been this close to a shifter before. Well, not in this form I mean. I know it's you, but you're fucking huge. You're kind of intimidating.'

'You're not afraid of a little wolf, are you?' She tilts her head to the side almost as if she's jeering him.

'*Little* is something you are definitely not.'

She closes the distance between them, coming to a stop right in front of them, her head a few inches below theirs. Quill holds out his hand but pauses, a little unsure if he should touch her or not.

But she takes the decision away from him by sliding her head underneath his palm. He laughs as he runs his hand over her thick dark hair. 'This is the most surreal thing I've ever done.'

'In our world that's saying something,' Bannon says, stroking the top of Sorcha's head.

'You really are beautiful,' Quill says, kissing the top of her head.

'Are you ready to do this or what?' she asks, taking a step back. *'I've been looking forward to this for too long.'*

Bannon smiles, and nods enthusiastically. She can never get enough of seeing that stunning vampire smile like that. He's happy. Both she and Quill can see the change in him. He's being heard now and it's making such a difference to him. Quill is still learning how to sign, even though they can now communicate in other ways. He just wants to make sure he can always hear what Bannon has to say, no matter what, and they both love him all the more for doing that.

Bannon walks back over to his bike, propped up on its stand by the wall. *'I'm so ready. How about you Quill? You think you can keep up?'*

Quill pulls off his hoodie, then pushes his shoulders back, releasing his stunning wings. He stretches the huge green and blue limbs out to either side of him, looking so much more attractive than any vampire should. Bannon also notices, his eyes narrowing as he smiles seductively.

'Oh, I think I can keep up. You two need to worry about yourselves. I'll be up there,' he says, pointing to the sky. 'You two have terrain to deal with. I'll be back home with a cup of coffee before you get to the halfway point.'

Sorcha gets to her feet, slowly walking around him, her green eyes locking on his. *'Four legs and two wheels. We'll be fine. Actually,'* she says as she stretches, getting ready to take these two vampires down. *'I'll take you both. Four legs will always beat wings and wheels.'*

Bannon grins as he starts his bike, then slips on his helmet. *'How about we all stop stalling?'*

'Couldn't agree more,' Quill says, pushing off the ground and hovering above the two of them.

'Gorgeous,' Sorcha says as she watches the huge vampire soaring above her.

Quill smiles down at her. 'Stop trying to distract me. Let's do this.'

Sorcha looks over as Bannon brings his bike next to her. Quill swoops low, taking up position above them.

'Count of three,' Sorcha says, crouching low to get a good start. *'Three, two, one!'* She pushes away from Bannon, her paws hitting the grass, her claws digging in to clear more ground.

In her head she can hear Bannon laughing as he catches up with her. Sorcha smiles when a shadow passes her as Quill soars over their heads and quickly takes the lead.

She wants to win, but that's not what this is about. This is about freedom. This is about three broken people finding themselves, about finding love in spite of all the shit that life has thrown at them.

Bannon and Quill are her life now. She has no doubts about that.

She is completely in love with both of these males and knows they feel the same about her. That doesn't happen often in life. Finding that one true love is something to be grateful for. Finding two is a miracle she will never take for granted for even a second of her life.

They've been lucky enough to find each other through the darkness. Wolf. Vampire. It doesn't matter. She's found her mates and will kill for both of them, die for them, and love them as long as she lives.

EPILOGUE

MURT

The grass is damp and cool under his paws as he makes his way around the back of the castle. He moves along the headland, leaving the grounds of Darkhaven, and safety behind. Far below him, waves crash against the rocks. The sea is particularly angry tonight, the wind coming off the coast ruffling his dark fur.

Murt never thought his life would take the path it has. But it's not something he's upset about. Having a purpose again is better than he could have hoped for. He's also looking forward to training with the Blackjacks. He trains his clan. Has for years. It'll be a good test to see how they fare against the vampires. Being able to use equipment designed for the purpose will also be a welcome change. Doing pull-ups on trees works, but he won't turn up his nose at a proper gym.

As soon as he rounds the headland and the castle disappears from view, he picks up the pace, covering the next few miles in no time at all. His hip complains, the old injury Dav's father gave him protesting as he runs.

Then he picks up on their scent. Instead of turning around and heading back to safety, he continues on his way, closing the distance between them. He smiles to himself when he senses their surprise. Fuckers probably thought he'd run back to safety. He probably should. From what he can make out there are five individual scents in front of him. One against five isn't exactly reassuring odds.

Murt slows as he approaches the forest. He's not going to go any further. Let them come to him. He also doesn't fancy being stuck in the forest where they can sneak up on him. Better to keep things out in the open.

Deciding on the right spot, Murt stops and stands facing the trees. He tilts his head back and howls. Less than a minute later, the five wolves step out of the trees, coming to a stop a few feet from him.

The one in the middle takes a step closer to Murt. The brown fur around the wolf's eyes and muzzle is greying. Murt is heading towards five hundred years old, but is still a youngster compared to the rest of the Elders.

'You came alone, Murtagh? Does that make you stupid or brave?' The wolf's voice is low and harsh in his head.

'You know me Donnacha. I like to be unconventional.'

The Elder nods slowly, 'Given your current situation I would have to say you're stupid. If we choose to take you in, how will you stop us?'

'You're not here to take me in. If you wanted to do that you would have done that when we were on Mount Leinster.'

'Your attitude is a continuing irritation to me.'

'Just like your constant stench in the air behind me irritates me. What do you want?'

Donnacha growls and bares his teeth but gets control of himself quickly. Can't have an Elder losing his temper. That just wouldn't do.

'Leaving your lack of respect aside, I would like to clear up something. When you and your clan were banished to Mount Leinster, were you under the impression it was an optional relocation?'

'Oh, I know it was permanent. Like I said, I'm not a fan of being conventional.'

'And you didn't think that disobeying us would have repercussions?'

'Oh, I know that too.'

Donnacha looks around them, the chuckle coming out like a low growl. 'Yet here we are. Are you intentionally trying to anger us?'

'Would you believe me if I said no?'

No response. He's pushing his luck with Donnacha, but he's beyond caring. His sole purpose over the last few years was finding Sorcha and keeping his brothers safe. Job done. Whatever happens now he'll take it. But that doesn't mean he's going to bow and scrape to these fuckers.

'Why are you keeping an eye on us?' Time to stop with the games and get straight to the point.

Donnacha takes a step closer to him. He's not as tall as Murt, but he knows the Elder can take care of himself. And it's not like he's alone. He's got his four mates to watch his back.

'Go back to Mount Leinster.'

'No.'

'That wasn't a request Murtagh. A punishment isn't optional.'

'I said no.'

'Wolves do not live with vampires. Especially in that castle. We have been incredibly tolerant with you up until now, but you are pushing all our buttons Murtagh. For the last time, take yourself and your clan back to Mount Leinster and stay there.'

Murt takes a step closer, sensing the others closing rank when he does that. He looks Donnacha straight in the eye, making sure the Elder can see his defiance. *'Last time, no. We're not planning to cause you any trouble. All we want is to be allowed to live our lives in peace. That's it.'*

'Consorting with vampires. Swearing allegiance to vampires. Living with vampires. How exactly is that not causing us any trouble? Our rules are clear. You are breaking them.'

'You banished us. Cut us off. What the fuck does it matter what we do?'

'Stop arguing with me. Rules are rules, Murtagh. Abide by them, or we will have to take things further.'

These stubborn fools aren't going to back down. Realistically he didn't think they would. Hoped certainly, but there really is no changing the past. They see vampires as the enemy, and that will never change.

He's not going to back down, though. He can't. The Blackjacks are a sound group of vampires. He considers some of them friends. And Sorcha's new relationship with Bannon and Quill deserves a chance. It shouldn't matter what race they are.

He's so fucking envious of what his sister has found. He has not one doubt Bannon and Quill would give their lives for her. That's the way it should be. It's what he'd do, if he was ever lucky enough to find a mate of his own.

It's who he is. At his core he puts himself second to everyone else he cares about.

'Let me make my position clear, Donnacha. I don't give a fuck about some ancient feud between immature idiots. What I do give a fuck about is my clan and my friends. You know me. You know what I'm capable of. If you come after my pack, or my friends, I will unleash a fucking nightmare on you. I won't stop until each and every one of you are rotting corpses. Leave us alone.'

Donnacha stares at him in silence for a long time, before slowly nodding. *'Very well. Now let me make our position as clear as you've* made yours. We will leave your pack out of this. With a leader such as yourself, I doubt they have much choice but to follow your rules. However,' he says baring his teeth. 'That does not mean you will be spared. Your life for theirs Murtagh.'

He should have guessed that would be the solution they'd come up with. He might be on board with giving his life for his family, but not like this. Not because these fuckers demand it.

'Strangely enough I'm not on board with that.'

'I wouldn't expect you to be. But that is the only option. I will give you four weeks to get your affairs in order. After that time, you will meet us here and quietly come with us. Do you understand?'

'And if I refuse?'

'Then we attack the castle to get to you. You know we won't stop until we have you. If you really want to risk your new friends, or your pack, feel free. That will be on you Murtagh.'

He nods, showing his teeth, amazed he managed to not sink them into Donnacha's neck. 'So, I guess I'll see you in a month.'

The Elder seems surprised by that. 'I thought you would fight me on this.'

'Just keep my clan and the vampires out of this. Nothing that happened was on them. As you said, I'm the pack leader.'

'You have my word.'

'One month then. Can't wait. Now fuck off and leave me alone.'

Donnacha turns, walking away with the rest of the pack. 'You know what?' he says, turning to look back at him.

'What?'

'I'm going to enjoy killing you Murtagh Whelan.'

Murt waits until he can't pick up on their scent any longer, before he turns around and heads back to the castle. He keeps to a walk, trying fucking hard to get his anger under wraps before he gets back to Darkhaven.

Well, that's his cards marked again. He knew the Elders would catch up with him sooner or later. If they hadn't banished the Whelan clan, they wouldn't be brave enough to come after him like this. It was generally frowned upon to try to kill one of the clan leaders - especially one of his standing - or former standing. Murt knows he has support in the other clans, but no one is willing to stand up to the Elders. Banishing his pack would have convinced anyone tempted to rethink their plans.

Fuck walking back. He needs to get this out of his system. Murt runs, pushing his legs hard, his paws thudding against the grass as he uses all his anger and frustration to help him run faster.

He won't be in that clearing in a month. No fucking way! That leaves him four weeks to get Quill, Bannon, his clan, and everyone else in Darkhaven trained and ready to fight. The Elders probably won't take on the castle inhabitants, just to get to him. They're not going to face a battle with the Blackjacks, either. They're idiots, but they're not stupid.

But just to be sure, he's going to have to take himself away from his clan. Lead the Elders somewhere else, far from the castle.

He stops at the corner of the headland, watching the castle a few miles ahead of him. Lights fill most of the windows. He has to give it to Thea and Fergus. They've managed to turn a lump of stone into a home. A home for everyone he cares about.

But it's a home he's going to have to leave.

He takes off again, racing around the headland and through the castle gates. He shifts back into human form in the stable where he left his clothes, then goes back into the castle. He's limping badly after the exercise, but his leg should recover in a few hours with rest.

He finds Sorcha in one of the living rooms, curled up on the couch in between Bannon and Quill. Bannon is going through some sign language with the two of them and, as usual, Quill's patience is in short supply.

'That's what I signed!' he says, pointing to the page.

'No,' Sorcha says. 'It's like this.' She shows him the correct movements and he gestures to her hands.

'That's what I signed!' he repeats as Bannon and Sorcha laugh. 'Oh, you two can knock it off. This isn't easy.'

'Relax. You're doing great,' she says, rubbing his hand. She looks over at the door and smiles when she notices him in the doorway. 'Hey Murt. You okay?'

'Yeah. Just went for a run along the headland.'

'I did that earlier. It's stunning around here.'

'Yeah,' he agrees. 'It is. I'm going to head to bed.'

He turns away, stopping when she runs after him. 'Are you sure you're okay? You look distracted.'

He pulls her into a hug, holding on to her for a long time. He can't believe he's just got her back in his life, and this happens. He's not ready to say goodbye to her again in four short weeks.

'Yeah. I'm great.'

Thank you for reading *Sorcha.*

I hope you enjoyed spending time with Sorcha, Quill, Bannon, and the rest of the Whelan clan. There's plenty more to come!

The sequel, *Murtagh,* is coming next.

Do you fancy staying updated with news about my books?

• Join my mailing list at: www.kafinn.com/

• Like me on Facebook: www.facebook.com/kafinnauthor

• Follow me on Instagram: www.instagram.com/kafinnauthor/

• Keep up to date with new releases: https://books2read.com/ap/nE2Kdj/KA-Finn

Also, if you have a moment, I'd appreciate if you could review *Sorcha* at the store where you purchased it. The Whelans and I would love to know what you thought of the book.

Thanks for your support!

K.A. Finn

Coming next.

STONE WOLVES BOOK 2

K.A. FINN

www.ingramcontent.com/pod-product-compliance
Lightning Source LLC
Chambersburg PA
CBHW030744030726
47497CB00001B/121